Just BUSINESS

Just
BUSINESS

BER CARROLL

POOLBEG

Published 2005
by Poolbeg Press Ltd
123 Grange Hill, Baldoyle
Dublin 13, Ireland
E-mail: poolbeg@poolbeg.com

A catalogue record for this book is available from the British Library.

ISBN 1-84223-185-5

Typeset by Magpie Designs in Goudy 10.5/14 pt
Printed by Norhaven Paperback, Denmark

www.poolbeg.com

About the Author

Ber Carroll was born in Blarney, County Cork, in 1971 and until recently worked as a finance director in the Information Technology industry. She lives in the Northern Beaches of Sydney with her husband and their two children.

ACKNOWLEDGEMENTS

Many thanks to Paula Campbell, Gaye Shortland, Brona Looby, Claire McVeigh and everybody else at Poolbeg for your support and enthusiasm. Thanks to Brian Cook, Anna Kassulke, Jane Newbury, Amanda Carroll and Koren O'Donnell for your invaluable comments and suggestions. The technical assistance of the following people was much appreciated: James Young, Scott Mortimer, Denis O'Mahony, Matthew Longmore, Tomoko Katatura, and Ann from Schizophrenia Fellowship of NSW. Finally, I would like to acknowledge my family and friends who went to such amazing lengths to spread the word about my first novel, *Executive Affair*.

Dedication

To Rob, for allowing me to put my feet up and become a full-time mother and writer!

Chapter One

No reason had been offered for the impromptu Monday morning gathering but most knew it wasn't good news.

The auditorium of HDD Ltd hummed with nervous conversation as five hundred employees filed in. The back rows filled up first. The front rows, where eye contact could be made from the lectern, were less popular. The rebellious snubbed the vacant seats and stood along the walls. On the podium, five empty seats stared into the expectant crowd.

When they had mostly settled, Niamh Lynch walked across the platform and sat in the far seat. She was followed by her colleagues, their faces solemn as they took their seats in turn. Malcolm Young, the CEO, only appeared when his executives, his buffer, were all in place. He stepped up to the lectern and looked down at his minions. "Good morning."

His greeting was met with a defiant silence. He cleared his throat, the microphone amplifying the unpleasant sound, and looked down at his notes. "Today we will lose 10 per cent of the workforce in Australia. I am sure that each and every one of you is aware of the downturn in the IT industry. HDD must respond to that downturn and adjust its staff levels accordingly. This is a business decision, nothing to do with the individuals who will leave our employment today." He briefly looked up to reiterate his point. "It's *just business*, nothing personal . . ."

Niamh inwardly cringed at his choice of words. Of course, it was personal. She could see the faces of the people in the first few rows of the auditorium and it was clear they thought it was personal too. It was their jobs he was talking about, their livelihood.

As head of human resources, Niamh had tried to counsel Malcolm on the most sensitive way to deliver the bad news. It seemed he was disregarding her advice. She sighed to herself and folded her arms across the front of her fitted jacket, which had the collar of a plain white shirt flaring over its neckline. Her curly blonde hair, usually with a mind of its own, was tied back from her face. A smattering of freckles underneath her tan made her look younger than her age, thirty. Being a female in the male-dominated IT industry was hard enough and looking younger than her age didn't help.

Malcolm was gathering momentum, his voice becoming progressively more domineering and loud. "The share price has been falling steadily over the last year and our head office has made it our number one objective to reverse that trend. They have committed to the analysts that each and every subsidiary of HDD will make a profit. You must view this restructure as the first step towards profit and a strong share price . . ."

Niamh had been with the Australian subsidiary of the Japanese multinational for a year now. She enjoyed the work; the progressive IT market and the conservative Japanese influence set a unique human resources environment. However, on a social level the role was much less fulfilling. The executive team didn't gel together. They were a disparate group of individuals who seemed to lack the initiative to find a common ground outside work. It didn't help that Malcolm himself was new, only two months in the job, and that teambuilding didn't appear to be one of his strengths.

Malcolm moved away from the lectern out to centre stage, giving each employee a bird's-eye view of their leader. His oversized frame had been brought about by too many liquid lunches and didn't fit comfortably into his pinstripe suit. His body looked as if it was ready to retire from the workforce and his hollow words were just as jaded. "The Australian subsidiary *must* return a profit . . . we must keep this goal in mind with every action we take over the next few months . . . "

Phil Davis, the finance director, sat next to Niamh. He nodded on cue when Malcolm mentioned "profit". Phil was also new to the company. A protégé of Malcolm's in a previous life, he was comfortable with the reality that he didn't need to prove himself. Tall, with the physique of a rugby player, his good looks were being threatened by an unhealthy lifestyle: late nights, too much booze, not enough exercise. His attention span was short at the best of times and his eyes soon wandered to the shapely legs of Lucinda Armstrong who sat tantalisingly close.

Lucinda, the internal legal counsel for HDD, was rigid in her chair, her beautiful face inscrutable as she listened to Malcolm. She had been with the company three years and this wasn't the first restructure she had seen in her tenure. Lucinda agreed with Malcolm: it was "just business". It was a natural part of the company's evolution – if you didn't change then you didn't survive. The beautiful woman with the long legs possessed a sharp practical mind with just the right element of ruthlessness to make her a damn good lawyer. She worked long hard days and psychologically had more testosterone than any of her male colleagues. Phil Davis leering at her legs didn't go unnoticed but it didn't bother her in the slightest.

Bruce Knight, the services director, sat next to Lucinda. Divorced and bitter, her legs held no interest for him. It was common knowledge that he still grieved for his ex-wife, the woman who had cheated on him for years before filing for divorce to marry her lover. As a consequence, Bruce smoked too much and worked too hard – his lined face bore the effects. If it were possible, this morning he looked more miserable than usual as he watched Malcolm strut across the stage.

"I'm confident we can put these hard times behind us," the CEO claimed in a now booming voice. "I'm confident we can win new business and push the share price back up …"

Maybe it was just his pessimistic nature, but Bruce wasn't as confident as Malcolm about winning new business and returning to profitability so soon. The CEO was new to the company and didn't fully understand the market behind their product, hard-disk drives. Bruce had been in the business all his adult life and knew that investment in technology was low on the priority list of customers as they struggled with the slowdown in the economy. He reckoned it would be at least a year before the profits bounced back and he had tried telling Malcolm this on a number of occasions. But Malcolm was trying to prove himself to Japan. He had promised them profits over the next two quarters and didn't want to hear anything to the contrary.

The last seat in the row of executives was occupied by Yoshi Murasaki, Japanese liaison director. This was the man who was paid a lot of yen to keep tabs on the Australian management team. In any other culture he would be called a spy; to the Japanese he was a crucial cog in the machinery of doing business outside the mother country. Yoshi's youthful complexion belied his age. He would be forty when this eighteen-month assignment to Sydney expired, the same age as Bruce Knight, but Yoshi didn't have a current or an ex-wife to cause worry-lines on his smooth face.

Yoshi frowned as he listened to Malcolm's monotone. "HDD has a solid future in this country – Japan is committed to its investment in Australia. Shedding 10 per cent of our workforce will make us infinitively more competitive and will ensure that the head office earns a return on their investment here."

Yoshi was starting to have doubts about the new CEO. He could pick up the insensitivity of Malcolm's words even though English wasn't his first language. He understood that achieving the right balance in the address was difficult – how to show empathy for those who were leaving while motivating those who were staying, but Malcolm didn't seem to be trying for any balance. His brashness was alienating the audience. Yoshi also noticed the ill-fitting suit, the jacket stretched across the CEO's midriff, the trousers too short in the leg, and thought that Malcolm must have neglected to look in the mirror before leaving for work.

The executives, like the audience, were getting fidgety. Niamh saw their legs and arms cross and uncross. Some of their faces she could read, some not. She felt fundamentally different to them and this wasn't the first time she wondered why. Was it nationality? The discerning ear could identify Irish origins in her accent but her name was the more obvious clue. When she had started with HDD, her new colleagues had struggled to get their tongues around the strange Celtic name. Niamh. Nee-uv. Most of them could say it correctly now. Yoshi was the other non-Australian on the team, his cultural differences much more pronounced than hers. Set apart from the others, it didn't mean they were close and neither did it mean there was a distinguishable inner circle.

Malcolm was winding down and he returned to his earlier position behind the lectern. "We'll be sorry to see the 10 per cent – um, the people – leave us. Human

Resources will meet with those impacted today ... we're hoping to make it as painless as possible ... it will be business as normal tomorrow."

Niamh thought to herself that Malcolm had inadvertently made it as *painful* as possible. He had blithely belittled the people who were losing their jobs by repeatedly referring to them as a percentage of the total workforce. He had explained the restructure as "just business". In reality, he saw it as an opportunity to prove his worth to the Japanese head office. Niamh knew his involvement ended with this speech and the dirty work, facing the people involved, was her department. Don and Jessica, two of her managers, had already labelled the day as Black Monday.

The auditorium emptied, the staff disgruntled and edgy. Niamh returned to her office but she didn't reach straight for the phone. She needed a few minutes to psych herself up. If there was one part of her job she hated, it was this – making people redundant, telling them they were no longer needed, pulling their financial security out from under their feet. There were twenty people on her list, fifteen each for Jessica and Don. Fifty people in all. That sounded a lot more than Malcolm's "10 per cent", particularly when those people had names.

Niamh didn't need to look at her list to remind herself of the first name. It was Scott Morgan, one of her staff. She had hired him a few months ago to manage the recruitment function. Mid-thirties, enthusiastic, he had fitted straight into the department and was already highly regarded. She wasn't at all happy about losing him but last in, first out, seemed to be the fairest policy in the circumstances. She took a deep breath and dialled his number.

She looked out her window as she waited for him to come round. The mass of skyscrapers broke to show an alluring slice of the harbour bridge and the water underneath. The slice was rich with colour: blue sky, navy water, yellow and green ferries. An artist would depict the skyscrapers as the grey corporate intrusion on the natural beauty of the harbour. It was a riveting scene and Niamh stopped a few times a day to look at it.

Scott's work station was just down the hall and it wasn't long before he was standing in her office – tall and athletically lean. She looked away from the window and into a pair of angry blue eyes. "Hello. Can you take a seat, please?" She nodded at the only spare seat, should he not see it.

"I don't need to sit down to be told I'm losing my job," he said sarcastically.

"I . . ." Looking up at his barely contained fury, Niamh was thrown off course. His handsome face was set in a scowl, his broad shoulders taut with tension. She wished that she knew him better because then she would have some chance of mollifying him.

"Come on, Niamh. After that debacle in the auditorium, I can only assume that I'm one of the unfortunate *10 per cent.*" His eyes pierced through her. Disconcerted, she looked downwards to her notes.

"Yes, I'm sorry to say that your position has been made

redundant in the restructure. We've looked throughout the organisation for alternative positions –"

"Oh, for Christ's sake, cut out the standard script – I know it off by heart – I work in Human Resources, remember?"

"I'm sorry." He was right; there was no need to read the script word by word.

"And I'm pissed off," he retorted.

"That's understandable," she said, trying to pacify him. Up until today, they had spoken only with the polite distance that came with a new working relationship. She had never seen him like this. She was distracted by the virility of his anger and breathed a sigh of relief when he finally sat his six-foot-plus frame into the seat.

"You hired me," he accused. "Only two months ago you offered me this role. How the hell is it redundant in the space of two months?"

"You're the last person to join our department so your role was the first one we examined to see if we could manage without it," she explained. "Our plan is to decentralise recruitment out to the business units so we won't need a senior recruitment manager role in Human Resources."

"And when was this inspired decision made?"

She ignored his sarcasm and answered him as honestly as she could. "A few weeks ago the head office realised we would have to restructure in order to make a profit for the next two quarters. As Malcolm said, the share price won't sustain any more losses."

"I understand all that – but someone in this company

must have known this restructure was coming when I was hired."

Niamh now saw why Scott was angry and where his argument was headed. What he was saying made perfect sense but, if the company was at fault, then this wasn't the place to admit it.

She avoided answering his question directly and said, "That's not necessarily true."

"Niamh –" he sighed, running his hand through hair that was highlighted from the sun, "I don't want to argue with you. I appreciate that you were probably not directly involved in the decision to restructure but you have to see where my issue is. Only two months ago I gave up a well-paid job for what I thought was a good opportunity with HDD. Now I'm unemployed. I've got a mortgage and a child to support. This has serious implications for me – I'm not just being difficult here!"

He had never mentioned his child before now and the unexpected insight into his personal life made it even harder for Niamh. He knew exactly what emotional buttons to push – he had worked in the HR profession for long enough.

"The company provides you with a retrenchment package that's as generous as we can be in these hard times," she said, her tone business-like.

"How many weeks' pay do I get?"

"You'll receive the equivalent of eight weeks." She handed him the calculation sheet.

"That's not good enough!" His voice was harsh; he didn't even look at the piece of paper. "It's coming up to

Christmas and the IT market is really struggling. It will take me months to find something else."

"I'm sorry, that's our standard package for somebody with your length of service. We'll also provide you with an outplacement counselling service." She sounded lame even to her own ears. She waited for him to explode but he didn't.

"Outplacement isn't going to pay my mortgage." His eyes were obstinate as they locked with hers. "Eight weeks just isn't enough to compensate me in these circumstances."

"This is the best I can do. If you sign here I can give you the cheque today." She knew he wasn't going to sign; she was just following the script.

"I'm not signing anything!" He stood up and was looking down at her again. "I want to consider my legal position."

"OK," she had to tilt her head backwards to meet the intense blue eyes, "that's your prerogative."

He left, shutting the door behind him with more force than necessary. She took another deep breath. That wasn't a good start and she still had nineteen more names on her list. Black Monday could only get worse.

Helen Barnes's face was void of expression and Don McAlister was acutely aware of his inexperience as he read through the script. Recently promoted, Don was usually an easy-going guy who liked to talk. But he was totally out of his comfort zone today and the right words were hard to find. Had Helen spoken, he would have felt more confident, more effective. But she remained stubbornly silent as she was told that her position was redundant and there were no alternative positions in the company. Her silence ran straight through the meeting, not even a muscle moved when Don explained the basis behind her termination-payment calculation. The exercise was a farce and he didn't blame her for not contributing. After five years of managing the Finance Department, Helen knew these calculations better than anyone. There was also no doubt that she had been at the other side of the table many times in her career.

Everybody in HDD knew and liked Helen. With short chestnut hair and dominant hazel eyes, she looked like the proverbial girl next door. Yet she cajoled the managers into a reluctant responsibility for their financial results and was pleasantly uncompromising on ethics and compliance. Finance directors came and went but there was always Helen, holding the department together and managing it better than any of her bosses. Don could only conclude that her silence masked a massive shock at losing her job.

When there was nothing more for Don to say, Helen found her voice. "I can't believe Phil has done this."

Her words were so quiet, Don had to strain to hear. "Phil" had to be Phil Davis, the finance director, Helen's boss. He was a big beefy man who had only been around a few months. Don fidgeted with his tie, daunted by Helen's anger. It enveloped the whole room, made all the more ominous by her low tone.

"He can't get away with this."

Colour was starting to flood into her face. Don watched her, rapt.

"Get away with what?" he prompted when she didn't continue of her own accord.

Helen's eyes fixed on the inexperienced HR manager who had the unfortunate job of telling people that their jobs had been axed.

"He sexually harassed me. Now he *thinks* he's found a convenient way to get rid of me."

Don felt like upping and running. He was only three days promoted; this was entirely out of his league.

"Have you made a complaint?" he croaked.

"No. But I told Phil that I would when it happened again last week."

Don nodded when she paused, setting his expression to empathetic, wondering what "it" entailed.

"But he found a way to shut me up – by retrenching me – the *bastard*!" Helen checked herself before repeating, "He's not going to get away with this."

Don glanced at his watch; he had ten more people to see before the end of the day.

"I'm sorry, Helen. I have to finish up. I think you should lodge a formal complaint in the next few days … I'll tell Niamh that you'll call her, OK?" he said, only too aware that he was out of his depth with a sexual harassment suit against a senior executive like Phil Davis.

"Thanks, Don – I will talk to Niamh. I know this hasn't been easy for you. Thank you for handling it all so professionally."

With that she left, her poise intact, her anger no

13

longer evident on her pleasant round face. Don's confidence was restored with her words of praise and he picked up the phone to call the next victim to the gallows.

Jessica Simpson found herself staring at Denis Greene's limp greasy ponytail. The hair drawn through the elastic band was grey and split. She had an urge to get the scissors from her desk drawer to snip the thing off. A ponytail on a man of his age had to be a statement of some sort – God only knew what!

She waited while Denis read through his calculation sheet, a series of expressions fleeting across his face, racing off before she could identify what they were. He took his time, studying the numbers with the care of someone who isn't too good at maths.

Denis noted they had rounded his years of service up to four – he supposed that was generous enough. He had got five weeks in lieu of notice and seven months' redundancy. The overall number was appealing; there were things he could do with the money.

"Do I take it that the figures are agreeable to you?" Jessica asked, aware of precious time ticking by.

"Don't put words in my mouth," he was quick to reply, his voice loud with a rough Yorkshire accent. He was anxious not to appear agreeable. In his experience, the more trouble you were, the more you got. He generally made it his business to be troublesome.

"Look, Denis," Jessica stifled an irritated sigh, "if you have issues, now is the right time to air them."

Denis frantically tried to gather his thoughts, not sure

if he wanted to complain or take this money and walk away. The girl, Jessica, hadn't mentioned his business visa. He guessed that it wouldn't be valid if he was no longer working for HDD, the sponsoring employer. But he wasn't sure what would happen to his outstanding application for permanent residency. He had made that application two months ago; only a few people knew about it.

"Denis?" Jessica prompted, her impatience now revealing itself.

"You're pressuring me! Give me time to think, lass!" he snapped. Denis, oblivious to Jessica's surging temper and his own rudeness, continued to weigh things up in his head. If the application for permanent residency fell through, the worst case would be that he and Lily would have to return to England. They had been arguing about that for ages anyhow, with Lily's mother getting older and constantly whingeing that her only daughter lived on the other side of the world. But this retrenchment might be forcing the issue prematurely. Denis's plan to go back had been a medium-term one, not short-term like Lily's.

Jessica gave a deliberate cough just as Denis reached a conclusion. He decided he would take the cheque and walk away from HDD. Things had been getting too complicated there and this was the perfect reason to back out. If that meant they had to go back to England, then it was a pity but he could live with it.

"No issues." He looked at her with narrowed eyes before adding, "For now," just to be mean to the stressed HR manager.

15

As he left, Jessica relaxed from a tension the extent of which she hadn't realised until her office was free of his obnoxious presence. When she was calm enough, she made her next phone call.

Five o'clock came and HDD was lighter by fifty people. Black Monday was over for most but Niamh had one final meeting in her office.

"It's been a tough day," she said to Don and Jessica when they came in. They both mumbled their concurrence. Their faces spoke volumes; they wanted to get as far away from HDD as possible.

Niamh knew they all shared the same thumping headache and spoke quickly. "I wanted to touch base before we head home. I need to know if you have any issues to report, anyone who is likely to get legal."

"I have one," Don replied.

"Who?" his female colleagues asked in unison.

"Helen Barnes."

Niamh took a sharp breath. She had been very surprised to see Helen's name on the retrenchment list. The previous finance director had once said she was a sterling employee, someone you would move heaven and earth to keep. But Phil Davis, his successor, had offered her name up like a lamb to the slaughter. Said that these were hard times and he couldn't justify her large salary. That had surprised Niamh, but with so many others going she hadn't challenged his reasons. Now she wished she had.

"She says that Phil sexually harassed her and put her on the retrenchment list because she wouldn't play his games," said Don.

The faint thumping in Niamh's head got more insistent. She knew Helen and she wasn't the type of woman to make an idle accusation of sexual harassment. She massaged her aching forehead. "Sexual Harassment is always so difficult – there are usually no witnesses and it comes down to one person's word against another."

"Phil Davis is a creep – it doesn't surprise me at all that he's made a pass at Helen." Jessica folded her arms in disgust. She was famous for her temper that was in sync with her red hair. She always had difficulty keeping her opinions to herself.

"You should know better than to jump to conclusions like that without knowing the facts," Niamh admonished half-heartedly.

Jessica wasn't listening. "What did Phil do to Helen? Did he –"

"Jessica!" Niamh's next admonishment was sharper. "It's none of your business . . . Don, is Helen going to make a formal complaint?"

"She said she would. I asked her to give you a call over the next few days . . ."

"Thanks . . . now, Jessica, do you have any issues to report from your meetings?"

"No. Nothing."

"Good. That means we only have two potential cases. Two out of fifty isn't bad."

"Who's the other one?" Don asked the obvious question.

"It's Scott Morgan – he says he wouldn't have left his

old job if he knew that he would lose his role here after only two months. He wants to think over his legal position – I'm fairly sure he'll sue."

Don and Jessica were silent. Scott was their colleague; he was new but he was popular. He was doing a great job at streamlining recruitment and without him they would be going back to the old chaos.

"Please keep that information confidential," Niamh warned unnecessarily. "I don't want any word of Scott's situation –"

She was interrupted by a knock on the door and it opened to reveal a peroxide head.

"Are you all finished now?" Sharon, her personal assistant, asked.

"Yes, just done." Niamh started to clear her desk, moving files into the drawer where they could be locked away.

"I brought some drinks – thought you could do with the numbing effect of alcohol after a day like today," Sharon said as she opened the door fully and walked in carrying a bottle of wine and a stack of plastic cups.

Jessica took the bottle of wine from Sharon's grasp, nodding with approval at the label. "Mmm – Shiraz – where did you get this?"

"Malcolm's office," Sharon admitted with a shameless grin. She was an excellent PA despite her haphazard appearance and personality. Her hair was peroxided to death and it clashed with her cheerful red face. Her life was a seesaw of diets and binges. The wine indicated she was currently on the crest of a binge rather than in the depths of a diet.

18

Jessica opened the bottle and poured four equal shares to the very rim of each plastic cup. Niamh raised her cup in a toast, saying, "Not sure what we're celebrating, but cheers anyway."

"We're not celebrating; we're commiserating," Don corrected his boss.

"Yeah, commiserating at losing the only good-looking man in the department," said Jessica, then seeing Don's fallen face added, "Sorry, Don, don't take it personally but you can't compete with Scott. He's a *sexy beast* – isn't he, Niamh?"

Niamh felt all eyes turning to her direction. In her head she was thinking of blue eyes, berry-brown skin and the lean muscle across his shoulders. Scott *was* incredibly sexy but she wasn't going to admit that to anyone but herself. She had registered that he was attractive at the very first interview. But then he became a member of her staff, putting him in a no-go zone even if she had been single. Outwardly, she hesitated only slightly before saying, "I'm not qualified to comment on sexy beasts – I'm married."

Everyone laughed but Don. He was in his early twenties and his attractiveness to the opposite sex was paramount in his life. He didn't fancy Jessica but he thought he should at least feature on her list of good-looking men.

Jessica, oblivious to Don's feelings, was getting worked up. "Yeah, typical of a smug married person to get rid of the only sexy beast we've had around here in ages."

Niamh grinned at her. "Sorry – but it was a last in, first out policy, nothing to do with sexiness."

"How did Scott take it, Niamh? Was he OK?" Sharon asked. Not many people knew that there was a very caring person underneath the scary hair.

"Not great," Niamh confessed with a grimace. "He was pretty pissed off. And I didn't handle him very well. I was thrown off course –"

"I should hope you didn't *handle* him!" Jessica picked up on Niamh's unfortunate choice of words and burst into a fit of giggles.

"How many times do I have to tell you?" Niamh pursed her lips with a mock primness. "I'm married."

Married! Yes, she was married but it didn't feel like it. It must have had something to do with living with a stranger. After one plastic cup of Shiraz, she left to go home to that stranger.

Traffic on the bridge was bad even though rush hour was over. Niamh hated sitting in traffic, edging forward in millimetres. She put on a CD to stop herself getting agitated and to stop the analysis of how she and Chris had become strangers.

It was a full hour before she turned into their street in Manly. Light filled the windows of their two-storey house. Chris was home before her and that was nothing short of amazing. She parked next to his silver BMW in the double garage. He loved that car in the same way he loved all the other symbols of his success as an up-and-coming solicitor. He was gunning for partnership and was within striking distance of his goal. She should have been proud of him.

20

"Hi, honey, this is a nice surprise." She kissed his cheek. He was cooking dinner, a rare occurrence.

"How did it go?" he asked, not reacting in any way to her kiss. He was asking about the restructure. She often shared confidential work matters with him. Being a solicitor, he could be relied on to keep his mouth shut. She kicked off her shoes before answering, the coolness of the tiles a welcome balm to her feet. "It was terrible – Malcolm made a total mess of the address. He told everyone it was 'just business', nothing personal. He kept referring to 'the 10 per cent', as if they weren't real people. He doesn't know the meaning of sensitivity! He doesn't care that Christmas is just around the corner and the job market is already starting to die down for the holidays."

"They'll be damn lucky to find work within the next three months – they would be fools to think otherwise," Chris commented with an indifferent shrug.

She stole a piece of pepper from the chopping-board. She was hungry; there had been no time for lunch. "I think most of them were trying to be optimistic. With the exception of Scott, that is. He knew damn well he'd be out of work for some time."

"Who's Scott?" Chris asked absently and Niamh felt a warning stab of frustration. She had already mentioned Scott numerous times. Chris had a faultless memory when it came to his own life but a hopeless one when it came to anything she told him about her work or her family.

21

"He is, I mean *was*, the recruitment manager in my department. He's only been with us two months and he was really mad at being made redundant – I kind of lost control of the meeting with him – I think he's going to sue us . . ."

Chris was somewhat of a perfectionist and the admission of an error by his wife fully caught his attention. "For heaven's sake, Niamh," he gave her an exasperated look, "you're the human resources director – you can't afford to lose control!"

"I know, I know – but I could understand why he was angry, I really could. He's got a child to support and he'll be out of work for a few months for sure . . . I felt sorry for him . . ." She stared back at Chris, knowing full well he wouldn't be interested in the mitigating circumstances but telling him anyway so he could prove just how uncaring he was. He didn't let her down.

"Don't let it bother you so much. You have outplacement counsellors to deal with that messy stuff."

"Messy stuff" meant personal and home issues and they clearly didn't rate with her husband. Niamh lost her tentative hold on her temper. "Of course, it bothers me! We sent fifty people home to their families today – that's *fifty* people who had to tell their partners they have no income and no job prospects until after the holiday season!"

"All I'm saying is that you have to distance yourself from all that. Human Resources exists to hire and fire – if you can't –"

"Thanks for summarising my job in such a crude way,"

she interrupted. "I do a *lot* more than hiring and firing – my job is about *people* – people management, development – and I care about *people* – there's nothing wrong with that – just because all you care about is money and your bloody partnership – "

"Stop!" he cut her off. It was clear he didn't want to engage in the emotion of another fight. "Look – I know you've had a bad day but don't bring it home, eh?"

She swallowed a response because he was right. It was late, it had been an awful day and she didn't need to round it off with an argument. Most of their conversations these days involved someone raising their voice in frustration before they descended into a full-blown argument. It was history repeating itself. Twenty years ago it had been her mum and dad fighting; now it was Chris and her.

She watched him, letting go of her anger, her disappointment in him. The hard lines to his face were set in concentration as he wielded the chopping-knife, mincing the peppers to a pulp. His dark hair had a few grey strands at the temples, his skin the pallor of a man who sat at his desk for most of the daylight hours. At that moment it was difficult to find any love for him inside her. She didn't want to think thoughts like that so she went upstairs to change.

Chris had a stir-fry ready by the time she came back down. They ate in silence. Afterwards he watched TV and she went to bed. Sleep came but it wasn't peaceful. Her dreams were full of yelling, arguing, screaming. Her mum and dad were there, Uncle Tom standing between them. Chris was in the background, waving the chopping-knife around, as was Scott, who kept yelling, "I'm going to sue you. I'm going to sue you!". The anger was ugly, hurtful, except for Scott. His anger was passionate. He was fighting for something that was noble, worthwhile, fighting for his child.

"Can I see the child?" she asked and everybody stopped screaming at each other.

Scott turned to pick it up.

"Here –"

Then everyone started screaming again for the child's face was black and starved of oxygen.

Denis Greene got a call at 8pm that night. He had been expecting the call but Lily happened to be passing when the phone rang and picked it up before he could get to it.

"Denis!" she yelled from the hall where the phone was mounted on the wall.

"I'm coming!" he replied, pressing mute on the TV so there wouldn't be too much background noise.

He took the phone from Lily. "Hello?"

"This is not a good situation."

It was the same voice as before. Denis knew the voice but had not met its owner.

"It's not my fault," he said sulkily. "How was I to know I'd get kicked out on my ass?"

There was a brief pause before the uncompromising response from the caller. "You were in the middle of a critical job. That job needs to be completed."

Denis didn't like being spoken to as if he was a naughty

child.

"Can't you ask someone else to do it?"

"Don't be an idiot!" The caller was dismissive. "We can't approach another employee at this late stage."

"What's the solution then?" Denis asked with a sinking premonition. He was starting to have a bad feeling about how this was all going to end, notwithstanding the fact he didn't have any real information on the endgame.

"The solution is that you've got to get your job back."

The caller hung up and Denis went back to the TV, pretending to watch it. He flicked from channel to channel, his mind far away. He had over a hundred thousand dollars in his bank account now. They would pay him more if he completed the job but he wanted out. It was too risky and the longer it went on, the more likely it was he would get caught. He had thought that being retrenched had got him off the hook – it was a perfect excuse to walk away. But it seemed the caller had other ideas, and for the first time Denis was worried that he was out of his depth with these people. Pots and pans clashed in the background as Lily cleared up the kitchen after dinner. There was no risk she would sense his anxiety; they had not been on the same wavelength for years.

Helen Barnes didn't go home after work. She didn't want to have to face her mother. The old lady didn't understand words like retrenchment and sexual harassment and tomorrow would be time enough to enlighten her. She was at her friend Tina's house when her mobile rang. It was eight thirty and there was a hot pizza waiting for her attention.

"Hello. I'm ringing to see how you are."

"I'm OK." Helen was surprised. The caller was not someone she was expecting to hear from.

"I was personally disappointed to find your name on the hit list today."

"Were you?"

"Of course." The voice was insistent. "It doesn't seem very fair considering what you've contributed to the company over the last five years."

"I don't think a single one of the fifty people today felt it was 'fair' to lose their jobs so close to Christmas," Helen said tartly, feeling she was being patronised but not entirely sure.

"But *you* more than the others – you so *much* more than the others."

There was a strange pause.

"Why do you say that?" Helen asked suspiciously. Did the caller know about Phil? Had her claim of sexual harassment leaked out already?

The caller didn't answer her question, only said, "If you want to take this any further, you have my full support."

Again, there was another strange silence as Helen tried to read between the lines. "Thanks for the offer but I can handle it myself," she responded after a few moments.

The conversation ended and Tina topped up their respective glasses of wine.

Helen drank some before saying, "What a bizarre

phone call!"

"Who was it?" Tina asked, taking a bite from an over-sized slice of pizza.

"Someone from work."

"Was it that man – what's his name again – Phil?" A full mouth never prevented Tina from asking questions.

"No, not him." Helen shuddered.

"Is Phil married?"

"Yes, poor woman. I bet she has no idea what her husband gets up to behind her back."

Tina finished the slice of pizza before commenting, "You didn't sound very pleased to hear from that person who called you."

"I wasn't," Helen replied, lifting her glass to take another sip of the wine. "It was someone who seems to have an agenda I don't quite understand."

Scott Morgan was trying to put Jenny to bed when his mobile rang. It was nearly nine o'clock, two hours past her usual bedtime. She was putting up a commendable performance and he could barely hear the person at the end of the line.

"Hello."

"Hello – Jenny, stop that – I said stop it – hello, who is this?"

The caller responded as Scott retrieved Jenny's teddy from the floor. He swore it was the last time. If she threw it out once more, the damn teddy could spend the night on the floor.

"What can I help you with?" he asked, turning out the

27

bedroom light one more time, waiting outside for the screaming to start.

"Are you OK after today? I presume it came as a shock."

"I'm OK as I can be under the circumstances." He could hear Jenny moving about in the cot but there was no screaming yet.

"I sympathise with your position. It's so much harder when children are in the picture," the caller said. "The financial strain is more immediate, the responsibility greater."

The purpose of the call wasn't yet obvious to Scott and he had a headache that could only be relieved with a beer. "Look, I have my hands full here. Is there any particular reason for your call?"

"I'm merely offering my support," was the response. "I want to ensure you get a fair outcome considering your circumstances."

He should have asked more questions but it was late. He was tired. He needed that beer. "I've got to go."

"OK. We'll talk again."

When he hung up he realised he hadn't heard Jenny for a few minutes. He dared to peek inside her room. She was horizontal. She was asleep. He went downstairs and got a beer from the fridge.

Chapter Two

It was after ten when Niamh got in the next morning. That was late, too late given the hoards of emails that were unanswered from the day before. She shrugged off her jacket and slid her laptop into its docking station. Sharon, her peroxide blonde hair even more awry than usual, arrived with a much-appreciated cappuccino.

"I thought I'd save you the trip to the coffee shop ..."

"Thanks . . . did you stay on much later last night?" As she had left, Sharon had been on her way to raid Malcolm's fridge for a second bottle of Shiraz.

"Malcolm's office was locked so we went to Jackson's," Sharon responded, stifling a yawn. "I didn't get home until after midnight."

Niamh laughed. "OK – I get the picture. I'll try not to disturb you too much today."

She was still smiling as she started to read the emails

that had banked up during yesterday's meetings. There was a knock on her door and she looked up to see Scott. Her stomach did an immediate flip which she did her best to ignore – the last thing she needed was to be thrown off course like yesterday. She noticed that the black bags under his eyes matched her own: they had a sleepless night in common. He and his kid had been on her mind half the night after that terrible nightmare.

"Good morning." She sat back from her keyboard, looking closely at him to gauge if he was still angry. His expression was sombre but it wasn't hostile.

"Hello." He sat down. They faced each other from the same positions as yesterday. He was dressed casually in a black T-shirt and navy Levis. Before she could help it, the *sexy beast* discussion from the night before came to the forefront of her mind. She remembered her cooling cappuccino and took a quick drink of it to hide her embarrassment.

"I just want to let you know that I will be taking legal action against the company." There was no anger this time, no accusations; he was just stating his intentions as impartially as possible.

"OK – thanks for coming in to tell me." It was no surprise. She knew he wasn't the kind of man to take a perceived injustice lying down.

There was a brief silence. It seemed that he had something else he wanted to say. "Look, Niamh . . . I don't have any alternative. I can't afford to be without a job – your responsibilities are greater when you have a family to support." Neither of them realised that he had unwittingly repeated the words of the caller the night before.

"It's OK, I understand – who's your lawyer?"

He grimaced. "I haven't got that far yet."

There was another silence and she was sorely tempted to ask him about his child, just to make sure that her nightmare wasn't some kind of terrible premonition. But he would think she was totally mad if she admitted to dreaming about him.

He stood up, saying, "I guess I'll see you around . . ."

"OK . . . bye . . ."

As he left she caught herself admiring the firm muscles of his upper arms. The black T-shirt was tight across his shoulders, the back of his neck an even deeper brown than his face. Luckily he didn't turn around to see her staring but Sharon, who sat right outside her door and had a bird's-eye view into her office, did. She gave her boss the thumbs-up. Niamh pretended not to see.

What's wrong with me? she thought to herself. *Are things so bad with Chris that I've resorted to leering at every attractive man that comes my way?*

She went back to her overflowing inbox. Even more messages had come in. She wasn't making any progress on yesterday's backlog.

She had just started to get somewhere when her phone rang. "I've got a call on hold," Sharon said tentatively, she could see from her desk that Niamh was absorbed and wouldn't welcome the interruption.

"Tell whoever it is that I'm unavailable this morning."

"I did – but he insists that it's important."

"Who is it?" Niamh asked with a sigh.

"A solicitor, Paul Jacobsen."

"I don't know him."

"He says he's representing Denis Greene."

Denis Greene – he was one of the people retrenched yesterday. He had been on Jessica's list. "Put him through."

Sharon obliged.

"Niamh Lynch speaking."

"Paul Jacobsen, I'm acting for Denis Greene."

Niamh's reply was curt. "I wasn't aware that Denis is taking an action against us."

"That's the purpose of this call." Paul Jacobsen had a smooth voice. "I'll be following through with a letter."

"What's Denis's issue?" She couldn't help the uncharacteristic terseness in her voice. The digital clock on her screen was evidence of the morning slipping away.

"Denis is currently on a business-sponsored visa – obviously HDD is the sponsoring employer. The term will be up in six months and he took the initiative to apply for a permanent residency so he could stay in Australia."

"I don't know Denis personally and I wasn't aware of his visa situation," Niamh admitted when Paul Jacobsen paused.

"I'm sure the company wouldn't have terminated him had they thought through the implications for Denis and his family," was his patronising response.

"That's not what I said," she corrected him immediately. "I said that I wasn't aware that he was on a business visa or that he has an application in progress for permanent residency. However, that is all irrelevant to this discussion as the company's decision to retrench Denis was based on the fact that his position is no longer needed."

The lawyer made his tone more amiable. "Denis has lived in this country for almost four years and wants to make it his home. As a result of his redundancy, his business visa will no longer be valid and he will have to be repatriated back to England. His wife, in particular, is devastated at the thought of leaving her friends and house."

Niamh absorbed the lawyer's words before questioning, "What about his application for permanent residency?"

"The Department of Immigration will turn him down if he isn't resident in the country at the time his application is being considered."

Again, Niamh wondered why Jessica hadn't foreseen the issue. She was normally very perceptive but then yesterday had been a stressful day. There hadn't been time for perceptiveness.

"Where is all this leading to, Paul?" she asked eventually.

"I believe a mutually acceptable solution to this problem would be to find Denis a similar role in the company. Then he will still be employed by HDD and living in the country when the Department of Immigration examine his application."

"I'm afraid it's not that simple," Niamh said firmly. "Retrenchment is not a decision we take lightly and we look for alternative roles as a matter of course. I can assure you there is nothing else for Denis at HDD."

"Let's not debate the issue here," he urged. "I'll send a

letter in the next few days and then we can meet to talk it over face to face."

He hung up and Niamh didn't waste any time before calling Jessica's extension. "I thought you said you had no legal issues from yesterday?"

"I didn't." Jessica was indignant at the edge in her boss's voice. It had been a late night with Don and Sharon in Jackson's and she had a pain in her head that could be a hangover.

"I've just come off the phone from Denis Greene's solicitor."

"Denis Greene?" The first thing Jessica thought of was the greasy ponytail. "He didn't say a word yesterday about a solicitor!"

"Apparently Denis was applying for permanent residency and being retrenched has thrown a spanner in the works. The solicitor said he was on a business visa, sponsored by us. Is that true?" Niamh asked, moderating the frustration in her voice. It wasn't Jessica's fault; Denis had the prerogative to sue any time he wanted and had no obligation to tell them of his grievance in advance.

"Yes. It's one of those four-year visas."

"How much is left to go on the term?"

"A few months," Jessica answered after taking a moment to think.

"Paul Jacobsen said six months."

"Does it matter how many months are left?" Jessica was defensive. "We've done a legitimate corporate restructure and Bruce Knight doesn't need as many engineers as before. Surely we have the right to pull out of a business visa if we no longer have a position for the individual?"

Niamh didn't answer the rhetorical question. "How much termination pay did we give him?" she asked, trying to come from a new angle.

"Seven months, including notice."

"That's well over the statutory minimum," Niamh commented. Her unvoiced opinion was that Denis Greene was already adequately compensated for any inconvenience.

"I can't believe that we can be held responsible for his personal and family circumstances beyond what we've already forked out." Jessica was in agreement but more vocal than Niamh.

"The solicitor isn't asking for money, not yet anyway. He wants us to reinstate Denis."

"That's a joke. Is he saying Denis loves his job so much that he can't bear to leave it?" Jessica was sarcastic.

"I think Denis only wants the job as a means to get the application for residency approved. He's using us. The question is whether we owe him . . ." Niamh sighed, wishing that employment law wasn't such a minefield. "I guess Lucinda Armstrong is the only person who can tell me if we're in trouble or not."

"I'm sorry, Niamh," Jessica said. "I completely forgot that Denis was on a business visa – I just don't know why he didn't say anything yesterday – I asked him *twice* if he had any issues – but he gave no indication that he would do this."

"OK. Look, can you write down what you recall from your meeting with him? It may become important later."

Hunger pangs told Niamh that it was lunch-time. Sharon had gone out while she had been on the phone to Jessica and she'd missed her chance to give her a food order. She peered out the window. The slice of sky between the two skyscrapers had heavy clouds – it looked like she should take her jacket.

Her escape was foiled by a fresh-faced Japanese man. Yoshi Murasaki paused at the door of his office when he saw Niamh hurry through the executive area.

"My sources tell me that we may have some legal issues that have come out of yesterday's retrenchments."

There was no acknowledgement, no greeting, just a statement of fact that came out sounding very like an accusation. His English was good but it was formal and stilted.

"Yes, that's true. So far, we have three potential legal actions." Niamh was curt. She didn't see why she had to justify herself to Yoshi and he was standing between her and her lunch.

"I need to understand the specifics of these legal actions as soon as possible," said Yoshi.

"I'll let you know the details as soon as I get them. I have nothing in writing yet."

"It could be weeks before you get anything in writing," he dismissed her offer. "I can't wait for that. I need to let Japan know as soon as possible if we have any exposures down here."

Niamh's frustration bubbled over and hardened her voice. "Yoshi, I was in back-to-back meetings for all of yesterday and I've had interruption after interruption this morning. I'll summarise the issues when I get five minutes of peace – but I have to talk to Malcolm and Lucinda before I release the details to you."

It wasn't often that Yoshi was challenged. It was less often that the challenge came from a woman almost ten years his junior.

"I need immediate notification of all such issues – I take offence that you insist on updating Malcolm without including me." His voice was more stilted than usual, a sign that he was uncomfortable with the difficult conversation.

Niamh met his black eyes. "There is no need to be offended. The last time I checked, Malcolm was still the CEO of this company. Has something changed?"

There was a tense silence. Niamh's gaze didn't falter. Yoshi was surprisingly the first to relent. "You are correct, of course. I apologise. However, I would consider it a personal favour if you could include me in your initial summary of the issues. My boss in Tokyo is extremely anxious that we return a profit over the next two quarters and I have to let him know of any risks to that profit."

Niamh awarded him with a smile. An apology from the haughty liaison director was not to be belittled. "OK, Yoshi, I will do that favour for you. Just be patient while I catch up on the work that has piled up from yesterday."

He nodded and backed out of her way so she could pass. He watched her as she walked past the lifts and made for the fire-exit. She was small in stature, like the Japanese women, but any similarity ended there. There was a steely determination underneath her youthful appearance and he had witnessed her fighting with passion whenever profit was put ahead of employee rights. Yes, she was a very different creature from the well-dressed, softly spoken women in the Tokyo office who showed him such fawning respect. She opened the heavy door of the stairwell and he heard her heels echo as she descended the four flights of stairs. The stairs ended in an alley off George Street and were used by those too impatient to wait for the lifts.

Yoshi returned to his office and shut the door. After a few moments of thought he dialled Malcolm's extension. When there was no answer he tried his mobile.

"Hello." Malcolm was barely audible above the laughter and music in the background. Wherever he was having lunch, it sounded like a lot more fun than the sushi Yoshi would have at his desk.

"We have some legal issues that have come about from the restructure," Yoshi stated, speaking loudly in recognition that Malcolm would find it difficult to hear.

The CEO didn't need to ask the identity of the caller: the stilted voice of the uptight Japanese spy was very distinct. Malcolm excused himself from the table of prospective clients. The background noise became fainter as he moved towards the foyer of the establishment.

"Yes, Niamh alerted me to that late yesterday. It was fifty people after all – some legal action has to be expected."

But his philosophical response did not satisfy Yoshi. "Niamh said that there are three cases – do you know who the people are?"

"No, I don't need to know the details yet," Malcolm said. "It's too early in the day – anything could happen."

It was the wrong answer. "The whole purpose of the restructure was to ensure we made a profit for the rest of the year," Yoshi preached. "These claims could threaten the small profit we've committed to Japan – I'm sure Nishikawa Shacho expects you to know the details ..."

Malcolm was starting to get sick of Yoshi looking over his shoulder, threatening him with the expectations of the vice-president up in Tokyo. It was time to show him who the boss was.

"Yoshi, I'm lunching with prospective clients right now – I'm sure you'll agree that Nishikawa Shacho also expects me to bring in new business . . . The lawsuits are only talk right now, there are no written claims and no information on the amount of money involved. Let's allow Niamh and Lucinda to deal with them for the time being . . ."

"I disagree with the priority you are placing on this." Yoshi wasn't going to give up.

"I must return to my clients." Malcolm was already walking back to his table, the background noise becoming louder. A girl screamed in laughter just as he hung up and Yoshi was left wondering what den of iniquity he was patronising for lunch. His sources had told him that the CEO had a weakness for the topless bars in Kings Cross.

Yoshi's instincts were telling him that they had made a mistake when they appointed Malcolm Young as the person who would lead the Australian subsidiary through one of the toughest years in the technology industry.

There were already some warning signs that he was not the right man for the job. Was it too soon to feed this information back to Nishikawa Shacho? Yoshi mulled it over as he ate his sushi.

Jenny was continuing her rebellion by refusing to eat. Scott tried everything, even singing *Twinkle Twinkle* as he attempted to force spoonfuls of mush into her mouth. But her lips remained stubbornly shut and each time she flicked the spoon away with an angry hand. In the end there was food everywhere: on her hair, the walls, even the phone.

After the aborted lunch, he called the childcare centre to let them know that Jenny wouldn't be coming back. He was a realist; it was going to take a few months to find a comparable role to the one in HDD. It was unsettling for Jenny, especially so if a place in the same centre wasn't available when they needed it in a few months' time. But the plain truth was that he just couldn't afford to keep her in care while he was out of work.

They had a long crabby day together and he put her to bed early. They went through the same teddy-chucking ritual as the night before – the poor kid could sense there was something wrong and this new ritual was her only way of making that known. When she finally dropped off, he rang his sister.

"How's my gorgeous niece?" Deb asked without even returning his "hello".

"Out of sorts . . . just like her dad."

"What's wrong? Is she coming down with something?"

Deb ignored Scott's negative reference to his own well-being.

"No – she's fine really – the problem is me."

"Why? What's happened?"

"I got retrenched yesterday."

"But you've only been in that place two months! How can you lose your job already?" she exclaimed in supportive outrage.

"I know. Hard to believe, isn't it?"

"Oh no – that's just your luck –" she bit off the rest of the sentence when she realised how bad it would sound out loud. It was too late.

"Yeah, rounds off a great year. I started with a wife and a job. Guess how many I've got left?" He let loose on the sarcasm; it made him feel marginally better.

"I'm sorry. I didn't mean it that way. Do you need any money? Damn, that came out wrong too. Why don't I just shut up?"

Scott ignored her babbling and asked after her better half. "Is Brett there?"

"Yeah, he's sprawled in front of the TV."

"Tell him get off his arse. I need someone to keep me company while I drown my sorrows. Will you come over and watch Jenny for me?"

"Is she in bed?" Deborah was an adoring aunt but not very hands-on. Getting Jenny off to sleep wasn't within the realm of her experience.

"She's sound asleep," he promised. "You won't hear a peep out of her."

Scott heard Brett yelling something in the background.

"What's he saying?" he asked his sister.

"He wants to know where you're taking him."

"Tell him we're going to the city," Scott decided. "I need to get far away from all things domestic!"

"OK." Deb sighed at the likelihood of a hungover husband the next day. "Your drinking buddy and baby-sitter will be there within the hour."

"Thanks."

Denis and Lily Greene were building up to a brawl. There was nothing new in that. Their personalties were absolute opposites and they annoyed each other in ways that not even they could predict. Denis carried his aggressive personality everywhere with him; it wasn't exclusive to home. But Lily, meek to those outside her immediate family, was a bully within the walls of her own house.

"Money, money – that's the only thing that means anything to you. You've no respect for anything else!" she spat at him from her position behind the kitchen counter. She chopped the vegetables viciously.

Denis regretted telling her about the lawsuit with HDD. She didn't need to know and he should have anticipated that she wouldn't approve. Lily, albeit not having worked for many years herself, had a fixation about respecting the company that paid your wage. She thought suing it was disrespectful. Logic never counted for anything with his wife; it didn't matter to her that HDD was no longer his employer.

"It's a good thing money means something to one of us – hell, if it was you in charge of finances, we'd be broke!" he yelled, keeping his head turned away from her as he watched the TV.

"Don't you start that! You wanted your wife at home, cooking dinners, cleaning – yet you keep throwing it in my face   I can walk right out of here and get a job – leave you to cook your own meals and clean your own mess," she threatened, knowing even as she spoke that the prospect of returning to the workforce terrified her. It was over twenty years since she had a job.

"That'd be the happiest day of my life – I wouldn't have to listen to your crap any more," Denis shot back, calling her bluff – he knew she was unemployable.

"Crap? Crap?" Lily screamed in rage, leaving the kitchen counter with the knife in hand to stand over him as he sprawled on the sofa. "I'm the one who's been listening to crap. Six months, you said – a six-month holiday in Australia. And here we are – *almost four years later* – with my mother still waiting for us to go back!"

Lily thought she knew it all and it often amused Denis that she knew so little about what was really going on. She didn't have the first idea of the technology industry and what he did day after day as a software engineer. She didn't know about the hundred thousand dollars that he had earned on the side, quietly accruing interest in a term deposit account. She didn't even know about the application for permanent residency. Boy, that would make her mad!

"Damn you and your mother – you're both too stupid

to see what opportunities there are in this country," he snorted, reaching for the remote to change the channel. Denis was much more flexible than his rigid wife; he could happily live in either Australia or England. The decision came down to money; it was as simple as that. He had applied for the residency as an insurance, just to give him some options should he not want to go back to England when his business visa was up. A few months ago he had told the caller about his insurance policy. That was when the phone calls had been simpler. Instructions, not threats as they were now. He had only been making conversation; the caller didn't need to know his visa status. The caller had retained that information and was now making the application for permanent residency pivotal to the lawsuit. He wasn't given the chance to say that he wanted out of the whole arrangement.

"Ha, opportunities my ass!" Lily screeched triumphantly, pointing the knife at him. "You've been doing the same thing since the day we got here – I haven't seen any extra money from '*opportunities*'!"

With that winning line, she returned to the kitchen counter to finish off the dinner.

She didn't hear him mutter, "You have no idea what money I've got, you stupid cow!"

Denis knew they behaved like trailer trash but he threw himself into the arguments wholeheartedly. After a brawl of this magnitude, they wouldn't be on speaking terms for at least twenty-four hours. That alone was worth the aggravation. Life would be peaceful without her incessant nagging and he could pretty much do as he pleased.

Lucinda Armstrong had a 6pm appointment with Niamh Lynch and her offsider, Jessica something. Lucinda had a bad recollection for names and was too arrogant to make an effort to become better at remembering them.

Her office was swamped in paperwork and folders that were begging to be filed away. They were stacked in every available space and it would take weeks of work to get them in order. She had been surviving without a personal assistant for two months now. Scott Morgan had been handling the recruitment of the position and his departure would undoubtedly cause further delays. The fact that Lucinda didn't come across well in interviews didn't help. Many of the applicants were petrified of the arrogant solicitor and didn't proceed with their application after the harrowing interview.

Niamh and Jessica arrived with several files of their own and there was a flurry as some space was cleared on the table to accommodate them. Denis's employee records were substantial. There had been a number of minor performance issues and his boss, Bruce Knight, had documented each one in detail. Niamh had read the file and guessed that Bruce was quite happy to see the back of Denis.

The records confirmed that HDD had sponsored Denis for a business visa and that there was six months left to go on the visa. Niamh felt optimistic, mainly because the company had paid him seven months of pay on termination.

"Look, we've paid him out past the date of his visa. I can't see how we can owe him anything else," she stated, handing Lucinda a copy of the visa.

Lucinda took the copy but only gave it a cursory glance. "It's a complex issue. No doubt it will be black and white to the Department of Immigration – they stick to their rules like glue. They're a typical government department who can't see outside the box. If there's no job, then there's no valid business visa and he has to go back to where he came from. Simple! On the other hand, employment law is much more lenient. He has lived in Australia for long enough to consider it home. We have deprived him and his family of their future in this country – and we didn't give him enough notice to make alternative plans."

"Doesn't common sense prevail here?" Jessica interrupted with passionate practicality. "Denis's job is genuinely redundant – we've had a downturn in our maintenance business and need fewer engineers than before."

Lucinda shot her a withering look. "Common sense never prevails in law. What's more, I'm pretty sure we have no other cases to use as precedent."

There was silence as Niamh and Jessica absorbed the injustice of the situation.

The lawyer broke the silence. "We shouldn't have retrenched him until next year. Another six months and his business visa would have expired – we would have had no further obligation to him. You should have thought of that before you put him on the retrenchment list."

The accusation hung in the air and Niamh wasn't

going to let Lucinda get away with it. "Contrary to popular opinion, Human Resources didn't handpick the people who were retrenched. That was the choice of the business units. And looking at Denis's performance record, I can fully understand why Bruce wanted him on that list."

"I'm sorry – this has happened because of me," Jessica muttered, her eyes downcast. "I knew about the visa – I just didn't think it would be relevant."

"Oh well, it's by the by now. Pointing fingers isn't going to get us anywhere," Lucinda said dismissively, ignoring the fact that she had started the finger-pointing exercise.

"What happens now?" Niamh asked to bring the conversation back to the core issue.

"Let's wait and see what his lawyer sends through," Lucinda replied.

"Do you know Paul Jacobsen?" Niamh knew from Chris that the law scene in Sydney was incestuous.

"Not very well – but I do know he's got a good reputation." Lucinda looked at her watch. It was clear she believed the meeting was over.

Niamh did some quick thinking. She had been working with Lucinda for over a year now. The only two females on the executive, they should have been allies. Should have – they weren't. They needed to build a better working relationship.

"Look, I don't know about you guys, but I've had a really hard day and I wouldn't mind going for a beer. Any takers?"

"OK," Lucinda shrugged.

"How about you, Jessica?"

"No, thanks. I had too much wine last night . . ."

Niamh went back to her office to lock up. She met Lucinda in the lift foyer and suggested the fire stairwell as the fastest way out.

"I never think to use this," Lucinda commented as her heels clicked on the bare concrete.

"I call it the coffee link," Niamh said. "It's the fastest way to get from level two to the coffee shop."

When they hit the alley, Lucinda paused to ask, "Forbes?"

"Why not?" Niamh shrugged and they walked up George Street without talking.

Forbes was belting out deafeningly loud music to cater for a crowd that was a decade younger than the two women. Niamh felt out of place yet Lucinda seemed to be perfectly comfortable.

"What would you like?" Niamh asked as she nudged her shoulder through the crowd at the bar.

"I'll have a Hahn."

"Draught?"

"No, bottle."

There was a considerable wait before Niamh caught the attention of the barman. She ordered two bottles of Hahn and handed one to Lucinda. "Look, why don't we stand over there?" she suggested, pointing back towards the door. "There seems to be a little more room."

Lucinda, tall with chiselled glamour, didn't seem to mind the jostling crowd as she led the way through.

"Are you a regular here?" Niamh asked when they reached the last available standing space.

"I come here every now and then," Lucinda answered vaguely.

Niamh realised that small talk wasn't going to get the other woman to open up and she tried a more direct personal question. "How's your little boy? Jack, isn't it?"

Bingo, Lucinda came to life. "He's great, he's a joy to us both. I can't believe my baby will be four next month!"

"Is he in a childcare centre or do you have a nanny?"

"My husband has been the nanny for the last few years. It's working out well for all of us."

"I haven't met your husband – what's his name?"

Lucinda hesitated as if she was being asked a difficult question. "Marcus."

"So you recommend motherhood?" Niamh hoped this would be her connection with Lucinda, a conversation point that would ease the tension she felt between them.

"Best thing I ever did – you should have a word with Chris."

"Chris is too busy chasing after a partnership to think of starting a family," Niamh answered. Since the day they married, Chris had put the subject of children on the proverbial shelf.

"I've seen him in here a few times."

"Who?"

"Chris, who else?" Lucinda smiled. It didn't reach her eyes.

"In here?" Niamh frowned, looking around the bar filled with twenty-somethings.

"Yes," Lucinda nodded slowly as if she was speaking to an idiot. "Doesn't he work close to here?"

"Yeah, he's on King Street."

Chris never spoke about going to bars after work. He worked late, all lawyers did. Niamh didn't mind him going for a drink after work but she did mind being told by Lucinda Armstrong rather than him. And she'd be really mad if he was driving home when he was over the blood-alcohol limit.

Scott saw her the minute he walked into the pub. He stopped dead and Brett ran into his back.

"What's wrong, mate?"

"My ex-boss is here."

"Where?"

"She's the blonde one, over there."

They stood for a few moments watching her. Unruly curls framed her dimpled face.

"She looks too young to be your boss."

"Looks can be deceiving."

Brett's eyes moved to the tall dark woman. "Who is she talking to?"

"That's Lucinda Armstrong, legal counsel."

Brett was already starting to feel conspicuous without a beer in his hand. "What do you want to do? Go somewhere else?"

"No, I've nothing to be ashamed of," Scott decided. "Come on. I'll introduce you to them."

Conversation with Lucinda had dried up when Niamh

felt a light tap on her shoulder. She turned around to see Scott Morgan. The subdued lighting cast a shadow on his face and he looked different to the man she had seen in her office that morning.

"Oh . . . hello." She was totally caught off guard and couldn't think what to say to him. Lucinda looking on didn't help.

"Look," he seemed awkward too, "I don't want any hard feelings – can I buy you a drink?"

Niamh's bottle was empty; she had no good reason to turn him down. "OK, I'll have another beer. Make it a light one – I have to drive home."

Scott turned to Lucinda. "What about you?"

"No, thank you, Scott. I need to go now." She said goodbye and the crowds parted to let the beautiful woman through.

Brett stepped forward and introduced himself to Niamh. "I'll go to the bar, you two can talk," he offered. "A light beer, isn't it?" he double-checked and she nodded.

She was left alone with Scott. The crowd had swelled even more and now it pressed around them. She was close enough to see the glisten of fresh stubble on his face. Close enough to smell the erotic scent of his after-shave. She took a deliberate step back from him.

"Is Brett a close friend?" she asked.

"He's my brother-in-law."

"Oh, your wife's brother?"

"No – my sister's husband."

"Oh."

51

The music pounded away through the brief silence between them.

"Niamh, I want to apologise for yesterday – for losing my temper like that."

"You don't need to apologise," she told him. "I met a lot of angry people yesterday – it's an understandable reaction to the circumstances."

"Yes. But I should know better. I work in HR, I know you were only doing your job –"

"Don't say any more." She stopped him with a smile. "It's forgotten, OK?"

His eyes held hers. "OK."

The crowd chose that moment to surge and she was pushed up against him. His hand reached out to steady her. It was just a brief innocent touch but it sent shock waves through her body.

What is wrong with me? she thought for the second time that day and looked around to see where Brett was at with the beer. He was handing cash to the barman – he'd be back soon to act as a badly needed buffer between them.

"I feel a bit old for this place," Scott remarked, looking around at the twenty-something crowd.

"Me too," she admitted. "Mind you, Lucinda seems to like it . . . and apparently Chris, my husband, comes here sometimes."

"Does your husband work close by?"

"Yes, he's in one of the law firms."

"Oh, a lawyer . . ."

"Yes, one of those, I'm afraid!"

They had a quick laugh at the expense of all lawyers.

"How about your wife? What does she do?" she asked, starting to relax a little.

"My wife?" He seemed to be taken aback with the question. "We're separated, soon to be divorced."

"Oh, I'm sorry, I didn't mean to –"

"Don't worry about it . . ."

Niamh had another look for Brett. He was edging through the crowd, one step forward and two back.

"He's taking his time, isn't he?" Scott said, following her eyes to Brett. "I should have ordered two beers instead of one. I have the urge to get very drunk tonight."

She giggled. "You couldn't get drunk here if you tried. It takes too long to get served."

His lips twitched in amusement. "Probably just as well. My little girl wakes at dawn, not a good situation if you have a hangover."

Niamh couldn't resist the opportunity to find out more about his home life. "Does your child live with you, then?"

"Yes – her mother isn't part of the family picture."

Brett made it back with the beers before she could ask any more questions. He shouted over the music, "Hey, this is a happening place!"

Scott and Niamh shared a smile; it seemed they were the only ones who felt out of place.

"What's so funny?" Brett asked, looking from one to the other.

"Private joke," Niamh told him.

He gave her an odd look and muttered something

about needing to buy cigarettes.

"Is he all right?" she asked, watching him dart through the crowds as if he was being chased.

"Yeah. I suspect that, somehow or other, he's come to the conclusion I'm hitting on you – so he's trying to make himself scarce," Scott said with an embarrassed laugh.

"That's very considerate of him – pity his efforts are wasted on this occasion." Niamh raised the bottle of beer to her lips. It didn't taste as nice as the full-strength one she had earlier.

"It's my sister's fault," Scott explained. "She's obsessed with finding me a girlfriend and it's rubbing off on Brett. The two of them need to be taught a lesson about interfering in other people's love lives."

He started to talk about his family – Deb, his big sister and Jenny, his little girl. Niamh didn't have a happy family life to tell him about so she let him do the talking.

"Jenny's got attitude now — I can tell already that she'll give me hell as a teenager."

His voice was full of indulgent love and Niamh ignored the maternal tug at her heart. She focussed on Scott, his contagious laugh, his intoxicating proximity. She wasn't looking out for Brett at all and was disappointed when he rejoined them. He opened the cigarette pack that had taken so long to buy and offered one to Niamh. She shook her head. He lit up, his eyes studying them both, trying to sense what had happened while he was gone.

Niamh felt her old wicked sense of humour come to the surface. She winked at Scott before she said, "Thanks for the beer. I have to go. My husband will be wondering where I am – he gets very jealous."

Brett's face fell at the realisation she was married. Niamh couldn't resist teasing him further. She sneaked another wink at Scott before she stood on her toes to kiss his cheek. "Call me." She felt the glistening stubble under her lips, saw the fine lines on his face. She pulled back quickly. The joke had backfired; it felt far from funny.

What am I thinking of?

"Come on, I'll walk you to your car." Scott, thinking the joke was still on, took her hand in his and led the way to the door. The air outside was heavy with the stirrings of an electrical storm and sticky heat hit her in the face. Scott, still holding her hand, was laughing. "You've got a quirky sense of humour," he grinned down at her. "Did you see his face? He's convinced he's caused me to get involved with a married woman – Deb will kill him when he tells her."

Niamh faltered, about to say that she got her sense of humour from her dad, the king of practical jokers. "Brett was an easy target," she said instead, reclaiming her hand from his grasp. She pressed the button at the pedestrian crossing. "I'd better get back to my car before the rain comes."

"Let me walk with you to the office."

The idea of spending another minute with him spelt danger. She couldn't believe she had kissed him. It didn't matter that it was meant as a joke. She had kissed him and she didn't dare to analyse the feelings that came from that kiss.

"No, I'm fine. Go back to Brett."

"Are you sure?"

"Yes. Thanks for your company tonight. It was fun," she smiled and the green man beckoned her to cross.

"Hang on!" He reached out and touched her arm. "I've been blabbing about myself all night. I want to ask you a question before you go."

"What?" she asked. The little man was now flashing for crossers to hurry.

"Your name – Niamh – where does it come from? What does it mean?"

"It's Irish. It means 'brightness'."

She crossed, her pace brisk as she headed back towards the office. She didn't look around to see if he was still there, even though she was very tempted.

Niamh woke on the couch. Her head was sore with a vague hangover.

Chris was peering down at her. "Hey, you had me worried! What are you doing on the couch?"

Niamh tried to remember. When she got in last night she had indulged herself in another beer to complement the ones she had in Forbes. She had spent a few hours sitting on the couch, looking at her life from a critical distance. She was the classic product of a broken home, confident at work yet hopelessly insecure in relationships. She was as much to blame as Chris for the way things were. She argued with him, but she didn't talk to him or share what was deep inside her. Her desire to have a different marriage to her parents had probably made her expectations of him too high from the start. A few more beers and she had a plan. She was going to be a hundred per cent honest with him, put all her issues on the table. He could do the same. If they couldn't work it out together, they could get counselling. It didn't have to be impossible to save a marriage. Happy with her plan, she settled down on the couch to have one of the best sleeps she had in weeks.

Chris was waiting for an answer. "I went out after work," she said. "I revived my taste for beer and had a few more when I got home. I must have dozed off . . ."

Chris glanced at the empty cans on the floor and grinned. "You obviously need to get out more. It might stop you from going off the rails like this when you do."

Niamh sat up, her curls flattened, her eyes sticky with yesterday's mascara. She *had* gone off the rails. She had been flirting with Scott Morgan. She had *kissed* him; it didn't matter that it was in jest. And she had felt weak at the knees when he held her hand on the way out of the pub. It all made her realise how dead things were with Chris. That's what had sparked the beers and the strategy session on the couch when she got home.

"You know, that's exactly what I was thinking. *We* need to get out more, spend more time together."

She went upstairs to have a shower. When she came down he was gone. There was a fresh cup of coffee and a note on the bench top.

Try not to go off the rails today.

She felt a surge of optimism. A cup of coffee and a note

– small gestures but they proved there was something left to save.

The traffic didn't punish her for being late. Manly to the city was a forty-minute run using the bus lane. The bus lane was Niamh's vice: she figured the time it saved was worth the fine should she get caught. For the last year she had been whizzing past the cars stuck in the other lanes and she hadn't been caught yet.

She was approaching the bridge when her mobile phone rang. She inserted the ear-piece of her hands-free kit. The call was from Helen Barnes.

"Hello, Helen. How are you?" There was kindness in her voice but it was checked so that it wouldn't be patronising.

"I'm angry. Very, *very* angry." There was no doubt that the mild-mannered Helen was furious.

"Don mentioned that you had a – complaint – against Phil . . . do you want to come in and talk about it?"

Niamh liked and respected Helen. She had already berated Jessica for taking sides before the full facts were known but she knew Helen wasn't a liar. Jessica's assertion that Phil Davis was a creep was probably right on the mark.

"Yes. That's why I called you." Helen sounded slightly calmer. "I want to talk before I drag a solicitor into the picture. I hope we can come to a resolution without chewing up resources and money in lawyers."

Niamh appreciated her practicality. Solicitors were a waste of money for both sides. "That sounds reasonable. Why don't we meet later today? I'll ask Lucinda

Armstrong to come as well."

Helen was slow to respond. "Is that necessary?"

Niamh heard the hesitation in her voice. It seemed that Lucinda didn't click with Helen either. "I'm afraid it is – she's our internal legal counsel and she needs to be across all potential legal issues – but I'll make sure she keeps to the background and that the discussion is between you and me in the main."

"If you insist." Helen was still reluctant. "Is three this afternoon OK with you?"

"That should be fine."

Helen knocked on Niamh's door at precisely three o'clock. There was no sign of Lucinda and they made small talk as they waited.

"It's hot out there today," Niamh commented, the weather seeming a suitably neutral topic to talk about. It had been over thirty degrees at lunch-time and now the slice of indigo sky visible from the window promised that the heat would dissolve into another electrical storm.

"It's sweltering – but it's still not as hot as Bourke, where I was brought up." Helen's face was flushed and it could have been due to the heat or an anger that was simmering beneath her calm exterior.

You could tell that Helen was damn good at her job just by looking at her. Her whole aura was that of competence and she had always interacted well with Niamh and the other executives when setting the budgets and monitoring performance. Phil Davis wasn't hands-on and didn't get involved. Or, considering the allegations Helen was making, maybe he was indeed hands-on but in all the wrong ways.

Lucinda arrived, slamming the door behind her. Her expression was impatient with "Do I have to be here?" written across her face. She sat down and crossed her remarkable legs without even a sideways glance at Helen. Niamh gave her a few moments to apologise for her tardiness: however, no apology was made.

"OK, let's begin." Niamh took the floor. In many ways it suited her that Lucinda wasn't in a participative mood. For a start, she could rely on the lawyer fading into the background and Helen would be happy with that. "Helen, first of all I want to assure you that we are taking your allegations against Phil Davis very seriously and we will conduct a thorough investigation. The first stage of the investigation is an interview with you. This will be followed by an interview with Phil."

Niamh paused and Helen nodded her acceptance of the outlined process. There was no reaction from Lucinda.

"Depending on the outcome of those meetings, it may be necessary to hold further clarifying meetings before we consider the evidence and reach a conclusion. All meetings will be minuted and we will give you the minutes of this meeting to review in a few days' time."

Helen nodded again, looking from Niamh to Lucinda as she said, "Do you want me to start now?"

"Yes, please." Predictably, Niamh was the one who answered the question.

"OK, my complaint doesn't relate to just one incident.

There are at least four occasions where Phil . . . made advances."

"I need you to describe each one of those incidents specifically," Niamh said while thinking to herself that Phil Davis would find it very difficult to explain away four separate incidents of misconduct.

"OK. He touched my breasts . . . twice," Helen's flush deepened, "Both times were in his office. Unfortunately, there was nobody else around at the time so it's my word against his."

Niamh didn't speak immediately, giving Lucinda a courtesy opportunity to contribute. The beautiful lawyer maintained a bored silence.

"Did you say anything to him to indicate that his behaviour was unwelcome?" Niamh's voice was overly kind to make up for Lucinda's lack of interest.

"The first time I was so shocked I didn't react at all," Helen admitted with an embarrassed shrug. "I wasn't sure if it was an accident or not. He was walking past me – there seemed to be plenty of room – but it happened so quickly. The second time was about a week later and there was no mistaking what he was doing. He put his hand on my hip and quite deliberately slid it upwards to my breasts, looking me directly in the eye."

"What did you say to him?" Niamh asked, pen poised to note Helen's response.

"I told him that if he ever touched me again – anywhere – I would have no hesitation in making a sexual harassment claim against him." Helen's voice was hard with anger. "And I would make sure his wife knew all about it."

Niamh scribbled furiously; she was no good at shorthand. She could have asked Sharon to take minutes but she was sensitive to how Helen would feel about another person being present. She was absorbed in her note-taking when she heard Lucinda ask, "What about the other incidents?"

"Well," Helen cleared her throat to answer the lawyer, "after my threat about sexual harassment, he behaved himself for a few weeks. I often thought he was leering at me but I couldn't prove it. About a month later, at the end of October, he came back from a long business lunch quite inebriated. It was about six in the evening and most people had gone home. He came and sat on my desk – asked if I would go for a drink with him – somewhere quiet – where we could get to know each other better. I said 'no'. He said he knew that I liked him and I should stop wasting time with the chase. I told him he was mistaken about my opinion of him. He didn't get the chance to retaliate. Donna Howard, who was also working late, was listening to our conversation from the other side of the room. When it sounded to her like I needed help, she popped her head over the partition to ask if I wanted a cup of coffee. Phil nearly fell off my desk with shock. But Donna's face was so deadpan, I think he convinced himself that she hadn't heard what had been said."

"Did she hear *everything*?" Niamh queried with raised eyebrows. Phil would be truly stuffed if there was a witness.

"Yes – and she's happy to talk to you about it." Helen

gave a lightning smile.

"OK. I'll make sure to catch up with her over the next few days." Niamh returned the smile. "Now, there was one more incident?"

"Yes, the week before I was retrenched. Again, I was working late." Helen's tone was wry now. "We had a budgeting package that was due to be sent to Japan that night and I had to go into Phil's office to get the go-ahead to send it. He must have seen me coming and was waiting to pounce. As I approached his desk, he stood up suddenly and I was trapped between him and the filing cabinet. He was trying to kiss me when Malcolm Young walked in. Malcolm made some disapproving comment about 'a time and place'. I told him that Phil was trying to force himself on me and that I would be lodging a formal complaint."

"What did Malcolm do?" Lucinda asked. Finally, a shred of interest in her voice.

"Oh, you know Malcolm," Helen was sarcastic. "The gravity of the situation was lost on him really. I'm sure he found my threat a bit unpleasant but thought it was nothing that Phil couldn't handle. He said something like 'Lay off her' to Phil and went on his merry way. When Malcolm had gone, Phil turned on me. He said there was no need for all the fuss – I was far too sensitive to be in a management position – I'd better stop my threats about harassment – if I didn't, he just wouldn't be able to work with me any longer."

Helen paused and the other two women waited for the final chapter of her story. "I told him he could go to hell.

His wife was going to be a lot more sensitive than me and the fuss hadn't even started. A week later I was retrenched. I have no doubt that Phil thought it was a clever way of shutting me up and I'm willing to bet that I was a last-minute addition to the retrenchment list."

Helen finished to a silence. Niamh was trying to get it all down on paper. Lucinda was churning it over, starting to pick holes.

"Why didn't you make a complaint straight away?" the lawyer asked. "You only brought the issue to our attention on the day you were retrenched – you had a whole week before that to do something about it."

"Look, I know that seems odd but I wanted to wait for the weekend so I could mull it over and decide what to do," Helen replied, looking Lucinda straight in the eye. "His implied threat that he couldn't work with me clouded my thinking. I have a mortgage like everybody else and I didn't want to risk my job without giving the situation due consideration."

Lucinda didn't stop to acknowledge the response, ploughing ahead with another question. "Has it occurred to you that it may be possible that these *incidents* had nothing to do with your retrenchment? Phil had to cut back like all the other executives and may have legitimately decided that the finance department didn't need both you and him."

Helen raised her chin with pride as she said, "You both know I have a very busy job – mainly because Phil sits on his fat ass and delegates everything. I work a twelve-hour day and I can guarantee you that my role still exists – Phil will never be able to cope without me. Wait and see: he'll be in here asking Niamh to recruit a replacement finance manager before the week is out."

Niamh was about to say that Phil could ask all he liked. Without Scott as recruitment manager, all hiring had been decentralised back into the field and Phil would have to sort out his own mess. However, Lucinda's reply was first past the line. "I'm sure Phil understands the consequences of a retrenchment and the fact you can't rehire someone else to do the job," she said patronisingly.

Helen gave her a scathing look. "You give him too much credit. The man is an idiot. He thinks he's immune to sexual discrimination laws and he doesn't understand the first thing about running a finance department. Let's face it, there's no way he would have got the role of finance director if he wasn't a mate of Malcolm Young."

Helen left soon afterwards. Lucinda lingered on. Niamh was busy reviewing her notes to see if they were decipherable when she heard the lawyer say, "This is all a waste of time, isn't it?"

Niamh glanced up from her notes with a frown. "You think she's lying?"

"I can't help thinking it's possible – she's not exactly the *femme fatale* type, is she?"

Niamh looked at her in shock. How much callousness was there underneath the glamorous exterior? "I'm surprised at you, Lucinda. How can you, as a woman, make such a biased statement?"

Lucinda got to her feet, unconcerned by Niamh's disapproval. "Modern women need to know how to handle unwelcome advances. I'd be very rich by now if I had sued every male colleague who came on to me."

She was gone before Niamh could vocalise a furious response. Niamh realised then that no number of drinks after work would make her connect with the lawyer.

Scott Morgan groaned when he heard Jenny stirring at 5am.

Go back to sleep . . . please . . . please . . . just another hour . . .

He hadn't slept very well. He had been thinking about her all night. Niamh. He remembered finding her attractive when she first interviewed him: her halo of blonde curls, coffee-coloured eyes, cute freckles and lovely accent. When he worked with her he saw the confidence and intelligence that had got her to director level at a relatively young age. But last night a new chemistry had started to ignite between them and the professional distance had fallen away. He had seen her giggle, tilt her head backwards as she drank from the beer bottle, show a quirky sense of humour. He had seen her fun side and when it was added to the qualities he already admired, it was hard to stop thinking about her. However, there was one big problem with Niamh Lynch. She was married. To a lawyer.

"Da-da! Da-da! Da-da!"

Scott groaned again and swung his legs over the side of the bed. His daughter was ready to start the day and it didn't matter how he felt about it. "I'm coming," he called out to her.

Jenny was standing up in her cot, rattling the side, wanting out. She gave a huge welcoming smile when she saw him come through the door. He lifted her clear of the cot and hugged her close, kissing her head.

"Mik!" she said.

"Did you say 'milk'?" he asked.

"Mik!"

She got another hug for her new word and they went to get her milk.

He and Jenny had carved a life for themselves without Ann, her mother. They didn't have much of a routine, he gave her too many biscuits and he dressed her in whatever was close to hand. It was Deb who usually pointed out these shortcomings in his parenting. Deb admitted she knew little of the practicalities of caring for a child but claimed she had a "woman's eye for detail". She took it upon herself to substitute for some of Scott's shortcomings and the child thrived despite her mother's continued absence from her life.

Jenny made up for yesterday's rebellious behaviour by being particularly angelic. She ate all her breakfast and played on her own while Scott updated his résumé on the computer. When that was done, he logged into *Seek* to see what jobs were out there. His search had only three hits, all contract positions. He did an online application for two of them.

"OK, Jen," he said when he had finished, "work's all done and it's time to have some fun. Want to go to visit Auntie Deb?"

His sister worked from home but was always open to

distraction, particularly when it came to her beloved niece. As he drove down to Manly, Scott's thoughts went back to Niamh. He realised now that he had done most of the talking and she hadn't revealed much about herself. He wanted to know more about her: where she lived, why her family had emigrated from Ireland, if she was happy with her lawyer husband. He realised that he was unlikely to ever know the answers. He'd probably never see her again.

He rang the bell of Deb's two-bedroom unit in Manly and she buzzed him in. Her apartment was three floors up and she was waiting for him at the door, a frosty look on her face.

"I heard you had a good time last night," she accused, whipping her niece from his arms to give her a possessive cuddle. Jenny wriggled free and toddled off to find something to destroy.

"Yeah, I needed those beers. I'm feeling more optimistic today. I've already updated my résumé and applied for –"

Deb cut him off midstream. "Why have you dressed Jenny in those terrible clothes?" she asked sourly.

"Purple and pink go OK –"

"No, they don't. She looks like an orphan."

He shrugged; his daughter was happy, that was all that mattered. "Want a cup of coffee?" he asked, going into the kitchen. His sister was a lousy hostess. If you wanted coffee, you had to make it yourself.

"No," she answered shortly, keeping a careful eye on her niece as she sized up the TV unit.

"What's put you in such wonderful humour this morning?" he shouted from the kitchen as he filled the kettle.

"You fooling around with married women," was her terse reply.

Scott laughed. "Brett's been telling tales."

"She's your ex-boss too," Deb continued, as if that added insult to injury.

"Nothing happened," Scott told her. "In fact, we were playing a joke on Brett. He's so gullible we couldn't resist. In fact, you are *both* so gullible you make a perfect couple."

"What do you mean?" Deb was outraged enough to come to the kitchen door.

"I mean you should stop pushing me into the arms of every woman in sight. I'm perfectly capable of finding myself a partner . . . when the time's right. Just because I fucked up once doesn't mean I'll do it again."

Deb was about to come back with an indignant reply when there was a crash. Jenny had pulled the DVD player off its shelf. The wiring saved it from hitting the floor and it dangled precariously in mid-air until Deb came to its rescue.

Chapter Three

"Busy day?" Niamh asked when Chris came in.

"Yeah. There's a big case coming up in January and a hell of a lot of work to do between now and then." He loosened his tie and opened the top buttons of his shirt.

She intercepted him with a deliberate kiss on the lips. There was a smell of beer from his breath and Lucinda's smug smile flashed into her head. Had he been in Forbes mingling with the twenty-somethings?

"Did you go for a drink after work?" Her question was carefully casual but she was inevitably bestowed with a sharp look.

"No. I had a beer at the office. I presume you don't

71

have a problem with that."

"Of course not. Here," she handed him a bottle of red wine, "Open that, will you?"

"What's the occasion?"

"We shouldn't need an occasion to share a bottle of wine," she replied, taking a dilapidated casserole-dish from the oven and serving its contents onto two waiting plates.

They sat at the table, facing each other. "Cheers!" she said, raising her glass.

He echoed her words but his voice lacked enthusiasm. They ate without speaking. He was hungry, digging in. She chased her food around the plate.

"Chris, we need to talk . . ." she said, splitting the silence apart.

He frowned, unhappy with the interruption to his thoughts. "What do you want to talk about?"

"Us."

"What about us?"

He wasn't going to make it easy and Niamh summoned up the energy to persevere. "We seem to be stuck in a rut where we argue rather than talk, we don't go out socially, we don't make love . . ."

"Anything else you want to add?" he asked sarcastically.

She jumped in at the deep end. "And we haven't even tried for a baby."

He pushed his plate away as if suddenly turned off by the food. "Are you interested in what *I* think at all?"

"Yes, of course, I am," she said earnestly. "That's why I

started this discussion. I want us to put everything out on the table –"

His expression was harsh, his voice even more so. "I think you're caught up in this dream you have of the *ideal family life*. It's a life where people don't have the pressures of real jobs, they have lots and lots of babies, and they live happily ever after on fresh air. You have no appreciation for what you and I have in the *real* world – our careers, our house –"

She interrupted him. "A career and house are material things. They come after relationships, love . . ."

"That's your values, Niamh, not mine. I'm not you."

They stared at each other. Niamh broke the stare by taking a long drink of her wine. She used the time out to counsel herself to stay calm, keep an open mind. She put the glass down and said, "I know we're very different, Chris. I just don't want to be so different that we end up with nothing at all in common."

There was any number of responses that he could have given to meet her halfway. But all he did was get up to stack the half-empty plates and put them on the counter.

"Don't walk off on me, Chris. We need to talk about this stuff."

He was unrelenting. "Look, I've got work that I have to do tonight – I have a conciliation meeting in the morning. But regardless of that, I've nothing else to contribute to this 'talk'. Maybe if you think about what I've said then we could try again some other time."

She stayed at the table, topping up her glass of wine. He wanted her to think about what he had said. To think about careers and houses and how important they were. He wasn't prepared to talk about their relationship or why they didn't make love any more. Part of her felt like throwing her hands up in defeat and walking away. But another part of her, a bigger part, said that if she gave up that easily she would be no better than her mother.

The familiar nightmare terrified Niamh from her sleep. The black face hung from the ceiling of the dingy garage. The mouth gaped open but no words came out. The body beneath the face was limp, dead with no hope of resurrection.

The black face and the garage had lived in her subconscious for over twenty years, as vivid now as when she was a child. She lay in the dawn-lit room, wondering if they would ever go away.

As a child, she would refuse to go into the garage alone. Her dad would laugh at her and, taking her hand in his, he would open the rotting doors. There was a long narrow window at the back. Blackened with dirt, it didn't let in much light. Flicking the switch inside the door gave some dim light from a bulb that dangled by a flimsy wire. Her dad was a tradesman and it was mostly his tools that were kept there. He also used it to store a few pieces of furniture that he called antiques and her mother called firewood. The chairs and tables sat there for years, foolishly believing that one day they would be restored to their former glory.

Often, when he saw she was scared, he would tease her with his spookiest voice but was always disappointed that he couldn't secure the smallest smile from his youngest and most devoted daughter. Niamh was convinced that an evil witch lived in the darkness. Because the witch's face was black, she blended into the murky corners. The blackness of her face wasn't because of her race; she wasn't from Africa or anything like that. It was a bruised kind of black. There was white underneath.

The garage had regularly featured in her childhood nightmares before it became the stage for the destruction of all their lives. Her mother told her it was normal for kids to have occasional nightmares and to try not to think too much about it during the day. It would fade away from her dreams over time. Her mother was wrong.

It was an old-fashioned garage, standing separate from the house with no form of heating. It would have been cold in there, even in the height of summer. Her dad hated the cold. He often said that he must have Mediterranean blood rather than Irish. He lived for the fickle Irish summer, dragging them seventeen miles to Youghal beach at the first sign of sun. He dreamed of leaving the perpetual winter behind and making a new life in a place where the sun shone all year round. As a young child, Niamh had heard her parents talk seriously about emigrating, about going to Australia. They always had the discussion in winter, when Dad was at his lowest. It was all forgotten by the time summer came around. Then her mother and Uncle Tom had stolen the idea for their own, leaving her dad with a dream he could never realise.

Often Niamh would replace Tom in her memories of

their first day in Sydney. It would be her dad immediately in love with the harbour and Opera House. It would be her dad running into the sea at Manly only two hours after touching down. It would be her dad proudly telling real Australians about his daughters' names and what they meant. Aisling meant "dream-vision" and Niamh "brightness." He had chosen those names long before they were born and convinced her mother not to even consider anything else. He often said his girls were everything to him. It was heartbreaking to think of him without his "vision" and "brightness", alone in the cold of the garage. Dead.

Chris's breathing was heavy beside her and she concentrated on its rhythm until the fear and guilt subsided. He didn't know about the nightmares; she had never woken him, no matter how terrified. She knew he would find it melodramatic that she still had these dreams, that she couldn't put it all behind her.

The sun was fully up now and Niamh got out of bed. She tried to shower the images away. She skipped breakfast and made good time in the bus lane. The freeway leading up to the bridge was the only slow part of the journey and she was able to look across at the harbour as she waited in the queue for the toll. There were only a few wisps of cloud to blot the perfect blue sky. But there was a strong breeze; the ferries had to ride up and down on white surf as they made their jagged way to Circular Quay. The toll queue was moving slowly and her thoughts inevitably moved to Chris.

He didn't see her problem, didn't want to talk. How

could she get past that? Counselling? Would he agree to go? When should she broach it with him? The last thing she needed was for him to walk off like he did last night. She had to get him to stay around long enough to listen.

She reached the top of the queue and paid the toll. The rest of the journey took only a few minutes.

As she hurried through the executive area, she saw that Willem Boelhoers was waiting outside her office. Willem was the head engineer; he reported to Bruce Knight. He was an academic-looking man with a narrow frame that could benefit from a few more kilos.

"Hello, Willem. How are you settling in?" she asked. Willem was a new hire – Scott had recruited him last month.

"I must talk to you . . . it's urgent," Willem responded with an inflection in his voice. His English was accented; as far as Niamh knew he was originally from Holland. However, today beneath the accent there seemed to be a thread of panic.

Niamh shot a questioning look at Sharon. "What does my diary look like this morning?"

"I've explained to Willem that you're very busy," Sharon shrugged. "He said it can't wait."

Willem nodded fervently. "Yes, it is imperative that we speak immediately."

"OK," Niamh said as she unlocked her door. "Come in."

She hung her jacket up and took her laptop from its case. When her system was loading, she sat down and asked, "How can I help you, Willem?"

He followed her lead and sat, perching on the very edge of the chair. His movements seemed to be heavy. Niamh's curiosity was starting to kick in; his behaviour was a little odd to say the least.

"No, I'm here to help you," he responded, his eyes intense behind silver-framed glasses.

"How?" she queried, watching him closely. His face was drawn with a permanent tiredness. She guessed he was a bad sleeper.

He looked over both shoulders, as if he expected someone to have crept up behind him. "There's a conspiracy," he whispered when he was satisfied that the coast was clear.

Niamh's first instinct was to laugh – there was something sadly comical about the way he was behaving.

"A conspiracy?" She couldn't suppress a smile.

"It's not a joke," he admonished when he saw the smile. "There are bad things happening in this company."

"What are you trying to say, Willem?" she said seriously, recognising that he was distressed.

"They're after the money – they're making big plans to blackmail the company–"

"Who?"

"I don't know."

Niamh allowed a considerable pause before she said, "You have to help me out here, Willem. You're saying there's a conspiracy – but you don't know what or who! Where did you get your information from?"

"I heard it . . . I heard voices." He sounded unsure of himself.

"Where did you hear the voices?" she asked gently.

"In my office."

Willem's office was around the corner from the executive area.

"When did this happen?"

"The voices?" He seemed confused for a few moments, then said, "Sometimes there's nothing. Other times I hear them a few times a day."

Niamh was looking at him perplexed when Sharon knocked on the door.

"Sorry, Niamh, Willem's sister is here."

"Willem's sister?" Niamh wondered if she was stuck in some strange dream. Nothing had made much sense since she had got to work. A petite lady, with the same chestnut curls as Willem, followed Sharon into the room. Her office was becoming cramped with the circus.

"I'm very sorry, Mrs Lynch. I'm Regina, Willem's sister. He forgot to take his medication last night."

"He did?"

Willem hung his head.

"Yes, Willem is ill – he has schizophrenia. It's extremely important that he take his medication – sometimes he works late and he forgets – he doesn't do it deliberately. His mind gets preoccupied with work and he forgets the Zyprexa – so I always check in the morning – I count the pills left in the pack, every morning . . ."

It was becoming clearer at last. "Willem was telling me about a conspiracy . . ."

"It's all in his mind," Regina explained. "He gets paranoid when he forgets his drugs – he rants and raves about conspiracies – and spies – and secret agents bugging his phone." She paused to give Willem a withering look. "You can't afford to forget those pills – you'll lose your job if you aren't careful – you should apologise to Mrs Lynch for wasting her time."

"I apologise. I'm truly very sorry." Willem looked at her earnestly. "However, it doesn't change what I came to tell you. There are bad things –"

"Willem!"

The Dutchman jumped to his feet when he heard the warning in his sister's voice.

Regina had one final thing to say. "Don't worry, Mrs Lynch. The illness is under control. Willem understands it, the family understands it – the professionals say that having an insight into the illness is half the battle – and once he takes those two Zyprexa, there's no problem at all."

The brother and sister left. Niamh and Sharon were left looking at each other, speechless.

The events of the rest of the day were dull when compared to Willem and his sister Regina. After a whirl of meetings and phone calls, the letter from Paul Jacobsen arrived on her fax machine. It was brief.

I act for Denis Greene.

I understand that he was retrenched by HDD on Monday 15 November 2004. I believe that the circumstances surrounding the termination of his employment

constitute unfair conduct and I am hereby requesting that you immediately reinstate him in his employment.

I look forward to meeting with you to discuss this matter further.

Yours faithfully,
Paul Jacobsen.

Niamh could see that Paul Jacobsen had also sent Lucinda a copy of the fax. She tried the lawyer's number. It was busy so she called Bruce Knight. The services director had been in Tokyo for most of last week and knew nothing about the threatened litigation.

"Yes!" Bruce barked as he picked up the phone. The surly forty-year-old didn't believe in the niceties of telephone etiquette. But he had a lot of personal baggage and everyone cut him some slack because of that. They had all felt his agony when his wife left him. Especially Niamh. Bruce reminded her of her dad – a man broken by divorce. Only difference was that Bruce was using cigarettes to kill himself.

"It's Niamh. I have a letter here from Denis Greene's solicitors."

"What? Don't tell me he's suing?"

She heard him mutter a swearword under his breath and she smiled. Bruce was of the old school: he would never swear in front of a lady. It was a pity; Niamh quite liked to swear but couldn't find a receptive colleague.

"Not exactly. It seems he wants to be offered an

alternative role in the company."

"That's not going to happen. I was glad to see the back of him."

"Why?" Niamh had read the file. She knew why. She just wanted to check that the verbal reason matched the performance reviews in his file.

"We've had some performance issues," Bruce replied with a weary sigh. "He was abrupt and rude to our customers. He was downright provocative with his colleagues. And he was insolent to all management, particularly to me. In summary, Denis Greene is a troublemaker."

Rude. Provocative. Insolent. With performance issues. Niamh was willing to bet Denis's request to be reinstated wasn't kosher. If they offered to take him back, it could well flush out his real motivation. Call his bluff.

"Look, Bruce, Lucinda says this is an untested legal area. If we end up in court we could lose and it would cost us a lot of money. It might be easier all round if we took him back. Are you sure there's no other job that he can do in your business? Maybe a role that isn't client-facing?"

"There's nothing." Bruce wasn't going to budge. "His skills are quite specific and they aren't transferable without intensive retraining. Regardless of all that, I would rather take my chances in court than have to reinstate an *arsehole* like him – pardon my language."

"OK. It's your business that will wear the cost should we lose," she warned. "I want you to know that before we embark on this."

"I'm quite prepared to take that risk," he replied, his voice clipped with obstinacy.

"OK, that's officially on the record. Now, Bruce, there's just one more thing . . ." Niamh said quickly.

"What?"

"Willem Boelhoers."

"What about him?" Bruce didn't have much patience for people who didn't come straight to the point.

"How's he going in the job?" Niamh thought it best to ask that question first. It was important to get an unbiased opinion.

"Very good. The customers seem to like him. That's everything when you're an engineer. The customers are already cranky that their equipment is faulty – you need to be able to calm them, keep them buying from us – and keep them paying for maintenance."

"Good. It's great he's doing so well," she enthused before throwing in the grenade. "Did you know he has schizophrenia?"

Silence.

"No."

More silence. Bruce digested the news.

"That puts a different light on things," he said slowly. "I'm not sure I want a schizo facing our customers. God knows what he is capable of doing – or saying."

Niamh had a response prepared. "For a start, don't call him a 'schizo'. That's an offensive term – he's ill and he's on medication for that illness – the drugs work and it should be OK for him to have a client-facing role."

"How can you be so sure he won't go crazy in front of

a customer some day?"

"I'm not totally certain but he deserves a chance. If he's doing his job OK then we have nothing to worry about. And if he doesn't do his job, well, then we'll talk to him about it."

"OK, let's see how it goes with him." Bruce was guarded but willing. Despite his notorious ill temper, he was fundamentally a kind man. And, hell, did he know what it felt like to have personal problems.

Helen's apartment was a box but it was in the heart of the city. After a childhood and teenage years in the depths of the countryside, she loved being part of the urban action. The traffic on the freeway never stopped. The bars never closed. The tourists never went away.

Helen was a farm girl who had grown up two hundred kilometres outside Bourke. It was an isolated life on the sheep station and every Saturday morning the Barnes family would drive into town to stock up on groceries and social contact. Weather had dominated her family's life. The drought cycle brought dead animals, parched paddocks and hard times. The flood cycle brought grazing stock, healthy crops and celebratory drinks with the neighbouring farms. Winter or summer, the sun shone for over three hundred days a year and celebratory drinks were a rare occurrence.

Helen's first years of education were under her mother's supervision and the crackling of the radio. The Distance Education Centre ran three lessons a week over the radio and bestowed homework that the daughter of

84

the house devoured. There were no brothers, sisters or neighbouring children to distract her from her school-work. When Helen was twelve years old she left the farm for boarding school. Shy from only her mother and father's company, she soaked in the sense of community in the school. It took some years before the shyness faded to be replaced by a quiet confidence. The clever farm girl was well-liked and made some life-long friends from her time at the school. She and her friends applied to Macquarrie University and her parents almost burst with pride when she was accepted to do a Bachelor of Commerce. After her degree she secured a graduate posi-tion in a big company in Sydney and gradually, as the years passed, her trips back to Bourke became less frequent.

Losing her job had topped off a bad year for the farm girl. Her father had died in January, the extreme temper-atures too much for his heart. They buried him under an intense summer sun in Bourke, the town where he had been born, educated and married. There was a huge turnout at the funeral of the quiet farmer despite the suf-focating heat that hovered around forty-seven degrees. Helen knew fewer than half the people who shook her hand and offered their condolences.

Following the funeral, Helen's mother became sud-denly petrified about living on the seventy thousand acres she had previously managed and co-owned. She wanted to sell and there was nothing that Helen could do to change her mind. The farm was put on the market. Within days a neighbouring farmer put in a decent offer and it was sold. It left a gaping hole in both Helen and her mother. It also left her mother homeless.

Of course, her mother didn't want to live in Sydney. It would be too noisy, cluttered up with people and cars. And she didn't want to live in a retirement home. Those places were for people without any families, people who were queuing up to die. It took Helen a number of weeks to get through to her that it had to be one or the other. Sydney or a retirement home in Bourke. There were only two options. The day before she was due to move out of the farm her mother agreed, with great trepidation, to live in Sydney. With Helen.

Her mother had been living in the box-like apartment for nine months now. Helen felt an increasing sense of failure with every passing month. She was in her early thirties and single. In fact, there had been no serious relationship in her life at all. She wasn't the flirtatious type and her sheer aptitude scared off many men. Now, with her mother as a flatmate, she felt even less likely to meet someone and settle down.

Old Mrs Barnes was conscious of the fact that her presence in the apartment was all the more uncomfortable now that Helen was at home all day. It really wasn't big enough for two people. The apartment had a tiny balcony and Helen spent a lot of time out there after she lost her job. She said she needed space to think. Some days dinner was the only time they talked. Mrs Barnes would cook and be inevitably disappointed when Helen would only pick at the food.

"You need to eat. There's no point in starving yourself."

"I'm not hungry, Mum."

Then there would be silence and Mrs Barnes would try to spark more conversation. "Have you talked to anyone at the company today?" she asked this time.

"No, not since last week." Helen's features were tight with tension.

"Right." Mrs Barnes chewed a mouthful before saying, "When do you think they'll let you know what's happening?"

Helen sighed before giving a forced response. "I don't know. It's complicated. They've got to interview him – and probably Donna too."

Old Mrs Barnes didn't know how to help her only daughter. Helen had never been in any trouble and neither mother nor daughter knew how to handle the current situation. Helen had lost her job; she had been retrenched. As far as Mrs Barnes knew, "retrenched" was a fancy word for being fired. Then there was the sexual harassment business. By Helen's boss, a senior executive and a married man. Old Mrs Barnes was a countrywoman who had lived all her life in Bourke; she had no experience of issues such as these. Life on the farm had been hard but simple.

"Mmm," Mrs Barnes took it all in as if it was the first time she was being given the information. "I suppose they'll retrench him once they've done the interviews."

"No, Mum," Helen snapped, dropping her fork with a clatter. "They'll *fire* him. I keep telling you that retrenching someone is different to firing them. What's so hard to understand?"

She felt immediate guilt when she saw her mother's face cloud over.

"I'm sorry, love. I'm just a silly old woman who only knows about animals and farms. Commerce and business are out of my grasp and I shouldn't be bothering you with questions to which I'll never understand the answers."

Helen abandoned the rest of her dinner and went out to the balcony. She stayed there as dusk turned into night and Darling Harbour was fully lit up. The Harbour Side shopping mall was to her left, buzzing with tourists. The opulence of the casino was on the right, healthy crowds trawling in but still a few hours to go before its peak business. Inside, her mother was a ghostly figure as she cleared the table and hand-washed the dishes. She was like a silent maid, cooking, washing up, dusting, all the while trying to fade into the background and not be an imposition on her single daughter's life. When there was no more housework to be done, the old lady settled in front of the TV.

Helen got up from her seat to stand at the railing. Two floors above there was a party with the crowd spilled onto the balcony. For a while she eavesdropped on the lively conversation and laughter. It made her feel lonely so she went back to her thoughts. Helen had a logical mind that was well accustomed to problem analysis. She knew instinctively when things didn't add up and the balcony was the only quiet place to try to figure it out. The night of the phone call she had been distressed with the news of her retrenchment and and a little tipsy from the wine.

It was difficult to piece the phone call back together and identify exactly what had got her hackles up. She had a few theories about the motivation of the caller but needed her job back before she could follow them up. She knew it was only a matter of time before she was working for HDD again but the waiting was hard. She had always been bad at sitting things out, this latest tiff with her mother no exception. She checked her watch: it was nine fifteen already, time to go inside.

"What are you watching?" she asked the old lady.

"Detective Frost. It's a good story tonight."

Her mother loved crime and mystery. She was not daunted by gruesome corpses or body parts that had been separated from their owners.

"Want a cup of tea before you turn in?"

"I'd love one."

Helen made the tea, feeling another wave of depression. It was Friday night, for heaven's sake. And she was having tea in front of the TV with her mother. Before Black Monday she had a respectable social life. Now, with the cloud of unemployment hanging overhead, she had lost the desire to go out. Phil Davis had attacked her self-esteem on all levels and she was determined the bastard would pay the ultimate price for his actions.

"Your solicitor's name is Paul Jacobsen. He's got a solid reputation but he's not too much of a high flyer. It's important this looks authentic."

Denis didn't respond, it was late in the evening and he was tired. He had spent the day at home, bickering with Lily. There was nothing more futile or exhausting than arguing with his wife. She was in his face all day long – having so much time together would drive them both crazy.

"Are you listening to me?" the caller asked sharply.

"Of course," Denis responded with an equal abruptness.

"We've also retained the services of a barrister – Steve Jones."

"I thought you wanted everything to look authentic," Denis interrupted. "Isn't a barrister a bit over the top? I'm a mere software engineer – where does someone like me get the money for a barrister?"

There was a pause. The caller didn't like to be questioned. "The barrister shows you are very serious about your request to be reinstated. It should speed up the process considerably."

"Whatever you say." Denis was deliberately vague as Lily passed him in the hallway on her way to bed. It was a relief to see the back of her as she stomped up the stairs.

"You need to let them know that you won't fade away into the background," the caller continued. "Make some noise. Call some people – call the CEO. Yes, call the CEO. Scare him with the legal costs, the damage to the company's reputation. Tell him there are journalists who want to run the story."

"Listen, you're wasting your time with all this." Denis kept his voice calm with great effort. "Bruce Knight doesn't like me. There's no way he'll allow me to come back."

"Bruce Knight's opinion will be unimportant," the

caller said confidently. "The CEO will take the path of least resistance when he is faced with a massive lawsuit and bad publicity. He'll tell Bruce to take you back and Bruce will do as he is told."

"For Christ's sake!" Denis's temper boiled over. "Haven't you thought about this? How can the CEO think that this is a *massive lawsuit*? They've already given me seven months' pay – that's beyond the expiry date of my business visa. No judge will award more than that."

"I told you the last time – forget the business visa," the caller ordered. "It's your application for permanent residency that matters now. There's big dollars involved when you try to deprive a family of the chance to live in Australia . . ."

"Aren't they going to smell a rat?" he said, again appealing for logic. "I didn't say anything about all of this the day I was retrenched. I was asked if I had issues – and I said I didn't. A few days later, I not only have a lawyer but a barrister to boot."

"If they smell a rat, it will only be because you haven't convinced them," the voice was dangerously smooth, "and, don't forget, there are two other lawsuits to distract them. You can be assured that your case won't stand out when there is so much other litigation on the table."

Denis knew nothing about the other lawsuits so it was unlikely he would "forget" them. The call ended and he hung up. He rested his head against the wall, feeling it was all spiralling out of his control. He was a pawn to them, their only means of access to the remaining sites. They wanted him to finish the installations and he was no match for their determination.

He knew from the reflected light on the landing that Lily was reading in bed. He was dead tired but didn't want to go up until she was asleep. In the meantime he would do as the caller instructed and contact the CEO.

Chapter Four

On the following Monday morning Malcolm Young burst into Niamh's office, his outstretched hand thrusting a sheet of paper in her face.

"Neeeve," Malcolm was one of those people who could not get his head around her name, "can you tell me what the *hell* this is all about?"

"It's Niamh, *Nee-uv*," she said, his rudeness goading her to correct his pronunciation of her name for the hundredth time. She took the sheet of paper from him and wrote *Nee-uv* on the back. Holding it up so he could see, she said again: "Nee-uv."

"Neeeee-uv," he repeated.

It was close enough and she turned the sheet of paper the right way around so she could read it. It was an email from Denis Greene, addressed to Malcolm with a copy to

Yoshi Murasaki. The message had been sent over the weekend.

Malcolm,

We haven't met but by now you will be aware that I was one of the 10 per cent retrenched from your workforce. I am writing to let you know about my unusual circumstances in the hope that you will use your authority to enable me to continue my employment with HDD. I have been working in Australia under a business visa for almost four years. My wife Lily and I have made Sydney our home and we have applied for permanent residency so we can continue to live in this beautiful city. The untimely termination of my employment means that I will have to return to England before the Department of Immigration has the chance to assess my application for permanent residency. This will be emotionally and financially devastating for me and I have no option but to take legal action against the company. This is not my preferred approach and I would be delighted to stop the litigation if you were to use your influence to find me an alternative role in the company. It is very likely that Bruce Knight and Niamh Lynch have not considered my flexible skill base when assessing my suitability for other roles. You may be asking yourself why you should intervene in this matter. For a start, you could save the company a considerable settlement sum and legal fees. As you must be painfully aware, the company is going through hard times and can ill afford these costs. Also, if you step in now and resolve this issue, you will save the company bad publicity on national television. A current affairs programme has expressed an interest in my story. Obviously, I won't speak to them until I hear from you.

Denis Greene.

"I hadn't read this before now but, yes, we do have an issue with Denis. I got a letter from his solicitor last week. I'm surprised he saw the need to send a message like this in addition to the solicitor's letter." Niamh was calm as she put the document down.

"Why didn't I know about this until now?" Malcolm asked, the red veins in his face protruding with impatience. It was embarrassingly obvious that the map of veins on his cheeks were induced by his fondness for whiskey.

"You already informed me that it was too early to brief you on the details of the legal issues that fell out of Black Monday," Niamh responded, her tone matter-of-fact. "But I did give you a summary of the issues, remember?"

After her discussion with Yoshi, she had prepared a brief memo outlining the basis and status of the three lawsuits against the company. Yoshi, Malcolm and Lucinda had all received copies of the memo. There had been no response from the latter two.

"You should have come to see me," Malcolm reprimanded, recovering the page to wave it in the air. "I'm a busy man. I can't read everything that comes across my desk and I expect you to use your common sense if the matter is important. I should have got some forward warning of this."

Malcolm didn't reveal that he had just come from a nightmarish meeting with Yoshi Murasaki. The Japanese liaison director had ruthlessly dissected their phone conversation last week. Malcolm had been out to lunch at the time and could barely recall it. Yoshi had no such problems with his memory, listing a tirade of complaints against the CEO: socialising in inappropriate places, not knowing the names of the people who were suing the company, not alerting Japan to the threat the lawsuits posed to the Australian profits. It had gone on and on and even though Malcolm had fought his corner, the message was clear. Yoshi, the Japanese spy, would use his influence to get rid of him unless he reformed.

"I had no idea that Denis would send you a message," Niamh shrugged, unaware of the intensifying power struggle between Malcolm and Yoshi. "And I don't see how this case is any more critical than the other two we have."

Her logical answer took the wind out of Malcolm's sails.

"He copied Yoshi on the message. He's made me look like a fool in front of him," he said, somewhat petulantly.

"I think you're overreacting. Denis is doing whatever he thinks is necessary to make you pay attention to his 'circumstances'. He copied Yoshi for impact, not to make you look like a fool."

There was a pause. Outside Sharon cleared her throat to alert them to the fact the door was open. Malcolm moved to shut it and sat his heavy frame down with a sigh.

"Niamh, let me be honest about things for a moment. I'm new and still trying to prove my value-add. Yoshi undermines me at every turn, looking over my shoulder, letting his disapproval be felt. He's dangerous, Niamh. Not just to me, to all of us. He feeds his version of events back to Japan and, *bingo*, our whole future gets decided . . . are you with me?"

Niamh gave the smallest nod, dispassionate as she watched him.

"You must help me. Anticipate his actions and cut him off at the pass. Don't give him the chance to complain to Japan about us. Don't let emails like this one here fall into his hands. Soon I'll get the company back in the black and I'll be in a strong enough position to boot him out . . ."

Niamh's last shred of belief in Malcolm dissolved when she heard his words. He had it all wrong – Yoshi would never go. It was the Japanese way of doing business; Yoshi was their eyes and ears on the ground. If Malcolm didn't understand that, he would not last the distance.

"Now, tell me, how do you think I should respond to this message?" His face was void of ideas.

"Just say that you believe his lawyer has already communicated with us in writing therefore it is inappropriate for you to enter into any dialogue on the matter at this point in time."

"OK," he nodded, relieved to have a spoon-fed response. "I'll say that . . . now, before we go any further,

97

is there any way we could take Greene back?"

"No, over Bruce's dead body. He said Denis was a rude, insolent troublemaker. I've alerted him to the fact that his business will wear the cost if we lose the case and he is perfectly prepared to take that risk."

Malcolm stood up, his voice regaining its strength, the tone of the confidant discarded. "I support Bruce," he said with bravado. "And this rubbish about TV – no current affairs programme would waste their time –"

"There's a chance they might," Niamh warned him. "But we shouldn't let ourselves be threatened by that."

"Certainly, that's what I'm saying," he said in a no-nonsense way. "If Greene's trying to threaten me, he'd better think again." He opened the door and left on that note.

Seconds later, Sharon appeared at the doorway. "Everything OK . . . Neeeeve?" she grinned.

"Very funny," Niamh said, handing her assistant the email. "As you're here, can you send a copy of this to Lucinda?"

If the dispute made it to national television, the lawyer would need to have a statement on the company's position ready for the journalists.

Yoshi Murasaki put through a call to his boss in Tokyo as soon as he read the email from Denis Greene. It was mid-morning in Japan and lunchtime in Sydney. Yoshi usually had lunch at his desk. With most staff preferring to eat outside the office, he found it a peaceful opportunity to catch up on his work. It was also a convenient time to call Japan. However, on this occasion his boss, Nishikawa Shacho, wasn't there to take his call and Yoshi had to leave a message with his secretary.

He read the email from Denis Greene again. It was a very ugly situation and it would undoubtedly save the company both embarrassment and legal fees if they could reinstate him. Yoshi knew that Bruce Knight would also be working through the lunch-hour and he punched out his number on the phone.

"Bruce, it's Yoshi."

"Hello." Bruce was guarded, it wasn't often he received a call from the Japanese liaison director. When he did, there was usually trouble afoot.

"This employee of yours, Denis Greene – he's sent me a message."

Bruce swore loudly. Yoshi cringed at the obscenity.

"What was this message about?"

"He wants us to find him another role in the company."

"Not that again!" Bruce exclaimed in frustration. "I've already been through this with Niamh. There's no way he's coming back. Trust me. We don't want his sort working for us."

"Performance issues?" Yoshi posed the leading question.

"Yes. Rude to customers. Rude to colleagues. Rude to management."

"I understand your reluctance to take him back," Yoshi conceded. He was a company man and could not abide lack of loyalty in others. But he sensed there would be trouble with this engineer, Denis Greene. There was an underlying aggression through the email and it ended with a blatant threat about the TV programme. And Greene was correct when he said that the company could ill afford the costs should the litigation continue.

"I understand your reluctance," Yoshi repeated, "but we may have no choice. We are under immense pressure from Tokyo to return a profit for the next two quarters. These legal costs could jeopardise our chances . . ."

"Reinstating Greene would be a foolish thing to do, no matter what the circumstances," Bruce responded, an icy edge to his voice. He hung up before Yoshi had the chance to tell him about the TV programme.

Yoshi sat back in his seat, his lunch forgotten. Sometimes Bruce was abrupt to the point of being offensive. Yet there was an appealing honesty to the man. He had ethics he didn't compromise and Yoshi respected that. The Japanese liaison director gave a deep sigh. The Australian executive team needed an overhaul and the problem was squarely on his shoulders. There was bickering, rivalry and division amongst the directors. It wasn't surprising that the quarterly results were falling short of the targeted profit. And with Malcolm at the helm, it didn't look as if the issues would be resolved anytime soon. Yoshi was resigned to the fact he would have to discuss it with Nishikawa Shacho on his next visit to Tokyo. His boss wouldn't be happy. He had spent a lot of money getting Malcolm Young on board and he was waiting expectantly to see a return on that money. Yoshi was scheduled to go to Tokyo in the New Year and he would have to be extremely diplomatic in the way he communicated the issues to Nishikawa Shacho.

To be truthful, Yoshi was not enjoying this assignment to Sydney. He was of the opinion that the Australians and the Japanese were simply not compatible and liaising between the two was almost impossible. He made a conscious effort to stop the spiral of negative thoughts and made another lunch-hour call. This time the recipient was Lucinda Armstrong. He expected her to be in her office and she didn't disappoint him. Lucinda worked longer hours than any of the executives.

"Have we responded to the letter from Paul Jacobsen yet?"

"No," Lucinda was curt, "but I will get to it – soon."

Yoshi swallowed a rebuke, saying instead, "I am forwarding you an email that I received from Greene this morning. He's threatening to take the story on national television."

"There's no need. Niamh already sent me a copy."

Yoshi waited for a few moments, hoping she would elaborate with a legal opinion on the issue. When she didn't, he found himself asking the obvious question. "Is there anything we can do to stop it?"

"Not really." Her rely was nonchalant. "If he wants to go on TV, that's his right. The last thing we should do is panic about it and let it influence our decision."

The call ended and Yoshi sat back in his seat again. He was annoyed with Lucinda. The lawyer had the Paul Jacobsen letter for a week now. He knew she was struggling without a personal assistant but responding to the letter should clearly take priority over everything else.

Yes, he thought, *there's no doubt that the Australian executive team needs an overhaul.*

Lucinda was becoming desperate to find a secretary. She was literally drowning in a sea of administration and Yoshi wasn't the only unhappy customer. But she must have sensed what the Japanese liaison director was thinking in relation to her place on the executive team for she immediately drafted a response to Paul Jacobsen. She diplomatically copied Malcolm, Niamh and Yoshi for their comments before it was sent out.

We confirm that our position in relation to the matter of Denis Greene is as follows:

HDD has terminated the employment of your client with an effective date of 15 November, 2003.

HDD has undergone a significant restructure, reducing our headcount in Australia by 10 per cent. The overall aim of the restructure was to reduce cost and therefore redeployment of your client is not an option for the company.

Subject to our obligations to the Department of Immigration, we will not take any steps which will prejudice your client's application for permanent residency.

We trust this clarifies our position in relation to this matter.

Yoshi was the first one off the mark to call her. "I do

not understand your reference to the Department of Immigration. What obligations do we have to them?"

"We must inform them of any change in the employment status of a sponsored employee," she replied. "We are obliged to give them the employee's name, notice period and last day of employment. They cannot take action until twenty-eight days after the last day of employment."

"What do you mean by 'action'?" Yoshi questioned further.

Lucinda's teeth gritted together – she found Yoshi's obsession with detail very annoying. "The Department will request Denis to take the first available flight out of Australia."

Niamh's phone call was hot on the heels of Yoshi's. "Are we going to get an external firm of lawyers to review this letter?"

"No!" Lucinda's patience was hanging on by a mere thread. "We don't need an external firm at this point. I'm quite capable of handling it myself."

"I wasn't questioning your capability. Employment Law is a very specialised area and I thought it would be good to get an external opinion. But if you don't see the need, forget I said it."

"I will – anything else I can help you with?"

"Yes, in fact, there is. What did you mean by our obligations to the Department of Immigration?"

"Why don't you go and ask Yoshi?" Lucinda snapped. In the ensuing silence she realised she had been unacceptably rude and said, "I apologise, Niamh. I have just been through it this minute with Yoshi. We need to inform them when the employment status of a sponsored employee changes."

"Thank you." Niamh was painstakingly polite.

Lucinda had just dived back into her enormous workload when Malcolm called.

"Read the note," he said. "I've no changes to recommend . . . good job."

"Thanks." Lucinda was stunned. Malcolm rarely gave feedback on her work. She wasn't aware that the CEO had recently had his fingers rapped by Yoshi and was showing a cursory interest in all matters he believed the bosses in Tokyo expected him to be conversant with. The open litigation seemed to be a hot subject with the Japanese so Malcolm was putting his personal stamp on everything that happened in that area.

The phone was ringing as Niamh came in but it stopped before she could pick it up. Intuition told her it was her mother. The house was eerily silent after the ringing and Niamh switched on the TV. She had no intention of listening to the presenter of the current affairs programme; his sole purpose was to drown out the silence. Then, when she should have been making a start at dinner, she sat on the couch and thought about Chris.

She had made numerous attempts to resume their "talk" but he refused to be engaged. Even their arguments had eased in frequency. A few times she had deliberately tried to goad him into a debate but he seemed too indifferent to be risen. If she was totally honest with herself, a part of her was indifferent too. She hugged a cushion to her body and tried to remember what she felt when they first met. It had been a whirlwind romance, accelerated by the fact they were both approaching thirty and wanted to settle down. At the time she told everyone she loved him. Now she wasn't sure. For a start, she hardly knew him before they raced down the aisle. Two years later, she didn't know him any better. And it was hard to imagine that the indifference of today had once been love.

Yet, she couldn't give up on it. She didn't want to be like her mother, the one who walked out. Even more so, she didn't want to be like her father, the one who fell apart. So it seemed the only course of action was to try and salvage the marriage. If he wouldn't talk to her, then maybe he would open up to a counsellor. It sounded like a reasonable plan but she knew deep down that he would go crazy if she suggested it.

Her conscience told her she should call her mother and she got up from the couch with a sigh.

"Hi, Mum, it's me. Did you call earlier?"

"Yes. And I called yesterday – and the day before." Her mother's tone was dry. "I was beginning to think you'd been abducted!"

"You should have left a message," Niamh told her.

"I feel stupid talking to a machine," was her response.

"We've had some redundancies at work and I've been working late," Niamh explained. "And Chris has some big court case that he's been buried in."

"I thought you'd call around over the weekend at least."

"I'm sorry."

"I only live five minutes down the road, you know, not in Timbuctoo!" There was a serious thread to her mother's flippancy. She was housebound with rheumatism and the only way she saw people was if they came to her.

"I'm sorry," Niamh said again. "I promise we'll do better . . . how's Tom?"

Tom was her stepfather, the man she loved and hated with all her heart. She loved him because he was kind and he had done his very best for them. She hated him because he had stolen her mother and, as a consequence, killed her father.

"He's grand."

"And have you heard from Aisling?"

Aisling, her sister, was her best and only close friend. She was living in Ireland now, married. As young children they had bonded in their grief, their guilt shutting them off from others. Now, her best friend was thousands of miles away and she hadn't seen her in over two years. Niamh missed her, terribly.

"She phoned last week," her mother said. "The child's started to sleep a good stretch at night so they're all feeling better."

"Did she say if she'd bring the baby over to see us?" Niamh asked, aware that she was treading on dangerous ground. Aisling would have to come to them because it was unthinkable that they go to Ireland.

"No. No, I don't think she'd be up to travelling for some time yet."

Niamh then enquired after her stepbrothers and their

children. Once she had a full account of everyone, they talked about Christmas dinner.

"What do you want me to bring?" she asked.

"I know how busy you are. It will be hard enough for you to bring yourself and Chris *on time*, not to talk about any food."

This time her mother's flippancy made Niamh laugh. "You're probably right. But I can't come empty-handed – I'd be totally shown up by the others. Can't you give me something easy?"

It took her mother a while to think. "Why don't you bring the bread?" she said eventually.

"Yeah, I should be able to manage that!"

Niamh hung up after promising to call to see her before the end of the week. She loved her mother; she really did. The problem was that she couldn't forgive her.

Phil was missing Helen Barnes. The monthly financials were late and none of his staff seemed to know the process from start to end. He was feeling harried and under pressure when his secretary reminded him that he had a four-thirty meeting with Niamh Lynch and Lucinda Armstrong. The girl hadn't bothered to find out the purpose of the appointment and Phil didn't bother to take her to task. In truth, they were as lazy as each other and well suited.

Phil made his way over to Niamh's office and found that Lucinda was already there. He took a seat and looked to his female colleagues to explain the reason for this inconveniently timed meeting. He liked to have a drink in Forbes before catching his train home. He often left work before five so he could squeeze in the drink, admire the twenty-something girls and still be home on time. His wife had become very suspicious in the last few weeks and sometimes rang the office to check up on him if he was late. This meeting meant that he'd have to miss out on Forbes and go straight home. And after a hard day trying to figure out the monthly financials, that didn't make him happy.

Niamh and Lucinda began to speak simultaneously. Niamh hadn't expected the lawyer to take the lead; she had taken a back seat in the meeting with Helen. She gestured to her to go ahead.

"Phil, we've had a complaint . . . and it's rather sensitive in nature," said Lucinda.

"Mmm . . . that doesn't sound good." The smile on Phil's florid face was uneasy. A large man, an ex-rugby player, in his youth he had been quite handsome but too much hard living had made his body and face sag prematurely. In a few more years he would be a clone of Malcolm Young, whose appearance also told a tale of excess.

"It's Helen Barnes. She says you sexually harassed her." Lucinda seemed almost apologetic.

"That's ridiculous!" Phil's face quickly darkened. "How dare she say that!"

"She has described four separate incidents," Niamh intervened. "Two were in your office. She says you touched her breasts . . ."

"That's bullshit. She doesn't have any breasts!" Phil shot back and Lucinda stifled a laugh.

Niamh glared at them both. "She claims to have witnesses to the other two incidents. She says you asked her out for a drink . . ."

"That's true. It was late, I felt like a drink and I'm sure she did. I was just being a thoughtful boss." He relaxed a little into his seat; the cheap joke about Helen's breasts had made him feel better.

"She also claims you tried to kiss her in your office. Malcolm walked in just on time . . ." Niamh was looking at Phil carefully. He leaned out from the brief comfort the seat had offered, floundering at the directness of the allegation.

"Look, ladies, I didn't intend to embarrass her . . ."

Lucinda responded, her tone uncharacteristically compassionate.

"In sexual harassment the intention of the alleged harasser is not relevant. The fact is that your advances were obviously unwelcome."

Phil realised his mistake. "Hey, don't take me literally. I'm reeling from all this – you haven't given me time to consider my response."

"I appreciate that," Lucinda agreed. "Look, why don't you take a few days to think it over? We can meet again next week."

Niamh tried not to show her annoyance at the early termination of the interview. They had barely asked him about the allegations and now Lucinda was releasing him to think about it. She was handing him time to come up with lies to justify his behaviour.

"Phil, I've taken minutes of this meeting. I'll send them to you later today for you to look over," she said, exasperation not far from displaying itself. Phil left and Lucinda got up to follow him out.

"Just a minute!" Niamh stopped her. "I can't help but get the feeling that you're not impartial about this sexual harassment case."

"Excuse me?" The lawyer's face was impassive.

"When we met Helen you were indifferent to the point of rudeness. Yet you were fawning all over Phil today."

"I'm sorry if you got that impression." Lucinda's voice sounded sincere. "I wasn't having a good day when we met Helen. To tell the truth, I'm struggling without a personal assistant and I've been short with everyone."

"Why did you give Phil more time just like that?" Niamh wasn't going to give up. "He either did it or he didn't – what's there for him to think about?"

"We have to be fair. It's a huge accusation and a lot to land on someone in one go. Imagine how you would feel if you were told you were being accused of harassment? You've had no prior warning and, like all harassers, you believe you did nothing wrong! It would be an enormous shock and it's unfair of us to expect a complete response straight away."

Niamh had to admit that Lucinda's explanation made sense.

"Look, Niamh," the lawyer continued, her voice even more amicable, "I've been so busy that I've been rude to everyone, even Jack. Speaking of the little mite, it's his birthday today and I have to get home. I'll see you tomorrow, OK?"

There was nothing Niamh could say in the wake of such an eloquent apology. The lawyer was indeed a chameleon with a continuously changing mood. Niamh just couldn't even start to figure her out.

Lucinda did a quick check on the time as she hurried away. She had promised Jack she would be home early. He had been half asleep when she kissed him goodbye that morning. Her heart had ached because her child missed out on so much. He didn't realise it yet and Lucinda hoped that their family life would be normal before he was old enough to know. She couldn't wait to get home to make a fuss of him now.

Jack's birthday party was just for the family – Jack and his mum and dad. They didn't know any of the children who lived in the neighbourhood; didn't *want* to know them. Jack longed for someone to play with but they couldn't take the risk. Rover Avenue was going to be a temporary address and they just wanted to fade into the background as much as they could.

Lucinda was in the process of logging out when her fax-machine started to creak with an incoming document. She regretted picking it up – if she had left it sitting on the machine she wouldn't have had to act on it until tomorrow.

The fax was from Paul Jacobsen. It read:

I acknowledge receipt of your letter by fax earlier this week. By way of response, I advise that:

My client does not accept the termination of his employment.

Considers your conduct to be unfair under S106 of the NSW Industrial Relations Act.

Is willing to accept any other position with your company that is comparable in salary to the position presently held by him.

Lucinda called Jack first, explaining to her son that she would be a little late for his party. Then she called all the stakeholders, being Yoshi, Malcolm and Niamh, to her office. She wasn't a fool; it was wise to respond to this letter in a more prompt and timely manner than she had to the first. She had heard Yoshi's criticism loud and clear

"This fax is merely regurgitating what Mr Jacobsen said in his first letter," Yoshi complained, frowning as he cleared a chair of its debris so he could sit. "We don't appear to be progressing."

"That is to be expected," Lucinda explained, totally unembarrassed by her untidy office. "Both sides have taken the hard line in the written correspondence. When we meet face to face, it will be easier to soften."

"What does Section 106 of the Industrial Relations Act say?" Niamh asked her. Lucinda turned from Yoshi to give her only female colleague a dazzling smile.

"It gives the Industrial Relations Commission the power to vary or declare void any contract of employment or *related action* if it is unfair, harsh, unconscionable or against public interest."

"So it can force us to rehire Denis Greene?" Yoshi jumped in ahead of Niamh. She didn't mind; his question was the same as hers.

"In theory, yes. In practice it would be unlikely as the Commission can only enforce an act if it is necessary to preserve its own jurisdiction. I think we can safely assume that we will not be forced to rehire Greene."

"So it's down to money," Malcolm declared with a booming self-importance.

"Exactly!" Lucinda rewarded his obvious statement with a smile. "The Commission are much more likely to award Greene reasonable notice of termination or payment in lieu."

Yoshi's smooth brow creased in a grimace, seeing the profits of the Australian subsidiary dwindle even further. "How much could he get?"

"The judge will consider a number of factors: length of service, age, position, status and prospects of obtaining re-employment. My guess is that Denis would do well across all of these considerations."

Yoshi was depressed, Malcolm only superficially interested, Niamh defensive.

"But we have already given him seven months' pay," she objected.

"That's generous," Lucinda granted. "But maybe not generous enough. There's no doubt that we had an obligation to give extended notice in this case. Given the fact that he may have to leave the country, we should have given him adequate time to consider his options.

What constitutes adequate time is in the eye of the
beholder. The beholder will be the judge."

There was a sombre silence.

"What should we do?" Malcolm asked.

"We meet Greene and Jacobsen," Lucinda responded.
"And we negotiate. We have no legal precedents to go on
and, if we want to limit our costs, there will be some compromise required on our end."

The meeting broke up and Lucinda drove home. She
darted through amber lights when she should have
stopped. She weaved from lane to lane, seeking the
fastest moving traffic. She got to their house in the
Western suburbs by six thirty and raced in the door to her
beloved son.

Scott found a solicitor through the recommendation of a
former colleague. Frances King was a tall sturdy redhead
with a London accent. Large spectacles added more
angles to her already gaunt face. Her mind knew every
trip and trap of Australian Employment Law. The fact
that she was one of the best in her field was not reflected
in her modest fees.

Scott apologised for bringing Jenny along to their
meeting but Frances wasn't at all bothered by an unsteady
toddler exploring her office.

"Thanks for seeing me at such short notice," Scott said
when they had finished making small talk about how cute
Jenny was.

"No problem." She was matter-of-fact. "Lawsuits are
not something to procrastinate over."

"I'm not sure I want to sue yet," Scott replied, keeping a careful eye on Jenny's activities. "I would prefer to come to a mutual agreement, a settlement for what I think is a fair notice period."

"OK, it's good that you're being reasonable," she said, approval lighting up her serious face. "Too many people come to me gunning for some court action."

"I don't want to end up in a courtroom over this." Scott was firm, adding by way of explanation, "I separated from my wife earlier this year. Our respective lawyers have been sparring with letters over the last few months. Something tells me we're going to end up in a real ugly brawl. I want this dispute with HDD to be resolved amicably . . . no courtroom fracas."

Frances glanced at Jenny who was absorbed in the pages of a law journal. "Custody issues?" she asked.

"Far from," he answered with a bitterness that surprised the lawyer. "My ex-wife would faint if she had to take custody. She never came around to the idea of motherhood and the so-called restrictions it brought to her life. Custody is the last thing she wants. It's assets. We're arguing about who gets what. We're arguing about a townhouse in Dee Why."

"So the last thing you need right now is to lose your source of income," Frances commented, neatly returning to the relevant issue. Deviations yielded interesting background information but time was precious in her field. It was after four in the evening and there were two more people she needed to see after Scott Morgan. She couldn't afford to take her eye off the clock.

"That's right. I would have never left my previous role if I knew this was coming. Security means everything to me – I remember making that clear to Niamh at the interview."

"Who is Niamh?"

"The HR director, my ex-boss."

"Oh, the bitch who retrenched you without a second thought," Frances remarked, beginning to type notes on her dated Pentium. Her unexpected aggression was a rousing douse of cold water, its sole purpose to obtain an unguarded reaction from her new client.

"Hold on a second," Scott jumped in. "She's not a bitch. She didn't know anything about my personal circumstances – and the restructure certainly wasn't at her instigation."

"Whose idea was it?" the red-haired lawyer fired the question without a split second of thought and Scott got a glimpse of what Frances King was like in the courtroom. She was still typing; she was a multi-tasking cross-examiner.

"Japan – the restructure was ordered by the owners in Japan. The CEO had to get rid of 10 per cent of the staff in Australia. Not negotiable! That's fifty people and I was one of the last in so my role was examined straight away. They decided that they could decentralise recruitment and manage without me."

"You sound sympathetic," Frances challenged, looking up at him from under her glasses. Her fingers still moved on the keyboard, taking notes.

"In one way I am," he confessed. "I understand why my

116

role had to go. All the IT companies are finding it tough with the downturn in the economy. I just think that someone should have known this was coming and should have prevented me from being hired in the first place."

"That's a very good point." Frances nodded just as there was a thud. Jenny was the culprit, a textbook the victim. Scott picked her up before she could cause further damage. She squirmed in his arms, desperate to get back to the fun the bookshelf offered.

"I'm sorry," he said.

"Don't be," Frances smiled. "Now, where were we? Yes, now, how many months' termination pay did you get?"

"Two – well, almost. Eight weeks."

"That's not bad." She looked at him; the enormous glasses had slid downwards to rest on the tip of her nose. "Why do you think you deserve more than that?"

"I'm a relatively senior manager. In the IT industry it's common practice to pay managers six to twelve months' termination, cognisant of the time it will take them to find a comparable role in the market place."

Frances nodded in agreement, using her index finger to slide the errant glasses back up the bridge of her bony nose. "I can't recall if you told me the name of the company?"

"It's Hard-Disk Drive Ltd – HDD – the Australian subsidiary of a Japanese parent," Scott told her as Jenny wriggled down off his knee. She thought about her next move for a moment before deciding to crawl under the lawyer's desk.

Frances gave the little girl at her feet a benevolent

smile before she said, "Japanese companies are traditionally conservative, tight with the purse-strings. They've paid you two months; you're looking for six. The difference could be eaten up in legal fees very quickly. I'll send them a letter, but do you think they'll come to the party?"

"Yeah," Scott replied, his thoughts on the phone call he had received the night he was retrenched. "I have an insider who assures me they'll come to the party."

Chapter Five

There was a thriving coffee shop on the ground floor of the HDD tower. Rumour was they sold over two thousand coffees a day. That was a lot of caffeine.

At ten thirty Sharon came into Niamh's office, guilt written all over her face. "Are you going for a coffee this morning?"

"Yes, just about to go down there now."

She bit her lip. "Can you get me a muffin, a chocolate one?"

"No worries."

Niamh left level two by the fire stairwell to make her routine contribution to the coffee shop's profits. The alley was deserted but on George Street the pavement was full of aimless tourists and rushed business people. HDD had a great location, smack bang in the thick of the CBD buzz.

The coffee shop had added mince pies and fruitcake to its selection of pastries and Niamh toyed with the idea of substituting Sharon's muffin for something more seasonal. She decided against it. Sharon was quite regimented about her binges and wouldn't like to be surprised.

Niamh had just placed her order when she noticed Willem Boelhoers further up the counter. He was holding a sterile mineral water.

"Hello, Willem, how are you?" she asked with a friendly smile to banish any residual embarrassment he may have had since their last meeting.

"I'm OK," he responded flatly, handing the assistant cash.

"Taking any holidays over Christmas?" she enquired as she waited on her cappuccino.

"No. ANZ is coming up for contract renewal and I'm heavily involved in that."

Willem seemed to be waiting for her and when Niamh's cappuccino was ready, she nodded in the direction of the only free table outside. "Would you like to join me?"

"Thank you."

They sat down. The soaring buildings across the street cast dark oversized shadows across the tables of the coffee shop but she could still see Willem clearly. He was deathly pale; the fingers that were wrapped around the mineral water seemed to have a tremor. All in all, he didn't look healthy.

"I want you to know that my door is always open and

you can talk to me at any time," Niamh said with a gentleness that seemed necessary to placate the troubled man.

Willem looked at her, the eyes behind the silver-framed glasses as anxious as the last time they spoke. "Thank you, Mrs Lynch."

"Niamh, please."

"Thank you, Niamh. I know what I said last week was bizarre and, yes, I didn't take my medication that day. However, the voices I heard were on days where I *had* been taking my medication."

"I'm afraid I know very little about schizophrenia," Niamh said, remembering to take a sip of her cappuccino. "Does your medication work completely?"

"Yes, that is why I am worried," he said. "Also, the voices I heard were Australian voices. The other voices in my head, the ones that occur because of my illness, they are speaking Dutch."

Niamh laughed before she could stop herself. "I'm so sorry, Willem. You'll probably think I'm being insensitive – but you must know how funny that sounded. Australian voices! Dutch voices! All in your head!"

Willem's pale face broke into a smile. "Schizophrenia has its funny side and it is refreshing when a joke is shared with me rather than made behind my back."

There was a pause and Niamh drank the last of her cappuccino. She noticed that Willem had barely touched his mineral water.

"How long have you lived in Australia?" she asked him. She had noticed that his English, although accented, was grammatically perfect.

"The family moved when I was eighteen. I developed schizophrenia when I started university a year later." He shrugged. "I guess I wasn't able to cope with so many life changes in such a short space of time."

Niamh would have loved to stay and find out more about Willem but her watch told her that Denis Greene and his solicitor were due to arrive in five minutes.

"I need to get back . . . hey, you've made me curious about those Australian voices. Can you write down what they say the next time you hear them?"

"I will do that – for you," the Dutch man promised.

They shook hands over the table and went in opposite directions. Willem headed for the conventional lifts, Niamh went down the alley. She swiped her access card and pushed in the heavy door. She was out of breath by the time she got to the second level. When she had first met Chris they would go to the gym together a few nights a week. The workouts had fizzled away as he got more and more entrapped by his partnership quest. She was now totally out of shape, just like their relationship.

Denis Greene's booming voice could be heard well before he appeared in the boardroom. He was wearing a mafia-like black suit, his hair swept back in his trademark pony-tail. With his aged face, the whole look had something seriously amiss. He was flanked by two men who also wore dark suits. Niamh guessed the younger man to be Paul Jacobsen. She wondered who the older one was. This was going to cost Denis a lot in legal fees. No doubt he would be planning to palm off those costs to HDD if he won his case.

Denis introduced his companions before they sat down. "This is my lawyer, Paul Jacobsen."

There was a flurry of handshakes and a nod of recognition between Lucinda and Paul.

"And this is Steve Jones, my barrister."

The legal fees would indeed be horrendous, Niamh thought as her hand was squeezed in a relentless grip.

Lucinda greeted the barrister with a peck on the check. "Hi, Steve. Long time, no see."

It was obvious to all that Lucinda and the barrister were more than distant acquaintances.

Sharon offered the visitors tea or coffee. There were no takers and she looked relieved as she took a seat to minute the meeting.

Paul Jacobsen cleared his throat and began to speak. "As I said in my letter, I believe that your termination of Denis's employment is unfair conduct –"

"We've read your letter," Lucinda cut him off, picking up the fax copy in front of her. "Maybe you can explain the basis of your conclusion."

"The company has reneged on my client's business visa before its natural expiration date –"

"We have no obligation to employ your client for the full term of his business visa," Lucinda interrupted the other lawyer for the second time.

"With all due respect, three and a half years have passed on the visa and any judge in the country would consider it reasonable for my client to expect that the final six months would also pass without incident." Paul

Jacobsen was a short man. The board table dwarfed him but he spoke with confidence. Lucinda's raised eyebrows indicated she was getting ready for another challenge and he forged ahead to prevent it. "My client has a pending application for permanent residency and your untimely termination of his employment has placed that application in jeopardy."

"Denis never informed us that he was making an independent application for residency." This time it was Niamh who dissented.

"Let's stop scoring points off each other," Paul suggested with a smoothness that glossed over his annoyance at the constant interruptions. "If you let me finish what I have to say, I will gladly give you the same consideration when you wish to put your side forward . . . now, back to my client. Denis wishes to remain in Australia. He has cut his ties with the UK and his family has settled well into the Australian lifestyle. His wife, Lily, loves living here and is distraught at the thought of leaving her close friends . . . I believe my client's request is a reasonable one. Remember, he isn't asking for money. This is a lifestyle issue not a monetary one. He just wants to be reinstated."

"We've already checked across the company," Niamh said. "We have no open positions for which Denis would be suitable."

"That's bullshit!" Denis burst into the conversation with an aggression that had been waiting to be unleashed. "What about the ANZ Bank deal? HDD will be recruiting more than twenty people when that contract is renewed in January."

"Correct me if I'm wrong," Niamh's voice was icy, "but this is *December*. As you said, the contract won't be renewed until January."

"It's practically in the bag," Denis argued, a menacing figure as he leaned forward.

"You're way out of line," Lucinda warned the Yorkshire man. "We do not have a signed contract with ANZ Bank and are not in a position to review the roles to see if you would be suitable. End of discussion."

"Forget ANZ, so. What about the other roles you've advertised recently?" Denis wasn't going to concede to a woman. "I have a very flexible skill base – I explained this to Malcolm Young –"

"I'm aware of your email to Malcolm," Niamh stopped him short. Paul Jacobsen was looking confused so she directed the remainder of her response to him. "I would appreciate if you could advise your client not to communicate with the CEO or any staff member in the company about this matter. All communication should be directed through me."

Paul nodded, caught off guard. He knew nothing of the email and didn't like surprises.

"It would also be helpful to this process if your client declined from speaking to journalists," Niamh continued. Yoshi had specifically asked her to bring up that point. He was paranoid about the current affairs programme and the damage it could do to the company's reputation.

Paul nodded again, fully intending to pull Denis into line after the meeting.

"Now, I hope we are clear on the fact that there isn't an alternative role that Denis can perform in HDD." Niamh reiterated her position, meeting the eyes of the three males in turn.

Steve Jones spoke for the first time. "Let me suggest an alternative." He had a deep educated voice. They listened. "Why not keep Denis on your books for six months, until May. Then he can voluntarily resign when his application for residency is approved."

Denis looked as if he was about to say something but swallowed his words after a glare from his barrister.

Niamh thought for only a moment before objecting, "But we don't have a role for him between now and May."

"He doesn't need to be in the office," the barrister countered simply. "He just needs to be on your payroll."

"Are you suggesting we pay him to do nothing?" Lucinda asked with a smile.

"I guess I am." Steve returned the smile, having a pleasant recollection of what it had been like with her in the old days.

Niamh didn't see the humour. "We've just retrenched 10 per cent of our staff to cut costs. Paying someone to do nothing seems very hard to justify."

"If this goes to court you will find that six months' pay will barely cover the legal costs." The older man's voice held a soft threat.

"That's if you win," Lucinda was quick to say.

There was a respite in the debate and it gave Niamh time to think.

"There's another issue," she said slowly. "The

Department of Immigration. I'm sure they won't be happy with a cover-up like this. Denis would be getting his residency on the false pretence that he still works for HDD."

"The Department of Immigration doesn't need to know." It was Paul Jacobsen who spoke the loaded words.

When Lucinda didn't tackle him, Niamh said, "HDD takes professional ethics very seriously. We will not entertain any propositions that involve misleading a government department."

"We all appreciate that," Steve Jones said reasonably. "Why don't you think over your options? There may be a way to achieve the desired outcome with the Department within the boundaries of your corporate ethics."

The meeting ended and Sharon scribbled furiously as the opposing parties shook hands.

"What do you think?" Niamh asked Lucinda when the visitors had left.

"I don't have time to think. I've got another meeting I must go to. It's an interview with a personal assistant . . . hopefully this will be the one!" She stood up, gathering her paperwork together.

"Don't you think it's time we hired an external lawyer?" Niamh persisted. "He has a barrister on his side . . ."

"I'm not intimidated by Steve Jones," Lucinda declared arrogantly. "I've known him a long time. Anyway, we're only sparring at the moment and it would be a complete waste of money to hire an external lawyer."

Niamh turned her attention to Sharon who was still writing notes. "Did you get everything that was said?"

"No – there were too many people speaking at once."

"I'll check it for you later – I wrote down a few of the important points. Maybe we should tape the next meeting to ensure we have an accurate transcript of what was said. Barristers make me nervous."

Niamh's last comment was a shot at Lucinda who was on her way out the door.

Donna Howard was a junior accounts clerk and the all-important witness to the sexual harassment case. She passed Denis Greene and his legal advisors as they stood out the long wait for a lift. Only the most observant would have seen the smile between the distinguished Steve Jones and the twenty-one-year-old.

Niamh, on her way back from the boardroom, found Donna waiting in her office.

"I guess you know why I want to talk to you," Niamh began, locking away Denis's file in her desk drawer. The file on Helen Barnes was considerably smaller.

"Yes, Helen phoned to tell me what was happening. Where's Lucinda?" she asked, looking around. "Helen said she would be here too."

Lucinda's absence and continued lack of interest in the sexual harassment claim was a sore point that Niamh brushed over.

"Lucinda has another meeting this afternoon. She was happy for me to talk to you alone."

"OK. You want to know what I heard that evening?" Donna leaned forward with an innocent eagerness to help.

"Yes." Niamh got ready to take notes. Sharon hadn't stayed on for this meeting. Even though she trusted her assistant implicitly, this matter was too sensitive for her to know about.

"It was a few weeks ago. It was late. I was finishing off some month-end work and had my head down. That's why Phil didn't see me. He asked Helen if she wanted to go for a drink with him. I tuned into their conversation straight away – I'm a sucker for company gossip." Donna gave a brief grin. "He said they could go somewhere quiet. I heard her say 'no' quite clearly. He said he knew she liked him and she should give up the chase. She told him *again* she wasn't interested. I could hear from her voice that she was getting upset so I made my presence known. I stuck my head up and asked her if she wanted a coffee. His face was a picture!" Her grin was bigger this time. "He wasn't sure if I had heard or not and didn't know which one of us to look at. He skulked back to his office pretty fast."

"Would you say that Helen encouraged the invitation in any way?" Niamh asked, looking at the young girl carefully.

"Certainly not!" Donna shook her head vehemently. "She was very firm with him and she looked quite upset when I saw her face."

It was a solid account of events that matched Helen's story exactly. Niamh had one more question. "Do you think he *intended* to offend her?"

"Sure he did!" The response was unwavering. "He was totally insulting when he said she should 'give up the chase'. I would punch him in the face if he said something like that to me."

"OK," Niamh smiled at her. "Thanks for your time, Donna."

"I'm glad to help in any way I can. Will it go to court?"

Her question caught Niamh off guard. She answered it honestly.

"I'm hoping that we can resolve it internally."

"Good. I saw Steve Jones in the foyer earlier – it looks as if you already have your hands full of litigation and don't need anything else to happen." And with that puzzling statement, the junior accounts clerk was gone.

Niamh checked through her notes, adding a few extra comments. She was getting closer to a recommendation. She had to meet Phil again but she wasn't expecting much from that. Malcolm, and an account of what he had seen, was the main outstanding matter. Niamh's thoughts went back to her last discussion with the CEO. Malcolm was fighting to prove himself; he could easily see an interview as a slight on his authority and refuse to co-operate. She'd have to think carefully about the best way to approach him.

It was after seven when she finished up at the office. There was no need to rush; she would still be home before Chris. His hours were getting longer and longer, explained away with the impending court case. There had been no opportunity to talk to him about counselling.

Yoshi Murasaki was also on his way home. He stood at the lifts, rigidly holding his briefcase. "Hello, Niamh.

How was your day?" he enquired with guarded politeness.

"I had that meeting with Denis Greene and his lawyers," she told him.

"How did it go?"

The lift came and Niamh waited until they were inside before answering. "They suggested we keep Denis on our payroll for six months while his application for residency is processed. Putting the cost issue to one side, I'm of the opinion we would be misleading the Department of Immigration if we did that."

Yoshi took a few moments to think. "I agree. That is not a palatable solution."

"Denis is waving some considerable legal costs in our face," she told him. "Not only did he have a lawyer there today, he also had a barrister."

Yoshi frowned, deep lines creasing his smooth forehead. "A barrister seems over the top at this stage."

"I think it's a threat. As far as I know, barristers rarely make appearances outside of court. Denis is trying to intimidate us." Niamh bent her head as she searched through her handbag for her car keys. "There's also the current affairs programme, another threat. As you requested, I did ask Denis not to speak to any journalists . . . however, I wouldn't count on it." She found the keys in the depths of the bag. When she looked up she noticed that Yoshi's frown had got deeper.

"What does Lucinda have to say about all of this?" he asked after a while.

"I didn't have the chance to talk to her – she was rushing off when the meeting broke up. However, she's still adamant we don't need an external lawyer – and you heard her the other day – she thinks we will have to compromise, what with no legal precedent –"

"What do *you* think?" Yoshi's black eyes were boring into her.

"I think we've paid him enough," she replied. "Quite frankly, compromising doesn't appeal to me. Lucinda's been extremely busy – I don't know how much real thought she's put into the situation. I'm going to make some discreet enquiries myself to see if we can come at this from another angle."

The lift finally shuddered to a stop and they both got out.

"What about the other disputes? Has there been any progress on those?" Yoshi asked with trepidation. Running a business in Australia was like a military exercise, ducking and dodging fatal missiles that came from all directions: aggressive employees, demanding customers, complicated federal and state governments. Every day there was something new to fill him with worry. These lawsuits, the latest missiles, were a real threat to the slim profit they had forecast for the remaining two quarters of the year.

"I had a meeting with a witness to the sexual harassment issue this afternoon," Niamh answered. "Her story fits with Helen's. Phil did ask Helen to go for a drink and was offensive when he got 'no' for an answer. Donna heard every word that was said. To be truthful, I can't see a way for Phil to redeem himself now."

"It's a shame," Yoshi said with unexpected emotion. "It

is a shame that any lady should be put in a situation like that ... I presume we will be releasing Phil of his duties?"

"I have to meet Phil again to give him the chance to respond fully to the allegations. And I have one more piece of evidence to check out before I can make a recommendation. Apparently, Malcolm walked in on one of the advances that Phil made to Helen –"

Niamh stopped short, an idea forming. Malcolm was threatened by Yoshi and, if caught off guard, was unlikely to cover up for Phil. And something told her that Yoshi was tracking Malcolm very carefully and wouldn't mind the opportunity to get a further insight into the man and his values.

"Have you asked Malcolm about what he saw?" Yoshi asked on cue.

"Not yet. Phil is an old friend of his and I am conscious that might –" she paused, searching for the right words, "might . . . cloud his judgement."

"Can I help in any way?"

"Yes, yes, you could," Niamh said as if the thought was just occurring to her. "You could ask Malcolm what he saw. I know he holds you in high regard and will give you a proper response."

Yoshi nodded, "It's not a problem. I'll find an appropriate time to broach the subject . . . Goodnight."

He made to walk away but Niamh stalled him.

"Yoshi . . ."

"Yes?"

"I don't think you should give him advance warning of what you want to talk to him about. I want to get an unguarded response from him."

"Very well. Goodnight, Niamh."

As she got into her own car, Niamh realised she had forgotten to update Yoshi on Scott Morgan's case. A letter had arrived from his solicitor, Frances King, that morning but had been brushed aside with the focus on the meeting with Denis Greene. Niamh watched Yoshi as he walked across the carpark to the reserved spot that held his Mitsubishi Verada. It was probably for the best that he didn't yet know that she would be recommending a settlement with Scott. She knew he would resist any outlay that would threaten the profit for the next two quarters.

Denis's home phone rang at 9pm, the same time as the night before. The phone calls were annoying Denis and making Lily suspicious.

"You did well today – bringing up the ANZ renewal got quite a reaction, so I heard . . ."

Denis's response was a grunt but his thoughts were running wild. Who was feeding the information back to the caller? Out of the four others in the boardroom that day, the most obvious informant was Paul Jacobsen. He was the lawyer the caller had hired: he must be the caller's spy.

The voice at the other end continued to speak over his thoughts. "Just keep the pressure up – don't let them think you're going to take this lying down."

"I'll do as you say, but you're wrong about all this. The more trouble I am, the less likely they are to take me back. Can't you see that?"

"Denis! Denis!" There was a sigh evident in the voice. "You've always been trouble to HDD. Why should you have a personality change now? Don't I keep telling you that this has to be authentic? Today you acted true to character – you were a difficult bastard. Keep that up and let me worry about the overall strategy."

Denis seriously doubted the caller's ability to strategise. He knew there were some strong personalities in the executive who would fight to the very end rather than take him back. Yet the caller seemed to think it was a decision based solely on money.

"Yeah, they're under pressure now!" The caller was practically gleeful. "They're worried about what it could cost to settle. Soon they'll be ready to compromise, to take the cheap option and give you your job back."

"They talked about another option," Denis said, remembering how the meeting had concluded. "Steve Jones suggested they put me on the payroll but I wouldn't need to turn up for work – that would be no good for us."

"They won't take that option," the voice assured. "If they have to pay you, they'll make you work for it – Steve Jones doesn't know a lot – he's just there to give them a scare about the potential legal costs. I bet they're squabbling already about hiring their own external legal representation to match up to Steve."

The call ended with the caller's promise to "talk soon".

"Who was that?" Lily appeared at the hall doorway the instant Denis hung up the phone.

"Someone from work," he answered.

"Why are they calling you at this hour?" she asked with an unattractive frown.

"They need my help on something. They were a bit too hasty to get rid of the old engineer. They may need me back!" he said. There were certain people who were desperate to get him back to finish the job he had started. But it wasn't the same people Lily would think it was.

"Was it Bruce?" Lily asked with narrowed eyes, thinking she was with the programme because she could recall his boss's name.

"No. Bruce doesn't call the shots."

He made for the stairs before she could ask any more questions. He would go to bed first tonight. He would read for thirty minutes before turning out the light and he knew Lily would wait downstairs until she was sure he was asleep.

Around the time Denis received the phone call, his barrister was sitting with a Scotch in the quiet of his study. Steve was reminiscing about Lucinda Armstrong. He remembered her as a graduate. Beautiful. Clever. Unfathomable. He had been the managing partner in a firm of four hundred gunning lawyers. It was rare that the partners knew the graduates by name but Lucinda stood out from the crowd.

She was bright; she had breezed through her articles. And she put in long days until she became the top fee-earning lawyer in the firm. But it was more than intelligence and hard work that fast-tracked her to senior associate. Everybody knew that Lucinda Armstrong had committed mentors at the partner level of the firm who cared about her career.

Steve couldn't deny that he was flattered when she flirted with him. He had been as married to Mary then as he was today. They weren't going through a bad patch. Life was steady and the only unpredictability was provided by the antics of their twelve-year-old son, Adam. Of course he had been tempted by Lucinda's come-on. She was a fresh poppy next to the staidness of Mary. She seemed to find greying hair and deepening facial lines attractive. Later it transpired that she must have also found baldness and extra kilos a turn-on. Then again, maybe it was the aura of power that made the older partners attractive to the stunning young woman.

Steve knew for certain that she had slept with two of the partners. They had individually boasted to him about how hot she was. Steve had listened with an impassive face but a sick stomach. His affair with Lucinda had not been a physical one, but it had been real in his mind as she rarely left his thoughts. He had seriously considered leaving Mary and Adam to free himself to respond to Lucinda's flirting and wherever it led. Listening to his colleagues, he realised that he had almost left his family for a tramp. No, he was being unfair. She was young, free and single with a high sex drive. He was the married one and he was the faithless one for thinking like that about a young woman who was fifteen years his junior.

Steve poured himself another Scotch of generous proportions. Seeing Lucinda today had completely thrown him. She looked every bit as beautiful as when he had last seen her, three years before. And he had felt every bit as helpless in the face of that beauty.

Scott pushed Jenny in her stroller as he jogged the walkway along Manly Beach. She loved the wind in her face and the same wind carried her squeals of laughter back to him. The sun was blazing, he was out of breath but the exercise made him feel good.

Frances King had sent the letter to HDD and the waiting game had started. The letter had asked for payment of six months' notice, a period that was appropriate for the managerial level of his role. They had decided against asking for more and negotiating back. Scott couldn't afford the time it took to play those kinds of games. With some luck, the case would be settled quickly and he and Jenny could enjoy this unexpected time together before he rejoined the workforce.

It had been this time last year when the first cracks in his marriage became apparent. Jenny was a few weeks old; Ann wasn't happy. She resented the night feeds, the endless washing, the unpredictability of the baby. Scott did his best to make it easier for her, shouldering a lot of the night feeds, fronting up for work the next morning after only a few hours' sleep. As the weeks passed Ann got more and more resentful and, eventually, when Jenny was three months old, she decided to go back to work. Initially she worked nine to five and seemed much happier. But after a while the hours got longer or there were drinks after work. More often than not, she would miss Jenny's bedtime. Scott slowly realised that Ann didn't love Jenny unconditionally. As a consequence, he loved Ann less and Jenny more. It all came to a head when Ann was offered a three-month assignment in Malaysia. She was keen, it was a great career opportunity and she would love to see the country. Being separated from her family had not been a deterrent in her decision to take the assignment. They agreed to start divorce proceedings before she left for Malaysia. It had been a detached unemotional discussion and he hadn't seen her since. There had been a gift and a phone call on Jenny's first birthday but that was all. The three-month assignment stretched to nine months with letters from Ann's lawyer being the only form of contact. The letters were urging a *de facto* property settlement prior to the divorce application. Ann wanted her half of the townhouse in Dee Why.

As he jogged along the walkway, with Jenny's squeals floating back in the wind, his eyes focussed on a familiar face coming towards him. Niamh. He had been thinking about her a lot since that night in Forbes but had never expected to bump into her out of the blue like this. Blonde hair whipped across her face; her brown eyes were cast downwards. She was with a tall good-looking man – obviously her husband. Scott was about to give a resounding "Hello!" when she met his eyes and shook her head to warn him off. He swallowed his words and jogged past his ex-boss without any visible acknowledgement that he knew her.

He got to the esplanade and he and Jenny shared an ice cream as they sat in the sun. They laughed as they took turns with the cone but he wasn't fully there with his little girl. He was back on the walkway, analysing the expression on Niamh's face. Something about the set of her mouth, the stiffness of her body, told him she had been having an argument with her husband.

"Our Christmas party is on next week," Niamh had said a few minutes earlier. Chris walked next to her but their bodies didn't as much as brush against each other.

"What night?" he asked after a considerable pause.

"Saturday." She had told him about it a few weeks ago. Pleading loss of memory was very transparent but he didn't seem to realise that.

"Are you going?" His voice was muffled by the wind that was gusting in from the ocean.

"We *both* are," she said tersely. "Your secretary has put it in your calendar."

They lapsed into a silence and Niamh mentally rehearsed how to broach the subject of counselling. She had asked him to come on this walk thinking it was an opportunity to have the meaningful discussion that was proving impossible within the four walls of the house. But so far he was as brusque as ever and she didn't think he would react well when she brought it up.

She put her head down, striding into the wind, her face set in an obstinacy that he couldn't see. Five minutes later she was ready.

"Chris, I think we need to see someone, a counsellor."

For a while the only sound she could hear was the wind. She wondered if he had heard.

"Chris, I –"

"I heard you the first time," was his response.

She turned her head to look at him. He was staring ahead, his profile stern, his shoulders tense. "Well, will you go?"

He left her waiting for his answer. "Counsellors are overrated. It's not as if they can wave a magic wand that will change your family history and all your hang-ups . . ."

She stopped dead, a cold fury washing over her. "Are you saying this is all about me?"

He stopped a few paces ahead. He looked around to see if there was anybody watching. "Look, this isn't the time or place . . ."

"What do you mean?" She raised her voice, undaunted by the public stage. "You won't talk at home – do you have some *special place* we can go where you'll open up?"

"Niamh –"

"Don't you *dare* say this is all about me!" she yelled, walking past him. A few moments later he fell into step at her side but they didn't speak.

She almost didn't notice Scott, jogging towards her with a stroller. The little girl was shrieking with laughter and Niamh was aware of the other walkers' indulgent smiles as they took in the happy scene. The child had the same berry-brown skin and fair hair as her dad. Niamh's eyes moved up to Scott who had recognised her and was starting to slow down. She shook her head in a moment of panic, signalling that it wasn't a good time to talk. She saw confusion cloud his face, but he kept going and they passed each other on the walkway without exchanging words.

The silence with Chris went on for the rest of the walk home and she was free to analyse the brief glimpse of Scott. Sweat had gleamed on his face and torso. His thighs were firm, his stride long. He had been enjoying the heady effect of running against the wind every bit as much as his little girl. When she saw him next she'd have to apologise for not stopping to talk. It would be hard to explain, though. How could she tell him she had reached a dead end with her husband only moments before? How could she tell him that she didn't want him to stand next to Chris? She would feel compelled to compare the two men and she knew that Chris wouldn't come off the better.

Phil Davis did everything he could to avoid the follow-up meeting on the harassment accusation. The meeting was to give him the chance to make a considered response to Helen's allegations. Despite his lack of co-operation, the investigation of the facts was coming to an end. The next stage was to assess the evidence and make a finding on the balance of probabilities. So far the balance of probabilities weren't stacking in his favour.

After a number of false starts, the meeting went ahead the Friday before the Christmas party. Phil sat down with an insolent impatience. Niamh found it peculiar that he didn't want to commit the time it would take to clear his name.

"I'm too busy for this rubbish." His opening statement wasn't promising.

"This meeting is in your interest," Niamh reminded him as if he was a child. "It's your chance to respond to

Helen's allegations."

"It's all crap."

"You need to be more specific than that, mate." Lucinda encouraged him with a smile.

He shifted his bulk around in the seat, then fidgeted with his loud tie. "Look, the attraction between me and Helen was mutual . . ."

"There's a witness who says that Helen resisted your advances," Niamh told him. "Our evidence doesn't appear to support a mutual attraction."

Phil realised he was caught. "What witness? Who?"

"I'm not at liberty to say." It was fun to play cat and mouse with him, fun because he was so transparent. Niamh knew she was guilty of taking sides but it was hard to be impartial when one party to the dispute was so pathetic.

"How do you know they're telling the truth?" He was petulant, his lower lip thickening in a pout.

"Her account matches Helen's exactly."

It took him a few moments to summon a response. "Well . . . I genuinely thought the attraction was mutual. I thought I was getting all the right signals," he stated, his gaze alternating between Niamh and Lucinda, fishing for some support.

"Do you have anything else you want to say?" Lucinda asked, prompting him to make a better attempt at his defence.

"I could apologise to her if you want – maybe that would make her go away," he said, hope lighting up his flushed face.

Niamh shook her head. "She won't be going away, Phil. You've admitted to making sexual advances and there's a witness who confirms that they weren't welcomed by Helen."

Hope was gone; now Phil was scared. "What are you saying?"

"We need to assess your future with the company," she replied.

He paled and Niamh felt a wave of amazement that the possibility of dismissal hadn't entered his thoughts before now. "For Christ's sake! Can't we just pay her some money to go away?" Phil was angry now, his face an open book as the different emotions chased each other across his broad features.

"No, sexual harassment claims don't work like that. We're obliged to take disciplinary action," Lucinda said quietly.

Phil marched out of the room and went in search of his mate, Malcolm. He found him in his office.

"You've got to tell those two bitches to get off my back!" he said, helping himself to a seat.

Malcolm looked up from his screen with a frown. Calling two female executives "bitches" was unacceptable even to him.

"Have some respect, eh? There's no need to talk like that."

"There's every need! Niamh told me she was going to assess my future with the company – who does she think she is?"

Malcolm didn't respond straight away. He didn't need Phil and his insatiable sex drive to add to the pressure he was already under. Yoshi Murasaki, the Japanese spy, was taking note of everything he did and every word he said. And it was all being fed back to Nishikawa Shacho, the humourless vice-president up in Tokyo.

"Look," he said eventually, "I'll speak to Neee-uv and make sure your ass is saved this time. But if you do something like this again, I'll be the first in line to boot you out. Got that?"

Phil's jaw dropped open and it was a few moments before he sufficiently regained himself to ask, "What the hell's got into you?"

"You ask what's got into me?" Malcolm's stare was unwavering but his voice was rising. "This is one of the worst years ever in the technology industry. If that wasn't bad enough, we have litigation flying at us left, right and centre, threatening our profits even more. I have the Japanese watching every step I take. Need I go on?"

Malcolm didn't like to be watched. He was a top-level guy, keeping out of the detail as much as he could. The Japanese obsession with micro-managing was driving him crazy. He wanted to tell the Japanese spy and the vice-president to go to hell. He wanted to but he couldn't.

Phil reacted to the telling-off in the only way he knew how. "I'm going to stop in Forbes on the way home for a drink. Want to join me?" he asked, standing up, his profile showing a significant beer belly. His wife would be furious that he was late but he was past caring.

Malcolm shook his head. After Yoshi's tongue-lashing,

he felt compelled to tone down his social activities. He was also beginning to acknowledge that he was getting too old for Phil's wild tastes. The finance director remained married to the same woman but bedded any willing female without remorse. Malcolm had been relatively faithful during his two marriages and was in awe of Phil's alley-cat ways. Waitresses, strippers, lady taxi drivers, Phil had stories to tell about all of them and, boy, did he love it when he had an audience to listen!

Malcolm went back to his work. He was tired of the pressure, tired of coming to the office to get beaten up every day. But he had to do this for one more year. Just one more year of raking in a CEO's salary. That was all he needed before he could retire. His two kids by his first wife were going to the best private schools in Sydney. They had expensive ways, just like their mother. His second wife wasn't getting alimony but she had nearly sent him broke when they divorced. He was soured by marriage and wouldn't be doing it again. He found it an inflexible and expensive arrangement.

Malcolm recognised that he needed to win over his executive team if he was to survive as CEO for the next twelve months. He'd had a shaky start but it wasn't too late to make amends. Phil as finance director was a bonus; he would be onside once he got over his sulkiness after today's telling-off. Lucinda Armstrong would also be OK; she was one of those few women who didn't demand too much. Bruce was harder to read: he ran his business without consulting with any of the team. He looked mildly surprised when Malcolm asked him the odd question, but at least he wasn't hostile. Then there was Niamh who he hadn't figured out yet. He sensed that she and Yoshi had shared opinions and he feared a future alliance between the two. The Japanese spy was the biggest threat of all – watching every move from the side-lines, feeding his version of events back to head office. The CEO had a plan to deal with Yoshi. First he would create an executive team that was so closely knit it would collapse if Yoshi tried to take him out of the equation. Then, when the team was pulling in the same direction, the results would get better, the Japanese would be more amiable and Malcolm would insist that Yoshi be sent back to Tokyo.

Chapter Six

Jessica and Sharon were having an impromptu consultation at Sharon's desk.

"I wonder if he'll go," Jessica mused.

Sharon knew she was talking about Scott. There was no need for names. "I doubt it," she replied bluntly. "He's suing us – he'll feel that he isn't welcome."

"Maybe we should ring him – let him know we'd like him to come," Jessica suggested, sitting on the desk.

"Let him know *you'd* like him to come, not *we*," Sharon corrected her, haughty as she flicked back her peroxide fringe from her eyes.

"Come on – let's phone him now," Jessica urged. "You have his number."

"I'm not phoning anyone."

"Oh come on, Sharon! You're the extrovert – he won't

think anything of you phoning him. He'd think it was weird if it was me."

"OK, OK," Sharon relented, looking up the number in her diary. "Anything for a peaceful life."

She dialled the digits and the phone on the other end rang six or seven times before it was picked up.

"Scott!" Sharon gave Jessica the thumbs-up. "Hi, it's Sharon – and Jessica . . . yeah, we're good . . . how are you?" Sharon listened for a few moments before saying, "Did you get your invitation to the party? You know, the Christmas party . . . Are you coming? . . . Why not? . . . I'm going . . . and Jessica and Don are going. We're planning a big night out – it would be great if you could come too . . ."

"What's a big night out?" Scott asked on the other end with a laugh.

"You know, the usual Christmas party stuff – getting outrageously drunk and making total fools of ourselves."

It sounded very appealing to Scott. His social life had been limited over the last year.

"Is Niamh going?" he asked as casually as possible.

"Yes . . . is that a problem?"

"No, not at all," he said quickly. "We're on good terms . . . I was just asking."

He expected that Niamh's husband would be there. Maybe when he saw them together it would put a stop to this stupid crush he had. So he told Sharon he would go.

In preparation for the "big night out", Scott organised for Jenny to sleep over with Deb and Brett. It was the first time they would spend a night apart in fourteen months and it was with mixed feelings he delivered the toddler, her pram, nappies and toys to her adoring aunt. Deb looked amazed when she saw the baggage that came with her niece.

"I tried my best to think of everything," he said.

"Knowing you, your best won't be good enough," was her critical response.

Scott couldn't help grinning to himself. Deb truly thought she was more organised than him but she had no idea what she had agreed to with this sleepover. She vaguely knew that Jenny rose with the birds but she would expect something different under her own roof. She was in for a rude awakening.

Lucinda was ready, stunning in a backless red gown that touched the floor. She stood regally at the doorway of the living-room. Her husband was absorbed, brochures strewn across the carpet where he knelt.

"I'm ready now."

"OK . . ." Marcus looked up reluctantly. His mind was over in London, or maybe Paris or Rome. He had brochures on all the big European cities; each one had been read several times. All going well, they would be in Europe for the summertime of the Northern Hemisphere. It would be their first holiday as a family. He was going to make it very special.

"Jack in the car?" he asked and Lucinda nodded. Their child, some would say the only thing they had in common, was waiting in the car. Those people didn't understand commitment or marriage vows. Through good times and bad.

"Right." He fumbled in his trousers' pocket for the car keys. Marcus was only ten years older than his wife but the last few years had not been kind to him. When they had married he had been at the crest of his career as the owner and founder of a successful software company. He was the super-brain who had written revolutionary anti-virus software and poured all his energy and business acumen into selling licences to big-name companies. Lucinda and her new husband had enjoyed two prosperous years of marriage before the company came crashing down with all the other dotcoms in 2000. Millionaires one day, bankrupt the next.

Marcus hadn't been able to dust himself off and start over again. He had lost his confidence and fell into a cycle of depression. His hair whitened, his face creased with premature wrinkles. After a couple of dark years, he started to accept what had happened and with that came the feeling that he was ready to move on. The European holiday was the milestone, the boundary between the old and the new life. Lucinda and Marcus poured their collective energy into the itinerary. What cities, when, every detail was very important. With two brilliant minds sharing the planning, it would be as close to perfect as they could get.

They held hands as they went outside to the car parked in the drive of their anonymous house. There was a warm silence as Marcus drove the forty-minute run to the city. When he pulled up outside the hotel, Lucinda gave him a lingering kiss.

"I'll be late."

"Enjoy yourself."

He meant it – Marcus wasn't possessive and was quite happy for Lucinda to go out alone. She was the bread-winner and all jobs had a social side. He preferred to stay at home with Jack rather than get into conversations with her colleagues about what he did for a living. There wasn't much to talk to strangers about when you stayed at home all day.

Lucinda watched Marcus slide back into the traffic, giving him a last wave. It was a modest car compared to the Mercedes he had when they met. But Jack was asleep in the back and he was their greatest asset.

Helen's initial reaction to the invitation was to throw it in the rubbish bin. It had come anonymously in the post and she guessed that all the others who were retrenched got one too. The social club was run independently of the company's management and would issue invitations to anyone who paid their subscriptions for the year, retrenched or not. Helen thought about the party over a few nights as she sat out on the balcony and she decided to go. She had every right to be there and wouldn't allow herself to use Phil Davis as a reason for not attending. She was sure he would be there; he was not one to miss a social occasion. In her mind she could already see what he would be like: his face flushed against a white shirt opened at the collar, his laugh raucous above the hum of conversation, his eyes assessing every female in the room.

It was daunting but she wasn't going to let the thought of facing him scare her away.

She had her hair done and bought an expensive new dress.

"You look very nice," her mother said from the arm-chair.

"Thanks – God knows I spent enough on this dress," Helen smiled at her. There was a pause and she could guess what was coming next.

"Is *he* going to be there?" her mother asked with narrowed eyes. "*He*" meant Phil Davis.

"Probably." Helen's earlier smile was frozen now and she was wondering why on earth she was going. "Don't worry. I'll slap him across his fat face if he comes anywhere near me."

With that parting promise, she kissed her mother's wrinkled cheek and left for the party.

She saw Phil as soon as she walked in. His shirt was white, like she expected, and his face was flushed with the contents of the empty wineglass in his hand. There was an attractive woman by his side. His wife. Helen went to the far end of the room, picking up a glass of chardonnay on the way. It wasn't until there were a few hundred people between her and Phil Davis that she relaxed a little. She was chatting to Donna and her boyfriend when she saw Donna's eyes widen. She knew straight away that Donna could see him coming in their direction.

"I need to talk to you," Phil whispered in her ear.

"Go to hell," she hissed at him, her voice low enough

not to be heard by Donna.

"What do you think you're doing with this sexual harassment business?"

"I said go to hell – I'm not going to talk to you."

"You're being a stupid cow – drop it now before it does any more damage –"

"What part of 'go to hell' don't you understand?" she asked, raising her voice.

Phil realised he was getting nowhere. And he had limited time before his suspicious wife would seek him out.

"I'll call you," he said, walking away before Helen could tell him to "go to hell" for the fourth time.

Niamh looked around for Chris as Malcolm waffled on beside her. Where was he? He had excused himself at the end of the meal and hadn't come back since. She would kill him for leaving her alone with Malcolm. The CEO was trying to be charming, smattering his monologue with "Nee-uv's" to demonstrate how proficient he had become at pronouncing her name. Niamh's eyes fell on Scott as she searched the room. He was with Jessica; there was a lot of laughing going on at their table. This wasn't the first time in the evening that she'd looked in his direction but on this occasion he caught her eye and smiled. She returned a desperate smile that signalled she needed to be rescued from Malcolm who had been fawning all over her since the moment she arrived. Scott read the signal and made his way across the room. He looked fantastic in black tie and, despite herself, Niamh felt her heart start to race.

"Would you like to dance?" he asked, his hand held out to help her to her feet.

"Why not?" She injected surprise into her voice. "Excuse me, Malcolm."

Malcolm looked put out as Scott led Niamh to the dance floor. He had been trying to bond with the HR director, trying to ensure that she was on his side rather than Yoshi's. He felt he had been making ground with her and didn't at all appreciate the interruption to their conversation. He was also very annoyed to see Scott Morgan and Helen Barnes at the party and intended to have harsh words with the social club committee about their lack of sensitivity.

There was a jazz band playing; most of the numbers were slow and seasonal. Scott's arms were loose around Niamh, a formal distance between their bodies.

A couple of minutes passed before he said, "You look really nice . . ."

She was wearing a black cocktail dress that stopped above her knees. Her hair was casually pinned up, blonde wisps escaping at the back of her neck.

"Thanks."

Chris hadn't commented on how she looked. They had been in a rush to get out on time. Saturday was his golf day. He hadn't played well and the eighteen holes had taken longer to complete than usual. He was home late and put forward a few lame reasons not to attend the party. Determined, she had stamped them out one by one. She got her way, her reluctant husband by her side as they arrived at the city centre hotel. But only for a short while it seemed.

Scott's hands were resting on her hips and the skin underneath her dress burned. She could see rather than feel his chest rise with each breath. Her whole body ached to move closer.

"I'm sorry we haven't responded to Frances King yet," she said, grasping at the first safe thought that came into her head. "I haven't had the opportunity to discuss your case with Lucinda."

"Don't worry about it," he replied as if his solicitor was the furthest thing from his mind at that point.

There was a lengthy silence. "Is Jessica your date for tonight?" Niamh was conscious of her looking in their direction. More than once.

"Jessica *and* Sharon – they both had a part in persuading me to come."

They continued to move in slow circles, the distance between their bodies closing ever so slightly. Every now and then their legs would brush against each other.

"I'm sorry for not stopping to talk that day in Manly," she said, tilting her head back to look up at him.

His fierce blue eyes locked with hers. "Was it a bad time?"

"Sort of . . . I was . . ." She was lost for words under the closeness of his stare. She could do nothing but tell the truth. "I was having an . . . argument . . . with Chris."

His eyes told her he understood. He didn't ask why she was arguing with her husband and she was thankful to him for his tact.

"Do you live in Manly?" was his next question.

"Yes – do you?"

"No, my sister does so I spend quite a lot of time there. I have a house in Dee Why – it's just a small town house – about twenty minutes' walk to the beach – perfect distance for Jenny in the stroller."

"She's a gorgeous child, Scott. She was having a great time that day with you pushing her into the wind."

He smiled proudly, saying, "Yeah, my girl likes the rush of speed. If she could talk properly she'd be saying, *faster, faster!*"

The band finished the last tune in the set and announced they would be taking a break. Niamh stepped back from Scott's embrace and gave him a conspiratorial grin. "Thanks for helping me escape Malcolm."

"No problem."

Then, on a mad impulse, she leaned forward to kiss him. His lips were warm with a faint taste of stout. For a few seconds she savoured the sensual smell of him. "I probably won't see you again so have a Happy Christmas."

He wished her the same and watched her go, disappointed with her haste to get away. She didn't go back to her table, presumably because Malcolm was still sitting there. She moved around the room, smiling and nodding at colleagues but not stopping to talk. He guessed she was looking for her husband.

Yoshi had taken Niamh's empty seat next to Malcolm.

"Enjoying the music?" he asked as a conversation-warmer.

158

"It's OK," Malcolm replied, looking at him suspiciously. The Japanese spy was not known to engage in wasteful small talk.

"It's nice to see some old faces here," Yoshi commented, not put off by Malcolm's offhandedness. "Scott," he nodded towards the dance floor, "and Helen . . . and some of the others who left in November . . ."

"They shouldn't be here!" Malcolm said sharply. "It's only creating bad feeling amongst the current staff."

"Come now," Yoshi gave the CEO a tolerant smile, "they are not . . . what do you call it? Lepers? They've paid their social club subscription, have they not?"

Malcolm's response was to light up a cigar with the intention of blowing smoke at Yoshi until he left him alone.

But the Japanese spy was not put off. "Now, Helen and Phil, I would think they are not happy to see each other –"

"She'll only cause more trouble by being here – she should have stayed away," Malcolm declared.

"Maybe Phil is the one who shouldn't be here?" Yoshi shrugged the shoulders under his well-fitted tuxedo. "Isn't he the one who made advances? And you saw him do it, didn't you?"

"Yeah." Malcolm reached across the table to pull over an ashtray. "Phil tends to get carried away around the ladies . . . I've had strong words with him, though. I expect he'll behave himself from now . . ."

"What did you see?" Yoshi asked.

"Why do you want to know?"

Yoshi was wise enough to know that Malcolm wouldn't

divulge anything if he pushed too much. "Just curious . . ."

They were silent for a few minutes. Malcolm was enjoying the cigar. He mellowed and answered Yoshi's question.

"He was kissing her. She was outraged, threatening sexual harassment. I told him to lay off her, in no uncertain terms."

Yoshi made some more small talk until he saw Niamh leave the dance floor. He then wished the CEO a good evening and made in her direction.

Niamh felt disorientated and took a glass of champagne from the drinks waiter. Where was Chris? She should be dancing with him, not Scott Morgan. She shouldn't have danced with Scott; it was asking for trouble. All the feelings in Forbes were back with a heightened intensity. It was everything about him: his muscled body, the highlights in his hair, the piercing blue eyes that she was almost afraid to look into. He was an outdoors man, unlike Chris who only saw the sun when he played his eighteen holes. But aside from the physical attributes, there was his passion. He adored the daughter he raised alone. He ran against the wind just for fun. Would he be as passionate in bed? She had kissed him – again. This time she couldn't pass it off as a joke, every part of her had wanted to taste his lips. She downed the champagne and got another from the waiter who appeared by her side at exactly the right moment. Where the hell was Chris? She was starting to get worried about him. She searched the room yet one more time and saw Yoshi coming her way.

"Good evening, Niamh. Are you enjoying yourself?" His voice was as formal as his well-fitting tuxedo.

"Yes." Niamh smiled absently as her eyes continued to scan the crowd for Chris. "It's good to see people are having a good time. HDD has been a rather grim place to work since Black Monday."

Yoshi nodded his agreement, then discreetly looked around to see if there was anyone within earshot. Satisfied that the coast was clear, he said, "I've spoken to Malcolm about that matter. I thought this would be a good place to talk as the alcohol would loosen his tongue"

Niamh gave up on finding Chris and concentrated on Yoshi. "What did he say?"

"He confirmed that he saw Phil kiss Helen and that she said he was harassing her." Yoshi's voice was so quiet Niamh had to strain to hear. "He told Phil to 'lay off her' and he expected he would behave himself in the future."

Niamh's temper flared up. "So that's it as far as he's concerned? Phil gets off the hook with a reprimand?" Her brown eyes were flashing.

"It seems so."

"How can I prevent sexual harassment in the company when I don't even have the full support of the CEO?"

It wasn't a question for Yoshi to answer. They sipped their drinks for a few minutes. Yoshi's was a red wine. He didn't drink much and had the same glass in his hand for the last hour.

"I don't think Malcolm sees it like you and I – a firing offence," he commented after a while.

"Well, then, it's obviously my job to educate him," Niamh's chin rose in determination, "Excuse me, Yoshi. I must go and find my husband."

"I saw him outside with Lucinda earlier. I bet they were talking shop," Yoshi said helpfully.

"Thanks. I'll look outside."

Yoshi watched Niamh as she made her way through stray tinsel and balloons to the French doors. Over these last few weeks he had come to like and respect her. He felt they had the same core ethical values and shared the same doubts about Malcolm. He didn't think that she would find her husband outside. It was quite some time ago that he had seen him talking to Lucinda.

Yoshi was a conscientious mingler. He looked around the room to see who he would speak to next. Helen caught his eye and he went to talk to her. His initial intention was to have a brief discussion before continuing to circulate. But somehow their conversation took an unpredicted path and he spent the rest of the night by her side.

There was a haze of smoke on the balcony, a separate party underway for the smokers who gathered there. Niamh couldn't see Chris and was on her way back inside when Bruce Knight caught her arm.

"I've been trying to get hold of you for a few days." He was alone, blowing smoke into the night air.

"Sorry, it's been meeting after meeting. I haven't read my inbox for days," she apologised, knowing he had a genuine grievance.

"Well, now that I have you, I'll take the opportunity to

update you with some interesting info on Mr Greene."

"Denis Greene?" Niamh asked, wearily leaning against the wall for support. It was the Christmas party, for God's sake. Why did Yoshi, Bruce and everyone else want to talk business? Where the hell was her husband? Chris should be saving her from this bombardment.

Some of the smoke from Bruce's cigarette blew back with the wind and his voice was hoarse as he said, "I think our friend has been stealing parts from the company."

Niamh coughed as the smoke also got caught in the back of her throat. "How do you know?"

"You know that blonde accounts clerk?"

"Donna?"

"That's the one. Nice girl," he said, wistful before becoming brusque. "She's doing an audit of our spare-parts inventory. There's a hell of a lot of parts out on loan to customers and Denis is the reference on all the loan documentation."

"Sounds like all the paperwork is in order then?" Niamh was finding it hard to summon up any interest. She wanted to find Chris. Had he gone home for some reason?

Bruce shook his head. "Not quite. The parts have been on loan for over six months, and that's against company policy."

"What kind of parts are they?"

"Hard-disk drives – for mainframes."

"What would Denis want with those? Do they have a resale value?"

"There's a very strong second-hand market for them," Bruce said, turning his tired craggy face to look at her. She wanted to ask him how he was going to spend Christmas yet she knew he would be offended by such a personal question. He didn't want her pity. The nicest thing she could do was to act interested in what he was saying.

"Why would Denis put his name down on the loan documentation if he was misappropriating the parts?" Her brain felt sluggish after two heady glasses of champagne.

"We've got *thousands* of spare parts," Bruce explained. "The company has never performed an audit of our loan inventory before now – the risk didn't warrant the effort. Denis would have had no reason to think anyone would look at that loan documentation ever again."

"Why are you doing an audit now?" she asked.

"Helen Barnes – she thought it was an exposure and committed Donna as a resource to look into it. That was a few months ago. Donna is only starting to uncover some of this stuff now." He shook his head in disapproval as he inhaled the last of the cigarette, crushing the butt against the balcony wall. A waiter with a tray of drinks handed him a neat shot of whiskey. It was a smooth transaction that had happened many times before.

Niamh finally caught sight of Chris through the French doors. He was still talking to Lucinda, as he had been when Yoshi saw him earlier. The two lawyers were deep in discussion; their serious expressions could only mean they were talking about work. Lucinda was stunning in red; she was by far the most beautiful woman in the room. Chris was just as striking, tall and confident.

Niamh watched them for a few moments before saying, "Look, Bruce, I can't talk about this any further right now. All I can say is that we would have a hell of a time proving it . . . but maybe if we insinuate some issues to Paul Jacobsen, they may back down on the lawsuit . . . I have to go now."

Bruce followed Niamh's eyes to Chris and Lucinda. "Have a Happy Christmas," he said but he was frowning hard as he watched her walk away. He saw her take her husband's hand and lead him to the dance floor.

Lucinda was left standing alone, her narrowed eyes watching the dance floor. She could tell by Niamh's face that she wasn't happy with her husband's behaviour.

"Your glass is empty – we can't have that."

It was Malcolm, cigar and all. He called over a waiter and got a long-stemmed glass of champagne for his beautiful legal counsel.

"Any of those left?" Lucinda nodded at the cigar.

Malcolm was delighted to oblige her by taking one from his inside pocket. The CEO said to himself, not for the first time, that there should be more women like Lucinda: beautiful, easy-going, smart, with a man's mind.

Scott watched Niamh dance with her husband. There was no distance between their bodies; they didn't look unhappy together. The foundation to his fantasies about Niamh was that she wasn't happily married. He had come to this conclusion by reading too much into a few things she had said and it seemed he had got it all wrong.

He suddenly wanted to pick up Jenny from Deb's and take her home. The only thing that stopped him was the time. It was midnight; he couldn't turn up on her doorstep at this hour of the night. The only other alternative was to stay and get totally smashed. The drinks waiter came around and this time he took a whiskey instead of a stout.

Jessica watched Scott as he watched Niamh and realised she was wasting her time with him.

Phil watched Helen as she danced with Yoshi. He had an eye for detail when it came to women and he had noticed earlier that her hair glinted with a new colour. Her dress was flattering and all in all she looked good. But she was still a trouble-making bitch. She had been flirting all night, making damn sure she was in his line of vision. Taunting him. Mocking him.

"Who are you staring at?" his wife asked, noticing that his eyes were fixed on the dance floor.

"Nobody." He dragged his eyes away, resisting the urge to march over to Helen and cut in on her dancing partner. He needed to finish the conversation he had started earlier, warn her against pursuing those ridiculous claims. But he wasn't going to get the opportunity with his wife watching his every move. He'd have to get hold of Helen next week and talk some sense into her then.

The jazz band had hiked up the tempo and the dance floor was dense with bodies. Chris's eyes were far away, his body rigid.

"I couldn't find you for ages – where on earth did you go?" Niamh said after a few minutes when he hadn't volunteered an explanation for his absence. She had to raise her voice to be heard over the music.

"I was circulating, chatting to your colleagues."

"To Lucinda?"

"And others."

His clipped response only served to get her hackles up even more. "You should have said you'd be gone for a while – you left me there, cornered by Malcolm . . ."

Chris lowered his head and whispered in her ear. "Come on, you've found me now – stop overreacting, OK?"

If he was intending to pacify her, he had chosen the wrong words. She pulled away from him. "I'm sick of this," she hissed. "I'm sick of always being the one in the wrong!"

He stared down at her for a moment, his dark eyes remorseless. "I've had enough of this *party*. I'm going home," was his comeback.

He walked off, leaving her alone in the midst of the dancing couples. She could feel their eyes watching her and she left the dance floor, taking the opposite direction to Chris. There was no way she was going after him. Her steps were quick as she made for the nearest exit. It led to the garden, dimly lit, empty of partygoers.

"Niamh?" she heard from behind and recognised

Scott's voice.

"Niamh?" This time she felt his grip on her arm. "Are you OK?"

She nodded, her eyes downcast. The hand on her arm led her further into the garden, towards a stone bench set back from the main walkway.

"Let's sit here for a while," was all he said.

It was sometime later when she told him, "Chris and I had another argument."

"It looked like that."

"Oh, no!" She covered her face with her hands. "How embarrassing! Everybody has seen."

"No, only me." His arm hugged her shoulders, offering comfort but stirring up so much else.

"It's all falling apart and I don't seem to be able to stop it." Her voice was barely audible from behind her hands.

His arm squeezed tighter. She drew in its warmth, its strength. She couldn't remember the last time Chris had hugged her.

She stopped hiding behind her hands and her eyes were drawn to his.

"Sometimes you can't stop it; it's inevitable," he said.

It was clear he was talking about his own situation and she asked, "Is that what happened with your wife?"

The arm around her shoulder tensed. "Ann didn't enjoy motherhood – she resented how it tied her down. She wanted her sleepless nights to be a result of partying till dawn and not because of an unpredictable baby. It got worse when she went back to work. She didn't think it was important to be home before Jenny went to bed.

She's in Malaysia now – on a three-month assignment that's been extended to nine months."

"I'm sorry. It sounds like she's the one missing out." Niamh didn't quite know what to say. She felt an overwhelming sympathy for the baby, Jenny. The baby without a mother. Niamh only knew what it was like to lose a father.

"You're right. She is."

It took Niamh a while to think of a question to open up the conversation without being too invasive. "Jenny is such a cute name – it suits her."

"Yes," his eyes clouded with a memory. "Ann and I spent months and months debating names. Jenny was the only name we agreed on – we were lucky it wasn't a boy."

Niamh wanted to know more. She wanted to determine exactly what she and Chris were missing out on. "What's it like being a father? Did it change your life?"

"Yes, but I love it – I love her. It's a fierce love, enough to make up for her mother. How about you?" His eyes were looking deep inside her. "Do you want to be a mother some day?"

"Yes, some day." She played with the hem of her dress, repeatedly smoothing it down over her thighs as she shared a small part of her demons with him. "It's a way of starting over, isn't it? A new baby – a new life to help everybody forget the past. My sister, Aisling, she has a new baby, a new start –"

Niamh stopped dead and Scott sensed she had already revealed much more than she was comfortable with. She was private; it would take time to get to know her. Would she allow him that time? Even as a friend?

He steered the conversation to what he thought was safer ground. "Aisling, I've never heard that name before . . . what does it mean?"

"Aisling? It's Irish, of course . . . it means 'vision'."

Denis Greene didn't attend the Christmas party. For once he had prevailed over the caller. And it was all due to Lily and her bout of bronchitis. The caller wasn't pleased, pointing out numerous times that the party was the perfect informal occasion for Denis to remind the decision-makers that he wasn't going to go away. But Denis could not be budged. He was adamant that his wife was too ill to leave at home alone.

Lily was a good patient. She complained less than she did when she was well. She slept a lot and only called him when she needed a fresh glass of water. It gave Denis time on his own to think. The night of the Christmas party was a warm one and he sat out on his back veranda with a cold beer. They lived close to a main road and the traffic was noisy but it didn't bother him. Despite his outward aggression, there were only two things in life that really bothered the engineer. The first was his wife. She was always sure to work him up and invariably made him see red within moments of opening her mouth. The second thing was money. He cared about money and was always striving to earn that extra dollar. It had been his sole motivation when getting involved in the racket at work. He was no fool; he understood the consequences of what they expected him to do. But the money was awesome. Three years' salary for ten successful, albeit illegal, installations.

It had started off on good terms. They gave him cash and he did what he was asked to do. There was minimal contact. Now it was a different game. There were the nightly phone calls. There was the solicitor. For Christ's sake, there was even a barrister! They were deliberately intimidating him and that freaked him out. And the big question was what would happen if he refused to co-operate? Would they carry out the unspoken threat?

He had two more beers before he came to a conclusion. This operation had been planned to the finest detail. They had identified the clients, they had decided on the date, they had even created the enabling virus. And with him, the engineer, they had access. There was no doubt these people had back-up plans. If he didn't conform, they would hurt him until he did or they would take him out of the picture.

It was a worrying thought and Denis drowned it out with the rest of his six-pack.

Willem Boelhoers tried to live a calm and healthy life. He avoided parties and alcohol as they only served to aggravate his illness. The following Monday he smiled politely as his staff told him what a great party he had missed. By mid-week the hype had quietened down and everybody was thinking about the impending holidays.

On Christmas Eve Willem was alone in his office when he heard carols drift through his open window. It reminded him he had shopping to do, gifts to buy for his beloved niece and nephew. He eventually became conscious of the voices that could be heard whenever there was a lull in the carols. He remembered what Niamh had said about writing down what he heard and he diligently took a notepad from his desk drawer. He wrote down the words as they floated past, faint and disjointed. That was the strange thing. The voices he heard because of his illness were so powerful that he had to do whatever they commanded him. Yet, he could hardly hear these voices and they didn't seem to be commanding him to do anything at all.

It stopped after a few minutes. Willem looked at the words; they didn't make any kind of sense. His face was puzzled when his boss, Bruce, walked in.

"I've received a written complaint from the ANZ Bank." Bruce was frowning; the festive season never got in the way of his work.

Willem forgot about the voices and told his boss what he knew about the bank's grievance. "Yes, I know they aren't happy. We didn't have a critical part when they needed it last week."

"How did that happen?" Bruce snapped.

"The part was on loan. To Denis Greene." Willem paused before adding, "We shouldn't allow our stock to go below minimum levels because of customer loans."

"Too right we shouldn't. What part was it?"

"It was a hard-disk drive – for their mainframe."

Bruce was thoughtful – the interrogation of Willem stalled as he let his thoughts focus on Denis Greene and the parts out on loan. Willem misread the reason for his silence.

"Don't worry about the ANZ," he said reassuringly. "We had a great relationship until this happened and we'll bend over backwards to win their confidence back."

"Their contract term is up in January," Bruce reminded the head engineer. "This is not a good time to be getting written letters of complaint. We must keep ANZ sweet – Japan is counting on the contract renewal."

"Why?"

"Apparently it's the biggest deal in the region at the moment." Bruce, looking very preoccupied, left as suddenly as he had arrived. Willem was left alone to face the words he had written. There were two words that stood out because they had been said more than once: "money" and "virus". He resolved that he would continue to write every time the voices filled his head. Maybe it would all make sense over time.

For now, the voices seemed to have ceased and all he could hear was a rousing version of "Jingle Bells" from the street below. He decided to have an early lunch and get stuck into his Christmas shopping.

Across in the executive area the Christmas carols couldn't be heard and there was no evidence of the festive spirit. Niamh and Lucinda were cocooned in Malcolm's office and anger was bouncing off the walls. Malcolm was speaking.

"Why can't Phil just say sorry to her and let that be the end of it?"

Niamh found it hard to temper her response to his

incredibly stupid suggestion. "For a start, if we don't deal with this properly HDD can be held responsible for Phil's behaviour," she said with surprising restraint.

"I think you're making a mountain of a molehill," Malcolm accused, folding his arms in dissension.

"Quite the contrary!" Niamh's patience was hanging by a thread. "It's *your* behaviour that places us at risk. A mere apology is not appropriate. There must be disciplinary action. Senior management has to get behind the company's sexual harassment policy – if they don't, we can be held legally responsible for acts of harassment by employees."

"Of course, I support the policy." Malcolm was indignant, jumping forward in his chair.

"Your actions don't demonstrate that support." Niamh's voice rose a few notches. It seemed that shouting was the only way she could get the CEO to hear what she was saying.

"Why don't we have some time out, guys," Lucinda intervened.

"It's not –" Malcolm started to protest.

"Let's take a break, OK?" Lucinda gave him a placatory smile and called his secretary to organise some coffee.

There was a tense truce until the coffee arrived. The secretary included some seasonal mince pies but her efforts were wasted. The pies were not touched but at least the coffee jug was emptied.

After allowing a few minutes for the caffeine to take effect, Lucinda, the calmest, reopened the discussion. "Malcolm, I have rarely seen such a clear-cut case of sexual harassment. Helen Barnes can take us to the cleaners – if we reinstate her we will save the company a lot of cash, not to talk about embarrassment."

Niamh was totally taken aback. She had assumed that she wouldn't get any support from the lawyer, especially after her derogatory comments about Helen. She bit her tongue to stop herself from asking Lucinda what had changed her mind. Maybe she just liked to play the devil's advocate. Maybe that was how she got results.

"I'm not saying you can't reinstate her," Malcolm said, his voice getting defensive again.

"Good, that's settled." Lucinda gave a nod of approval. "Helen comes back. Now, regarding Phil –"

"Phil stays," Malcolm stated with the weight of all his authority as CEO. Phil was his ally on the executive. He would be naked without him.

"No, Phil must go." Lucinda was firm. "If you want any credibility in this company you have to say goodbye to him. His actions are unforgivable. There's no going back for him. *He must go.*"

Niamh saw a slow acceptance come over Malcolm's demeanour and felt a reluctant admiration for Lucinda. The lawyer had pulled all the right strings, making him realise there were no other options. All without re-igniting his anger.

"What will we do without a finance director?" Malcolm's question proved his defeat.

"Helen Barnes can do that role standing on her head," Niamh said. "Hasn't she been second-in-command for the last five years?"

"Hold on, now." Malcolm looked from one woman to the other. "Just a moment ago we were only reinstating her – why can't I hire a new finance director?"

"It's up to you." Niamh shrugged, deliberately nonchalant. "As you know, we're all trying to boost the profit for the next two quarters – a new hire will cost you dearly in recruitment fees."

Malcolm was trapped into saying, "OK – give her the job – I just hope she appreciates all that we've done for her."

"I think it will go a long way to alleviate the hurt and embarrassment she's had to endure." Niamh met his eyes squarely. "And I think she'll be an outstanding finance director."

She left it to Malcolm to break the news to Phil. He had hired him and it seemed appropriate that he fire him. While Malcolm was busy doing that, she called Helen and asked her to drop in to see them.

This time Lucinda was punctual and Helen was the one who was late. She was flustered when she arrived. "The traffic is horrendous. There's been an accident on the bridge –"

"We've investigated your claims regarding Phil Davis," Lucinda cut short her traffic report. "From the evidence we've obtained, we agree it is probable that the sexual harassment occurred."

"Probable?" Helen questioned, looking outraged as she sat down.

"Yes, the sexual harassment code of practice requires us to make a finding on the balance of probabilities."

Lucinda's smile was patronising. "Don't take it personally – it's just a relevant way to describe the outcome of our investigation under the code."

"If you say so."

There was an undisguised dislike between Lucinda and Helen. At the last meeting it was Lucinda who was the agitator. This time it was Helen. Niamh wondered if there was a specific issue or if Helen, like her, found it impossible to connect with the lawyer.

"Phil has been dismissed," Niamh said, not wanting to leave Helen in suspense for any longer than necessary.

"Good," she nodded with satisfaction. "It's no more than he deserves."

"And we would like to offer you his role," Niamh continued.

"The finance director's role?" Helen asked, her eyes wide as she checked for clarification.

"Yes – that's the one! Our offer is with the same salary and terms as it was with Phil." Niamh smiled when she saw Helen looked happy about the proposition.

"Well, I'm flabbergasted . . . I accept your offer, of course. When do I start?"

"We'll send you out a letter tomorrow and you should be able to commence your duties after the Christmas break," Lucinda said as she stood up. "I'm afraid I have to go now. I have a function to attend this evening."

Niamh noticed that Lucinda was wearing a cocktail dress underneath her fitted jacket. She knew that the lawyer took the social side of her role seriously. She made sure she was seen at all the important seminars and functions in her field. She circulated with diligence, she networked with flair, she formed relationships with the people who mattered. But Niamh couldn't imagine what function would be more important than her own child. Surely four-year-old Jack would be waiting for his mother to come home on Christmas Eve?

"I had better go too." Helen jolted her out of her thoughts about Lucinda's family life. "I have to take my mother for a check-up this afternoon. Her GP warned me to get there early before he has his seasonal tipple . . . Look, Niamh, thanks for all your support these last few weeks. I really appreciate it."

"No worries – I'm looking forward to working with you."

Helen left quickly, seemingly overcome by it all. She had only been gone for a few moments when Niamh heard the shouting. She rushed out of her office, hoping that the booming voice didn't belong to Phil Davis. Her hopes were in vain. She stood by Sharon's desk as she helplessly watched the confrontation unfold.

"You stupid fucking cow! Look what you've done!"

Phil had cleaned the contents of his office into a small box and now he dropped it to the floor so he could square up to Helen. Niamh and Sharon flinched in sync with the thud on the carpet.

"Get away from me!" Helen stepped back from his fury.

"You'll be sorry you did this, you stupid bitch!" He closed the distance between them by taking another threatening step towards her.

There were many things Helen could have said in

response, cutting replies that she had rehearsed in private a thousand times. But none of them were appropriate for an audience to hear.

"Just leave me alone!" was all she said before she turned on her heel.

Phil stood there for a while, his broad rugby shoulders heaving in anger. Then he picked up the box and left the executive area for good.

"Bloody hell!" Sharon's hair seemed to be standing on end. "He's a scary man! That was bad timing to have Helen come out of your office then."

"It shouldn't have happened," Niamh replied through gritted teeth. "I told Malcolm to have Phil out of here within the hour – I don't know why he delayed."

"Where's the Christmas spirit gone this year?" Sharon enquired, her humour resurfacing.

Niamh looked at her watch, grinning as she said, "Why don't you head home now? You've a big night tonight, what with Santa Claus and all."

Chris didn't come home from work that Christmas Eve. He rang at six to say he was having a drink at the office and that was the last Niamh heard from him. She watched an old movie and went to bed at ten. She slept soundly until the next morning, waking to find his side of the bed hadn't been touched. Her first reaction was panic. Jumping out of bed she checked the answering machine for a message. Nothing. Then she checked her mobile. Ditto. She racked her brains. Had he said something? Had he told her he wouldn't be coming home and she had been too preoccupied to register? No – he had definitely said nothing. Had he been in an accident?

She rang his mobile, her heart pounding. For some reason she was caught off guard when he answered.

"Hello." He sounded tired but he didn't sound hurt. "Hello," he said again. "Is there anyone there?"

"It's me," she managed to say.

"Hello, 'me'. I thought you were a crank caller." He gave a hollow laugh.

"Where are you?" Her words were choked.

"At the office. I couldn't get a taxi last night – the drivers stopped work early. I was over the limit so I bunked down here."

"Any reason you didn't call me?" A strange nausea was starting to work its way up through her body.

"I thought I was coming home. It was about 3am when I realised I had no hope of getting a taxi. I didn't want to alarm you by phoning – I knew you'd be asleep."

She could see him in her mind: he would be shrugging, confused about why she was making such a fuss. "You're so damn thoughtful!" she said, her tone dripping with sarcasm. "Didn't you think I would be worried to death when you weren't here when I woke up?"

"No . . . sorry."

There was remorse in his voice but it was too late. She hung up on him; she didn't care if she was being childish.

She started to cry – helpless tears because she could see now, after months of trying to pretend differently, that they had no future. Their lives were too far apart, so distant that Chris didn't think he needed to tell her if he wasn't coming home. He had stayed away the whole night.

Oh God!

A dreadful thought came into her mind.

Has he been with someone else?

She thought of all the late nights, put down to the big court case. She thought of their non-existent sex life. Then she thought of her mum and dad and the infidelity that had cost them all so much. The alarm on the bedside table was flashing 8am. She wiped the tears from her face and straightened up. She didn't have time to think about it now. The bakery would be sold out if she didn't get there quickly.

Niamh sprinted down the street but it was too late. An apron-clad man was locking the doors.

"Sorry. We had hundreds of people come this morning."

"Don't you have *anything* left?"

"Not a single bread roll."

"Damn. Mum will kill me."

It was the only thing her mother had asked her to bring to the family dinner. Fresh bread. The others would undoubtedly bring complex starters and salads. Niamh's job had been so simple and she hated the thought of letting her mother down.

Her mobile rang. The number displayed wasn't a familiar one.

"Hello," she said, breathless after her futile sprint.

There was no response.

"Hello," she said again.

This time she heard a familiar voice in the background.

"Jenny, who have you called? Jenny – give Daddy the phone."

"Scott?"

"Hi, Niamh – sorry," he sounded embarrassed, "Your number is programmed in my mobile and Jenny somehow called you . . . she's got all these wonderful toys from Santa but all she wants to do is play with my mobile."

It seemed that Scott had uncanny timing, turning up every time there was an altercation with Chris. Showing up everything that Chris wasn't. And this time giving her a glimpse of what normal family life should be like on Christmas morning.

She heard him speak to Jenny in a solemn tone. "The mobile's off limits, honey –"

Jenny obviously didn't like things being off limits and made sounds that sounded like the start of a tantrum.

"Here, eat your toast. That's a good girl."

"Scott, is there a bakery near you in Dee Why?" Niamh asked suddenly.

"There are a few up on Howard Avenue," he responded, with surprise in his voice at her strange question.

"Are they open this morning?"

"I don't honestly know."

"OK – have to run – hope you and Jenny have a lovely Christmas!"

She had a weird feeling in the pit of her stomach as she

hung up from the call. Hearing his voice but not being able to see or touch him was strangely poignant. For the last week, since the party, his face was in her mind, his arm still around her shoulders. It was her only comfort, her only escape from the impasse with Chris.

She ran back to the house to get the car. There was a chance she would be lucky enough to find fresh bread over in Dee Why and would be saved from arriving empty-handed to the family dinner.

Chris was home when she got back, fumbling through the kitchen drawers for some magic pills to ease his headache. She put him out of his misery by finding him the Panadol and then pouring him a glass of water.

"Thanks. God!" he groaned, "I haven't been that drunk in years." Chris rarely got drunk. He liked to drink but always knew when to stop. "Sorry about last night," he said when he finally noticed she wasn't speaking.

"Sorry isn't good enough."

"What do you want from me – blood?" he asked irritably.

"I want to know who you were with."

"I was with my colleagues – I was at the office – I've already told you that."

"And I'm meant to just accept it, right?"

"Come on, for God's sake!" He threw his hands up. "It's Christmas morning – let's not start the day with a fight."

She could tell by his face that she wasn't going to get anything out of him. But she was determined to have the last word. "If you stay out like that again, don't bother to *ever* come back here."

He went upstairs to shower, unbuttoning yesterday's shirt on his way. She made herself a cup of coffee and brought it outside. The house had a generous courtyard out the back. Flowers edged along the base of the fencing, framing the terracotta tiles. Niamh sat down at the wrought-iron table and allowed the coffee to calm her because she didn't want to be fighting with Chris when they arrived at her mother's. She wouldn't be able to bear it if her mother guessed what was going on.

He came outside twenty minutes or so later. He was clean-shaven and was obviously feeling the first pangs of hangover hunger. "What are we doing for dinner?" he asked.

"We're going to Mum's," she responded as if for the first time. Chris never absorbed the details of their personal lives, knowing that when he needed to ask, Niamh would be there to repeat the information.

"Let's get going, then. I'm starving."

Her mother still lived in the family house they had bought a month after arriving in Sydney. It was a modest, three-bedroom, single-level house. A few minutes' walk to the beach. An ordinary house in anybody's terms, yet worth an absolute fortune in the current property market. It was only fifteen minutes' walk from their place but Chris insisted on driving his precious BMW.

They were the last to get there. The gift distribution had already begun, with Uncle Tom dressed as Santa Claus. The kids were dying for their turn to sit on his knee and were too engaged to greet their auntie. Her mother was in the kitchen, looking flustered as she always did on Christmas Day. Her knees were swollen with rheumatism and standing for any length of time brought a lot of pain. But it was Christmas Day, there was dinner to be served and she wanted to be in the thick of it.

"I've got the bread," Niamh declared as she put the loot on the counter.

"That's great . . . I like to have fresh bread on Christmas Day."

"I know – that's why I went all the way to Dee Why to get it."

"Dee Why?" Chris asked with raised eyebrows before adding, "I wouldn't mind one of those bread rolls – I'm famished."

He helped himself and her mother cut some ham so he could have a sandwich. One of the kids wandered in, his small face lit up with excitement at the parcel he had received from Santa. The kids were too young to twig that Santa was just their granddad sweating in the heavy red suit.

Her mother saw Niamh's expression as she looked at her nephew and said, "You shouldn't leave it too late for a baby."

Chris bit into his sandwich and Niamh bit into her lip. They both said nothing.

There were no exceptions – even the adults had to sit on Uncle Tom's knee and swear that they had been good for the year. Niamh sat on the lap of the well-padded fig-ure, looked into the familiar face, had a brief fantasy of what their lives would be like if it was her dad sitting there rather than Tom.

"Ho, ho, ho! And what does this little girl want for Christmas?"

"Something outrageously expensive, Santa," she joked.

Just to be happy, she thought to herself. *Like I was when I was a little girl in Ireland. Before you came along and ruined everything.*

Chapter Seven

Chris's big case was going to court in the first week of January and he spent most of the Christmas holiday in the office. Some nights it was after midnight when he came home. The court case seemed to come with a social side as the next morning telling alcohol fumes would engulf the bedroom.

Her suspicions well and truly roused, Niamh found herself going through his pockets. And one morning, while he was in the shower, she searched his wallet. But if there was another woman, he hadn't kept any obvious evidence.

The holiday dragged on. She spent long lonely days thinking about divorce and, considering her past, wondering if she would ever have the courage to go through with it. A few times she picked up the phone to call Aisling, hoping her older sister might give her that courage. But it always seemed like the wrong time to call

Ireland: dinner-time, the baby's bedtime, too late at night, too early in the morning. Niamh spent a few afternoons with her mother but never told her what was happening with Chris. And she started to exercise again, running along the walkway in Manly, always on the lookout for Scott.

She was relieved when it was time to go back to work; she needed a routine she could hide behind. On her first morning back she was speeding up the bus lane when her mobile rang. This time she recognised Scott's number when it appeared on the screen of her phone. She struggled to get the ear-piece in place so she could talk hands-free.

"Hi there." He had such a nice voice – warm, friendly, everything that Chris's wasn't.

"Oh, it's just you this time – not Jenny."

He laughed. "Yes, it's just me. Did you have a good Christmas?"

Before she could answer, the bus in front stopped suddenly and she had to jam on the brakes. "Shit! God, that was close!" She took a steadying breath. "I nearly ran into a bus!"

There was a pause before he asked, "Are you OK, Niamh?"

She knew his question was much broader than the incident with the bus. She was tempted to tell him everything: her growing suspicion that Chris was having an affair, her inability to walk out on their marriage, her dad dying alone in a garage. The bus moved off and she came back to the real world.

"I'm fine. How can I help you?"

"I have a favour to ask," he said. "I know I'm suing HDD – and I would understand if you didn't want to do this – but I wanted to put your name as a referee on my résumé."

Niamh thought about it. Scott was a damn good employee and if it had been her choice she would never have retrenched him. He deserved a good reference. "No problem. It would be a pleasure."

"Thanks, Niamh. I appreciate your help."

The rest of the journey to work was uneventful. Sharon looked up to say "Happy New Year" as she passed her desk.

"Same to you," Niamh replied, looking at her closely. "You look different . . ."

"Fatter?" was her automatic response.

"No, silly. It's your hair . . ."

"Oh, I got some more highlights . . . you look different too . . ." She tilted her head to one side. "You've *lost* weight!" she accused.

"I've been jogging over the holiday," Niamh offered by way of explanation.

"It's just not fair," Sharon muttered as she resumed her typing. In her head she was wondering how many kilos she could lose if she took up jogging. Maybe she'd lose so much weight she could eat whatever she wanted.

Niamh buried herself in work. It was therapeutic; in the office she was in control, at home she wasn't. The morning sped away and it was midday when Bruce burst into her office.

"I've an idea!"

"Good for you!" She was flippant; sometimes she could be like that with Bruce.

"Let's hire a private investigator!" He was bursting with boyish enthusiasm.

"For what?" She was lost as to what he was talking about.

"To check out the parts on loan, you know, the disk drives," he explained. "Let's see if he can dig up what Denis Greene has done with them."

Niamh nodded, now recalling their conversation at the Christmas party. They had been talking out on the balcony and she had left him to dance with Chris. Then they had that fight and he had gone home. She became aware that Bruce was looking at her, waiting for a response. She said the first relevant thing that came to mind. "We have a meeting with Denis and his legal entourage again next week."

"Cancel it," he urged. "Let's take some time out to see what's going on with these parts. I have a hunch that all our problems will go away if we follow through with this."

She let his enthusiasm drag her in. "How much would an investigator cost?" she asked. "We're already up for a mountain of legal fees on this case."

"I don't know. But I can find out." His face was lit up with excitement. He was thrilled to be back at work with the loneliness of Christmas behind him.

"Who will we hire to do the job?"

"We used someone a few years ago . . ." His forehead crinkled as he tried to remember. "Helen Barnes hired him. But I can't recall why we needed him . . . or what his name was."

"I'll be seeing Helen in a few minutes; we're having lunch," Niamh said. "I'll ask her if you like."

Bruce nodded and went to walk away. But he turned around at the door. "I forgot to wish you a Happy New Year . . ."

"Oh, thanks, Bruce. I hope it's a good one for you too."

"And your Christmas, how was that?"

"It was OK," she said, her voice seriously lacking in enthusiasm. She could hardly say it was terrible.

"Did Chris have some time off?" Bruce still loitered.

"No. He was very busy – there's some big case on at the moment. I barely saw him."

"Right." He gave a little cough. "You'll let me know about that investigator, won't you?"

"Yes, of course."

She watched him go and wondered if everything was OK with him.

Helen Barnes was nervous. It was her first day back on the job and she was going to lunch with Niamh in a few minutes. It had been Niamh's suggestion; she felt that Helen's promotion to the executive team warranted a celebration. She joked that the kindred females needed to stick together and give the men hell. However, Lucinda, the third woman on the executive, didn't get an invitation.

It was a short walk to the popular seafood restaurant that jutted into the harbour waters. The restaurant had only a few patrons. The waiter liked the look of the two ladies and led them to the table with the best view.

"Can I get you any drinks to start?" he asked when they were seated.

"We're celebrating, so why not?" Niamh smiled and Helen felt her stomach churn. But she somehow managed to make small talk while the waiter made a performance of pulling the cork and pouring two glasses of icy-cold chardonnay.

"I'm sorry you ran into Phil that day in the office," Niamh said when their food order was placed.

"It wasn't very pleasant but I'll get over it." Helen grimaced and reached for her wineglass.

"You must be relieved you won't ever have to face him again."

Helen didn't respond, her shrug indicating she didn't want to talk about it. She didn't want to have to tell Niamh that Phil had called her mobile phone a number of times over Christmas.

"I have something to ask you." Niamh changed the subject and Helen's heart raced. This was it. Niamh obviously knew. Neither of them deserved to be in this awful situation.

"I'm looking for a good private investigator."

"What?" Helen's voice was sharp and Niamh looked taken back.

"A private investigator – you know, a PI," she repeated.

Helen almost asked her if she was getting a divorce. It was the first thing that came into her head. Niamh needed a PI to follow a philandering husband. Thankfully Niamh continued to speak, saving Helen from an unforgivable faux pas.

"As our newly appointed finance director," Niamh grinned and Helen gave a weak smile in return, "you should be aware that we have a contentious dispute with an ex-employee, Denis Greene. I won't go into the details right now – let's just say we think he's stealing from us. Bruce said you knew a private investigator."

"I used someone a few years back," Helen said slowly, trying to concentrate. "Keith . . . Keith Longmore."

"Was he any good?"

"Yes, he was very thorough," Helen nodded, "and, most importantly, he got the result we wanted."

"Great. Can you give me his contact details when we get back to the office?" It could have waited but Niamh was clinging to her work, creating as many reasons as possible to be home later than Chris each evening. It was somehow easier to be the last one home. They both knew it and it was a competition now. He was winning hands down.

"It was quite a while back but Donna should be able to find a phone number. She's a very resourceful girl."

"Thanks."

Their meal arrived and Helen raised her glass. "Thanks for suggesting lunch, Niamh. I'm looking forward to working with you on the executive team."

They toasted, the two wineglasses clinking against each other. Silence descended as they ate, both sets of eyes staring into the beautiful view, both feeling the mesmerising effect of the water as it lapped against the side of the wharf. Niamh was hoping that this was the start of a friendship. She had coffee friends, shopping friends, but no best friend other than Aisling. It had been that way almost from the very start. Coming to Sydney had taken the edge off their parents' divorce. Laughing as they were flattened by giant waves at Manly, they would sometimes forget about their dad and as they became busy with new friends, there was less time to write to him. But the phone call changed everything, their guilt immediately isolating them from their new friends. The guilt of allowing themselves to be wooed by a new country and forgetting about their beloved father who had been left behind.

Helen was also hoping for a friendship. She really liked Niamh and she appreciated all that she had done to see that Phil Davis got his dues. The only problem was that a friendship was impossible while she was keeping such a deplorable secret from her.

The lunch was finished in less than two hours and both women returned to work, going their separate ways when they reached the executive area. Niamh was passing Lucinda's office when the lawyer called her in.

"I've been thinking about it over Christmas and I've come to the conclusion we should re-instate Denis Greene." Lucinda stood up and came to the front of her desk. Her dark hair was drawn back in a stylish knot and her skirt stopped at just above her knees, showing her toned legs to their best advantage.

"Bruce doesn't *want* or *need* him back in the business," Niamh said from where she stood at the doorway. She noted that Lucinda didn't bother with pleasantries about the Christmas holiday; it seemed she had no personal interest in anyone but herself.

The lawyer tried a different angle. "Then why don't we do what Steve – his barrister – suggested – put him on our payroll for six months until his visa is sorted out?"

"No, for two reasons." Niamh moved further into the office until she was standing directly in front of Lucinda. "First: the Department of Immigration will almost certainly take issue to that approach. Second: I'm not going to put him on our payroll while he stays at home doing nothing."

"Then let him come to work, for heaven's sake!" Lucinda gave an audible sigh of impatience. "This is the real world – we can't always get a perfect outcome. Denis Greene won't disappear without some pain on our part."

Niamh threw the problem back at her adversary. "Why don't we hire an external lawyer to give us a different perspective on the issue?"

Lucinda's beautiful face flushed. "That's just chucking more money away. I've already explained that this is uncharted ground and there are no precedents to rely on. The legal fees of an external lawyer would be horrendous and we would have no guarantee on the outcome of the case. At least we can limit our costs if we take Denis back for six months."

Niamh just said, "I've thought of a third reason not to take him back. It sends the wrong message to other employees."

Lucinda smiled in a patronising way. "Other employees won't be as interested in this as you think."

Niamh disagreed. "Denis is an agitator, a troublemaker. Everyone will know about this the first day he comes back."

"Trust me, if we take him back he'll keep his mouth shut and behave himself for the six months." Lucinda's eyes were pebble-hard.

There was no doubt that the two executives were locked in a battle of will.

Niamh had no intention of giving in. "Taking Denis back doesn't have my support, not when we suspect him of other misdemeanours."

She got some satisfaction from the surprise on Lucinda's face.

"What are you talking about?"

"It may be nothing." She was deliberately vague as she turned back towards the door. "I'm just following a few things up. I'll let you know if anything comes of it."

She grinned to herself as she left Lucinda in a rare state of bewilderment. She knew it was immature to play a game of one-upmanship with her but it felt good. It was only as she walked away she realised that she had missed another opportunity to talk to her about Scott Morgan. His solicitor's letter had gone unacknowledged so far. It was probably for the best. Given that she and Lucinda couldn't come to agreement on Denis Greene, it was likely the lawyer would oppose any settlement to Scott. Lucinda would be perverse when thwarted.

There was a bright yellow envelope on Niamh's desk when she finally got back to her office. It looked like an invitation of some sort. She opened it.

Do you know what your husband did at the Christmas party?

The typed words were threatening on the otherwise blank sheet of A4 paper and her first reaction was panic. She turned the page over to check if there was something written on the back. She checked the envelope again. Both the envelope and note were evidently anonymous. What had Chris done at the party? Had he been with another woman?

No, she thought, *he couldn't have been, not while I was there.* Common sense kicked in and she realised that her insecurity about her marriage was taking over. No doubt this was a joke. Someone had thought up a series of clues that would end in a hilarious outcome. She spent a few moments wondering who the joker was and then went back to her work.

HDD had its headquarters in Mita, an hour outside Tokyo. Yoshi was staying with his parents on the other side of the city and the commute to the office was ninety minutes in total. Sitting on the crowded train, there was more time to think than he was used to. His sister still lived with his parents and all three had fussed over him since his arrival. There had been a big family dinner and a homemade cake. Yoshi felt very undeserving; all he could think about was his new lady friend back in Australia. He didn't tell his family about her. They would certainly disapprove.

He got to the office for seven thirty. The smoking room was full as he passed and it was a foreign sight to the man who had spent the last year in a smoke-paranoid society. It was an early start and it would be a late finish in the headquarters of the Japanese multinational. The staff worked their day around their superiors; it was important to be in before them and to go home after them. A young woman passed Yoshi in the corridor, giving a quick bow to acknowledge his importance. She, like the others, was very well dressed. The women spent a high percentage of their take-home pay on their clothes. Appearance was everything in Japan – it got you halfway to where you wanted to be. It was ambition that got you the rest of the way.

Yoshi made his way through the nondescript work stations until he reached the one occupied by Nishikawa Shacho. He couldn't help comparing the humble décor to the pretentious offices of HDD Australia. A direct comparison of the humble Japanese to the pretentious Westerners followed. Nishikawa Shacho was a vice-president and board member. He was infinitely more senior than Malcolm Young yet the work station he occupied was smaller than that of Malcolm's secretary.

In his late fifties, Nishikawa Shacho wore a charcoal suit with an immaculate white shirt. Yoshi bowed with respect and Nishikawa Shacho rose to return the greeting.

"Murasaki San," the older man sat down, "for how long will we have the pleasure of your company?"

"I plan to be here until the end of next week."

"We must have dinner one night," Nishikawa Shacho suggested as if it was a new idea. They always had dinner together whenever Yoshi was in town. In fact, nine times out of ten they would travel three hours outside Tokyo to Kyoto where Nishikawa Shacho liked to be entertained by the traditional geisha. There was one particular geisha that the vice-president liked to see. She was beautiful, articulate and very knowledgeable. His wife was unthreatened by the fact her busy husband was prepared to travel three hours to see another woman. She knew he went there for conversation, nothing else.

"Thank you. I will arrange it with your secretary," Yoshi responded.

"Please sit and update me on what is happening in our Australian subsidiary."

Yoshi had waited for the invitation and sat down with relief. Sometimes the formalities of the Japanese culture were cumbersome next to the relaxed way of life in Australia.

"As expected, the quarter has closed with a large loss."

"Yes, due to the restructuring costs," Nishikawa Shacho nodded. "Fortunately those costs are extraordinary in nature and the subsidiary should return to profitability next quarter when the benefits of the restructure are realised."

His shrewd eyes were all over Yoshi's face, pressing for his concurrence.

"I have concerns about our ability to return a profit over the next quarter," Yoshi admitted.

"Please explain your concerns." Nishikawa Shacho's expression was unyielding.

"There are a few lawsuits that have come out of the restructure. It may cost a considerable amount to settle with the individuals."

"I see!" The lines on the older man's face became tighter. "Was the executive team careless in the way they went about implementing the retrenchment pro-gramme?"

Yoshi was fair. "No. With the exception of one, the lawsuits are the result of a more litigious culture than we are used to in Japan. I can understand the complaints of the employees in question but I could not see the same cases making it to the courts in Japan. Our employees here are more accepting of authority and our legislation doesn't favour the employee as it does in Australia."

Yoshi's explanation appeared to offer some comfort but obviously not enough. Nishikawa Shacho probed further. "Are the executive team managing our exposure to these lawsuits in the appropriate way?" he asked, his tone grave.

"Yes, both the legal counsel and the human resources director are actively working on the claims," Yoshi replied. He was telling a small white lie but would call Lucinda later in the day to ensure his lie was made truth.

"Has the financial impact of the lawsuits been dis-closed in the quarterly financial package?" The shrewd eyes were still focussed on Yoshi and he sighed inwardly at the upcoming revelation.

"I'm afraid that the finance director was dismissed before Christmas and the quarterly reporting package will be delayed."

Nishikawa Shacho's eyes bulged with shock. "Why was Phil Davis dismissed?" The vice-president knew the Australian subsidiary's finance director by name; it was a senior position after all.

"He sexually harassed a female employee," Yoshi replied, not daring to look in Nishikawa Shacho's direction.

"This is outrageous!" Nishikawa Shacho was appalled. "Doesn't Malcolm Young have any control over his executive team?"

"It was Malcolm who hired Phil," Yoshi said. "He was his mate – his friend."

There was a brief pause in the heavy conversation.

"Have we made a mistake with Malcolm Young?" Nishikawa Shacho asked, his voice dangerously soft.

"I think we need to assess his performance very closely," Yoshi answered, drawing on all his diplomatic skills.

"I am not happy with what I am hearing. How can Australia achieve their financial goals if the executive team is not performing to the appropriate standard?"

There was something in Nishikawa Shacho's tone that implied he regarded Yoshi as part of the deficient Australian executive. Yoshi didn't retaliate; it wasn't the Japanese way. However, he was quite fed up with being held responsible for the shortcomings of the Australian subsidiary. When they had dinner later in the week, he would tactfully remind Nishikawa Shacho that he was a mere liaison director and not the CEO of the operation.

Willem Boelhoers was in his office, working through the numbers for the ANZ Bank. The contract was up for renewal and the proposed Service Level Agreements were much more risky than the old ones. Any system down-time would mean significant penalties for HDD. Bruce Knight had asked Willem to rework the numbers showing the worst-case scenario in terms of penalties. The result wasn't good.

It was late and Willem was just finishing up when the voices started. He had a headache; numbers were not his strength. He didn't feel like waiting on to hear what was being said but he owed it to Niamh. She had specifically asked him to write down what he heard.

Without the daytime office buzz, the voices were clearer than ever before.

"She's not co-operating . . . we're running out of time."

Willem started when his phone rang. He hesitated before answering it.

"It's me." It was his sister. He knew why she was calling; she rang every day to ask the same question.

"What time are you coming home?"

"I'll be there soon, I'm just finishing up here," he replied, trying to listen to the voices at the same time.

"We have four more sites to do before the deadline . . . if they don't take you back, we may have to find another way of getting in."

"OK," Regina said, "why don't you take your pills now, while we remember them, instead of later?"

"Good idea."

After his last lapse, Regina had suggested he carry the pills on his person rather than leave them at home. She thought it best for him to have access to the Zyprexa at all times of the day. She was obsessive about the pills and had every right. Her house, where he lived, was full of reminders of what happened when he didn't take them. There was the glass door through which he had stuck his fist, the phone he had ripped out of the wall, convinced it was bugged, and, of course, the TV. He didn't want to even think about the TV.

Now that he understood his illness, his forgetfulness about his medication was not intentional as it had been in the early days. But occasionally his workload over-whelmed him and he didn't get round to taking those two critical pills.

He took them as soon as he hung up from Regina and the voices stopped immediately. They must have been in his head after all. Panicked, he rang his psychiatrist, leav-ing a message on his paging service.

"It's Willem Boelhoers. I need to see you. I think I need an increased dosage of the Zyprexa. I'm hearing voices again."

Donna Howard flicked through the travel brochure on Fiji as her boyfriend, Adam, watched the TV. The next morning they were flying their way to five days of sun, sea and sand.

"Was it a good show?" she asked politely when Adam's parents arrived home from the theatre.

"No," Mary Jones responded as her husband said, "Yes."

Steve joined in the laughter, glossing over his tension about his son's upcoming holiday with his girlfriend. He knew that foreign holidays were a common enough thing for young couples these days. Yet he couldn't help feeling that there should be more of a formal commitment between the two before they jetted off together. He felt ashamed for being the fuddy-duddy father he always told himself he wouldn't be.

"Looking forward to tomorrow?" he asked Donna, as he sat down in the armchair with the purpose of trying to get to know the girl better.

"You bet," she grinned. "Hey, I never asked you about that day I saw you in the lobby at HDD."

Steve's face darkened. "Oh, I was representing a client, or should I say, an *ex*-client."

Adam peeled his eyes off the TV, sensing an opportunity to tease his father. "What happened, Dad? Did the guy fire you?"

Steve failed to see the humour. "Of course not. I resigned. The case had no merit. I have an ethical duty to the court, you know, not to waste its time with baseless cases."

Steve left the armchair, his good mood shattered. Donna watched him go, her mind already mulling over what he had said. Steve had been with Denis Greene that day in the lobby. Donna knew Denis as she sometimes helped out the payroll department. He was well known by payroll as he was always complaining about something. It was no surprise that Denis was suing the company but it was very interesting that Steve said the case had no merit.

Steve went to the study, pouring himself a Scotch before sitting into the worn comfort of his armchair. A barrister's reputation was only as good as his most recent courtroom win. It was professional suicide to take on a case where there was only a slim chance of success and he wasn't prepared to go out on a limb to defend someone like Denis Greene. The man was loud, obnoxious and had infinite ability to land embarrassing surprises on his defence team. Putting personalities to one side, the case was weak. The grievance of being forced to leave the country didn't stand up to close scrutiny. If it was true that Greene had applied for a permanent visa then he would have automatically received a bridging visa while his application was being processed. Following that line of logic, Greene should have been free to stay in the country. Steve always believed in telling his clients if they had no chance of success but Paul Jacobsen was of a different school. He would defend anyone if the money was right. And that was another thing that bothered Steve. Where did an engineer get the money to hire a lawyer and a barrister to defend such an unworthy case? There was certainly something strange about this one and he was glad he had pulled out.

If Steve was honest, Lucinda Armstrong also figured in

his decision to resign. She would be back in his life if he defended Greene. There would be a peck on the cheek every time they met to discuss the case. He didn't want to feel that yearning temptation again. He was getting too old for feelings like that.

He remembered Lucinda's engagement ring all those years ago. It was obscene, flashing in the faces of the partners, taunting them that the object of their desire was no longer available. Her betrothed was what one expected. Rich. Successful. Older. He bought her a Mercedes to match his. He came to some of the firm's social events, polite but aloof. Lucinda didn't stay by his side. He didn't expect her to.

The partners had a look of doom for weeks after Lucinda's fiancé hit the scene. The party was over and life in the office became very dull. She produced a son and heir exactly eleven months after the wedding. It was a no-fuss pregnancy. Even those who were allergic to childbirth were in awe of her splendid tummy. Steve couldn't help comparing her to Mary when she was pregnant with Adam. He looked for varicose veins in Lucinda's long legs. For blotchiness in her flawless skin. For emotional outbursts. For an insatiable desire to go to the bathroom. There was nothing. Lucinda was superhuman even in pregnancy.

A nanny was recruited and left to do the job of rearing the baby. Lucinda lived life as before. Worked the same hours and continued her ascent up the corporate ladder. Steve's curiosity about the baby was his sole motivation to go to the firm's children's party that Christmas. He had barely tolerated the party when Adam was a child. Now that his son was a teenager, there was no need to go. Mary knew that and was confused about why she was being dragged there.

Lucinda, the ultimate corporate woman, was in the thick of the festivities. There was no nanny hovering in the background. Lucinda fed, burped and played with her child while she mingled and charmed all around her. The partners almost had tears in their eyes as they looked on. Steve admitted defeat. The young female lawyer had him at checkmate. She was the very definition of inscrutable.

She left the practice a few months later to take a commercial role in a computer company. There was disbelief amongst the partners. Lucinda would have undoubtedly been the first female to make it to their ranks. Yet she changed direction with no warning and abandoned her partner aspirations to become legal counsel in the unpredictable world of high technology. They thought she was mad. Steve didn't know that the company she went to was HDD and all the old feelings had come back when he had seen her again. And it was for the better that he had resigned from the Greene case and didn't need to face up to her beauty.

Chris was engrossed in the late-night news when Niamh sat down next to him. "Can I ask you something?"

"What?" He looked wary, obviously thinking she wanted to reopen the aborted counselling discussion.

"I need your professional opinion on an issue I have at

work."

He visibly relaxed and she pressed the mute button on the remote control. The sound ceased, leaving them to stare at each other. It had been ages since they had a conversation of any kind.

She shut everything else out and focussed on the problem. "Let's say you have an employee on a business-class visa . . ."

"Yes . . ." he prompted, impatiently glancing at the TV to see what he was missing.

"And you retrench that employee because his position and skills are redundant given the future direction of your company . . ." She adjusted the cushions so she could sit sideways against the arm of the sofa and face him.

"I hope that you would only retrench under those circumstances anyway." He was righteous all at once.

"Of course," she indulged his ego. "Do you think the company would be liable because the individual on the business visa has to return to their home country?"

"Which is?"

"England. Yorkshire to be precise."

"So what does he want?" Chris raised his eyebrows. "Hefty relocation expenses?"

"No, he says he wants to be reinstated – he wants his job back. Do you think he has a case?"

He thought about it. "I don't know the full facts but, from what you tell me, I would say not," he declared with the arrogance of a lawyer who was almost a partner. "You have a *bona fide* redundancy. I don't think the Department of Immigration would be happy if you created a role for him that doesn't use the skills you sponsored in the first place."

"My feelings exactly." She leaned back into the sofa with a small smile. "He claims that he has an application outstanding for permanent residency and we're depriving him of the right to live in the country."

"No judge would fall for that sob story." Chris gave a short laugh, his eyes still fixed on the TV. "Can I put the news back on now?"

"After I ask you one more question, different topic," she said quickly.

"Well, go on . . ." The wariness was back.

"You went missing for a while at the Christmas party . . . where were you?"

He was instantly annoyed. "I was circulating – trying to make conversation with your colleagues. We've already been over this – why are you asking me again?"

"You were gone for a long time – over an hour . . ."

"So what? Are you saying I can't leave your side?"

She thought of telling him about the joker and the anonymous note by way of explanation. But his expression wasn't inviting.

"Were you talking to Lucinda all that time?"

"For Christ's sake, Niamh! What is wrong with you? I was only talking to her about some law society function!"

He switched the TV back on, his profile frozen as he watched the last few minutes of the news.

Niamh was thinking of Lucinda's snide comments about seeing Chris in Forbes. She was thinking of Lucinda in her cocktail dress on Christmas Eve. She was thinking of Chris not coming home the same night. And she was thinking of the Joker, and if he was joking or trying to tell her something. She wanted to say what was on her mind, spring the "Are you having an affair?" question on him. But she didn't have the courage to do it – yet.

She stood up to walk away.

Then Chris surprised her by saying, "That fellow is having you on. If he really applied for permanent residency, then he would automatically go on a bridging visa while he waited for it to be processed. There is no need for him to leave the country in the interim."

She stopped in her tracks. "Are you sure?"

"Of course, I'm sure."

"Why wouldn't Lucinda know this?"

His answer was a shrug as he turned up the volume on the news.

Niamh went upstairs and showered before going to bed. She fell asleep easily enough but the nightmare was there, waiting. The garage, the black face, the finality, the guilt. The climax, the gaping mouth, woke her from her sleep. Her heart thudding in her chest, she reached out to shake Chris awake, to demand comfort. But she stopped. He was the cause of the flood of nightmares, not the cure. Their relationship was deteriorating at such a rate that divorce seemed inevitable. Would the devastation be as bad as it was twenty years ago?

She had been ten, Aisling a year older. Her mother leaving her father to marry a stranger was incomprehensible and ultimately unforgivable. Both of her parents had offered reassurances. The divorce wouldn't change how much they loved her. Life would be better all round; there would be no more arguments. She pretended to believe them but she knew deep down there wasn't going to be a happy-ever-after ending.

The day of the phone call was sunny, a perfect winter's day in Sydney. She and Aisling saw their mother's face crumple as she spoke on the phone and they ran away into the garden. They cried for hours, for days, for years.

People didn't understand. They said he was selfish to do what he did. That's how they remembered her fun-loving generous dad. Selfish. Even when he was dead he didn't get the sympathy he deserved. But her mother and Tom knew they had blood on their hands. Their guilt permeated the whole house in Manly. There was no doubt that her dad would be alive had they not robbed him of his "brightness" and his "vision".

Aisling went back there. She was in her late twenties when she did the big European trip and she couldn't resist the lure of Ireland. She went to Midleton and she said she had put her ghosts to rest. After seeing the garage and visiting her dad's grave, she found the peace that Niamh couldn't find. But Niamh didn't have her courage and never went back to face the demons. She didn't even go back when Aisling met a Corkman and had a large Irish wedding. She didn't even go back when her niece was born a few months ago.

Chapter Eight

Denis's caller was pissed off. Things were not going to plan.

"We're getting more resistance than we thought."

"I could have told you that," Denis said smugly. "There's no way they'll take me back. I was a pain in the ass for them."

The caller carried on as if Denis hadn't spoken.

"We must keep the pressure up. Things have been too quiet since the meeting. It's time to increase your visibility. Write them a few more notes. Let them know you're still a problem and you're not going away."

Denis sighed in defeat and asked, "What about the deadline? Are you going to move that out?"

"No," the caller was firm, "the dates stay the same. We'll have to find another way to get you into those sites if they don't take you back within the next two weeks."

"I'm not breaking and entering – you hear that? I'm not a common criminal." Denis raised his voice, forgetting about Lily. He heard the bed squeak as she got out. The floorboards creaked as she made her way to the landing and looked down to the hall below.

"What's wrong? Who's that?" Her face was white and drawn; her bronchitis still hadn't cleared.

"Nobody," he snarled, crashing the phone down. "Go back to bed."

Denis had a study of sorts at the back of the house. It was a long narrow sunroom with some shelving and a computer. He logged onto the computer and dialled into the internet. His hotmail didn't have any new messages. He spent the next half hour typing, trying to do everything he could to get his job back. It was now clear that nothing would stand in the way of the caller and Denis would rather be reinstated than have to break into the remaining sites. When he was finished writing emails, he typed in the web address for Channel Nine. Up until now his threats about an interested journalist had been baseless. But with the latest developments it was time to make them real. He navigated through the website until he found the story-submission area. He filled in the electronic form and clicked the submit button. The windows in the sunroom rattled with wind. They were old and loosely fitted. They also let in a lot of the traffic noise from the main road and tonight he found the noise irritating. It usually didn't bother him. Upstairs, Lily was asleep and oblivious to what was going on in her husband's life.

Don McAlister, the newly promoted human resources

manager, was the first to see Denis's handiwork the next morning. Don was surprised to receive an email from Denis Greene. He was even more surprised when he read the message.

Please find attached my application for the project manager's role advertised in the company's web site yesterday. I am available for interview any day this week.

Don leaned over the partition and spoke to Jessica, his colleague. "You'll never guess who has applied for the project manager's job . . ."

"Denis Greene?" she replied without hesitation, shuddering as she thought of his grey greasy ponytail.

"How did you know?" Don was disappointed not to be the bearer of groundbreaking news.

"Because he has also applied for the sales person's role."

Jessica read the arrogant message out loud for Don's benefit.

Please find attached my application for the sales person's position recently advertised. You will find my skills an excellent match for this role. Please advise a suitable time for interview.

"Is he an idiot?" Don asked, shaking his head in disbelief. "He's been retrenched, he's dead and buried. Doesn't he understand that he can't come back here doing another job?"

"No," Jessica said slowly, "he's not an idiot. He's very clever. He wants to be reinstated and applying for roles for which he has no skills match is just his way of bullying us . . . *oh my God!*" she exclaimed mid-sentence, squinting as she stared at the screen.

"What? What's wrong?" Don asked urgently.

"He's copied Yoshi and *Nishikawa* on these applications. You have to admire his balls!"

Scott smiled to himself as he left the CBD building. The interview had gone well. It was a reputable company and a strategic role. He felt he was in with a good chance.

George Street was buzzing with lunch-time crowds. He let himself become part of the buzz. He missed the challenge of work and the thrill of the CBD. It was great spending this time with Jenny but it wasn't very stimulating.

He sat on a bench in Martin Place and called Niamh from his mobile. She picked up on the first ring.

"Hi, it's Scott."

"Hello there." Her sexy Irish-Australian voice made him feel even better about the day.

"I've just been for an interview. I'm ringing you in advance to let you know they may call you for a reference."

"It must have gone well then." She sounded happy for him.

"Yeah. It may be premature to say it's in the bag but I think I came across well."

"Great – can you excuse me a moment?" She put him on hold and he listened to a recording that pitched all of HDD's wonderful products.

She came back after a few minutes. "Sorry about that. Sharon needed an urgent signature . . . right, where were we? Oh yes, can you tell me a little about the role so I can frame the reference to fit it?"

"Yes, it's a recruitment manager," he began, then stopped before saying, "Look, what are you doing for lunch?"

"Nothing – is that an invitation?" Her voice was receptive.

"I guess it is," he laughed. "It would be easier to tell you about the role face to face. Plus it's a glorious day and Deb is taking care of Jenny for the afternoon."

"All excellent reasons. Where can I meet you?"

"I'm sitting on a bench right in the centre of Martin Place."

"I'll see you in ten minutes."

Scott hung up. Niamh would be here in a few minutes and a sense of anticipation tightened his chest. He deserved some nice food and some decent conversation before returning to Jenny's baby world. But that was all this should be, some adult time out. Niamh was married; he mustn't lose sight of that.

Scott was easy to find. The sun glanced off his fair hair. He had taken off his jacket and rolled up the sleeves of his white shirt. Tanned and smiling, he mirrored the feeling of summer that radiated from the CBD of Sydney.

Something inside Niamh fluttered, a feeling that was alien after the bleakness of the last few weeks. But she still recognised it as the same feeling she had when she stood close to him in Forbes and danced with him at the Christmas party.

"Hi." He stood up when he saw her approach.

"Where are you taking me for this lunch?" She felt totally out of her ordinary self but decided to go with the feeling.

"I don't know. Do you fancy something suave and sophisticated or cheap and nasty?"

"Considering your state of employment, cheap and nasty," she joked.

He didn't take offence and laughed with her. "Look," he said, "we're quite close to Hyde Park. How about we grab a sandwich and sit on the grass?"

"Sounds like a good idea to me."

The park was full of city workers, grabbing their piece of summer during the all-too-short break from the office. Niamh kicked off her shoes so that her toes could curl into the soft green grass.

"I'm sorry that we still haven't responded to your solicitor. Lucinda's been extremely busy . . ." Niamh didn't meet his eyes because she wasn't a good liar. She couldn't tell Scott that she had decided to bypass Lucinda completely and go straight to Yoshi for clearance to offer a settlement. Trouble was Yoshi had been away in Tokyo.

"Don't tell me she still hasn't hired a personal assistant?" Scott knew all about Lucinda and the lack of willing secretaries to take her on. He had been working on the position when he left.

"I'm afraid not."

They shared a smile at the expense of Lucinda and the arrogance that scared away perfectly good candidates.

"Well, you'd better tell me about this job so I can do my bit to make sure you get it," Niamh said and over the next few minutes Scott gave some background information on the company and the position.

"It sounds like a great opportunity," she remarked when he had finished.

"Yes, I'm quite excited about it. And the job is here in the city centre – imagine, I might be able to bring you for a posh lunch like this again."

She laughed, thinking she'd rather be here in the sun than in any posh restaurant. There was no further conversation until they finished eating.

"How are things at home?" he asked. She felt herself freeze up and he must have realised it because he came back with an immediate apology. "I'm sorry. I didn't mean to overstep the mark. I was trying to be a friend."

"Are we friends?" she asked, her voice quiet.

He met her eyes. "I think we have the potential to be very good friends."

There's nothing wrong with confiding in a friend, Niamh thought. It took her a few minutes to summon up the courage and to find the right words to describe what was happening with Chris. "My marriage is crumbling around me. I know it's not going to last and I'm sure Chris knows too. But we're in this limbo where neither of us seems willing to make the hard decision."

"I've been through it and I understand how hard it is. I really do," Scott said. "But some day you will both reach a conclusion and you'll move forward."

She studied his face, the strong line of his jaw, the confidence in his eyes. He was tough; he could handle the failure of a divorce. She was different, more like her dad. He had let the failure take his life.

"Scott . . . my parents divorced when I was a child . . . I was ten."

"I'm sorry . . . that must have hurt you a lot."

"It hurt my dad . . . he hung himself," she said, baring her soul in the middle of the busy park.

"Oh, Niamh! " He took her in his arms, holding her tight against him as if he was trying to transfer his strength. Those same arms had got her through the whole Christmas holiday but they were for real now, not in her imagination. She could feel the warmth of his skin through the thin cotton of his shirt. She could smell the now familiar scent of his aftershave. She wanted to stay there forever.

She reluctantly pulled back to give him an embarrassed smile. "I needed a hug like that. I'm sorry if I stayed there too long."

He smiled back. "Nothing would be too long for you."

Now the punchline of the story was out, Niamh felt compelled to tell him the rest. "It was Ireland in the early eighties. Midleton was a small place then. The whole town was agog that Monica Curran – a woman with two young children – had left her husband for Tom Kenny.

The disapproval wore Mum and Tom down and they bailed out. We flew to Sydney and, sure enough, when we landed we were free from the scandal. Only trouble was we left my poor dad behind to face it all." She paused, watching the parade of workers come and go through the arching trees. "Aisling and I didn't want to come here at first – we didn't want to leave our dad. But we were gradually won over by the beach, our new friends. It all fell apart when we got the phone call. We felt so guilty. We felt we had betrayed him as much as Mum and Tom."

Niamh found it hard to leave the sunshine of the park. Found it hard to leave Scott. She could feel they were on the verge of something much more than friendship. On a precipice. Could she jump over without looking back at Chris?

Sharon was waiting for her back at the office; there were yet more letters that required her signature. It was only when Sharon left that she noticed another yellow envelope at the top of her in-tray. She stared at it with foreboding. The previous message was never far from her thoughts. She seesawed between seeing it as a joke and taking it as a threat. This envelope might help her decide which one it was. She took a steadying breath before ripping it open.

Your husband is keeping a secret from you.

It was Yoshi's last day in Tokyo. He battled through the crowds that swarmed Ginza and found himself surprisingly overwhelmed by the jungle of retail shops. Ginza was the exclusive home to the cream of fashion and was lined with sophisticated department stores, all stocking the most expensive brand names. It was the perfect place to find a suitable gift for his girlfriend.

He stopped to cross the street. The traffic sped past, all new models. An old woman was also waiting at the pedestrian crossing. She was wearing a kimono; the garment was a turquoise blue silk. He guessed that she was a geisha on her way to an appointment at one of the elite restaurants in the area. The geisha in Tokyo were harder to recognise than the traditional geiko in Kyoto.

Yoshi found himself staring at the old geisha in her youthful kimono. She was foreign to him. Had he been away from Tokyo for too long? He was aware that he was somewhat critical of Australians and their lifestyle. Yet the density of his home city was strangely irritating. The geisha's face would stay with him for the remainder of the day as he tried to rekindle his feelings for Tokyo.

Yoshi wasn't used to buying gifts for ladies. Over the years there had been a few casual relationships. But they had never stretched through birthdays or Christmas and consequently he was inexperienced in buying gifts for the opposite sex. Commitment wasn't something he avoided; it had just happened that way. When he had lived in Tokyo there were many women who made it obvious they were interested in him. But Yoshi knew that their interest was sparked by the desire to have an established businessman for their husband. Now he was glad that he hadn't settled. This lady was special. They had dated for only two weeks before he had to leave for this trip. In that time they had seen each other almost every day. They had shared breakfast, lunch and dinners. They had done romantic things like walking on the beach and swimming together in the pool of his rented house. They had done mundane things like buying groceries and watching television. They had talked and talked and talked. When they weren't together he found himself calling her late at night. Just to hear her voice. Just to have an aimless discussion about nothing much at all. It felt like a lifetime, yet it was only a few weeks. It felt wonderful.

He went into one of the department stores. Perfume, scarves and handbags were presented for sale against a backdrop of tasteful Christmas decorations that hadn't yet been taken down. What could he possibly buy? If the lady was Japanese it might have been easier. There were kimonos in the store, expensive kimonos with stunning colours. It would be an elegant but extravagant gift. However, his girlfriend was a Westerner. She was practical and her taste was far from extravagant. He approached a sales lady and told her about the Western lady he had only recently met but who was very dear to him.

He came back out into the crowds of well-dressed people. His purchase was gift-wrapped and safe inside his shirt pocket. His flight was leaving in two hours; he would pick up his bags from his parents' house on the way to the airport. His mother was unhappy that he was not staying for longer. He could have explained to her that he was hurrying back to his new lady friend in Sydney but he chose not to.

With his mother's tears fresh in his mind, Yoshi used the journey to the airport as an opportunity to catch up on some calls. It was his second time calling Lucinda from Tokyo and it was to ask the same question. "Have you written to Paul Jacobsen?"

He heard her sigh on the other end of the phone.

"I will get to it, Yoshi. I don't need to be reminded by you – or by Niamh," she said, having fended a call from the human resources director earlier that day on the same issue.

"Are you aware that Denis copied Nishikawa Shacho on his job applications?" Yoshi was furious that Greene was causing turmoil even as far away as Tokyo. "Nishikawa Shacho is extremely concerned. You must make this a priority – you must write to Paul Jacobsen today before his client does any more damage."

"I'm doing it right now, Yoshi," Lucinda said with another sigh, starting to type a letter on her keyboard. She still didn't have a personal assistant and was struggling to keep up. A detail-obsessed Japanese man was not helping the situation.

Your client has contacted various people within the company, applying for vacant positions notwithstanding our previous communication that we have no vacancies that are suitable to his experience.

In order to limit unnecessary involvement of additional personnel within the company, please ensure all future correspondence related to your client's employment is directed to Niamh Lynch, our human resources director.

She read it back to Yoshi and couldn't help smiling to herself. Denis Greene brought a new definition to the word bully. To apply for open positions was a stroke of genius she couldn't help but admire.

Yoshi didn't sleep much on the overnight journey to Sydney. His visit to Tokyo hadn't been very satisfactory from either a personal or business perspective. On the personal side, he had found himself thinking treasonous thoughts about Tokyo. That didn't make him feel good. And on the business side, well, he was unsettled by what Nishikawa Shacho had revealed at dinner last night. They had gone to Kyoto to eat, the vice-president's favourite geisha joining them at the exclusive restaurant. She sat next to Nishikawa Shacho at the table; Yoshi sat opposite. The mood was tense and the exquisite food didn't do anything to lighten it. The email from Denis Greene earlier that day had panicked Nishikawa Shacho. He was unaccustomed to being involved, even indirectly, in employee disputes. He was also deeply concerned about Malcolm Young's ability to lead the Australian subsidiary to a profitable result for the year. Dinner was over and they were having some tea when Nishikawa Shacho dropped a bombshell.

"Murasaki San, I want to get rid of Malcolm Young. In fact, I would like *you* to become the CEO for the Australian subsidiary."

Yoshi hadn't foreseen such an astounding job offer coming his way. The geisha's face was impassive, as if she knew in advance.

Yoshi swallowed his exclamation of surprise and bowed his head in respect. "I am deeply honoured you have considered me for such a prestigious role."

The vice-president sipped his tea, letting a few moments lapse before dropping a second bombshell. "I'm concerned, Yoshi. The company's share price is low. Our competitors are ready to swoop, buy us out."

Yoshi was thrown further off track, glancing at the geisha again, uncomfortable that Nishikawa Shacho was being so frank in her presence.

The vice-president continued to speak, oblivious to the fact he was saying things that should only be said in front of the most senior officers of the company. "We can't make a loss this year, Yoshi. We must make a profit, even if it is only a small one. That is what we have committed to the analysts and we must deliver on it. If they find out how close we are to negative earnings – well, they'll recommend to the shareholders to divest – the share price will drop further – then our competitors will make a bid on the company. None of us will have jobs then – do you understand me? Do you understand the situation we're in?"

Yoshi met the shrewd eyes of the older man. He felt he was being handed a poisoned chalice with this job offer.

I want you to be CEO. But I expect you to pull off a miracle to return the Australian subsidiary to profitability. Otherwise, there is a risk our competitors will make a take-over bid. Be thankful for the impossible opportunity I am giving you.

Of course, he didn't say what he was thinking out loud. "I understand. May I please have some time to reflect on your offer?"

The vice-president looked surprised but nodded all the same. Yoshi left soon afterwards so his boss could fully enjoy the company of the geisha he had travelled more than three hours to see.

The flight to Sydney landed right on schedule and Yoshi was tired but happy to be back. The terminal was thronged with the barrage of flights that had touched down within the first ten minutes of operation. The customs queues were long and painfully slow. As Yoshi waited for his bags to appear on the crowded carousel, he thought to himself it was high time the international airport lifted the curfew on early morning flights.

Helen was waiting for him. It was a wonderful surprise to see her waving at the end of the ramp. It was Sunday morning, and she liked to sleep in at weekends. He was very pleased that she had got up early to meet him. His steps quickened and he almost ran into her arms. He threw his usual reticence about public displays of affection to one side and their kiss was long and passionate.

He gave her the gift in the car. She didn't wear much jewellery and the black pearls were a gamble. There was

227

genuine pleasure as she held them up to her neck and adjusted the rear-view mirror so she could see them.

"Thank you, Yoshi. They're beautiful."

"So are you." It was an unoriginal thing to say but she was indeed beautiful. Not in the traditional way. It was her kindness, her sense of fun, her depth, her intelligence. Quite simply, his heart hadn't been in Tokyo while she was so far away in Sydney. The trip had been worthwhile only in that it clarified his intentions about their future together.

"How has HDD been surviving without me?" he asked.

"Let's not talk about work," she said and started the car.

After Lucinda's letter there was a reprieve on the Denis Greene case and, to everyone's relief, the job applications stopped coming through. A week passed by without any contact from Greene or his expensive representatives.

The private investigator, Keith Longmore, had been hired and given his briefing. Niamh was glad that Bruce had suggested calling in a professional after what Chris had said about Denis's case. Hopefully Keith Longmore would find an explanation for both the sketchy visa story and the missing parts. Niamh wanted to know how much time Keith had on his side and the only way to do that was to call Paul Jacobsen. Her call went directly through to him; there was no fielding by a secretary.

"Paul, it's Niamh Lynch. Happy New Year."

"And Happy New Year to you also," he responded.

There was a pause and it was easy for Niamh to take

the lead. "I've given due consideration to Steve's request to keep Denis on our payroll and I have decided that it is not an option for us."

Paul's response was not what she was expecting. "Steve Jones is no longer working on the matter."

"Why?"

"I'm not at liberty to say."

"Where does that leave us?" Niamh asked, wondering if the hot-headed engineer had fired his barrister.

"It changes nothing. You are refusing to reinstate my client, either in practice or on payroll only. Therefore, we will be seeking a hearing with the Industrial Relations Commission." Paul was gathering steam now. "We should set up a meeting to –"

"Hold on," she stalled him. "First things first. I will put HDD's position regarding the reinstatement in writing. Then I expect you will respond stating that your client will be seeking a hearing. Let's hold off any further meetings until we have all the paperwork in place."

"Of course," Paul said quickly, recognising he had possibly showed his hand too soon.

Niamh put down the phone having got what she needed out of the call. She now knew where Denis Greene was headed with this. The Industrial Relations Commission was confirmed as the next step. Now it was time to slow the pace. Keith Longmore, the private investigator, would need time to do his job.

Niamh dictated a letter for Sharon but told her to hold off sending it until further notice. Then she found herself in a lull – a rare moment in time where her inbox was clear, her phone wasn't ringing and the only thing outstanding was the last yellow envelope that was propped against her in-tray. Now her eyes focussed again on its distinctive colour. Where did it come from? Who ordered the stationery in this place?

Sharon told her boss that it was Donna Howard. It was one of the many tasks the resourceful accounts clerk was responsible for. Niamh-went around to her work station.

"Does this look familiar?" Niamh held up the yellow envelope without any introduction. She wanted to see her gut reaction.

"No." Donna looked up from her work, clearly puzzled.

Niamh tried a more direct question. "Have you ordered these envelopes for anyone in particular?"

"No, it hasn't come from our stationery."

There was a pause. Niamh realised the young girl deserved the courtesy of an explanation before going any further. "I'm sorry," she sighed. "I'll start again. Someone has been using this stationery to threaten another employee." She knew it was extreme and premature to use the word "threaten" but there was a sense of urgency about getting an honest answer. Something told her that these messages were the compelling event that would end her marriage.

"It's not ours," Donna repeated. "Everything we order goes through me. I've never ordered envelopes of that colour – trust me, I would remember."

"OK, thanks. Please don't mention this to anybody. I have a better chance of finding out where this came from if the perpetrator isn't forewarned."

"Of course."

Niamh was turning to leave when Donna stopped her. "Look, Niamh, on a different subject . . . I'm not sure if I should be saying this –" Her fair skin flushed as she struggled for words.

"Go on," Niamh prompted.

"It's about Denis Greene."

Niamh was taken aback. How and what did Donna know about Denis Greene?

"This may sound silly . . . but my future father-in-law said that Denis's case had no merit."

"Who is your future father-in-law?" Niamh was transfixed as she waited for the answer.

"He doesn't know yet that he's going to be my father-in-law." Donna gave a self-conscious grin. "That's a surprise we're going to spring on him soon . . . his name is Steve Jones."

"The barrister," Niamh said with amazement. "Denis fired him, didn't he?"

"He wasn't fired. He resigned." Donna was defensive about the reputation of her future in-laws. "He's very well respected in his field – he doesn't want business from people like Denis Greene. He only takes cases he has a chance of winning."

Niamh nodded mutely, eventually saying, "Thanks, Donna. That was very valuable information. Obviously, I'll be careful about how I use it."

That was two people who said that Denis Greene didn't have a leg to stand on. Chris and Steve Jones. What was Lucinda playing at by recommending he be reinstated? Was she plain stupid or did she have a different agenda to everyone else?

Willem balanced himself on the chair before pushing in the air-conditioning vent. His suspicion was confirmed: the voices were immediately louder and clearer.

"We're going with Plan B . . . too much resistance from Niamh on Plan A . . . we may need to deal with her . . . she could ruin everything."

Willem's heart thumped. What was Plan A and B? What did they mean by "dealing" with Niamh? Did they intend to hurt her?

He needed something with more height. Coming down off the chair, he pushed his desk underneath the vent. He was standing on the desk, ready to hoist himself up into the ceiling when Bruce walked in.

"What the hell are you doing up there?" The sight of the Dutchman standing on the desk was not one Bruce had expected to see.

"Can you hear anything?" Willem asked, looking up into the air-conditioning vent.

Bruce listened. "No."

The voices had lulled. Bruce was looking at Willem for an explanation.

"The vent isn't working," Willem improvised, thinking it was not a good idea to say he was hearing voices. "It's so hot in here I decided to have a look at it myself."

"You should call facilities. It's their job to deal with all building maintenance." Bruce had stated the obvious but Willem could tell from his demeanour that he commended the urge to fix the problem. They were of the same stock, kindred engineers. They spent their life fixing things.

"I've checked through the numbers for the ANZ Bank. With margins like these, I'm not sure we should go ahead with the bid for the contract renewal," Bruce said, sitting down at the displaced desk while Willem was still standing on it.

"You did ask for the worst-case scenario," Willem reminded him, coming down and pulling a seat up to sit opposite his boss. They both ignored the open vent for the time being.

"There is a possible upside," Willem suggested carefully. "At the moment the numbers only include what equipment is under maintenance contract. I think ANZ Bank has significant repairs that are handled on a time and materials basis. The margins would look better if we were guaranteed that business. We have all the infrastructure in place – it should be pure profit."

"I was assuming they would give us that business as a matter of course – we'll be the incumbent maintenance provider – who could do a better job of it than us?" Bruce was defensive. It hadn't occurred to him until now that ANZ Bank could go elsewhere with the equipment that wasn't under contract.

"Then we need to make the arrangement formal," Willem said.

"Yes, you're right," Bruce acknowledged. He was gaining a solid respect for his head engineer. "I need you to work on more numbers including that scenario."

"I'll start on it straight away."

"What the hell is that?" Bruce asked suddenly, looking around before his eyes veered upwards to the open vent.

"Voices." Willem took a risk. He waited for Bruce to tell him he was crazy.

"Well, I can hear that. Where are they coming from?" Bruce stood up, his eyes fixed on the vent.

"I don't know. It's been annoying me for a while," Willem admitted, feeling dizzy with relief that they weren't in his mind. He wasn't having an attack. He could tell his psychiatrist that he didn't need more Zyprexa.

Bruce couldn't resist the opportunity to get his hands dirty. His jacket was off within seconds. He climbed onto the desk and heaved himself up inside the vent. He stuck his head out after a few moments to say, "I'm just going to follow the duct back along the ceiling," and he was gone again.

Willem waited. Frustratingly, the voices ceased again. In the quiet he found himself panicking as he replayed the earlier threat to Niamh in his head. He took a calming breath; it was important that he didn't let his paranoia take over. He would take his time to piece this together to ensure he had a full grasp of what was going on. Then, and only then, he would talk to Niamh.

Bruce came back and there was a thud as he landed on the desk. He had streaks of dust across his blue shirt but a satisfied look on his face. "Your duct shares an air supply with two of the executive offices."

234

"Whose offices?" Willem asked, keeping his tone casual.

"Helen Barnes and Lucinda Armstrong. The sonic lining is missing from the duct – you should get facilities around to fix it." His attempts to brush the dust from his shirt served only to smear it in further.

Keith Longmore, the private investigator, parked outside an unimpressive house in the Western suburbs. Working on the joint brief from Niamh Lynch and Bruce Knight, he had received this address but little other information. Keith sat in his nondescript white Commodore for an hour, listening to the radio while his eyes remained glued on the door of the house. Finally, there was movement as a red open-top Saab emerged from the garage. Keith smiled. With a car like that, Denis Greene would be an easy target to follow.

The driver wore a baseball hat, his greying ponytail swishing in the wind as he took off down the road. After ten minutes of fast driving, the Saab pulled up outside yet another unimpressive Western suburbs house and Keith had his first good look at Denis. Tall and well built, he wore old work jeans and trainers. And, of course, there was the ponytail, a distinguishing feature that made a private investigator's job all the easier.

Denis rang the bell and the door opened. Keith caught a brief glimpse of a white-haired man and a young child. When the door was safely shut, Keith left his car to walk past the postbox. He picked the lock but his efforts were wasted: there was no mail inside to tell him the names of the residents. He walked down the street, looking at the ordinary houses set well back on square blocks of land. He hoped to run into a neighbour, one of the most reliable sources to find out what he needed to know. But there was nobody about and he went back to his car, turning on the radio again to pass the time.

Denis came out after twenty minutes or so. The white-haired man walked with him to the car. Keith was surprised to notice that the man's face was much younger than the colour of his hair. He was probably the father of the child rather than the grandfather as he had first thought. The two men spoke as the boy watched from the doorway. He was about four or five years old. Keith had his camera poised, ready to take the shot as the two men shook hands. It was a dull day and the flash went off. Denis looked around, his eyes narrowing. The child at the door pointed to Keith's car but thankfully nobody but Keith saw him.

Keith had to wait until the white-haired man went back inside before he could start the engine and follow the red Saab. It took a few precious moments before the front door of the house was shut. Keith doubted he would catch up with the Saab but he got lucky. It was first in the queue behind the set of traffic-lights at the end of the street. Keith joined the queue, annoyed with himself for not thinking of the flash. It wasn't often he made stupid errors like that.

This time he followed the late model Saab to North Sydney. It was a longer journey and much more tricky to keep his target in sight. It started to rain and Denis put up the soft top. As usual, parking in North Sydney was almost non-existent, the commercial stations full since early morning. Denis circled for a while until he secured a metered space on the Pacific Highway. Keith had no option but to park his white Commodore in a disabled spot. His target would be long gone if he waited for a legitimate park. Parking fines were par for the course in his job and one of his more significant expenses.

Denis got out of the car, turning his face up to the rain to see if it was heavy enough to warrant more protection than the baseball hat. He seemed to think it wasn't too bad and took a canvas bag from the boot of his car, balancing it on his shoulder as he headed towards Miller Street. Keith managed to take a shot of him, this time remembering to switch off the flash. The canvas bag must have been heavy as he stopped a few times to rest it on the footpath while he flexed his arms.

Denis's journey came to an end at the ANZ Bank, with another shot for Keith as he passed under the bank's signage before disappearing through the doors. He didn't queue at the counter, speaking instead to the lady at the information desk. She made a call and the security doors to the back office were opened to let him inside.

Keith quickly called his wife at home. After a brief conversation, he went inside and headed for the information desk. "I'm with the guy who just went through to the back office," he said with a cheerful grin.

"The computer-repair guy?" The clerk's voice was terse. It had been a busy morning.

"Yes."

"Where's your ID – if you're from HDD you should have a badge." She looked at him suspiciously.

Keith had found out all he needed to know for now and, with perfect timing, his phone started to ring. It was his wife. He listened to what she was saying, nodding occasionally for the benefit of the information clerk. Hanging up, he turned to the lady with a rueful expression. "I'm terribly sorry. I've been called out to another site. An emergency, or so they tell me. Don't worry – Denis can deal with the repair without me."

He left before she thought of asking any questions. Another customer was quick to take his place at the desk. The clerk would be kept busy and Keith felt sure she wouldn't mention the incident to Denis when he came back out.

Keith went back to his car and lifted the wiper to retrieve the parking ticket. The fine was sixty dollars. He shoved it in his pocket and checked his watch. It was one thirty. He decided that he had done enough for one day and would surprise his lovely wife by getting home early.

Denis's wife wasn't as lovely as Keith's. It was late when he got home from the ANZ Bank. He was tired and jumpy. All afternoon he had been expecting to get caught. Ironically, in the end it was Lily who caught him. She was ready to pounce as soon as he got in the door.

"Your lawyer called," she said as she sat on the sofa, her back to him as she faced the muted TV.

"Jacobsen? What did he want?" Denis pulled off his sweater; it was damp from the rain that was now falling heavily.

"It's very interesting what he wants – he wants a statutory declaration from me – saying that Australia is my home and I've cut off all ties with England."

She still had her back to him and Denis swore under his breath. The stupid lawyer, what did he go talking to Lily for?

"Oh . . . he only needs that for the Industrial Relations Commission – it doesn't mean we have to stay here or anything," he said.

"Oh, yes, *the Industrial Relations Commission*." She turned to face him. "And, of course, he told me all about your application for permanent residency."

Her face was expressionless and, for the first time in many years, Denis felt unsure of himself.

"Tell me now – just tell me and don't lie – *did* you apply for residency?" she asked, her voice a deadly whisper.

Denis could only nod. This poker-faced woman was a stranger to him.

"Without consulting me? Your wife? You applied for this visa without consulting your wife?"

She wasn't screaming. Usually she'd be screaming by now. But her voice was flat and that's what chilled him.

"I'm sorry." It was a decade since a word of apology had been used between the bickering couple. It hung in the air, out of place, unfamiliar.

"Sorry?" Lily repeated, not buying the apology. "Try again! You're not sorry. You're only telling me about the visa because you want me to sign this declaration thing for your solicitor."

It was true and there was nothing that Denis could say in his defence. Lily walked away, her slippered feet heavy on the stairs.

"What are you doing?" he called after her.

"I'm getting my things together," she answered as she walked along the landing. "You want to stay in Australia? You're welcome to. Me, I'm going home. I should have gone back a long time ago."

Denis stayed downstairs, listening to the floorboards creak as she went to and fro between the wardrobe and her suitcase. This had never happened before, not even after the most bitter of arguments. A suitcase had never been packed. He didn't know whether to stay downstairs or go up there to try to talk some reason into her.

He was still in the kitchen when she came down, some thirty minutes later.

"I'll come back for the rest of my things during the week." She rested the suitcase on the tiled floor that she mopped every day. She was in control of the situation, her faded eyes were even excited. She wasn't sad to leave him. She had been waiting for the guts to go. A car honked outside. "That's my taxi – I called myself a taxi."

She didn't drive. She had nagged Denis to teach her but he never got around to it.

"Lily," he said, "you've still got your slippers on."

She looked down. "So I have."

She kicked them off. Her feet were bare when she walked out on him.

Chapter Nine

Helen had rearranged Phil's office. Her pictures were on the wall, her name on the door. She was stupidly proud as she sat behind the large desk. She wore a flattering suit, a grey skirt with a short fitted jacket. It was part of the new wardrobe she had purchased in honour of her move to the executive level of the company.

The receptionist called to let her know that Keith Longmore was waiting in the foyer.

"OK, I'll come down and get him."

Keith was contentedly reading the paper when she got down to the foyer. It was a few years since they met but he looked the same. The hair he had left was still speckled with grey and his beard was still ginger. He smiled and showed teeth that were stained from cigarettes. His grip on her hand was tight as he shook it.

"I have another job for you," Helen said when they

were seated in her office, the door safely shut.

Keith gave a slight nod to indicate his interest. HDD was a premium customer; he was always happy to do business with big corporations.

"I want you to . . . *check up* . . . on one of our executives."

"What do you want to know?"

"I'm not sure. For a start, you could find out if there is a criminal record. Find out names of friends and family and do a criminal check on them also. Watch the house . . ." Helen grinned with a hint of conspiracy. "I'm sure you know the routine better than me."

"Do you have a photograph?"

"Yes."

Helen handed it over and Keith gave it an appreciative glance. It would be a pleasure to follow such a beautiful woman.

"How about a home address?"

"Damn, I meant to have that ready for you . . . hold on a moment."

Helen pulled her phone closer and dialled a familiar number. In the meantime, Keith admired the view. It looked as if the bridge was superimposed over the buildings. He had never seen anything quite like it; it was quite spectacular.

"Donna, can you look up an address on the payroll system for me? Lucinda Armstrong. Bring it to my office when you have it . . . thanks."

As soon as she put the phone down, Keith said, "Tell me, what does Lucinda Armstrong do on the executive?"

"She's our legal counsel."

"Right." Keith's eyes widened ever so slightly.

There was a knock on the door and a pretty young girl popped her head inside. "Here it is."

Helen saw a new ring on Donna's slim wedding finger as she held out the slip of paper. The engagement ring sparkled and Helen was dazzled by it. Momentarily distracted, she was uncharacteristically short with the accounts clerk. "Donna, can you keep this under wraps? Please don't mention it to Lucinda."

Donna nodded, wondering what was going on as she closed the door behind her. Two people had asked her to keep her mouth shut in the last week. She liked Niamh and Helen but didn't appreciate them treating her like a child. She was an adult; she was getting married soon.

"OK," Helen said when Donna had gone. "You have a photograph and home address. Anything else needed to get this under way?"

"Not for now." Keith stood up to go.

"By the way, did Niamh Lynch get in contact with you?" She was wondering if Niamh had used the phone number she had given her.

Keith was slow to answer. In his line of work you had to be perpetually discreet. "Yes, yes, she did," he said vaguely as he held up the slip of paper with the address. "I'll call you about this in the next few days."

Helen left work at six, the drive to Pyrmont taking much longer than it should. She parked her car in its allocated spot and took the elevator to her apartment.

As she opened the door, she was greeted with the mouth-watering aroma of her mother's cooking.

"Hello, love." The old lady looked up from straightening the cutlery on the table. Helen noticed there were two places set.

"Mum, I'm going out tonight. I won't be having dinner."

"Oh," her face dropped, "you should have told me."

"I did."

Helen was preoccupied as she changed out of her suit into a more casual skirt and top. Her mother was jaded from a lingering cold and now her sharp memory seemed to be slipping. Was it just the normal symptoms of old age or was something else wrong? She emerged from the bedroom, crossing the living-room to get to the mirror at the far end. The light was much better there for applying make-up.

'Have you heard anything more from *him?*" old Mrs Barnes asked from her armchair. The table had been cleared and there was no evidence of the dinner that had been prepared on Helen's arrival.

"Phil?" Helen asked, knowing full well who her mother was referring to. She saw the old woman's nod in the mirror.

"No," she lied but it was for her mother's own good. She wouldn't sleep at night if she knew that Phil was still harassing her daughter with phone calls, claiming he was going to get her back for all the trouble she had caused him.

"That's good – he was a nasty piece of work." Mrs

Barnes flicked through the channels until she got to the right one. *The Bill* wouldn't start for another ten minutes but she liked to be prepared. The story was ruined if the first few minutes of the show were missed by not being on the right channel. "Where are you going tonight?"

"It's just a work thing – it could go on quite late so don't wait up for me," Helen answered, not happy with her lipstick and putting on another coat.

"You've been out a lot these last few weeks."

"It's the job, Mum," Helen said lightly. "If I'm going to be paid a whacking finance director's salary, I've got to take on the social commitments."

Mrs Barnes nodded as if she agreed but inside she was questioning her daughter. Was it really the job? Helen had social engagements most nights of the week. She came home late and a few times her bed hadn't been slept in at all. And when she was at home, there were phone calls. She took them on the balcony and sometimes she was out there for an hour. It was true that she had purchased smart clothes to dress the part for her new role. She had her confidence back, plus some more. But was it really the job? Or was there a man? Surely Helen would tell her if she had finally met someone?

Helen saw the questions on her mother's face but wasn't inclined to answer them. Their relationship had always been very open but a distance had been building steadily over the last year. The box-like apartment didn't encourage honesty; instead it enforced a proximity that would kill the strongest of relationships. Helen knew she had to do something. They couldn't continue to live on top of each other like this.

"Do I look like a successful hardnosed executive?" she asked, doing a light-hearted twirl to take the look of worry off her mother's face.

"I've never seen you look better, love," her mother responded with a sad and proud smile. She was also acutely aware that she and her daughter were damaging their relationship by living together in the tiny apartment. But the only other option, a retirement home, still held no appeal for the old woman. She didn't want to live in a place where people with no families queued up, waiting to die.

Niamh arrived at the office after another night of tormenting nightmares. Sharon's head shot up as she passed her desk. "You look like you've been out on the town all night," she commented. Sometimes her perceptiveness was a pain in the neck.

"I wish!" Niamh gave a weak grin. "Any calls?"

"Paul Jacobsen – again," Sharon replied, pointedly emphasising the "again".

"OK . . ."

Niamh was on her way into her office when her assistant asked, "Aren't you going to call him back?" Sharon was getting fed up with being piggy-in-the-middle. She was a bad liar and found it hard to hold an accomplished solicitor like Jacobsen at bay.

"Not yet."

"Can I send him the letter?"

The letter had been sitting on Sharon's desk for over a

week. It formally stated that the company wasn't prepared to put Denis back on their payroll. Niamh had
been waiting for the right time to send it.

"Not yet."

Sharon gave a long-suffering sigh and went back to her
work.

Niamh sat at her desk and stared out the window for a
few minutes. Work was a sanctuary, a place where Chris
and her dad rarely entered her thoughts. Her bright office
didn't lend itself to sordid nightmares or negative thinking. Maybe the nightmares would go away if she slept
here. God knows Chris spent enough time in his office so
why shouldn't she do the same?

She called Keith Longmore's mobile phone while her
laptop was starting up. He answered without delay. The
reception was bad; he sounded as if he was in the car.

"Keith. It's Niamh Lynch. I'm just calling to see if
you've found anything on Greene . . . I can't stall his
solicitor for much longer."

There was some crackling then the line was clear. "I'm
just stopped at the queue for the toll so I have only a few
seconds before I lose reception in the tunnel. Last week I
followed your friend to the ANZ Bank in North Sydney.
The clerk at the information desk told me he's the computer-repair man."

"The computer-repair man?" Niamh frowned into the
phone. "How can that be? He doesn't work for us any
more . . . and ANZ Bank is one of our biggest clients."

"Yes, I know they are one of your clients. HDD was
labelled all over the hardware at the information desk.

And I'm guessing the bag that Greene was carrying contained the stolen parts."

"Has he been stealing our clients as well as our parts?" Niamh asked, her frown deepening further as she tucked wisps of her blonde hair behind her ear.

"I thought that too – but I soon realised it didn't make sense," Keith replied, reaching the front of the queue and handing the toll operator a five-dollar note.

"Why?"

"Because the clerk mentioned that Denis was using a HDD identification badge – he's pretending that he still works for you – I don't think he'd be doing that if he was stealing your business." Keith took his change from the gloved hand of the operator and the green light beckoned him to move along. "Look, I'm going to lose you as soon as I go into the tunnel. I'm confident I can nail him, I just need a little more time. In the meantime, you may want to make some discreet enquiries at ANZ."

Niamh put the phone down slowly, her stomach giving a growl of hunger. She had left the house without breakfast. "I'm going down to the coffee shop. Do you want something?" she said to Sharon.

As usual, it wasn't a simple question for her assistant. "It's not ten thirty yet. You're early," she accused, her resolve shaken by the unscheduled temptation.

"A muffin?" Niamh suggested, recognising the look of yearning on her face.

"Thanks." Sharon was clearly relieved that she hadn't said the damning words herself.

"Right you are," Niamh said, then added, "By the way,

it's OK to send that letter to Paul Jacobsen now."

Keith Longmore was closing in on Denis Greene. Unauthorised access to ANZ was an unforgivable offence and she was confident that soon they would have all the ammunition they needed to end the lawsuit.

Coming out of the fire stairwell, she had a headlong collision with Bruce who was on his way in. There was a fresh smell of smoke off him.

"I'm sorry." His weathered face was an embarrassed red as he stepped back from her.

"It's OK – I needed to see you anyway. I have some news on Denis Greene."

"What is it?" He was distracted, ill at ease.

"I'm just getting a sandwich from the coffee shop. Do you want to have a quick coffee with me and I'll fill you in on the latest developments?" she suggested.

"A coffee . . ." he repeated without enthusiasm. "OK. Maybe just a quick one."

They walked up the alley to George Street and were lucky to get the last free table in the thriving coffee shop.

"Keith Longmore saw Denis going into the back office at ANZ," Niamh said bluntly as soon as their order was taken. "The clerk said he was the computer-repair man. Keith thinks he had the stolen parts in the bag he was carrying."

The weight of the statement was enough to shock Bruce out of whatever had been distracting him earlier. "ANZ?" His face registered panic, his first thought being the contract renewal. The proposal was to be submitted to the bank later in the week.

Niamh helped him focus his thoughts by giving him the most relevant facts up front. "He has an HDD identification badge – ANZ think that he still works for us."

"He can't have an ID – he handed it back to me the day he left," Bruce said simply.

"He got one from somewhere," Niamh shrugged. "Any ideas?"

"No! What the hell can he be doing at ANZ? I don't feel good about this. The bastard's up to something . . . . and the proposal, damn it . . . the bank will have us out on our ear if they find out that an ex-employee is gaining access to their premises with a false ID." His flat white arrived just in time to stop him from blowing a fuse. He downed the coffee in a few tense seconds.

"Keith suggested we make some discreet enquiries at the bank," said Niamh.

"Willem and I have a final pricing meeting with them in the morning," he replied, getting to his feet. "While we're there, I'll get Willem to check our hardware and software to make sure it's all OK."

He lit another cigarette as he walked away. Niamh was left to eat her sandwich alone. Soon after, her mobile phone rang. It was Sharon.

"I've changed my mind about the muffin. Don't get me anything – I'm going to be strong for once," she said.

"OK. You're the boss," Niamh smiled. She finished the sandwich. Then she walked across the street to the post office. She needed to get a birthday card for Uncle Tom.

The man that killed her dad was sixty-five tomorrow.

The next morning Bruce inhaled a calming cigarette outside ANZ's North Sydney premises. Willem Boelhoers stood silently beside him, waiting for him to finish. They were both ill at ease, the upcoming meeting and the all-important contract renewal could swing in any direction.

The head of IT for the bank was remarkably young for his role. Bruce had met Martin Fitzgerald many times but it was Willem who had the day-to-day relationship. They were hoping that Willem's relationship would pull them through.

"We're very close to finalising our pricing," Bruce said when the introductory small talk was over.

"Closing date is Friday," Martin warned, smiling as he teased the incumbent service provider.

"Don't worry," Willem bantered with him. "We'll get it to you at four-fifty-five – just in time for you to read before the weekend."

Some of the tension ebbed away from the HDD representatives as they joined in the brief laughter.

"Martin, you know me. I don't beat around the bush." Bruce took an unsteady breath that was more related to his nicotine habit than anything. "We want to keep your business and we're trying to give you the best possible price. We can move the price down further if you commit to give your time and materials business exclusively to us."

Martin's face closed up and he assumed the bland expression of a negotiator. "We already have a contract with another party covering our T&M."

Willem left a respectful pause before saying, "We can drop our prices by 5 per cent if you contract it with us."

"That's a very lucrative offer," Martin acknowledged. "However, we like to have more than one IT service provider. It keeps them on their toes, makes sure they *both* give us the best possible service and price."

Bruce cleared his throat. "We work best when we have an exclusive arrangement with our client. We like to give an end-to-end solution, including time and materials. If you guarantee us the business, we'll drop the total price by 10 per cent – that's our final offer."

Martin adjusted his tie, an uncharacteristic fidget for the experienced negotiator. "I need time to absorb this offer and the consequences it has for the bank." His tone indicated he didn't want to discuss the matter any further.

"What numbers do you want to see on Friday?" Willem asked. "Including or excluding T&M?"

"Send me both," Martin responded, not willing to give anything away.

"OK. Will do." Willem glanced at Bruce before saying, "Just one more thing, Martin . . . we need to visit the computer room before we go . . . we have some work to do there. Can you let us in?"

Martin's face showed his puzzlement at the request. Bruce Knight and Willem Boelhoers were senior management in HDD and didn't usually muck around in the bank's computer room. That sort of work was left to the junior engineers.

"One of our engineers is giving cause for concern and we want to check over a job he did here a few days ago,"

Bruce said by way of explanation. He was committed to being as open as possible without unduly alarming his client. This conversation would be analysed over and over again if it transpired that Denis Greene had inflicted some damage on the bank's hardware or software.

Martin's frown was instantaneous. Bruce and Willem flinched simultaneously as they saw it descend. "That's not good."

The gravity of the situation was portrayed by the heavy silence.

"We'll give you a full briefing if we find anything," Bruce promised the bank's head of IT.

Martin was still frowning as he said, "We had an issue with a back-up tape last week. We recalled it from storage but it didn't hold any data. It was blank."

"That sounds like a mistake, a human error." Willem was reassuring. "One of your staff must have sent the wrong tape to storage."

"Let's hope it was a mistake – and nothing to do with your engineer," Martin replied darkly and the meeting ended. It wasn't on a good note.

Martin walked them to the bank's basement, the home of the computer room. He punched out his access code on the keypad and pushed the heavy metal door inwards. "Let me know if you find anything."

Bruce nodded and a blast of cool air-conditioning hit his face as he went inside. The computer room was a work of technological art. Miles and miles of cables connected the stacks of storage devices and the gleaming servers. White floors, walls and equipment blended together, the monitor screens adding the only colour to the room. "How many servers do they have in here?" he asked Willem.

"Last time I counted it was forty. Then there's the mainframe as well."

"We'll be here for hours."

Bruce had started off many years ago as an engineer but had spent the last fifteen years in senior management. His skills were too dated for today's technology and there was little he could do to help Willem. He looked on as the head engineer carefully checked all the hardware and software. Willem updated the virus files on the servers and ran the scans.

"OK, that's all the servers clear – now for the mainframe."

He spent almost an hour looking for any changes to the system made in the last seven days. Nothing unusual was revealed.

On their way out they passed by Martin Fitzgerald's office to let him know that all was in order. Once outside the bank, Bruce lit up and closed his eyes as he inhaled the smoke into his damaged lungs. He was reassured by Willem's checks but he couldn't get rid of the niggling feeling that all was not well. Denis Greene had a purpose when he illegitimately gained access to the bank's computer room. He hadn't gone in there just for the hell of it, that was for sure.

Weekends made the truth harder to ignore and this last weekend had been worse than the others. Chris played golf on the Saturday and spent most of Sunday in the office. But there was nothing they could do to avoid the wordless nights together. Scott's words stayed in Niamh's head. *"At some stage you will both reach a conclusion and move forward."* She had reached a conclusion and she was bracing herself to take the next step to move forward.

On Monday morning she hurried past Sharon's perceptiveness to the shelter of her office. It was only when she shut the door behind her she saw the yellow envelope sitting ominously on her keyboard.

It brought her close to breaking point. Who was doing this? Tears started to form in her eyes as she dialled Sharon's extension.

"Did you put a yellow envelope on my desk?"

"Yes."

"Where did it come from?"

"It was in your pigeon-hole this morning."

There was nothing else she could ask. There were five hundred employees in HDD who had access to her pigeon-hole. She opened the envelope.

Do you trust him?

It was a straight question and the answer was that she didn't. It was very obvious now that something had happened at the Christmas party. Chris had been with someone else. He had been gone for over an hour. It had to be Lucinda, all the other evidence stacked up. How could he humiliate her like that? She started to cry in earnest.

The phone rang and if she had been thinking straight

she wouldn't have picked it up. It was Sharon again.

"I have someone on the line who is looking for a reference on Scott Morgan."

She pulled herself together to say, "Put them through." She had been waiting for the call since the day in the park. She would do the reference, then plead sick and go home.

She spent the next fifteen minutes talking to the recruitment agent whose name she didn't catch. She gave Scott a glowing report and when she hung up she knew he had a very good chance of being short-listed. Her tears had dried into her face. She was feeling a hollow kind of calm and decided to stay in the office after all, realising there was no point going home to an empty house.

She had a productive day and called it quits at six. At home, she roamed around the kitchen doing trivial chores as she waited for Chris. It was after eight when she heard the garage door open, a few more seconds before the car door slammed and he came inside, juggling his briefcase and a massive lever-arch folder. "You look as if you've been waiting for me," he said when he saw that the TV wasn't on. Niamh always turned it on as soon as she came in from work. The noise made her feel she wasn't alone in the house as she waited for her husband to come home.

"I was."

"You should know better," he laughed as he slid the file onto the bench top and rested the briefcase on the floor. He didn't stop to see her sombre expression before he sat on the sofa, loosening his tie. She left the kitchen to sit next to him.

"Well, what's so important that the TV is switched off?" he asked.

His hair was freshly cut, making his face stronger, more handsome. She had a moment of detached admiration before plunging in. "I want to know what happened at the Christmas party."

"For God's sake, not again!" He threw his eyes to heaven.

"I know you were with someone." An outrageous accusation was the only way to get to the truth. He would get angry and if there was anything there, it would come out. She waited for his gut reaction. There was certainly shock on his face; was there guilt too?

"I'm sorry."

An instantaneous confession was not what she was expecting. After weeks of feeling numb there was a very sharp hurt.

"You had . . . *sex* . . ."

"No, it was just a kiss."

"Who? Who was it?"

"Does it matter?" he countered with a sigh.

"Of course, it does," she raised her voice to demand, "Who?"

He hesitated and then his eyes met hers as he said, "I'm not going to tell you. It doesn't serve any purpose."

"It's Lucinda, isn't it? You were talking to her when I found you."

"I'm not going to take part in a guessing game," he replied adamantly.

"I *know* it's Lucinda – you've seen her in Forbes, haven't you? And I bet you were with her on Christmas Eve too."

"What?" His face twisted with a frown. "Where are you pulling all of this from? It's not Lucinda, OK?"

"I don't believe you."

"Well, that's your problem."

"How long has it been going on?" she asked.

"It hasn't been 'going on'! It was just the Christmas party, that's all. I got talking to this woman on the way . . ."

He must have realised how tacky it sounded and didn't finish the sentence. Her husband was the kind of man who groped other women on his way to the gents'. While his wife waited for him to return. It was too humiliating to contemplate.

"Have there been others?" she asked even though she already knew what the answer would be.

"Yes . . . look, Niamh, I was never like this until we got married . . . now, women are like an addiction . . . the more forbidden the fruit and all that . . . you know, I'm glad this has come out . . ."

"You are?" Her sarcasm climaxed as she stood up. She needed the protection of distance, the distraction of pacing. Her husband was admitting to being some kind of sex junkie, someone who was obsessed with women. No better than Phil Davis.

"Yes, it's obvious I'm not marriage material – it brings out the worst in me – it seems I want every woman but my wife . . ."

258

It all made an ironic kind of sense. He didn't touch or make love to her because he was turned off by the fact they were married and it was boringly legitimate. Her voice flat, she said, "So what now? Are we going to get a divorce?"

"I think that's the right thing to do," he replied with an odd sincerity. "We both deserve happiness and if that's not possible together, I think it's best that we go our separate ways."

"*You* think it's best – *I'm* the one who brought this up – who found you out. What would have happened if I hadn't confronted you?"

Again, he seemed to be sincere when he said, "I've been waiting for you to bring it up – to break us up – I didn't want to be the one –"

"*What?*" She turned on him, incredulous at what he was suggesting.

"Well, with your family history, I didn't want to give you a *fait accompli* by leaving. I wanted you to be the one to suggest divorce."

"How *fucking* noble of you!" she screamed at him. "What were you afraid of? That I'd top myself like my dad?"

"Yes."

She was still standing, he sitting. Their eyes locked. There was no going back. This was it. It was over.

"Have there been any good times for you?" For some reason she needed reassurance that their time together wasn't a total write-off.

He considered her question for a few moments before

replying, "I'd say there haven't been any *bad* times . . . . it just hasn't felt right."

"Oh, I'm *terribly sorry!*" Again, she called on sarcasm as a defence to his indifference.

"So am I. You're a good person – you just married the wrong man. And I think you've known it for some time too. You would have called it off ages ago if it wasn't for the baggage of your parents' divorce."

He was right. God, he was so right.

"Why did we get married? Can you remember?" Her voice was barely audible. Flashbacks of her parents' divorce were making it hard to concentrate.

"Me?" This time his response was more considered. "I guess I thought that I should settle down, I was at that age. Now I have learnt enough about myself to know that I'll probably never be conventional and settle down with one woman. Now, *you* . . . you got married because you were trying to prove something. Trying to prove you were different to your parents and could make a happy family. I'm sorry I couldn't give you that happy family, Niamh, I really am. But we're both at fault, not just me. We both raced up the aisle without taking the time to know each other. If we had slowed down for a moment, we would have seen we weren't at all compatible."

She hid her face behind her hands. Because he was right again. It was harsh, but it was a precise and accurate assessment of their relationship in a way that only a lawyer could sum it up. They had never been in love and they had been in too much of a rush to realise it.

"When do you want me to move out?" he asked eventually. He could afford to soften his voice now that the finish line was close.

"Get out now – just get out and leave me alone – I can't believe you've done this, humiliated me in front of my colleagues like this . . ."

"I don't think anyone saw, if that's any consolation."

She took her hands down from her face, her voice furious as she shouted, "Somebody *did* see! How do you think I found out? They've been leaving me notes, little clues here and there . . ."

She was conscious of him standing up, collecting the briefcase and the folder from the kitchen. They were all he needed; he had a change of clothes at the office. Chris was doing the leaving. He was the one moving out. He was strong. He was in control. And he had no qualms, no second thoughts. If he hadn't been so determined that this was the end, Niamh guessed her own insecurity would have been looking for a way to work it out.

But she could hear her voice, still yelling at him, finding words of its own accordance. "I *hate* you – for going off with other women – for not even trying to be a husband – I hate you for wasting two years of my life!"

He only said, "I'll give you some space tonight. I'll be back in the next few days to get my stuff."

The door gave a humiliating bang. Short of breath, she continued to pace. She thought about the Joker. The Joker knew about Chris and Lucinda. Who else at the office knew? The laughing, painted face of the Joker was replaced with the image of her father hanging in the garage. She hadn't seen the scene of his death but her

261

mind had a vivid picture that flashed its horror whenever her defences were down. Shaking now, she headed for the phone. There was only one person she could call, even though it killed her to do it. Her mother.

Chapter Ten

Tom was at Niamh's door within fifteen minutes. Her
mother's rheumatism confined her to the house and he
had been her legs for years now. He was carrying a canvas
bag; it presumably held some clothes so he could stay
overnight. The bag was left in the hallway and Niamh sat
on the sofa while Tom made the tea. He was from the old
school where the first step in dealing with a catastrophe
was to make a pot of tea. There was no teapot in Niamh's
kitchen and he had to settle for two solitary mugs. He set
them down on the coffee table and the cushion next to
Niamh sank beneath his weight.

"If it wasn't for Mum and Dad I would have left Chris
ages ago," she said to him. "I was afraid of divorce, Tom,
of the hurt it brings. I was trying so hard to pretend it
wasn't going to happen to me as well."

"I know, girl." His arm squeezed her shoulders as they silently recalled the devastation of twenty years ago. They both forgot about the tea. It was some time before she spoke again.

"I can't believe Chris did that to me . . . in front of my colleagues . . . and there have been other women too."

"You're worth more than that."

"How can you say that, Tom?" She looked into his familiar face. "Wasn't Mum unfaithful to her husband with you?"

"No." He shook his head. "There was nothing like that – there was no sex until after she separated from your dad. We fell in love, Niamh. We had to follow our hearts . . ."

"Was it worth it?" she asked him.

He took his arm away from her shoulders and hunched forward with his hands clasped tightly together. "No."

"Haven't you and Mum been happy together?"

"How could we be happy, girl? Every day we think of him. And should we ever forget, there's you with his looks and his sense of humour to remind us."

It was the first time they had ever spoken about it and now that the embargo was lifted there were lots of questions to ask.

"How did you know about his sense of humour? Is that something Mum told you?"

"I was one of his friends," Tom confessed. "Your dad loved to joke around with his friends . . . where are *your* friends tonight, Niamh?"

"What do you mean?" she looked at him, confused by his left-field question.

"You called your mother for help. Was there any friend you could call if your mother wasn't there?"

"No – Aisling is the only one who's that close to me."

Tom didn't say anything but his clasped hands tightened, his knuckles whitening with the pressure.

"Are you ever going to go back to Ireland?" she asked him after a few minutes. "Even for a holiday?"

He shook his head sadly. "No, girl. Sure we've been exiled. The guilt back there is too much for any of us to face. You, me and your mother can hide over here, pretending nothing happened – but still unable to move on. Aisling is the only one of us that has any guts. And now she has a baby over there that we haven't even seen."

His raw grief brought her a strange comfort. A happy-ever-after ending for her mum and Tom wouldn't have been fair. Her dad's life and death had to mean something.

Tom woke her early the next morning. He believed that no personal trauma stood in the way of an honest day's work. His culinary skills were limited but a hearty breakfast was something he could manage. She devoured it before she set off for work, like an obedient child going to school.

Keith Longmore was intrigued. For a private investigator, he wasn't a very curious individual. He found that excessive curiosity wasted time. However, he had never been asked to trail an executive before. And a lawyer to boot. Most of the people he followed were lower down the food chain and too often they were oversexed husbands.

The first thing he found out about the beautiful Lucinda Armstrong was that the address that Helen Barnes got from the company payroll system was incorrect. He wasted two days sitting outside a North Shore house before he realised that the Asian family who lived there did not feature Lucinda. A neighbour confirmed that she had moved out over three years before.

One of Keith's contacts in the police department ran a check and confirmed the lawyer didn't have any criminal history. It was impossible to run a check on her family and friends for now. For a start Keith needed to know their names. Without her home address, it was not going to be easy to find out who she was close to.

The contact was reluctant to give an address to match the car registration and Keith didn't want to stretch the friendship by pushing him. Reluctant to go back to Helen without first using his own initiative, he decided he would follow the lawyer home from work. That was another brick wall. The woman drove like a maniac and he couldn't keep up with her. She sped through amber lights and weaved in and out of lanes while he got left hopelessly behind. For three evenings he followed her old Camry without any success. The furthest he got was Parramatta Road so he could only assume that her new home was in the Western suburbs somewhere.

Helen had asked him to keep her updated with his progress and he was treating the assignment with the sense of urgency he read from her that day in her office. When he got home after the Parramatta Road debacle, he typed a brief email with two fingers while his wife massaged his tired shoulders.

Helen,

Address that you have is incorrect. She moved on three years ago. She doesn't have a criminal record but I've made little other progress to date. Is she married? If so, do you know her husband's name?

Best regards,

Keith

It transpired that Helen didn't know the husband's name. She knew the son's name, Jack, but over the three years that Lucinda worked for HDD, her husband hadn't attended any of the social functions. And she never spoke of him.

The incorrect home address niggled away at Keith. If Lucinda had moved house three years ago, then all the company's correspondence had been addressed incorrectly from the day she started at HDD. Did she have a forwarding arrangement with Australia Post? For three years?

Helen was able to give Keith a consolation prize — details of Lucinda's previous employer. Someone there might know more about the nameless husband. Keith called them without delay. They were an old-style firm of lawyers with little staff turnover. He didn't have to go further than the receptionist to find someone who remembered Lucinda.

"I'm an old friend of hers," he explained. "I've been overseas for the last few years and I called at her house last weekend. A neighbour said she moved on years ago."

"Was that the house in Mosman?" the receptionist asked.

"Yes, it was!" Keith exclaimed, his hopes rising. It seemed the receptionist knew her stuff.

"That's the last address we have as well."

"Darn it," Keith said, making sure to coat his tone with deep disappointment. "Maybe I could try the phone book. She got married, didn't she?"

"Yeah, she was still with us when she got married."

"I never met her husband. Do you remember his name?"

"It's Marcus."

"Marcus Armstrong! Great – I should be able to find them in the phone book."

"No, Armstrong is Lucinda's maiden name. She didn't take her married name – I wouldn't blame her," the receptionist giggled.

"Tell me – what's so funny?" Keith encouraged, giving a chuckle himself for good measure.

"It's Diddams," she giggled again. "His name was Marcus Diddams. Wouldn't you think a successful businessman like him would have had the sense to change his name by deed poll or something?"

Keith liked this receptionist. His job would be a lot easier if there were more people like her in the world. "What did Marcus do for a living?"

"Oh, he had his own company – something in computers – don't ask me what, I'm not very technical."

"Listen, thanks for everything. I'll mention you to

Lucinda when I get hold of her." Keith hung up with a satisfied smile. He would have been well and truly stuffed without the assistance of the receptionist. He knew of people who went officially under cover but didn't conceal their tracks as well as Lucinda Armstrong.

Niamh's office was no longer a sanctuary and for once her work didn't offer distraction. She was unable to focus on even the mundane task of reading her email. She stared into the screen. Out of the corner of her eye she became aware that Sharon was casting curious glances in her direction. She got up and shut her office door. Scott! She'd call Scott. She needed to tell him about the reference check. Maybe he would come into the city and meet her and she could leave the office and Sharon's discerning eyes behind for a while.

Scott didn't take any persuading to come into the city at short notice; he didn't even ask why. They agreed to meet in Martin Place again but this time it was saturated with rain. He wore a brown leather jacket and didn't seem to mind the teeming rain on his bare head. Jenny sat next to him on the bench, appropriately dressed for the weather in a pink Barbie raincoat and gumboots.

"I'm sorry. This wasn't the best place to meet considering the weather," Niamh apologised from the shelter of her black umbrella.

"It's OK. We've been having fun while we waited."

Jenny's blue eyes fixed on Niamh with open curiosity. Niamh winked at her and was rewarded with a traffic-stopping smile.

269

"We've been looking at ourselves in the puddles," Scott laughed, cuddling Jenny closer.

Niamh's automatic reaction was to look down. She saw her blurred reflection. It was grim. "That company called me for a reference," she said as she sat down on the dripping bench.

"I know. They rang me this morning to call me back for another interview."

"Great." She smiled her first smile in days.

"It's thanks to you. The agent said your reference was spectacular."

"Glad to be of service."

There was nothing left to say about the reference and she felt foolish for asking him to meet her when they could have had the same conversation over the phone.

But he didn't rush away. He sat there with rivulets of rain running down his face and Jenny sat still too, as if she sensed that something big was coming.

"Chris and I . . ." Niamh faltered. "We . . . we've come to that conclusion you were talking about . . . we're getting a divorce."

"I'm sorry."

They stared at each other before she turned her eyes to the nearby fountain. She felt his free hand envelop hers.

"I'm very sorry, Niamh."

She was mesmerised by the gushing water as it escaped the top of the fountain and free-fell to the pool below.

"I wanted to tell you because –"

"Because you know I'm in the middle of a divorce," he finished the sentence for her. "Don't worry – it's a perfectly understandable reaction. I also sought out every divorcee I knew when Ann went to Malaysia. I wanted someone to tell me that life can go on."

It wasn't really that. It was because, with Aisling away, he felt like her only friend. Much to her embarrassment, she started to cry. His hand moved up to her face, his thumb wiping the tears away. The tenderness of the gesture was unaffected by Jenny's round eyes as she looked on from Scott's other side.

"I should go." He took his hand away and Niamh's face felt exposed without it. "Is it OK if I call you later in the week? Just so that I know you're OK?"

She nodded and he got to his feet, hoisting Jenny up on one hip. Niamh also stood up, a little unsteady. He hugged her to him, her face touching the wetness of his jacket, her nostrils filling with the scent of the leather, her eyes level with Jenny's. Then he was gone, Jenny held high in his arms.

Old Mrs Barnes was in hospital with pneumonia. The doctor said it was an unusual time of the year for such an illness. His casual comment terrified Helen that there might be something more serious wrong. Her mother hadn't been in the best health for the last month. Her lingering cold had turned into a lingering chest infection before the onset of pneumonia. She had been lethargic, barely leaving the armchair.

It was seven before Helen got to the hospital. "I'm sorry I'm late, Mum. Something came up just as I was about to leave."

"Don't worry, love. I was happy watching the TV."

She did indeed look happy. Helen pulled up a chair and watched the programme with her.

"I should be able to go home next week," her mother said when the break came on.

"That's great. What day?"

"The doctor doesn't know yet . . . That's a nice necklace – I haven't seen that on you before."

Helen knew her mother's comment about the necklace wasn't a casual one. Her fingers inadvertently touched the pearls.

"Yes, it's a gift. From a friend."

The old woman's eyes were knowing. "A boyfriend?"

Just as Helen was about to respond, the tea lady knocked on the door to ask if they wanted something to drink. Her mother chatted with the woman as she poured two cups of tea. Helen looked on, realising that her mother had more company and space in the hospital than she had in the box-like apartment. It was no wonder that she was happier.

"Yes, it is a boyfriend. I'd like you to meet him, Mum," she said when the tea lady had backed her trolley out of the room.

"Is it serious with him, Helen, love?"

"Yes. We haven't been seeing each other that long but it's very serious."

"When can I meet him?"

Helen was meeting Yoshi for dinner later in the evening. "I can ask him to drop by here before I leave."

"Do I look all right for visitors?" Mrs Barnes asked,

anxious now.

"I'll change your nightie and you'll look gorgeous," Helen assured her. "Just give me a minute to call him first."

Helen made the call, changed her mother's nightie and they resumed watching the TV. The programme was just finishing up when there was a knock on the door to the private room.

"Come in," they both said in unison.

Yoshi came in and old Mrs Barnes couldn't hide her surprise. He wasn't what she expected at all.

It was four days since Chris had left and Niamh was trying to keep busy. So far she had been successful in avoiding Lucinda but now there was a five-minute reminder box flashing up on her screen, telling her that she had an upcoming meeting with the lawyer. Sharon, not knowing any better, must have accepted the electronic meeting invitation and with everything that had been going on, Niamh hadn't seen it in her calendar. The subject of the meeting was Denis Greene.

Niamh felt panic rise like a wave. She had to face Lucinda in five minutes. How was she meant to talk about Denis Greene when all she wanted to ask was why Lucinda had kissed Chris at the party? She could see them in her mind, Lucinda in the stunning red dress and Chris tall and handsome. A striking couple – what did it matter that they were married to others? A horrible thought came into her mind. Was Lucinda the Joker? Would she get a kick out of playing games with the

273

cryptic clues?

Niamh was outwardly calm when she arrived at the lawyer's office and helped herself to a seat. Lucinda, as glamorous as ever, wore yet another knee-length skirt that showed off her remarkable legs. It seemed she had a wardrobe full of such skirts and must have realised a long time ago that skirts went further than trousers in business.

"I want to progress this case today." The lawyer started the meeting with purpose. As usual, no time was wasted on small talk.

"So do I," Niamh responded.

"So you will agree to a reinstatement?"

"No. That's not what I said. In fact, I've already written to Paul Jacobsen telling him that we won't be reinstating Greene."

"You've done *what?*" Lucinda's eyes narrowed, her voice giving promising signs of outrage.

"I've written to Paul Jacobsen telling him we won't be reinstating Greene," Niamh repeated with an indifferent shrug.

"You had no right to do that." Lucinda's face paled with anger. "You've gone completely against the advice I've given you on this."

"I had every right," Niamh corrected her. "Your role is to give me advice, not to tell me what to do."

She saw Lucinda struggle to keep hold of her temper as she said, "May I ask why?"

"You certainly may." Niamh just fell short of mimicking her clipped tones. "Why don't you read this?"

She handed her a progress report from Keith Longmore and watched her closely as she read it.

Denis Greene gained access to the computer room of ANZ Bank on January 28th on the strength of a HDD identification badge. I have evidence that Greene purported to be a current employee of HDD. This is a criminal offence and would be enough in itself for the police to bring charges.

Greene's previous ID was handed back on his departure from the company and the fact he has obtained another indicates he has an ally in HDD. I am looking at possible contacts right at the moment.

I believe that Greene had stolen parts in the canvas bag he was carrying and I am trying to determine the identity of the white-haired man in the enclosed photograph.

It took Lucinda longer than it should to read the report. Niamh's eyes moved from her to take in the mess around them. No secretary had been willing to take on the lawyer's arrogance and the office told a tale of neglect. Sooner or later the chaos would bring Lucinda her just dues. Sooner or later she would trip over her own ego.

When it was apparent that Lucinda was finished with the report, Niamh gave her the photographs. There were some nice shots of Denis, particularly the one of him going into ANZ Bank.

"This is totally stretching the imagination," Lucinda said, throwing the snaps away as if they were burning hot. They landed face down and were immediately lost in the layers of paper.

"I don't think so."

"You may think this is damning evidence, but I can tell you right now that it's far from adequate. This bloke – what's his name? Longmore? This is a rather shoddy job. He's proved nothing – he's just making ridiculous insinuations."

"Why don't we ask the police to investigate?" Niamh was being deliberately simplistic.

Lucinda's face darkened. "Unlike you, I'm trying to save the company legal costs," she hissed. "Yeah, you can get the police involved. Then we can add defamation to the wrongful dismissal claims and suddenly we have an army of lawyers in the picture. It may make you feel justice has been done. But it will cost us thousands – yes, thousands – and we have less than a fifty per cent chance of winning."

"I disagree," said Niamh.

The lawyer flushed, helpless in the face of her colleague's doggedness. "We're stalemate, then. I'm *very* disappointed we can't come to an agreement."

Niamh's answer was a nonchalant shrug. She was bursting to tell Lucinda that she knew Denis's case had no legal merit. Chris and Steve Jones, experienced lawyers, said the same thing when they had time to think about the ludicrous visa allegations. But it was too early to let Lucinda know all that.

"We need a mediator," Lucinda continued with an irritated sigh. "That will be Malcolm."

Niamh wasn't surprised that she suggested Malcolm.

The CEO was no match for his legal counsel and she would be guaranteed the outcome she wanted. Niamh was a step ahead with her counterstrategy. She was going to brief Yoshi. Lucinda was a fool for not understanding where the power in the company really lay.

"Whatever you want, Lucinda. But let me warn you, I will do everything in my power to ensure that Denis Greene does not come back here."

Niamh left Lucinda's office on that note. She couldn't slap her in the face. She couldn't say she knew about the Christmas party. She couldn't even ask her if she was the Joker. Her only revenge was to find out why the bitch was lying through her teeth about Denis Greene.

The ANZ Bank kept Bruce waiting on the outcome of the contract renewal. It had been many years since he felt this tense about a deal. Usually he was a dignified winner and philosophical loser. But this time he felt his reputation was on the line. Despite the fact that Greene was now terminated, he had been an employee for almost four years. The fact that he had got into the bank using a false ID was a personal blow to Bruce.

In addition to that, there was the pressure from Japan. The share price had dropped a few more yen. Nishikawa, the vice-president up in Tokyo, was calling Yoshi every other day to see if there was any new business that would redeem the company in the eyes of the analysts. Yoshi, in turn, kept asking Bruce if there was any word from Martin Fitzgerald. Everybody knew the ANZ contract renewal was the only significant deal in the South

Pacific. It was a five-year contract with an order value that was big enough to catch the attention of the analysts.

After a week of serious nicotine abuse, Bruce got the call from Fitzgerald. The news was good. Not only had they retained the client, they had also won the lucrative T&M business. Bruce felt a sweet relief. It was an old HDD tradition to announce a new deal by ringing a handbell. It was rare that Bruce followed this tradition; he was not a showy man. But this time he rang it loud as he walked through the work stations. He stopped outside his chief engineer's office to congratulate Willem on his pivotal role in winning the deal. Willem's door was shut and Bruce didn't think to knock before he entered. It took him a while to absorb what he saw. Huddled in the far corner, Willem had his head bowed as he muttered into his hands. Bruce was quick to shut the door behind him.

"Where do you keep your medication?" he asked. It was no surprise that Willem didn't respond; there wasn't even a pause in the ranting from the corner. Bruce started the search, rifling through the desk drawers first. He found the tablets in Willem's jacket and knelt down beside him.

"How many?"

Again, there was no answer, just muttering about someone spying on him, reading his mail, reading his thoughts. Bruce read the script that was labelled to the packet.

"*Two pills, once a day* . . . here . . . take these . . . now

278

who can I call to come and help you?"

Willem was calmer by the time Regina arrived. She was pale, her bare arm protective around her brother's waist.

"He only forgets his medication because he works so hard," she said defensively.

"I know."

"Please don't fire him. He lives for this job."

Bruce's smile was reassuring. "Don't worry. Willem would have to do a lot worse than this to lose his job. He's the best damn chief engineer I've ever had."

"Thank you." Regina's eyes were bright with unshed tears of gratitude.

Willem looked dazed, the whole conversation passing over him.

"Tell Willem I don't want to see him here for a few days," Bruce said, opening the door so they could leave. "He needs a break. And when he's recovered, tell him that we won the ANZ Bank deal. That should make him feel better."

Yoshi had a spring in his step and the confidence of a man who was making life decisions with remarkable ease. Those decisions were a direct consequence of his fateful trip to Tokyo. The first one was to ask for Helen's hand in marriage. After only six weeks of dating her, many would say he was losing his senses by jumping into a formal commitment so soon. Yet it was the urgency of his feelings that made him so sure of what he was doing. Not in his wildest dreams did he ever expect to marry a Westerner but he was realising that life was full of surprises.

The next decision was regarding where he was going to live. Sydney had won the battle that had started the day he saw the old geisha in Tokyo. He no longer felt a pull from his home city. There were many factors that influenced his decision but he pinpointed the main issue as being one of space. He had a house in Sydney. He had a garden to enjoy. He had a pool to relax in. It was unthinkable to go back to a tiny one-bedroom apartment in Tokyo. He was realising that he liked having space; he liked it very much.

His last decision related to HDD. He had decided to accept Nishikawa Shacho's offer and take on the role of CEO. He was fired up with plans to bring the Australian subsidiary back to profitability and do his bit to hike up the waning share price. Yes, Nishikawa Shacho was giving him a poisoned chalice but overall it was an opportunity that couldn't be turned down. Yoshi's first action would be to get rid of Malcolm Young. Then he would address the shortcomings of the remainder of the executive team. Some would have to leave with Malcolm.

Niamh could sense the difference in Yoshi from the minute she walked into his office. It was a considerable change yet she found it frustratingly hard to pinpoint. It could have been a sense of anticipation but that seemed absurd. Whatever it was, it was unquestionably a change for the better.

"Good afternoon, Yoshi. I haven't seen you since your trip to Japan – how was it?" Niamh said as she sat down.

His office was bare of personal effects. There was little to look at but the Japanese man himself.

"It was good, thank you for enquiring."

Niamh found herself responding positively to Yoshi's formal politeness after her meeting with Lucinda. The lawyer had a disregard for basic good manners in addition to her penchant for other women's husbands.

"I want to discuss the lawsuits with you. I've run into some problems and I'm looking for ideas on how to get past them."

"I'll help in any way I can," Yoshi said. Nishikawa Shacho would call before the end of the day to discuss all threats to the Australian subsidiary's flimsy profit. The vice-president made an art of cross-examination and Yoshi would need to be fully conversant with the status of each lawsuit.

"Let me start with the easy one," Niamh suggested. "Scott Morgan's case. You know the background: he was only with us two months when we retrenched him. I think we did the wrong thing by him and I'm recommending we offer him a settlement of six months' pay."

Yoshi's eyes contracted to black slits before he asked, "Six months? Why do you suggest that? It is a very significant amount of money."

He was known to be careful with the purse-strings. For that reason, Niamh had her argument well rehearsed. "Scott had a solid well-paying job which he left to come to HDD. As I said, he joined us only two months before Black Monday. He claims he would never have left his old job had he known what would happen in HDD."

"In business, one doesn't have the benefit of hindsight," Yoshi commented as he leaned back into a less upright position.

"Maybe," she conceded before continuing the debate, "However, Scott maintains that the company would have been planning the restructure at the point he was hired. You would know, Yoshi. Is he right?"

Yoshi was an honest man. "Yes, I believe he is correct. We didn't know numbers or departments at that point. But yes, we did know there would be cutbacks."

"So it's arguable that we should have taken more care with our recruitment activities," Niamh pushed and Yoshi could only agree.

"Yes. We should have frozen all new hires until the extent of the cutbacks were identified."

With an admission of guilt under her belt, Niamh pressed home her advantage, painting a background that would pull at the heartstrings of the hardest man. "Scott has a small child. Her name is Jenny – she's only fifteen months old. Her mother isn't around to support her and her father has been out of work for almost three months now. Morally, if nothing else, we owe this family."

There was a pause before the black oriental eyes fixed on her.

"I presume you have discussed this with Lucinda?"

She was prepared for the question. It was a perfect lead-up to the second matter she wanted to discuss. "No, I haven't. Lucinda and I are at loggerheads over the Denis Greene case. I also found her handling of Helen's complaint less than satisfactory. I'm not sure I can work effectively with her any longer."

Yoshi was poker-faced as he asked, "Why were you not happy with how Lucinda dealt with Helen?"

It was a direct invitation to hang the lawyer. Niamh didn't waste the break she was being given. "She was less than sympathetic to the victim, Helen, and overly compassionate to the perpetrator, Phil. She was of the opinion that all women should be able to brush off unwelcome advances. She also threw in a derogatory remark about Helen's appearance. Let me say, I was not impressed."

Neither was Yoshi impressed, his sallow face tinged with an angry red. "That is diabolical behaviour, utterly unacceptable – and to come from our legal counsel – Lucinda, of all people, should be above reproach on such issues."

Niamh had never seen the Japanese man show such strong emotion. With Lucinda's name mud, there was no better opportunity to tell him about the Denis Greene issue. "I came here mainly to ask your opinion on the Denis Greene case."

"Yes, yes." Yoshi was visibly trying to calm down.

"There are so many things that bother me about it . . . how about I start from the beginning?" Niamh looked briefly at Yoshi and he nodded. "When we retrenched Denis, he made no indication that he wasn't happy with his termination cheque. We were understandably surprised when his solicitor contacted us the next day saying that Denis wanted to be reinstated."

"Yes, I recall that. And Bruce was adamant he didn't want Denis back," Yoshi said, trying to concentrate on what Niamh was saying.

"The basis behind Denis's complaint was that his business visa was void after we retrenched him and he was being forced to leave the country before his application for a permanent visa was processed . . . however, two reliable sources tell me that he hasn't a leg to stand on legally."

"Who?"

"The barrister, Steve Jones." She was at the very edge of her seat. "He resigned because the case had no merit."

"Who's the other source?"

"My husb –" She faltered. "My ex –" She stopped again – they weren't divorced yet. "My husband, Chris – as you know, he's a lawyer. He said that if Denis had really applied for a permanent visa then, as a matter of course, he would have been issued a bridging visa until his application was processed. Therefore, there would be no need for him to leave the country in the interim."

"Why has Lucinda let this go so far if there are no legal grounds for damages?" Yoshi's question was matter-of-fact.

"That's why I came to see you." Niamh took a steadying breath. "Lucinda says that there is no precedent to rely on and we would only have a fifty-fifty chance in court. She point-blank refuses to engage an external lawyer to give us a second opinion. She's lying, Yoshi. I *know* she's lying."

"Why would she lie? Why would she risk her own job to get Denis Greene back his?"

"I don't know – yet."

There was a pause as they both took time out to think. Niamh's eyes fixed on a Ken Duncan photograph that hung from the inside of Yoshi's door. It could only be seen when the door was shut. It was a strange place to hang such a beautiful photo of Sydney Harbour at sunset.

"That's new, isn't it?"

"Yes." His colour deepened and she felt he was embarrassed. It was clear he wasn't going to offer any further details so she flipped back to the conversation they had left.

"Did you know that Denis gained unauthorised access to the computer room at ANZ Bank last week?"

Yoshi shook his head as his thin eyebrows descended in a frown. The ANZ contract renewal was going to be announced to the analysts next week. The bank was now their most critical client in the region – the deal with them would change the trend of the share price. What the hell was Denis Greene doing in their computer room?

"His identification badge was recovered the day he left," Niamh continued. "Someone in here must have given him another one."

"Are you implying it was Lucinda?"

"Who else would it be?" Niamh was becoming more and more animated. "She wants to have him reinstated – getting him an ID badge might be the next best thing."

"How did you find out that he got into the ANZ?"

"We've had a private investigator following him for a few weeks now."

"Who is 'we'?"

"Bruce and I. Bruce has a lot of logistics parts missing

from the warehouse and they have been loaned out under Denis's name. Bruce wanted to see what he was doing with them."

"Isn't it time to stop fooling around with private investigators and to get the police involved?" Yoshi asked bluntly.

"We could get the police involved for Denis – but we have nothing on Lucinda. If we turn Denis in we may never find out what Lucinda's role was in all this."

"Then what do you suggest we do?"

"We need to watch Lucinda – sooner or later she'll show her hand."

Yoshi didn't miss a beat. "You sound very sure."

"I am. Lucinda has a huge ego. The visa story was full of holes but she operates with the belief that nobody but herself has the intelligence to realise that."

Yoshi's head moved ever so slightly to the side as he considered what Niamh was saying.

"Now, the immediate problem is that she wants Malcolm to mediate between us. She's confident she can get Malcolm to take her side and reinstate Denis."

"Don't worry about Malcolm," he said. "Leave him to me."

"Thanks." Niamh gave him a big smile. "OK, I'll leave Malcolm in your capable hands. Before I go, do you agree to offer Scott Morgan a six-month settlement?"

Yoshi gave a small smile in return. "You make it hard to say no."

It had been a long week for Niamh. Now, as she drove her

car into the garage, she felt emotionally exhausted. When she opened the door the house immediately yelled at her that Chris had been and was now gone. Permanently gone. There were telling gaps in the CD rack and bookshelf, revealing spaces on the walls. She wandered from room to room, taking a mental inventory of what he had taken. She began to feel a dead weight lift away from her. Chris, and all the negativity that went with him, was gone. And she was OK, more than OK. She was relieved.

He hadn't taken anything significant. The furniture was intact and would be split in a civilised manner at a later point. It was the personal things that were missing. Things he had brought from his single life into their married life to become theirs. Now they were his again.

Her mobile was ringing downstairs. Her first thought was that it was Chris. She ran down the stairs, pausing at the end as she tried to remember where she had put the phone. The ringing seemed to be coming from the living-room and there it was on the coffee table.

"Hello," it was Scott, "I'm just checking in. I wanted to make sure you're OK."

She was so glad it was him and not Chris.

"I'm fine," she told him. "I've been kept busy with work."

"Is Chris there now?"

"No, he's moved out. The house feels . . . naked."

"You'll feel better when you can't see what he has taken with him," he said. "Find some old photos and put them up in the open spaces. Fill the bookshelf with textbooks."

"No, I'm OK with the spaces," she said, looking around as she spoke. "I'm OK with him going. I feel . . . relieved."

"Are you sure?"

"Yes. I think it was the thought of divorce that scared me more than anything. But now that he's gone, it's not as bad as I thought. Anything would have to be better than how we were living ... Maybe I'm more like my mother than my father after all."

There was a brief silence. Jenny's babble could be heard in the background. Scott spoke first.

"I'm happy to hear that you're OK. Remember, I'm close by if you need me to come over anytime –"

"Come over now," she said, cutting him off.

"What? Now?"

"Yes, now.'

He was there in half an hour, Jenny in one arm, an enormous bag in the other. The toddler was in her pyjamas, disgruntled at the upheaval to her routine. "Do you have a bed she can sleep in?" he asked.

Niamh, bemused by the invasion, led the way to the guest room.

"Teddy," Jenny said when she saw the bed.

Scott's face registered panic as he searched the contents of the bag. "Damn, I've forgotten Teddy. I always forget something."

"Teddy," Jenny repeated, standing her ground.

"There's no way she'll sleep without it," he said. "I'll have to go back and get it. OK if I leave her with you?"

Niamh nodded and he was gone, bounding down the

stairs, the door slamming in his wake. She and Jenny sized each other up. Seconds later the door opened again and he came back up the stairs.

"It was in the car."

She watched as he tucked his daughter in and put a pillow on each side of her. "Are you sure she won't roll off?" she heard herself ask.

"She's a big girl now. She knows how to get off the bed safely – the pillows are just to stop her rolling in her sleep."

Niamh nodded as if she agreed.

Downstairs, they avoided eye contact as they sat in an awkward silence. Niamh couldn't remember why she had wanted him to come over.

"I've –"

"Do you –"

They both jumped in at the same time and stopped dead.

"You go first." Scott was chivalrous.

"OK . . ." Niamh had decided to get off the personal platform of Chris and the divorce. "I've got some good news for you. HDD will settle your claim. I have authorisation to offer you six months' pay."

"That's great!" he said, his face breaking into a smile.

"Let's have a drink – to celebrate," she suggested, getting to her feet. There was chilled wine in the fridge and she went to get a bottle.

He followed her over to the kitchen. "Thanks for arranging the settlement . . . and please thank Lucinda for me too."

The mention of Lucinda's name jolted Niamh. Was there no escape from her? "Why do you want to thank Lucinda?" she asked sharply, dropping the bottle-opener with a clatter.

"Because she called me at home. She said she wanted to make sure I was treated fairly. I presume she helped you get authorisation to make me an offer." Scott sounded defensive.

Niamh's mind kicked into gear. She felt close to a breakthrough. Something that would explain Lucinda's lies about Denis Greene's visa.

"I think you'd better tell me exactly what Lucinda said to you," she croaked, looking up into his piercing blue eyes.

"She called me," he said slowly. "It was the night I got retrenched, before my solicitor was in the picture. As I said, she wanted to make sure I was treated fairly. I got the impression she would make things easy for me if I sued."

Niamh's mind raced, trying to figure out why Lucinda hadn't mentioned the key conversation with Scott, trying to figure out why she had called Scott in the first place. Indiscriminate kindness was not part of her character make-up.

She was practically encouraging Scott to sue. There has to be a reason.

"Did she mention anything about money?" Niamh started to pace around the compact kitchen area.

"No, she just gave a vague show of support. Said she understood the financial pressures when you have a family."

There has to be a reason … it's obvious that she was the motivation behind Denis Greene's lawsuit. But she also contacted Scott. Why would she want Scott to sue?

"Have you talked to her since that night?"

"Well, I saw her at Forbes – the night she was with you – but she barely spoke to me then and I haven't seen or heard from her since." His eyes stayed with Niamh as she walked back and forth.

She called Scott out of the blue and hasn't spoken to him since . . . it can only be that she got what she wanted from the call. . . the next morning he came in to tell me he was suing. . .

Scott put his hand on her shoulder, calling a stop to her pacing. "Tell me what's wrong . . . maybe I can help."

"I'm trying to understand why Lucinda encouraged you to sue – considering she's the company's legal counsel. It certainly wasn't very ethical of her."

"That day was a bizarre one and the phone call just added to it," he said. "I would have been more suspicious if I had been thinking straight. I hardly knew her – she had no reason at all to be concerned about my welfare."

"Knowing Lucinda, she had some reason – I wish I knew what it was!"

She was hitting a brick wall, couldn't figure it out. She went back to the wine, uncorked it and poured two glasses. She was handing him his when it came to her. "You were a decoy!" she cried out. "That's it! You were just a decoy. She wanted to take the attention off Denis Greene. The more lawsuits we had, the less time we would have to think about them in detail . . ."

"Denis who?" Scott was lost.

"It's a long story."

"Jenny will be asleep until at least five am," he grinned. "Is that enough time?"

"Should be . . ."

It took a full bottle of wine to tell the Denis Greene story. She had just finished when the phone rang.

"I should answer that," she said with a grimace.

This time it was Chris and his voice was officious. "I've been around –" he began.

"I couldn't help but notice!"

"I hope you don't mind what I took – it was just my things before –"

"You can have what you want. I really don't care," she cut across him.

"Do you want to do a settlement –"

"I can't talk about that now – there's someone here."

"Who?"

"You wouldn't know him," she said, being deliberately cruel. "Why don't you call back later in the weekend?"

She hung up and went to get a second bottle of wine from the fridge.

"Was that your husband?" Scott asked after a few moments.

"Yes."

"Do you think it will be an amicable split?"

"Probably," she shrugged, filling their glasses. "Once I get over my rage about him screwing around with other women . . ." She sat down and made a start on her fresh glass of wine.

"I can't understand that. I would never do –" Scott stopped short, his expression uncertain of the territory they were entering. For the first time it occurred to Niamh that her attraction to him might be reciprocated.

"You would never do what?" she prompted, studying him carefully.

"I would never do that to any woman but least of all to *you . . .*"

Their eyes met and she could see it. This wasn't just a friendship thing for Scott, it was something more. So she took the risk and leaned over to tentatively place her lips on his.

"What is it with me kissing you all the time?" she joked, her face very close to his.

But Scott didn't find it funny. "I don't want this to be on the rebound, Niamh."

"It's not," she assured him. "It's something I've felt for a few months now."

Her lips trailed along the fair-coloured stubble of his lower face. He turned his head and his mouth covered hers, strong and sure. Their first real kiss, full of passion, full of promise. He loosened her hair from its knot and entwined his hands in the falling curls. The sensation of his big hands massaging her hair was incredibly sexy. She wanted to touch all of him and pulled him back against the couch so she could feel his full body on hers. His weight pushed her against the cushions and she heard him give a soft groan. Their kisses got deeper, more intense. His hands moved down to her shoulders, then her breasts, cupping them through her cotton shirt. Her fingers had started to open the buttons when he pulled back.

His voice husky, he said, "We can't do this, Niamh. Not when your husband has just moved out. Let's wait until we have no cloud of doubt hanging over us."

The following night Scott asked Deb to take Jenny for a sleep-over. Deb knew what she was getting into this time but still agreed. Her niece, plus baggage, were delivered and Deb resigned herself to a 5am Sunday morning rise.

Scott and Niamh went to an Italian place on Dee Why beach and spent the evening getting to know each other. He told her about his parents, who had died young, and the legal wrangling with Ann over the house.

When the main course was cleared away, he said, "Niamh, you mentioned something yesterday, something about being more like your mother than your father. What did you mean by that?"

She looked down at her hands. "I meant that I was someone who could walk away, like my mother, as opposed to someone who can't cope, like my dad. My biggest fear over the last few months was that I would be like my dad. I look like him, we have, I mean *had*, similar personalities, and I was terrified that if I broke up with Chris I'd end up like him, falling apart."

Scott left a respectful silence before he asked, "Did your dad suffer from depression? Is that why he did it?"

"No. He had his ups and downs like everybody else. Particularly in winter because he hated cold weather. But he died in the summer, the time of the year when he was always on top of the world. No, he wasn't depressed . . .

you know, he had a great sense of humour – he was a real practical joker. You had to be very careful around our house – there were booby traps everywhere."

It had been years since she had talked about him out loud, given herself the chance to remember him. It was weird this was all coming out now. She was getting divorced yet all she seemed to want to talk about was her dad. First with Tom, now with Scott.

"Do you think he was selfish?" she asked suddenly. She wanted an outsider's opinion on the question that had been nagging her for twenty years. Was her dad a sad betrayed man, as she remembered, or was he a selfish man whose suicide was the ultimate form of attention-seeking?

"Pardon?"

"Do you think Dad was selfish to kill himself? Do you think he knew what it would do to us? That we'd never get over it?"

"No, Niamh, I don't." His voice was strong and certain. He must have sensed how important his answer was. "Not from how you've described him. He was a practical joker who loved his little girls. His death was sad. It was a waste. But I don't think it was selfish."

With his validation, another age-old weight started to lift away from Niamh.

The meal finished and Scott suggested a walk along the beach. The sand was cold and damp next to the water's edge. Harmless-looking waves crashed down with surprising vigour and several times they had to race to the softer sand to avoid getting wet. They were up the far end of the beach, far away from the lights on the main strip when he said, "You seem to have a love-hate thing going with your mother."

Niamh felt suddenly ashamed that this was apparent even to Scott. "I know. I blamed her, as well as myself, for what happened to Dad. I'm only starting to understand now that I had very unrealistic expectations of her. Now I know first-hand that some marriages can't hold together – no matter how hard you try."

Chapter Eleven

Denis Greene hadn't left the house too much. He needed to be there when Lily came back to get her things. The exception had been Westpac Bank. He had gone there, just as the caller instructed him to. But he had been jumpy from the moment he left home. He could see a white Commodore in his rear-view mirror and was convinced it was following him. He made a few sudden turns; it followed. Then he ran a red light and left it behind. He knew it was probably all in his mind but he felt relieved anyway.

He had paused before entering the Westpac building in the CBD. The caller said it was the last installation;

they were going to stop at eight sites instead of the initial target of ten. So far they had done the Australian Taxation Office, the Department of Health, the Department of Defence, the Australian Federal Police and three of the four major banks. Westpac was unlucky number eight.

There would be chaos across the country when the banks and major government departments were disabled with an unknown and deadly virus.

All Denis could see inside the glass doors of Westpac was a hole, deeper than the one he was already in. With a sudden moment of clarity, he realised he was the fall guy. The caller would be long gone when the systems came crashing down and he would be the one the police would go after. He didn't know the target date for the crash but it couldn't be far away if Westpac was going to be the last site. He started to walk away from the bank, his feet instinctively moving faster until he was close to running. He needed to get out of the line of fire. That meant getting out of the country as fast as he could.

It was lunch-time two days later when he heard Lily's key in the lock. He went out to the hall to greet her. She looked surprised to see him.

"Oh . . . I thought you'd be out."

"I haven't been out much since you went," he admitted sheepishly. "I've been afraid I'd miss you and wouldn't get to talk to you, Lil."

She looked around, approval on her face. "You've kept the place clean." It told her more than words ever could.

This was the man who hadn't lifted a hand to housework since the day they married.

"I've tried hard, Lil," he admitted with a catch in his voice. He was after spending fifteen long days alone, without the company of the woman he thought he despised. In her absence he had been the perfect husband, doing all the things she had nagged him about for years. The house was immaculately clean and the engineer had finally become acquainted with the washing machine, a piece of technology he wasn't previously familiar with.

"You want some tea?" he asked her.

She nodded, walking ahead of him to the kitchen. He brewed the tea, pouring it black, too embarrassed to ask how she took it. She put one spoon of sugar in. He committed that to his memory. Lily took one sugar.

"I've booked my flight," she said, her hands cupping the mug. "I'm leaving on Friday."

His heart lurched. "I'll come with you."

"What about your lawsuit . . . all the money?" she asked with a suspicious frown.

It wasn't the time to tell her about the banks, the government departments, the virus or the caller whose threat he had been living under for the last few months. "Damn all that. I don't want to be here without you."

He meant what he said. He would tell her the full truth when they were safely back in Yorkshire. The phone rang and because Lily was closest to the hall, she went out to answer it.

"It's for you," she said, coming back into the kitchen.

"I asked who it was and he said he was from Channel Nine. Smart-ass!"

Denis took a moment to think. It was ironic that the journalist from the current affairs programme would pick now, of all times, to call him. "Someone's playing a joke, all right. Tell them I'm not here," he said and Lily obediently went back out to the hall to pass on the message.

It was a busy Monday morning for Niamh and well after lunch before she had a free moment to call Keith Longmore. Lucinda's phone call to Scott had been at the back of her mind all weekend. She was sure the lawyer had used him as a decoy but still couldn't figure out why Lucinda was going to such lengths to get Denis Greene reinstated. She realised that she wasn't getting very far by playing detective herself and it was time to call in a professional.

As usual, Keith answered his phone without delay.

"Keith – it's Niamh Lynch – I want you to take another assignment."

"What kind of assignment?" he asked hesitantly. He was usually keen for new business but had his hands full for now.

"I want you to follow Lucinda Armstrong for me – she's the internal legal counsel here."

Keith's voice didn't let on that he already knew who Lucinda Armstrong was, although he was finding it damned hard to ascertain where she lived. It was a long time before his response came. "I'm sorry. That's an assignment I cannot take on."

"Why not?"

"I can't disclose my reasons," he said.

Keith hung up and spent a few minutes wondering what was motivating Niamh to investigate the elusive Lucinda Armstrong. He was relieved that he was finally making progress on the assignment that had already been given to him by Helen. He had asked his contact at the police department to run a criminal check on Marcus Diddams. The name got a laugh but the result still came back clear. Keith had then followed up on the receptionist's comment that Marcus owned his own company. He took a punt that Marcus would have been a director of the company and he called an old friend at ASIC. His friend gave him his first big break on the case. Marcus Diddams had been the director of a company named Virus Solutions Pty Ltd. The company had gone into liquidation over three years ago.

Keith's next port of call had been the Bankruptcy Court. There he confirmed that Marcus Diddams had been declared bankrupt in January 2002. Not a good way to start the New Year! That was why Lucinda and her husband had moved house – their home in Mosman had been repossessed by the bank. Keith read through the long list of creditors that Marcus Diddams had pissed off. A venture capitalist, who had put up most of the cash to get Virus Solutions off the ground, had lost twenty million. His name was Kel Sheridan.

But Keith still didn't have an address. It was no surprise that neither Marcus Diddams nor Lucinda

Armstrong were listed in the phone book.

After Niamh's phone call, the private investigator had a brain-storming session with the smartest person he knew: his wife. She massaged his tired shoulders as they threw ideas around on how to get the address.

"You could try your contact at Telstra," she suggested.

"It's a silent number – Telstra won't give me that kind of information unless it's an emergency."

"What about the wife? Doesn't the company have an after-hours contact number for her?"

"I bet they don't have her home number but they must at least be able to contact her after hours on a mobile." Keith closed his eyes as her hands worked their magic on the knotted muscles of his lower neck.

"And this couple have a kid, don't they?"

"Yeah, Helen said he's four."

"Then it's easy," she declared. "Keep calling the mobile after hours until the kid answers. He'll be able to tell you his address. He's old enough to know it."

Keith left the wonders of his wife's hands and went upstairs to send an email.

Helen,

Husband's name is Marcus Diddams. He founded and owned a company called Virus Solutions Pty Ltd. It went bust in early 2002 and Marcus and Lucinda lost their house. No criminal record for Marcus. No other progress to report but can you send me a mobile phone number for Lucinda, please?

Best regards,

Keith

He had an early dinner and when he went back upstairs there was a reply from Helen. It contained Lucinda's mobile number. The private investigator didn't waste any time, making two carefully spaced calls to the lawyer's mobile. Each time a confident female voice answered and he pleaded a wrong number. Then he handed the phone over to his wife. She hit the jackpot on her first call.

"Hello," she said when she heard the child's voice. "What's your name?"

"Jack Diddams," the kid stated confidently.

"And what age are you?"

"I'm four." She couldn't see him but she was sure the child was holding up four fingers to demonstrate his age.

"Oh, you're a big boy then," she said, hoping the praise would prompt him to volunteer more information to the stranger on the phone. "Do you know where you live, Jack?"

"Number 29 Rover Avenue," he said, proud that he knew all the answers to the questions he was being asked.

"Jack, who are you talking to? Jack? Give me the phone." Keith's wife heard the father negotiate to take possession of the phone and she got her story ready.

"Hello. I'm doing a survey on dishwashing detergents. Would you have ten minutes to spare?"

She guessed that ten minutes would be too long for any harried father, especially on the topic of washing detergents.

"I'm on my way out," he said abruptly. "I don't have

any time to spare even if I knew the first darned thing about washing detergents."

Keith's wife was left with a dialling tone. The married couple shared a giggle.

"You're superb – you can talk your way around any-thing," Keith said with admiration.

"That's how I got you to marry me."

They laughed again before Keith asked, "What's the address?"

"29 Rover Avenue."

The mirth drained from his face. "I know that address."

"Come again?"

"I know that address," he repeated. "I was sitting out-side that house a few weeks ago, waiting for Denis Greene. And there was a young child living there. And a white-haired man."

Willem Boelhoers was back at work but still shaky from his relapse last week. Regina wanted him to take even more time off but he had insisted he come back to work. His bones rattled; his eyes were sunken into his face. He was a slave to the illness. Those pills were his only chance of freedom and he couldn't afford to forget them ever again. Regina said that Bruce Knight had been support-ive and concerned but Willem knew that sympathy for schizophrenia never lasted long. Friends and family thought they could cope with the illness of their loved one but it always unravelled at the point when the ugli-ness was fully revealed. It seemed obvious to Willem that

Bruce would soon run out of patience. It was amazing that Regina still hung in there.

The voices started, faint at first, then getting louder. Willem stood on his chair and pushed the air-vent into the ceiling. Now he could hear nearly every word and some of his questions were finally answered.

"I've talked to Malcolm – I don't know what's got into him – it seems he's not going to support me – Niamh must have got to him somehow."

"It's water under the bridge, Lucinda. We had decided to stop anyway – eight sites will do it. Denis doesn't need to get his job back now."

Willem's heart stopped. Lucinda. The man had called the woman "Lucinda". Bruce had said that he shared ducts with Helen and Lucinda. It all added up: the voices were coming from Lucinda's office. It had been the lawyer all along.

"Denis hasn't confirmed Westpac – that means we only have seven. And he hasn't been picking up his phone. He's trying to hide from us." There was a brief silence, then Lucinda spoke again. "I think we should go, Marcus. Let's just do it now, this week. Pack up our things and start the rest of our lives. It's time to cut the kite loose."

"Will seven be enough?" Marcus sounded unsure. His voice was echoing and Willem suddenly realised he was on a speakerphone. That was why the voices were making sense: for the first time he was hearing both sides of the conversation.

"You said eight was enough a few moments ago," she

reminded him, a smile in her voice.

"I know, I know. I guess you're right . . . we'll have to sort Greene out, though. He could ruin it all if he spills the beans."

"And Niamh," Lucinda added.

"Look, I don't want any unnecessary blood on our hands," Marcus cut in.

"She knows too much," Lucinda insisted. "For Christ's sake, she even has a photo of you with Greene."

"But she doesn't know it's me."

"That photo is still lethal. It's all over for us if she can unravel what's going on before we get out."

There was another short silence; Willem could feel his heart pounding away.

"I'm going to call Kel Sheridan," Lucinda said. "It's time he pitched in."

"Is that a good idea?"

"This is his damn money – we're doing all of this for him." Her voice was hard. "He's had his debt collectors threatening us for the last three years. The least he can do is use those thugs to help us close this out."

"Greene is easy. We know where he lives." Marcus was thoughtful. "It would take us time to figure out how to get to Niamh."

"Don't worry about it," Lucinda said confidently. "I know exactly where we can get to her."

"OK." Marcus was reluctantly on board. "Are you sure you don't want me to call Kel rather than you?"

"No, I'll do it. You just book the flights and concentrate on the packing. Don't forget some toys for Jack. He'll need familiar things to play with when we get there."

The call ended and Willem took a long steadying breath before he came down off the chair. Niamh was in trouble. They wanted to shut her up. He needed to do something; he couldn't ignore the voices any longer.

He went home early, unable to concentrate on work after what he had heard. He sat in his room desperately trying to decide what to do. He was very aware that with his history he would find it hard to make anyone believe that this time there really was a conspiracy. And people would find it even more unbelievable that the internal legal counsel, Lucinda Armstrong, was orchestrating the whole thing.

Downstairs Regina's family were watching TV together. Willem didn't watch television. For a long time he had believed the presenters were giving him a message. Saying one thing to him while the others were hearing something else. It was overwhelming, terrifying. It was sometime later he learned that this was a classic sign of schizophrenia. Once he gained an insight into his illness, his life returned to a diluted version of normal. He led a quiet lifestyle, tried not to drink too much, tried not to let himself get too tired, and set his day around the routine of taking the pills. Once he was disciplined, everything was OK. But, despite being well, he never went back to watching TV. He was still terrified that the presenter's eyes would fix eerily on him and would command him to do something evil.

His family had migrated from Holland when he was in his teens. His illness had raised its ugly head at his first year of university. The psychiatrist said it was a common time to develop schizophrenia: university could be a scary and demanding place. The psychiatrist also explained that men were generally not very good at living with relatives who had the illness. Their coping abilities were less advanced than females'. That explained the reaction of his father who was horrified that his son had lost interest in his appearance, ate like a bird, ranted about their mail being opened by spies and repeatedly checked the house for bugging devices. The older Dutchman didn't care what fancy term the doctors gave his son's behaviour. He was a selfish, spoiled boy who was causing nothing but distress for his family. Relations in the Boelhoers' household were at crisis point when Regina stepped in. Newly married, she rescued her brother. Allowed him to live in her new marital home. Stood by him when he was officially diagnosed and stood by him every day since.

Willem rose from the single bed he had been sitting on. He went downstairs and yelled from the hall that he was going for a drive. The family understood that Willem never came into the living-room while the TV was on. It was just the way things were. Regina shouted at him not to be too late. He knew she was afraid he would get over-tired and have another attack on the back of the last one. She would go crazy if she knew he intended to sleep in his car that night. He would face the music with her tomorrow. Right now, he had to go to Niamh. Watch over her, do his best to protect her from harm.

This time Niamh wasn't at all bemused when she opened

the door to Scott, Jenny and their inevitable baggage. She was just delighted to see them. Both of them.

"Hi." Scott kissed her. Then, to Niamh's delight, Jenny followed suit.

"Come in."

She hadn't seen Scott since Saturday night. She took a few extra moments to drink him in. A white shirt hung casually over his denims, a few buttons opened at the neck. "I've missed you," she said, moving forward to kiss him again.

"Me too ... how did your thinking time go?"

The brief time apart had been his idea. He wanted to be a hundred per cent sure that Niamh wasn't on the rebound before they went any further.

"Well . . . I tried to tell myself that I didn't care for you . . ." she wrinkled her nose, "and that you weren't right for me at all. And that I was running into the first pair of arms after the break-up with Chris. But it didn't work. Sorry . . ."

"I'm glad."

Jenny had scrambled down by now and was off on her usual mission of destruction. She was wearing a pair of dungarees that stopped well short of her ankles.

"They look a size too small for her," Niamh commented and Scott laughed.

"What's so funny?" she asked.

"When you meet Deb you'll understand," was all he said.

They followed Jenny to the kitchen where she made a beeline for the rubbish bin. Niamh's mobile rang and she answered it as she steered the toddler towards the living area.

"Niamh . . ."

"Just a minute," she said to the caller before turning to Scott. "Why don't you help yourself to a beer? I shouldn't be long."

The accented voice on the other end of the phone sounded familiar but she couldn't readily put a name to it. "Niamh, thank goodness I've got you. I was trying your office all afternoon."

"I was in a meeting. Who is this?"

"Willem. Willem Boelhoers. I'm so glad you are OK."

"What are you talking about?" Niamh asked, using sign language to tell Scott where to find the bottle-opener.

"They are going to hurt you. You need to leave your house right away, go somewhere safe."

"Willem – your medication. Have you forgotten your pills again?"

"No. I have taken the pills. This is real – you are going to be hurt – the voices said so." The urgency was making his English less clear than usual.

"Who is going to hurt me?" Niamh asked, trying to keep an unexpected amusement from sounding in her tone. She was getting divorced and a schizophrenic was warning her she was going to get hurt. *I've already been hurt*, she wanted to tell him, *but I'm OK. I've come through it.*

"One of your colleagues."

"Why?" She wasn't really concentrating on what he was saying. Otherwise she would have asked "who" again instead of "why".

"I don't know."

"Willem," she said gently, "you seem to be having one of your attacks. Please call Regina –"

"I'm not hallucinating. Please believe me, you're in grave danger," he pleaded.

"OK," she conceded only because she couldn't seem to get through to him. "I promise to be careful. But you have to promise me that you'll tell Regina and your psychiatrist about this."

Willem did promise but his voice lacked conviction. Niamh hung up with the disappointed acknowledgement that she'd have to tell Bruce about the call. It seemed that Willem's problems were now starting to impact on his work relationships and that wasn't an acceptable situation.

Scott put Jenny to bed about an hour later. When she was settled, he came downstairs and got two more bottles of beer from the fridge. Sitting on the sofa, he handed Niamh a beer and then took her free hand in his. They were sitting very close, their arms and thighs fusing. Every part of her was aware of him as they drank their beers in silence. The noise from outside was an unwelcome interruption.

"What's that?" she whispered.

"What?"

"I heard something outside." She crept over to the window, pulling back the drapes. She could see nothing through the darkness but she listened hard. There was another sound, a minor sound, but they both heard it. Scott joined her at the window just as the view to the courtyard was suddenly illuminated.

"The lights have sensors. There's someone out there . . ."

She unlocked the back door and he followed her outside. Footsteps echoed down the side of the house.

"Who's there?" he called out. They both heard the side gate slam shut but there was no one around by the time they got to the front of the house. Niamh went out on the street, looking up and down. There were a few joggers and a man walking his dog.

"Don't worry. It's probably some kids," Scott said, coming up behind her.

"There are no children living on this street," she replied, looking around the front garden more carefully. The shadows at the side of the porch seemed unusually black. She went closer. There was someone there, flattened up against the wall. Someone with silver-framed glasses.

"Willem!"

"I'm sorry, I'm sorry," he said, his head hanging as he stepped out so he could be fully seen.

"What on *earth* are you doing? You've frightened the life out of me . . ."

"I was watching the house. I wanted to make sure you were safe."

"I told you I was OK on the phone!"

"That was over an hour ago – they could come and get you anytime."

Scott, who had been watching silently, joined in the bizarre conversation. "Who could come and get her?"

Willem faltered. If he said he had heard Lucinda, there would be no going back. And it would be the lawyer's word against his. "The voices," he replied weakly.

"Come inside, Willem," Niamh said, taking his arm. "And let me call Regina to come and get you."

"No. I have the car – I can drive myself home. I can go now I know Scott is here and you'll be safe."

He freed his arm from her grasp and walked up the drive. Niamh couldn't think of anything else to say to make him turn back. His car was parked down the street and they waited until they heard its engine roar to life. Then they went back inside and deadlocked the doors.

"Is there any truth in what he's saying? Could you be in danger?" Scott asked with a concerned frown.

"No. Willem has schizophrenia. Conspiracies and voices are all part of the illness. I wish I had Regina's phone number . . . I just hope he gets home OK."

They went back to the living area and resumed holding hands as they drank their beers. There was a long silence, one in which all her attention was focussed on the stroke of his thumb against her palm. Slowly, his thumb moved upwards until it was circling the back of her wrist. Anticipation filled her body.

"This time I don't want to stop at kissing," he whispered as he took the bottle of beer from her loose grasp to put it on the floor.

"Neither do I."

He kissed her forehead, her eyes, every inch of her face. "Have I told you I love those freckles?"

She shook her head.

"And your dimples . . . here and here." His lips brushed them in turn.

Again, she shook her head. Words were stuck somewhere in her throat.

He slipped her T-shirt up over her head and kissed along the line of her bra. "So beautiful," he muttered into her skin as he undid the clasp. The bra fell away, her breasts were exposed to his touch. His fingers grazed across the nipples and caressed the soft skin along the sides. "So beautiful."

The slow confidence of each touch, each whispered word, was making Niamh want him all the more. Her fingers were rushed as they unbuttoned his shirt. She pulled it down over his shoulders to reveal his chest, the same berry-brown as his face, broad and smooth. She ran her hands down his bare back, feeling the strength of him, pulling him closer so their skin touched. Then they kissed, the same deep intense kisses as before but this time with the added erotica of bare skin. His mouth was hot on hers as one hand finally left her breasts to run along the waistband of her jeans. She gasped when it slid inside and she felt its coolness against her warmth. Massaging, massaging, taking her to the very brink. The need to lie against him fully naked was overwhelming.

"Scott, wait . . ."

He stopped to allow her to remove both pairs of jeans, the denim falling to a pool on the ground. Her hand touched him and he moaned into her neck. She brought him to the very brink, just as he had done with her.

"You ready for this?" he mumbled, his voice thick with

314

desire.

She nodded – she had never felt so ready. There was nothing slow then, only a crazy urgency as she met each thrust of his body, their climax inevitable.

Much later on they moved from the sofa to the bed and she dreamt of her dad. But this time it was different. His face wasn't black and starved of oxygen. It was happy, laughing. And he wasn't in the dark, dingy garage. He was at the beach. There was no seaweed, evidence in itself that it wasn't Youghal. It took a while before Niamh could see it was Manly. Her dad was in Manly.

"The water's beautiful. Come in," he called to them.

"You're not real," she shouted back. "You're dead."

"What's dead?" he said with a rumbling laugh.

"Aisling!" He turned his attention to his eldest daughter. "Bring the baby in!"

"I'm not sure . . . she's only three months old . . ."

"Ah, sure, weren't you in the sea at Youghal at three months? Come on, now. Hold her up in your arms. Let her little legs trail along the water."

Aisling obeyed, wading in, wincing as the cool water lapped against her bare tummy.

Her dad held his arms out. "Here, sure, give the little one to me . . . I've been waiting all this time to hold her."

Niamh woke just as her dad took the baby into his arms.

"Dada . . . Dada . . .Dada . . ."

She could hear a baby. Aisling's baby? Here in Sydney? She shook the shreds of sleep away and realised it was Jenny. She was awake in the spare bedroom. Scott was dead to the world and didn't hear his daughter's summons. Niamh made an impulsive decision.

Let him sleep in.

Jenny was sitting up in the bed, looking unsure of herself in the unfamiliar surroundings. Niamh lifted her up. She was a solid child, made for cuddling.

"Hello, gorgeous girl," she said, kissing her soft face. Jenny looked uncertain but at least didn't scream.

"Now, what's in this huge bag your dad brought with you? We must have everything we need here, surely."

More than a little rusty, Niamh changed Jenny's nappy and carried her downstairs. Then she sat on the sofa with the child cradled in her arms as she drank her milk. Niamh thought of Aisling's baby and told herself that soon, very soon, she was going to pluck up the courage to go over to Ireland to see her new niece.

Steve Jones didn't know why he was parked outside Lucinda's house. It was a renovator's masterpiece in the exclusivity of Mosman. He had been in the house only once before, for a dinner party a few years ago. He looked at his watch. It was nine in the morning and the occupants had not yet left for work. He couldn't explain the urge that had compelled him to this spot two hours earlier. His brow furrowed when he thought of Mary and what she would think if she saw what he was doing. They were flying to Fiji tomorrow, on Adam's and Donna's recommendation. Steve had packing to do and some loose ends of work to tie up. He could ill afford to waste time like this but for some reason he couldn't leave.

At nine fifteen the garage door opened and a suburban Tarago edged out. He was just wondering what had happened to Lucinda's Mercedes when he saw that the driver was not her. He was totally shocked even while he acknowledged that it was perfectly reasonable for Lucinda to move house in the three years since she had worked for him.

A neighbour, clad in a fluffy housecoat, darted out to pick up the morning paper. Steve jumped out of his car and pounced on her anonymity.

"Lucinda Armstrong – she used to live next door to you," he began, pausing to give the embarrassed woman the opportunity to blurt out what she knew.

"Oh – she's gone – moved out years ago," she answered quickly, *Mosman Daily* in hand as she turned to go back inside.

"Do you know where she's gone?"

"No – only know that it would be somewhere less expensive than here."

Steve kept his face bland as he asked, "Why is that?"

"They went broke. The husband was involved in one of those dotcom companies. They lost it all."

"Oh . . . I didn't know that," Steve said, winded by the unexpected revelation that Lucinda's bubble had finally burst.

The neighbour forgot about what she was wearing and offered her own opinion. "She had expensive taste, the wife. She had Italian furniture in the house, imported directly. And the child only wore designer clothes."

"The baby," Steve muttered to himself, thinking of the

poignant image of Lucinda with the baby at the Christmas party all those years ago.

"He was a lovely child – I often took him myself when the husband was having a bad day – he suffered from depression after they lost the money."

"Thank you." Steve backed away and hurriedly opened the door of his car. He drove off but pulled over again just a few streets away. He couldn't think straight enough to drive. It seemed his old infatuation with Lucinda had crept back. Just like the last time, it made him want to do crazy things – like watching her house, like leaving Mary. He had more to offer Lucinda this time round. She was penniless with a depressed husband. The enigmatic, unflappable Lucinda was in an intolerable situation. Of course, she would be tempted if he offered her a way out. Poverty would not become her.

Scott pulled into the driveway of the townhouse in Dee Why. He was unstrapping Jenny from her seat when he became conscious of a moving shadow that signalled someone had come to stand behind him. He lifted Jenny out and turned around. He was face to face with Ann.

"Hello, baby" she squealed to Jenny, her arms outstretched. "It's Mummy."

Jenny got shy, turning her head into Scott's chest.

"Ever think of calling ahead?" he asked sarcastically, searching his pocket with his free hand for the house keys.

"I called a few times last night but there was no answer," she replied, her eyes noting Jenny's pyjamas.

"Looks like you had a sleepover. Did you stay at Deb's?"

"No." His response was deliberately short. He unlocked the front door and Jenny scrambled from his arms.

"She's got so big." Ann looked surprised when she saw Jenny standing upright. "Can I have a cuddle? Can you give Mummy a cuddle?"

Jenny ignored the outstretched arms for the second time, her legs unsteady as she toddled away down the hall.

"Doesn't she know who I am? Haven't you shown her photos of her mummy?" Ann asked, clearly disappointed with Jenny's lack of interest.

"Why should I do that?" Scott turned on his estranged wife. "I'm not going to do your parenting for you. If you can't be bothered to see or call your child, don't expect me to create a presence for you."

Scott went inside and Ann paused for a moment before following him through the open door.

"It looks so small," she said, sizing up the living area. "Hard to believe that a place as small as this can be worth so much. I guess that's the craziness of the Sydney real estate market."

If she was trying to make conversation, she had chosen a bad topic: the house, the subject of all those letters from her solicitor.

"Is that why you're here? The house?"

"Of course not – I came to see Jenny," she said, looking over at her daughter who was busy pulling books from the bookshelf. "Do you let her do that?"

"I let her go wild." Scott enjoyed being sarcastic. "There's

319

absolutely no discipline in this house, is there, Jen?"

Jenny looked up from the books to say, "Yeah."

"She can speak?" Ann looked overcome.

"Just a few words – the usual stuff for kids her age."

Ann went over to her child, crouching down beside her. "Hello, Jenny. It's *Mama*. I'm your *Mama*. Can you say *Mama*?"

"Dada," Jenny responded, pointing at Scott and ignoring her mother's prompts. Scott laughed out loud.

Ann straightened, giving him an angry glare. "Is that how it's going to be, Scott? Are you going to use our child to score points off me?"

"Don't expect to come back here after nine months and get the red carpet," he reprimanded her, his laughter gone.

"I have a right to see Jenny . . ." Her face reddened.

"I'm not going to stop that," he countered. "Just don't expect a warm and fuzzy reception from either her or me after nine months of no contact."

Jenny was at the books, laughing with glee as each one hit the floor.

Ann walked towards Scott. "I think I had post-natal depression. I think that's why I had to get away."

The admission wasn't made with sincerity and Scott couldn't find any sympathy for her. "You should have phoned us from Malaysia when you figured that out. Was that at the start of the nine months or the end?"

She didn't answer the question and abandoned the whole topic of post-natal depression with amazing speed. "We need to come to an agreement about the house," she said, her voice low. "Our application for divorce will be filed soon. It's better to have the house sorted out on an amicable basis before –"

"It's simple, Ann," he cut her off. "I don't have the money to pay you 50 per cent. In fact, I don't think you *deserve* 50 per cent as Jenny isn't living with you."

"You could sell to get the money –" she started to say.

"I'm *not* selling!" he shouted. "This is Jenny's *home*! She needs security, familiarity. This house is not being sold, got that?"

"Don't fly off the handle in front of her," Ann hissed, looking back at Jenny. The child was sitting amongst all the books, a large hardback open on her knees as she looked up at her parents.

"Look, I think it's time for you to go now . . ." Scott put his hand on the small of Ann's back to usher her towards the hall.

"I want this to be amicable," she protested.

"There's no chance of that if you persist with this idea of getting half of the house," he responded as he opened the door. "Unless you drop that idea, we're going to end up in court."

"Well, then," she stepped away from the arc of his arm, "why don't you tell me what *you* think is fair?"

"My lawyer has already told yours what my position is. Don't you read his letters?" Scott was mocking as he looked down at the woman who used to be his wife. He felt nothing for her. All he wanted was for her to go away so he could think over last night with Niamh.

"When can I see Jenny again?" Ann's mouth was in a thin line of frustration.

"Why don't you send one of those nice letters from your lawyer and we'll work it out from there . . ."

Niamh didn't see the black Honda outside her house the next morning. She reversed out of the garage and waited in the drive for a break in the stream of cars. When she was part of the heavy traffic her thoughts settled on Scott. What was happening with them? Was it love? Or was it, as he feared, on the rebound? So much had happened in the last few weeks it was hard to put a permanent label to anything. All she knew was that it felt good, it felt right. And the dream about her dad, where he was laughing on Manly beach, seemed like a good omen for a new start.

She flew up the bus lane and wasn't aware that the black Honda got left behind. She was thinking about Willem now. The hunted look in his eyes, his paranoia that someone was going to hurt her, the voices in his head. She would have to discuss it with Bruce. They couldn't allow Willem to prowl outside people's houses, no matter how good he was at his job.

She turned right inside the entrance to the carpark and automatically looked along the executive reserved parking for Lucinda's car. The lawyer wasn't in yet. Niamh parked and applied some lipstick before getting out of the car.

The lift had just arrived when she saw Bruce pull up in his four-wheel drive. She held it for him. As it was only the two of them, she took the opportunity to discuss what happened with Willem the night before. "I think Willem is starting to lose the plot."

Bruce was taken aback. "What do you mean?"

"He called me at home last night. He was saying that someone was trying to hurt me – later on I found him outside my house."

Bruce's frown was as fast as it was ferocious. "What was he doing at your house?"

"He was going on about voices. Voices that were telling him I was in grave danger." Niamh couldn't help a wry smile as she recalled their weird conversation.

"He may not be as mad as you think," Bruce said unexpectedly, his frown easing to a look of concentration as the lift arrived at the executive floor. "I've heard the voices," he confessed as he stood back to let Niamh out first.

"Not you as well," Niamh giggled as they walked side by side down the corridor.

"I'm being serious. They're coming from his air-conditioning duct – I heard them."

They stopped walking. They had reached Bruce's office.

"Are you saying that there's a chance these voices are real and not in Willem's head?" Niamh asked.

"Yes, definitely. I heard them loud and clear."

"Do you know who it is?"

"Willem's office shares ducts with Lucinda and Helen. It must be one of them . . ."

He trailed off but Niamh's mind sprinted ahead at the mention of Lucinda's name. Everything seemed to come back to the lawyer.

"Willem could hear what's being said in another

office?"

"The sonic lining is missing from the ducts," Bruce muttered. "I saw it for myself."

"Willem seems to think I'm in danger," she said thoughtfully. "I wonder what he heard. Maybe I've done him an injustice, assuming that his odd behaviour was related to his illness. I'll see if I can catch up with him later to talk to him properly."

Bruce seemed to be lost for words so she wished him a good morning and continued on to her own office.

Helen was locking her car when she saw a figure emerge from the shadows of the carpark.

"Phil . . ." Her heart pounded but she tried not to let fear sound in her voice. "How the hell did you get in here?"

"You won't talk to me on the phone – I had no choice." As he got closer she noticed a cold ominous sweat on his forehead.

"I have nothing to say to you," she said, looking past his broad frame to see if there was anyone else around.

"But *I* have something to say to *you* – I want you to realise what you've done to me – you've ruined me."

"You ruined yourself," she snapped. "You don't have me to thank for that."

"You're a stupid bitch – I did nothing to you."

"You harassed me – *four* times!" Helen corrected him, taking another quick look to see if there was anyone around.

"For fuck's sake – it was hardly anything. You must

be a real prude to say you freak out like this when a man touches you."

He advanced further and Helen was trapped against the car. There was no way out. "I don't want you anywhere near me – get away from me – you make my skin crawl!" Her voice rose in desperation.

But Phil wasn't listening. "I could kill you – I could really kill you for what you've done!"

Helen's mobile rang and his words were suspended in the air as they stared at each other. She plunged her hand into her bag and luckily it made contact with the phone, her lifeline.

"Keith . . . no, I'm in the carpark . . . I'll be in my office in a few minutes . . . can you hold a moment?"

She took the phone down from her ear but held it close to her chest. Keith being on the line was her only insurance she would get out of this situation unharmed. "I promised you something, Phil, that day in your office. I said I would tell your wife. But I haven't. If you don't leave me alone I'll do it. I'll tell her. Do you understand?"

"Don't threaten me!"

"I'm not threatening you, I'm *telling* you. If you think you're ruined *now*, what will it be like if she finds out why you lost your job? I bet you haven't told her the real reason you left HDD . . . don't make me do it for you . . ."

Phil backed off a little; he understood blackmail.

"Get out of here!" Helen pointed to the exit in case he didn't comprehend. "This is your last chance. Phone or harass me again *in any way* and I'll call your wife . . ."

She took a deep calming breath before putting the mobile phone back to her ear. "Yes, Keith, everything's OK."

"It doesn't sound OK," the private investigator said at the other end. "What's going on there?"

"Just stay on the line – call for help if I drop off or anything."

Only when she saw Phil walking away did she call the lift. For once, it came promptly. "I'm OK now, Keith," she said when she was safely inside. "Why don't you call me back later, OK?"

The lift arrived at the second floor and Helen got out. She made a beeline for Yoshi's office and breathed a sigh of relief when she saw him behind his desk. He automatically rose to his feet when he saw the tears welling in her hazel eyes.

"Helen? Why are you crying? What's happened?" He came around the desk to take her in his arms.

"It's Phil," her voice was muffled against his shoulder, "He cornered me in the carpark . . . he said he could kill me."

"Phil? You mean Phil Davis?" Yoshi looked confused even when Helen nodded. "What was he doing in the carpark? It's weeks since he left here."

Helen stepped out of his embrace and sat on one of his visitors' seats. "There's something I've kept from you. Phil's been calling me all the time . . . threatening me, saying I've ruined his life."

"Why didn't you tell me?"

"I thought I could handle it," she shrugged.

"I'm disappointed in you." Yoshi was clearly annoyed. "We're meant to have no secrets."

"I'm sorry," she said again but saw that he was still very displeased.

"How could you not tell me this was happening?" he repeated and for the first time in their short courtship, Helen lost her temper with him.

"Look, I said I was sorry. But I'm the one who should be upset, not you. And your role is to comfort me, not to make me feel even worse." She walked out and slammed his door shut for good measure.

It was much later that day when Keith Longmore called Helen back. "Everything OK now?" he asked.

Helen had just sat down to dinner with Yoshi and her mother. It was the old lady's first day home from hospital. She was making up for a year where she had spoken very little as she fired question after question at Yoshi. He fielded the onslaught well enough and threw some questions of his own back.

"Yes, thank you for calling when you did this morning," Helen said, vacating the seat she had just sat in. The old lady barely glanced in her daughter's direction before she dived back into the third degree.

"I was ringing this morning to tell you that there appears to be a connection between Lucinda Armstrong and Denis Greene," Keith explained.

"What? How can that be?"

"I saw Denis going into Lucinda's house last week. Only thing was, I didn't know whose house it was at the time."

Helen was out on the balcony now, looking down on Darling Harbour. "I don't know much about the case Denis is bringing against the company – I believe that he wants his job back so he can stay in Australia ..."

"By all accounts he certainly appears to be desperate to get his job back," Keith agreed. "The question is if Lucinda is helping him to get reinstated?"

"Heavens, that's a rather abstract question. You're the private detective – how will you go about getting an answer?"

Keith allowed himself a pause to gather his thoughts. Was this the time to break a lifetime habit of discretion? "Niamh Lynch might know something."

"Niamh? How?"

"Because she also asked me to follow Lucinda. She must suspect something too. We could see if she has another angle on this."

"I'll ask her about it tomorrow morning," Helen promised, turning to go back inside.

Keith spoke quickly, not wanting Helen to go away just yet. "I've spent the last two nights mulling over the Denis and Lucinda connection, trying to work it out . . . Denis, he's a software engineer, right?"

"Yes, I think his speciality is operating systems of large mainframes," Helen replied. She had worked in the company a long time and could match a role description to most names.

"Like the mainframe at ANZ Bank?" asked Keith.

"I suppose so." Helen could see through the balcony

doors that Yoshi was still in deep conversation with her mother. However, she didn't want to be rude by being gone too long.

"Denis got into the computer room at ANZ Bank a few weeks ago," Keith explained, once again breaking his golden rule on confidentiality. But he didn't think Niamh or Bruce would mind the details of their investigation being disclosed to Helen.

"You mean after the date he left our employment?"

"Yes."

"What on earth was he doing there?"

"That's what I've been thinking about all night – and I think Marcus Diddams might know."

Helen got distracted when she saw Yoshi leave the table. "Marcus . . . you mean Lucinda's husband?"

"Yes. I think I told you already that his company went bust in 2002 – it was called Virus Solutions – they wrote, manufactured and marketed anti-virus software."

"What's this got to do with Denis?" Helen asked, giving Yoshi a tentative smile as he stepped out on the balcony.

"Marcus was the brains behind the company – he developed the software himself," Keith said with a certain amount of awe in his voice. "Consider this for a scenario – what if Marcus was writing some software program and using Denis to install it in ANZ?"

"Dear God – don't even *say* that." Alarm shot through Helen. The ANZ contract was the most important one in the South Pacific. It was going to be announced to the analysts tomorrow.

"Don't panic yet," Keith warned. "My imagination can tend to run away with me – this is just a theory at this point."

"What do we do?"

"Why don't you talk to Niamh as we planned? She obviously suspects something. If we put our heads together we might get somewhere."

"OK. I'll ask her about Lucinda in the morning – and I'll call you as soon as I've spoken to her," Helen promised again and hung up.

"Is everything OK?" Yoshi asked.

"Yes."

"Your dinner is getting cold."

"I'm sorry. It was an important call."

"You're not keeping any more secrets from me, are you?" he asked with a wry smile.

"Well . . ." she hesitated. "I do need to update you on something but it can keep until the morning."

"Not another lunatic stalking you?"

"No," she smiled.

They were both a little wary after the scene in his office that morning. It was the first time they had exchanged angry words, their first argument.

"You seem to be getting along famously with my mother," Helen commented.

"I was telling her who would come from Tokyo for the wedding. She wanted to know if it would be appropriate to organise their accommodation. She heard of some weddings in Bourke where visiting guests . . ."

Helen laughed out loud as Yoshi related the rest of the

conversation. It seemed her mother had claimed him as a kindred spirit: they were two foreigners battling life in a big city far away from their homes. Tokyo and Bourke were hardly in the same league but there was no point in telling her that.

"Who *is* coming from Japan?" Helen asked, bemused that she didn't know. They had been dating less than two months and she was aware there were some things she didn't yet know about her future husband. But they had explored all the important issues of life: family, religion, politics, lifestyle. She wasn't worried if there were a few things they hadn't covered yet. But she should have told him about Phil, she acknowledged that.

"There's my immediate family, my parents and my sister," he replied. "And I will invite some people from the office in Tokyo – Nishikawa Shacho and maybe a few other colleagues. We shouldn't need to worry about their accommodation – it's not common to provide that in Japan . . ."

"Well, we have to make sure we do whatever they do in Japan," Helen mimicked her mother.

Old Mrs Barnes had been gobsmacked when she first met Yoshi at the hospital. A Japanese man was the last person she expected to see come through the door and, had Helen not risen to kiss his cheek, she would have assumed he was one of the hospital staff. Yet the old lady had adapted remarkably once she got over her astonishment. Yoshi had stayed in the hospital room for over an hour as she hounded him for details of his mother country, fascinated with his answers. She returned the favour by telling him all about Bourke.

Tonight they had told her about the wedding and the large house they were planning to buy where she could have her own living-room. Understandably, she was over the moon.

Marcus was very tired. It had been a long and stressful flight. Jack didn't sleep well and was uncharacteristically troublesome. He kept asking where his mother was.

It was the early hours of the morning when they got to Paris and pitch black even though dawn wasn't far away. With the sudden rush to get out of Sydney, Marcus had forgotten to put winter coats in their hand luggage. Some parts of the airport were blasting with heat and others were cold to the bone.

Their luggage was slow to appear on the carousel. There was one bag missing, the one that had Jack's toys. Marcus was queuing in the line for missing baggage when he realised he was taking an enormous and unnecessary risk. They left the queue and went outside to get a taxi. Jack would be disappointed about his toys but there was nothing that could be realistically done to get them back without jeopardising their new life.

They checked into a popular hotel in the Marais area. It was booked under their new surname, Ryan. Marcus had explained to Jack a few times already that there would be no more Diddams and no more Armstrong. Everyone in the family had the same surname now. Wasn't that good? Jack wasn't convinced it was a good thing at all. He had just learnt to say his old surname properly and he didn't want to change. He wasn't overly enamoured with Paris either. It was cold and dark. Jack wanted to go home. And he wanted his mother.

This was Marcus's second time in Paris. He had been in the autumn of last year but hadn't stopped to enjoy the charm of the city. His main purpose had been to set up an account with Banque de France. When that was done he had travelled to six other European cities and set up several bank accounts in each. Marcus Ryan made a modest deposit in each new bank account and the tellers barely glanced at his fake passport. Since then he had made a few more deposits. This was done remotely from Australia but who was to know that? Lucinda had worked out that part of their plan. If the bank accounts existed for some time and there was normal transactional activity, then it wouldn't stand out as much when a large deposit was made.

As Marcus unpacked their bags his thoughts were with his beautiful wife. He hated leaving her behind and would be on edge until they were reunited. There was too much going on in Sydney. Even though Lucinda would lie low while she waited for her flight, there was an undeniable risk she wouldn't get out on time. It was a pity they couldn't all get on the same flight but they had booked the tickets at very short notice. He looked at his watch, working back to Australian time. Greene and the HR woman would be dealt with soon, if not already. He felt no remorse for Greene. He had found him to be a greedy loud-mouthed man. It was Lucinda who had picked him. Without his knowing, she had matched up his qualifications and personality with their requirements. She had been confident that he would say "yes" when he was approached. But Greene never knew that Lucinda was the voice at the end of the phone. He had met Marcus a few times but didn't know that Lucinda was his wife. Marcus felt no remorse for the HR woman either. He had never met her. She was nothing to him.

They had travelled light and the unpacking was finished in no time. Marcus got his mobile phone and sat on the bed to type a text message to Kel Sheridan, the venture capitalist who wanted his money back.

$20m will be in your bank account by close of business tomorrow.

Marcus looked at the message for a few moments before pressing send. Twenty million for Kel Sheridan. Ten million left over. That was all they needed. It was the price of freedom. It was the price of a new life without Kel Sheridan and all the other creditors who would stalk them for as long as they lived in Australia.

They were going to spend a week or so in Paris before travelling around to the other European cities. Their schedule was flexible; they were in no hurry to settle. This was the holiday they had planned and waited for. It was going to be in the Northern Hemisphere's spring rather than summer but what did that matter?

Room service delivered some toasted sandwiches which Marcus and Jack devoured. The child started to get sleepy and they curled up together on the bed. They didn't see the sun when it came up. They slept straight through the day and it was dusk when they woke.

Marcus rugged Jack up and they went out into the cold Parisian evening. They searched the locality for a suitable internet café. They needed somewhere that would be open in the early hours of the morning. They needed somewhere that would be busy, where they wouldn't be noticed. They needed somewhere with fax facilities.

Chapter Twelve

Denis was on his way to the airport, the traffic moving well on this glorious Friday morning. The top of the red Saab was down and Lily's blonde-grey hair blew in the wind. Denis slowed to stop at the lights of a major junction.

"I need to call that lawyer," he told his wife. "Can you hand me the mobile?"

Paul Jacobsen's number was stored in the phone and Denis called it up. The lawyer answered after the first ring.

"I'm pulling out," Denis said, forgetting to introduce himself.

"Pardon?" The lawyer sounded confused.

"It's Denis Greene," he backtracked. "I'm going back to Yorkshire with my wife."

Lily's eyes met his and she smiled. She was truly delighted to be on her way back home.

Paul Jacobsen immediately tried to sway his client. "But our submission to the Industrial Relations Commission is ready to go. All we need is Lily's statutory declaration."

"Lily won't be signing any declaration," Denis said firmly. "We're going back to Yorkshire for good. Lily's mother is ailing."

Lily's mother was disappointingly healthy but Denis felt the lie was necessary to make his decision sound more believable to the lawyer. Lily didn't seem to mind the fib.

The car behind him honked; the lights had changed to green. "I have to go now," he said, putting the Saab into gear and handing the mobile over to Lily.

"Switch it off, Lil," he told her. "We'll dump it at the airport. It doesn't have international roaming – it won't work over in England."

Denis had arranged to meet a friend at the Qantas terminal to hand over the keys to the Saab. His friend would sell it and keep half the cash for his trouble. The house was more straightforward. They had handed the keys back to the landlord that morning. They would lose their bond due to the lack of notice but Denis didn't care – it was a small price to pay.

Lily couldn't stop smiling and now he was smiling himself as well. He was getting out, starting anew. He had a second chance, not just with Lily, with everything. This time he wasn't going to blow it. He became conscious of a motorbike in the lane to his right. It was very close, the passenger level with Denis and holding something white in his hand. Denis took his eyes off the road to have a better look. It was a gun nozzle, draped with a white cloth and it was aimed right at him.

"*Fuck!*" He braked hard and the bullet missed the side-window, slicing across the windscreen instead. The glass caved in and Lily screamed, shielding her face. There was a smell of burning rubber as the car behind reacted to the sudden slowing in pace. The motorbike still hovered, disadvantaged by being slightly ahead of the Saab. The passenger turned around; his beanie covered his head to eye level. Denis realised the gunman was about to have another go. He yanked the steering wheel to the left, lucky enough to find a gap in the traffic of that lane. A second shot sounded just as he made it across to the hard shoulder. He pulled Lily down below the dash while the Saab was still coming to a stop. He prayed for the first time in his adult life. Someone heard him and the bullet didn't hit its target.

He was shaking uncontrollably. Cars whizzed past.

"Why aren't they stopping?" Lily screamed, too scared to come up above the dash level. "Why won't someone help us?"

"It's OK. We're OK." He tried to calm her but didn't explain that anybody who had seen anything would have been caught up in the flow of the traffic. And the motorbike was gone; it would have been easy for it to get away.

"Call the police. We must call the police," she sobbed. There was blood on her hand as she tried to reach for the mobile.

"No, Lil." Denis grasped her hand, forcing it to be still. "We'd miss the plane. We can't miss that plane."

He brushed the fragments of glass off her clothes and squeezed her hand with his until she was ready to sit upright.

"See, it's all right." He indicated the flowing traffic with his free hand. "Now, I want to get off this hard shoulder. It's not safe to be parked here. OK?"

It was only when she gave him an uncertain nod that he finally let go of her hand. She studied the minor cuts on her fingers. He could feel stinging skin on his face and assumed he had some cuts too. His knee wobbled as he released the clutch and rejoined the traffic. He was angry with himself. The motorbike must have followed him all the way from the house and he should have been more vigilant. This was the caller's way of terminating their relationship after the failed Westpac installation. It was obvious now that today was the day of the crash. The digital clock on the dashboard told him their flight was leaving in two hours. They had to get on that plane to London. It was their only chance to walk away from this terrible mess.

When Niamh pulled out of her drive, she didn't notice that the black Honda was waiting for her again. It stayed close, never more than a few cars back. When she finally reached the bus lane she was able to zoom past the stationary cars in the next lane. The black Honda hesitated for a moment. It quickly became clear to the driver that he would lose her for the second morning in a row if he didn't also use the bus lane. So he changed lanes, pressing down heavily on the accelerator. It was too late when he realised that Niamh's car was stopped up ahead next to the flashing blue light of a police car. She was being booked and Willem Boelhoers followed her straight into the police trap, doing an unforgivable seventy kilometres over the speed limit.

Niamh finally pulled into the HDD carpark after earning three demerit points and a two-hundred-dollar fine. She wasn't too upset: she still felt the convenience of using the bus lane was well worth the fine. She was making her way through the executive area when Bruce called out her name from the door of his office.

"Niamh . . . can I have a minute?" He looked even more solemn than usual. She changed direction from her own office and followed him inside his. He shut the door and they both remained standing.

"I need to tell you something." His crinkled face was ill at ease. "It might explain why Willem thinks you're in danger."

He opened the top drawer of his desk to take out a distinctive yellow envelope. Holding it up, he asked, "Does this look familiar?"

Niamh felt weak at the sight of it and looked around for the nearest chair.

"Where did you get it?" she asked, her voice shaking as she sat down. "Whose is it?"

"It's mine," said Bruce quietly.

"But who . . . has someone been taking them?"

Then something in his expression told her the truth.

341

Bruce, of all people, was the Joker. She couldn't believe it. Bruce. Her life seemed like a play where actors had parts that bore no similarity to the people she knew and trusted.

"So you sent the notes," she said flatly. "Why?"

His response was simple. "Because I saw what your husband did at the Christmas party."

A red tinge crept up under the tan on Niamh's face. She could kill Chris for humiliating her like this. "Why didn't you just come out and tell me what you saw? Why did you fool around sending stupid cryptic notes?"

"I'm sorry. I didn't intend to cause you hurt." He paused, seemingly overcome with emotion himself. "My wife cheated on me for years. All our friends knew but I was the last one to find out. I didn't want the same thing to happen to you. The notes were an indirect way of making you question your husband's fidelity. I thought you had the right to know what happened at the party – I just wasn't sure how to tell you. It's a hard thing to put into words – that's why my friends never told me about my wife."

"What did you see? What were they doing?" she asked, holding her breath for the answer.

"They were kissing."

Niamh studied the sad man who had lost everything in his divorce. There was no question that his intentions were honourable despite his misguided means of putting them into action. "I should thank you, Bruce. Your notes did the job. Chris and I have split up."

A sheet of remorse passed over the older man's face but

Niamh said, "Don't be sorry. You did me a favour. Lucinda wasn't the first."

"Lucinda?" Bruce looked confused. "No, it wasn't Lucinda. It was Helen."

Dazed with shock, Niamh shook her head in disbelief. "Chris was with Helen? Kissing her? *Are you sure?*"

"Yes." Bruce sat down heavily. He stared at his own trembling hands. It was as if Chris had been unfaithful to him rather than Niamh.

"God, this just gets worse and worse. Why would Helen do this to me? I could understand Lucinda . . . but Helen?"

Bruce didn't respond; he looked shaken. Niamh had a thousand questions about what he had seen that night but she put them to one side. It was her problem, not his. And she couldn't bear to see the man in such distress.

"I assume from all this you think that Helen wants to harm me?" she said after a while.

He looked up from his hands. "I had the simplistic theory that she might want you out of the picture so she could have Chris all to herself."

"Commendable theory," Niamh acknowledged with a weak smile, "but knowing them both, I think it was a genuine one-night stand. They're like chalk and cheese . . ."

"OK. I guess it was a little far-fetched," Bruce admitted sheepishly. "Assuming Willem is right, who do *you* think is trying to harm you?"

"You said yesterday that Willem also shares a duct with Lucinda?"

"Yes."

"That's where I'd put my money – Lucinda."

"Why?"

"Because I know too much," Niamh said, getting to her feet. "I'm getting closer and closer to unravelling her motives. Problem is that neither she nor Willem came to work yesterday and I don't know how I'm going to get to the bottom of this if I can't talk to them."

"Willem called in sick yesterday morning." Bruce was looking even more worried. "And I haven't yet seen him this morning."

Niamh walked over to the door but paused before opening it.

"I'll keep an eye out for him," she said. "But will you be OK, Bruce?"

He was back to looking at his hands. "Yes, I'll be fine. This has just brought back some unpleasant memories of my own wife."

Niamh still lingered at the door. "Have I ever told you that you remind me of my dad?"

"No."

"Don't end up like him, Bruce," she said gently. "Don't let the grief consume you so much you don't want to live any more."

Helen was reading the *Sydney Morning Herald* and enjoying her morning coffee when she heard her door click shut. She looked up to see Yoshi and almost dropped the cup of coffee with shock. His right eye was a reddish purple, the swollen lid half shut.

"My God! What happened to you?"

"I went to see Phil after our dinner last night," he replied with a casual shrug.

"You did *what?*" she spluttered. "Are you crazy? He's twice the size of you!"

"But not half as fit as me," he grinned as he pointed to his busted eye. "This is nothing next to what I did to him."

"But why?" Helen looked at his face in dismay. "Why did you go looking for trouble?"

"I wanted to reinforce what you said to him – to keep away or else. He took the first punch, caught me by surprise. But I sorted him out fairly quickly once it became a purely physical argument."

"Have you put ice on it? Did you go to a hospital?"

"There's no need to fuss, Helen. It will heal soon enough."

She shook her head in amazement. "You're full of surprises, Yoshi."

"I have my secrets too," he smiled, tongue-in-cheek. "I used to do kick-boxing in my youth."

As Helen gazed at him wordlessly, he sat down and said, "Now, you have something else to tell me. Remember? Last night on the balcony? That phone call?"

"Oh, yes." She found her voice. "It's a long story, one that you might find a little hard to take in."

"I heard the end of your conversation last night," he prompted. "You mentioned Lucinda's name."

"Yes. I was talking to a man called Keith Longmore. He's a private investigator – he's been following Lucinda for me."

"Following *Lucinda*? Why was that necessary?" Yoshi asked, wondering why private investigators were so in vogue with the females on the executive team. He had only been speaking to Niamh about one last week.

Helen resisted a bizarre urge to giggle. Yoshi's speech became very stilted when he was upset or uncomfortable. He sounded like a very untalented actor in a B grade movie. "Lucinda called me the evening I lost my job," she said when her composure was regained. "We had a strange conversation. She implied that she thought I was hard done by and seemed, in a very roundabout way, to be saying that if I sued she would agree to a settlement. I wasn't sure if I was hearing right. It was a very mixed-up day. I avoided her after that, trying to deal with Niamh wherever possible. Once she realised I was giving her the cold shoulder, she became rather hostile to me."

"Niamh mentioned that she wasn't happy with the way Lucinda behaved towards you," Yoshi told her, feeling the same anger he had when he first learnt that Helen had been badly treated.

"Once I got my job back, I promised myself that I would look into Lucinda Armstrong," Helen continued. "It was extremely unethical for her to call me like she did. She's the company's legal counsel, for goodness sake. She's meant to prevent litigation, not encourage it. I couldn't help thinking that she had some other agenda." She stopped dead when she saw realisation hit Yoshi's face.

"Niamh says that Lucinda has been lying about Denis

Greene. She's had reliable information that he has no legal grounds to sue yet Lucinda has been advocating that we re-instate him," he said, his speech becoming even more stilted.

"Why, Yoshi?" Helen asked. "Why would she lie about Denis? What's he to her?"

He took a deep breath. "I don't know. This is all very confusing." He cautioned himself not to think derogatory thoughts about the Westerners' lack of honesty. He was, after all, about to marry one. Helen knew him well enough to guess what he was thinking and left him to his thoughts for a while.

"It seems you were just a – what do you call it? – a red fish?" Yoshi said eventually, looking at Helen to correct the metaphor. He knew he had got it wrong.

"You mean a red herring – why do you say that?"

"She didn't speak to you about the matter again. She achieved what she wanted," Yoshi muttered to himself as he fitted the pieces to the puzzle.

"And what was that?" Helen pressed.

"Something to distract us all from Denis Greene. Something to distract us from the fact his claim against the company was invalid . . . what's more, all that stalling when she was responding to the solicitor's correspondence – that must also have been a front. She didn't want to appear to be too interested in the outcome."

"Christ – the conniving bitch!" Helen apologised when she saw him flinch at her choice of language. "Sorry . . . I'm going to ring Keith Longmore right now to tell him this." She picked up the phone but Yoshi caught her wrist.

"Don't do that just yet," he cautioned her. "Let's talk to Niamh first."

Niamh sat at her desk, too preoccupied to do any work. She had tried Willem's number a few times but it had rung out. Unable to stay still, she went around to his office. As expected, he wasn't there. He was usually an early starter and his absence indicated that he wasn't going to come in. That was two days running.

Next Niamh found herself walking towards Lucinda's office. The door was still shut, the light switched off. She had been missing for two days running as well.

She was on her way past Helen's office when she caught sight of Yoshi. Then, as she watched, Helen touched Yoshi's face with a gentle hand. His expression confirmed that the two were more than colleagues. Witnessing the intimate moment brought an image of Chris and Helen right before Niamh's eyes. She flung the door open, not bothering to knock. Helen jumped back from Yoshi, a guilty flush on her face.

"What is it with you and every man that comes your way?" Niamh asked before she could stop herself.

"You know about Chris?"

"Yes. Thanks a lot." Niamh was deeply sarcastic. "It's just great that you and he hit it off so well."

"I'm sorry. I'm so terribly sorry," Helen whispered, her eyes bright with regret.

Yoshi looked from one woman to the other and quickly stood up from his seat. "I'll leave you two to sort this out."

It was only then that Niamh noticed his black eye. It was almost perfectly symmetrical, the handiwork of a well-aimed fist. He closed the door behind him, leaving the two women with no buffer.

"I didn't know Chris was your husband until later in the night when I saw you dancing together," Helen explained.

"You're not serious?" Niamh faltered.

"I am. Chris doesn't wear a wedding ring. I'd never seen him with you . . ."

She sounded sincere but that didn't change Niamh's need to exact some revenge, even if it was only with words. "I didn't think that groping a stranger in a public place would be your style – I know that Chris gets off on it – but *you*?"

The insult didn't entice a retaliation from Helen. Her response was genuine. "It's not. I was feeling pretty low after a confrontation with Phil earlier in the night. Chris is an attractive man. We got talking and he was very charming. When we started kissing I thought I was being impulsive, living for the moment. In hindsight, I think I was subconsciously trying to get back at Phil by being with someone else right under his nose. Maybe I thought it would make me feel more worthy . . . that was my mistake. It didn't. I felt like shit when Chris disappeared without asking for my number . . . and wanted to die when I saw him dancing with you."

There was nothing more that Niamh could say. Helen was being brutally candid. And she didn't have a partner that she had betrayed. Chris was the guilty one, the married man who kissed a stranger while his wife waited for him to come back from the gents'.

"What about Yoshi? What's going on with him?" she asked as another half-hearted dig at the woman who had proved beyond reasonable doubt that Chris had no regard at all for their marriage.

"Yoshi is the only good thing that came out of that dreadful party." Helen's smile was shy. "I got talking to him later in the night and we've been seeing each other since."

"Does he know about Chris?" There was a stinging bitterness in Niamh's question.

"Yes, he does. He knows everything about me, well, *almost* everything. We're getting married in June."

"Christ, this is all too much." Niamh shook her head in denial, turning back towards the door.

"Wait!" Helen called after her. "I need to talk to you about Lucinda."

"Lucinda? Look, I've had about as much as I can take for one morning. I'm going to get some fresh air. I'll talk to you about Lucinda later."

Niamh went back to her office to get her purse. It was ten thirty, time for coffee. "I'm going to get my caffeine fix," she said in a monotone to Sharon. "Do you want me to get you a muffin?"

"I've got Paul Jacobsen on hold for you," Sharon answered, holding the phone in one hand while the brightly painted index finger of the other was suspended over the transfer button.

"Try to –"

"Look, Niamh, he's not an idiot. He knows he's been getting the run around and I don't want to be piggy-in-the-middle any longer."

"OK. Point taken – put him through," Niamh relented as she went inside her office to take the call. Her over-loaded brain was trying to do some fast thinking. Did Jacobsen know that Lucinda was in cahoots with his client? Would a reputable lawyer knowingly get his hands dirty with a case like this? It was unlikely. This could be an unpleasant and embarrassing surprise to him.

"Paul. I apologise for not calling you. It's been a busy few weeks . . ."

"I'm sorry to bother you, Niamh, but I have an impor-tant update. Denis Greene has withdrawn – he's no longer suing HDD."

Niamh was stunned into silence.

Paul continued to speak. "He's decided he's going back to Yorkshire. His wife's mother is ill. I get the impression they won't be coming back to Australia again."

"I don't understand," she burst out. "How can he change his mind so abruptly after causing so much trouble?"

"Maybe it was his wife. Maybe she gave him an ulti-matum to go back to England when she heard her mother wasn't well."

There was a heavy pause.

"Paul," Niamh decided to be frank, "why did you take on this case?"

"What do you mean?" he stalled, his voice cautious.

"Denis had a bridging visa – there was no need for him

to leave the country before his permanent visa was processed. *I* know that – *you* know that – so why did you take the case when there was absolutely no legal grounds for him to sue us?" The next pause was longer. "If you satisfy my curiosity, I won't take this any further," she added, giving a concession to encourage his honesty.

It worked and he said hesitantly, "Without prejudice . . . let's just say I owed someone a favour."

"Who?" She shot the question straight back at him, limiting his time to think ahead.

"A guy called Marcus." He must have felt it was safe to disclose a first name. "You wouldn't know him."

He was wrong! It was obvious he didn't know that Lucinda Armstrong was married to a Marcus; Niamh remembered her saying so that night at Forbes. It couldn't be a coincidence.

"No, don't know any Marcus." Niamh laughed to distract him before asking, "What was the favour?"

"Look, I'm not . . ." He sounded extremely uncomfortable with the direction the phone call was taking, as if he regretted telling her anything.

"Come on, just answer the question," she urged him. "I'm not going to report you or anything – I'm just curious, that's all."

She had him in a corner; they both knew it. He had no way of knowing if she would report him to the Legal Services Commissioner and he would find it hard to defend himself if she did. As a lawyer, he had an ethical responsibility not to waste the court's time with baseless lawsuits. He had breached that positive ethical duty. Now he was screwed if he told her the truth, screwed if he didn't.

"He owed me some money a few years back. He paid the debt before the liquidators were brought in to wind up his company."

"OK – thanks for that – the morning has slipped away, hasn't it?" she kept her voice light, not wanting to alert him to the enormity of what he had just revealed. "I'd better go and get some work done."

He muttered a response and was the first to hang up.

Niamh went back outside to Sharon. "Last call for a muffin?"

"A fruit salad," she mumbled, then repeated with more certainty, "Yes, you can get me a fruit salad."

Paul Jacobsen stayed on Niamh's mind as she headed for the fire exit. She was getting somewhere now. There were some facts she knew for certain. On Black Monday it was likely that Lucinda had called Denis at home to encourage him to sue. She made at least one other call, to Scott, so that Denis wouldn't stand out from the crowd. She had arranged for her husband to call in an old favour in the form of Paul Jacobsen, who agreed to take on the flawed case. She was obviously desperate to get Denis reinstated into his old job. So it was reasonable to conclude that he had been doing something that directly benefited her while he was employed by HDD. The only remaining question was what?

Niamh decided she would go and see Yoshi after getting her coffee. She might even talk to Helen to see what it was she wanted to say earlier. There was no point in going now – her head was spinning and needed a coffee to set it straight.

Her footsteps echoed through the stairwell as she made her way down the four flights. She opened the door at the bottom, taking in only one breath of the fresh air before she was winded. She looked up only to take the next blow to her face. There was a crunch. There was blood. Her whole face was numb. Staggering back against the wall, she tried to steady herself to fight back. Her attacker was a heavy-set man with a face that was hard to put an age to. His skin had a sinister pallor. That was all Niamh registered before the unforgiving kick in her ribs. She was doubled over when she saw, through blurred vision, that he had a knife.

"Here . . . here's my purse."

He didn't take the purse. It wasn't money he was after. Their eyes met over the glint of the knife.

"What do you want? I'll give you anything you want," she said desperately.

He didn't answer but his eyes said it all. He had murder in them. Time was suspended as he came towards her with the knife. In those few seconds her thoughts were split between her past and her future. In the past there was her dad, she had never knelt to pray by his graveside: her mother, who she had misunderstood for so many years: Aisling, whose baby she hadn't seen. And in the future there was Scott and Jenny.

"Get away from her!"

They both turned to the sound of a new voice. It came from a familiar Dutchman who was racing down the alley.

"Get away from her!" he repeated, launching his full

body at the attacker without any regard for the knife. Niamh was more bewildered to see Willem than she was at being assaulted in broad daylight. She wanted to help him but she couldn't move. Her vision became more blurred, Willem and her attacker were one. She was on her knees, catching blood in her cupped hands as it streamed from her nose. Some people were starting to make their way down the alley.

"Help him," she screamed at them when it became apparent they were just happy to watch the spectacle.

She shocked them into realising it wasn't some sideshow and two of them helped Willem restrain the heavy-set man. The knife fell out of his hand and landed on the gully. Its metal blade shone with newness against the blackened rust of the drain.

Malcolm Young brooded in his office. It was Friday but he couldn't even look forward to the weekend. His teenage children were coming to stay with him. They were spoilt, insolent and self-absorbed. Malcolm didn't enjoy their visits. He felt guilty that he couldn't summon up any natural paternal love and usually ended up compensating for this with cash handouts. He was aware that this earned him even less respect. It was a vicious circle.

"Malcolm, I have an urgent fax here for you." His secretary appeared at his door, walking to his desk with precariously high shoes to hand him a single sheet of paper. She turned to leave and he admired the backs of her long, shapely legs. When he remembered that she was barely older than his teenage daughter, he stopped leering and cast his eyes downwards to read the fax.

Malcolm,

You'll have an important decision to make soon. Call your executive management team together. You'll hear from me again in fifteen minutes.

Malcolm noted that the sender of the fax had not put their name to it. He read the two typed lines again, slowly this time. His podgy finger ran along the digits of the fax number that was recorded at the top of the page. It was an international number. Someone, an anonymous someone, had sent a fax from an overseas country ordering him to call his management team together. It could be a joke. But his gut feeling was telling him it wasn't. He picked up the phone

"Call my team together," he instructed his secretary. "Tell them to get to my office as quickly as possible."

"Will do."

"And when you've done that, find out what country has a telephone access code of 33."

It took ten minutes to assemble the team. They crowded around the circular table in his office.

"Shouldn't we move to the boardroom? We'd have more space there," Yoshi suggested.

"No. We're waiting for a fax. Let's stay put." Malcolm enjoyed shooting the Japanese spy down. He preferred being in his office, his territory.

"Where's Lucinda?" Helen asked her colleagues.

"She's on holiday," Malcolm replied. "She called in yesterday to say she's taking a week off."

"So it wasn't planned?" Helen was instantly suspicious.

"What does it matter?" Malcolm said tersely. "Now, does anybody know where Niamh is?"

"I think she had to pop out for a few minutes," Helen answered. Her fair skin had a faint flush. Only Yoshi knew why.

With every executive member now accounted for, their eyes turned to Malcolm to explain the purpose of the impromptu meeting.

"The reason I asked you all to come here is because I got this fax a short while ago," he explained, his meaty hand sliding the page across the smooth surface of the table until it sat in the centre. Yoshi was the first to read it. When he was finished he passed it to Helen and she subsequently passed it on to Bruce.

"This is just a joke, Malcolm," Bruce declared confidently as he handed the fax back to him. "Someone is having some fun at our expense."

"I certainly hope so," Malcolm replied but his tone lacked conviction. He was a flawed CEO and leader but he had the instincts of a survivor. His gut was telling him that this fax was bad news.

They sat in silence for the remaining two minutes. Then there was a loud knock on the door and Malcolm's secretary brought in a second fax. "33 is the access code for France," she told Malcolm.

"Thanks," he said, waiting until she left before he read the second fax out loud to his senior management team.

To the executive management team,

A latent virus has been installed on the operating systems of seven of your most critical clients: ANZ Bank, Commonwealth Bank, National Australia Bank, the Australian Taxation Office, the Department of Health, the Department of Defence and the Australian Federal Police. This virus will become live in one hour and will completely destroy the application software and customer records of those clients. The country will come to a grinding halt for at least one day until disaster recovery processes are completed. Many records will be permanently lost, despite disaster recovery. You are contractually responsible for the hardware and software of these clients. Your contract clearly states you have responsibility to keep their systems virus free. They will sue you for billions.

Don't worry. There is some good news. You have the power to stop this from happening – for a very reasonable sum of money – A$30m. You have one hour to make your decision. As soon as you transfer the money to the bank account below, I will fax you instructions on how to find and delete the virus before it becomes active.

S Rodwell
ANZ Bank
Account no: 06-2799 280645659

Spend the next hour wisely! Remember, the money must be transferred <u>before</u> the hour is up. If you inform the police or your clients, you have no chance of mak-

ing this deadline. Good luck with your decision.

There was a moment's silence when he finished, then the room erupted.

"Jesus Christ, this is what Denis Greene was up to at the ANZ Bank." Bruce's voice was heard first. "The stolen disk drives – the missing back-up tape – he must have been testing the virus before he installed it for real."

"And Lucinda," Helen added softly. "Her husband is an expert on viruses. In fact, he used to own an anti-virus software company. Lucinda's not on holiday. She's flown the coop."

"Yes, yes . . . it all makes sense now," Yoshi agreed, "but we're too late."

Malcolm watched them in amazement. "How do you all know something about this and I don't?" he asked furiously.

His question stopped the jabbering of the team.

Yoshi was the one to respond. "It's a long story and we don't have the luxury of time to explain . . . Bruce, can you get an engineer to each one of the sites?"

Bruce nodded, his mobile phone already in his hand. "I'm onto it."

Yoshi then turned to Helen. "Can you call Keith Longmore and ask him if he knows where Lucinda or Denis are this morning?"

"They'll be nowhere we can find them," she replied with a grimace.

"Let's try anyway," he said, giving her a smile.

Malcolm was extremely peeved that everybody seemed

to be willing to follow Yoshi's instructions. "We should call the police. They'll be able to find out who sent this fax," he said, trying to regain control of the situation.

"I think it's *highly* unlikely that the Australian police would be able to contact their French counterparts and track this person down within an hour!" Yoshi's face showed his frustration at the time the CEO was wasting with the stupid suggestion.

"But what about the name on the bank account? S Rodwell – the police must be able to track the individual from that," Malcolm persisted, struggling to get his power back.

"The money will be gone out of that ANZ bank account within minutes of the funds transfer," Yoshi responded, his voice becoming more stilted than ever with the clock ticking the allocated hour away. "Undoubtedly, it will be routed through a plethora of other off-shore bank accounts until such point as it can no longer be traced. And I can wager that S Rodwell doesn't even exist."

"I'll bet they'll crash the ANZ regardless," Bruce said and all eyes turned towards him. "The funds transfer is to an ANZ account. If they bring down the bank's application software, it's likely that today's data will be permanently lost and there will be no trace of the money . . . I'd better get Willem out there – he's the best engineer we have."

Yoshi nodded in agreement before turning to his fiancée again. "Helen, can you also get the funds transfer ready to submit?"

"You're not going to pay this blackmailer?" Malcolm asked incredulously, looking at the rest of the group for support.

"Preferably not, but I will if I have to." Yoshi's black eyes were hard. "We know it's not a hoax and I doubt if an hour will give Bruce's engineers enough time to find the virus. If the banks and those government departments go down for a day, then you can be assured that HDD will go down permanently. We'd go bankrupt from the damages. I won't let that happen."

There was a heavy silence before chairs scraped back as the group dispersed.

"OK – a quick recap before we go," Yoshi said to the group. "Bruce, you're organising the engineers. Helen, you're contacting the detective and getting the payment ready. I'll call Japan and get approval to pay. Everyone back here in thirty minutes."

"What about me?" Malcolm asked petulantly.

"I suppose we must at least *inform* the police, even though I suspect they will be a hindrance rather than a help. Why don't you call them, Malcolm?" Yoshi replied, his tone dangerously bordering on patronising. "Just keep them away from the rest of us – we can't be distracted from what we have to do."

Chapter Thirteen

Someone must have called an ambulance. Niamh sat on the kerb. All she could see were feet, her head hurt too much to lift it to see the faces. A paramedic was down at her level, squeezing her nose to stop the bleeding. It hurt like hell. He was shining a light in her eyes to see if she had any concussion.

"What's your name?"

"Niamh."

"Date of birth?"

"22 Feb 1975."

"Can you remember what happened?"

"Yes, that guy was trying to kill me," she said, painfully lifting her head to point to the heavy-set man. His pale face was covered with blood, she wasn't sure if it was hers or his.

"What's your home address?"

She had no sooner said when he asked her to count to ten.

"Why?"

"I'm just trying to determine if you're concussed at all."

Niamh counted, feeling foolish.

"What's happened here?" A lady police officer had appeared, and crouched to Niamh's level. Niamh hadn't noticed the police arriving.

"That guy tried to kill me," Niamh repeated, wishing the paramedic and officer would just ask questions once.

"I think he was just trying to get your purse," the lady officer said with a kindly smile.

"No – I offered to give him my money but he still came after me with the knife," Niamh said, pointing to the knife that was still in the gully.

"She's right – he was trying to kill her." Willem had joined the party by the kerb. His voice was soft and there was a sudden quiet so he could be heard.

"And who are you?" the lady officer asked, giving him a haughty look for interfering with her investigation.

"My name is Willem Boelhoers. I was expecting this would happen and I have been keeping close to Niamh over the last few days." He turned to look at Niamh. "I followed you from home this morning. Just like you, I got booked for driving in the bus lane. But I was also caught speeding and my licence was suspended on the spot. My car was towed and I had to get a taxi to work. It was good luck that the driver pulled into the alley while I paid the fare."

Realisation dawned on Niamh. This was what Willem had been talking about that night outside her house. He had been saying that someone wanted to hurt her and he had been absolutely right.

The lady officer also gave the academic-looking man her full attention; it was clear that he knew about a more sinister motive behind the seemingly standard mugging.

Now that he had a more receptive audience, Willem continued to speak in his accented English. "Officer, I'm sure you will find that this man was paid to attack Niamh and seriously hurt, if not kill, her."

It was a heavy allegation and the accused bucked against the restraining arms of the male police officer. Niamh and Willem were locked on the same wavelength, filling in the jigsaw pieces.

"Lucinda?" Niamh asked, trying to ignore the pressure of the paramedic's fingers on her nose. "Was it Lucinda that you heard through the air-conditioning ducts?"

"Yes." Willem nodded.

"Do you know why she would do this to me?"

"Because you and Denis Greene know too much – of what I'm not sure."

"Can I stand up?" Niamh asked the paramedic. It was too hard to think sitting at street level. She stood up, her fingers taking over from his to staunch the flow of blood. "Willem, what else did you hear the voices say?"

"They talked about the number of sites . . . there should have been ten sites but they stopped at seven. It seems they were doing an installation of some sort at each site but sometimes the voices were very faint and I wasn't able to fill in all the gaps."

"I wouldn't mind someone taking the time to fill in some gaps with me," the frustrated lady officer cut in. She turned to Niamh. "You'd better go with the paramedic here and get your nose seen to. Can you give me your number so I can talk with you later today?"

Niamh still had her purse in her free hand and she gave it to the officer. "You should be able to find my business card in there."

"I'll come with you to the hospital," Willem said, putting a protective palm under her elbow. He was proud of himself; he had saved Niamh. Pride was a weird sensation; it was worlds apart from shame. He was more used to shame; it was part of daily life with schizophrenia.

"No, I'll be fine. You stay with the officer." Niamh was firm, reclaiming her elbow from his grip. She badly needed some space to come to terms with what had happened.

"Are you sure?"

Willem's troubled face almost made Niamh laugh, albeit hysterically.

"Yes, take the officer to see Yoshi – he's the best person to deal with this," Niamh instructed when she got a hold of her seesawing emotions. She thought of Yoshi's black eye and had the urge to laugh again. She took her purse back from the officer and followed the paramedic through the spectators to the waiting ambulance.

Willem wasn't happy about letting her go alone but

the lady officer was waiting with a look of expectation. He was about to suggest they go inside when his mobile rang.

"Bruce," he said when he heard his boss's familiar voice. Then he listened intently. "Damn, so that's what Greene was doing for Lucinda, installing a virus . . . Now that I think of it, I heard the voices talk about a virus too . . . Where is it? Servers or mainframe? . . . Shit! That will be hard. OK, I'll take ANZ . . . I'm on my way right now."

The officer started to get impatient and pointedly cleared her throat. Willem turned to her and said, "We have an emergency with a client. I have to go immediately." He ran back up the alley as fast as he had run down to save Niamh.

The officer called after him, "Wait! Wait! I need your phone number." She was sure he heard her but he didn't stop.

Helen stopped at Donna's desk on the way back to her office.

"I need you to get a payment ready." She was short of breath from the rush. "The bank details are here." She handed her a photocopy of the account details only, the letter of demand that preceded them was not for Donna's eyes.

"How much?" the young accounts clerk asked.

"Thirty million."

"Yen?"

"No, Australian dollars."

"You're joking, right?" Donna gave an uncertain

giggle.

"I wish I was."

There was a sobering silence before Donna said, "But we don't have thirty million in our bank account."

"Let me worry about that," Helen told her, already walking away. "Drop whatever you're doing. Just get the payment ready. Don't submit it to the bank – have it standing by."

Helen raced the remaining distance to her office. She riffled through her business-card collection for Keith's contact details. Her fingers were butter, the cards gluing to them. She couldn't see it so she turned the holder upside down, the cards falling to spread across her desk. The wayward card surfaced and she jabbed out the number on her desk phone.

"Keith – it's Helen – where are you?"

"Outside Lucinda's house. She hasn't left for work yet."

"Go up and knock on the door." Helen gave the instruction with an abruptness he had never heard from her before.

"That will give my identity away," he said reluctantly.

"It's too late to worry about her knowing who you are." Helen was dismissive about Keith's precious anonymity. "She's demanded thirty million bucks from us this morning."

"Thirty million bucks?" Keith's jaw dropped open. "Is she blackmailing you or something?"

"I haven't the time to go into the details. Can you just go up to the door and see if there is someone in there?"

"OK, I'm going. Do you want to stay on the line or will

I call you back?"

"I'll stay." Helen was firm.

Keith got out of his car and walked down the drive to the house. He knocked on the weathered door. When there was no answer, he rang the bell. Again there was no response so he circled the house, looking inside each window. There was no sign of life. "Do you want me to break in?" he asked in a matter-of-fact way.

"No, they're gone. I *knew* they'd be gone."

"Do you want me to check the airport?" he offered as he made his way back to his car.

"Yes. That's a good idea. Can you go straight there?"

"Yeah. International, I presume?"

"Yes."

"I'm on my way."

Helen looked at her watch. There was no way she would get back to Malcolm's office within thirty minutes. Her next call was to the company's bank manager, his business card was easier to locate. He was a man who was rarely at his desk but this morning she got lucky.

"Frank. It's Helen Barnes. Look, sorry for the rush, but we're trying to get something done here at short notice . . . how much free facilities do we have at the moment? Nine million? I was hoping it would be more than that! Whatever! Look, we may go into debit today . . . um . . . a net twenty-one million . . . yeah, that's right . . . I can get the extra funds from Tokyo tomorrow . . . would you honour the payment? It's just one day . . . no, no long-term requirement . . . great, thanks, Frank. Owe you one."

Helen came across as more grateful than she really was.

The bank had security over the company's premises and were well covered for a short-term extension of credit. She'd known from the outset that Frank would be OK.

She was already over time but she had one more thing to do before returning to Malcolm's office. She wanted to see if she could find Niamh.

Yoshi had also gone back to his office, the door shutting behind him with a bang. He sat down, his eyes glancing off the beautiful photograph of Sydney Harbour that hung behind the door. It was a gift from Helen, her way of telling him that his home was now in Sydney. He took a deep breath and dialled his boss's number. A sweet-voiced secretary answered the phone on the other end.

"Good morning," he greeted her. "This is Murasaki. I am looking for Nishikawa Shacho."

"Hello, Murasaki Bucho. Unfortunately, Nishikawa Shacho is not in the office this morning."

"I must speak with him." Yoshi's voice had a restrained urgency. "Do you know where he is?"

"I'm afraid not. I have not heard from him this morning. It is most unusual."

"OK. I will call his home number. Goodbye."

It took Yoshi a few moments to locate Nishikawa Shacho's home number. He never had occasion to call it before now. It rang for some time before a tremulous female voice came on the other end.

"*Moshi moshi*. This is Murasaki. I apologise for calling your home but I am looking for Nishikawa Shacho urgently."

370

"He's not here."

"I must speak with him urgently. Do you know where he is?"

There was such a long pause that Yoshi thought maybe she had not heard his question. He was about to repeat it when she said, "He's moved out. He's gone to live with the geisha in Kyoto."

Yoshi was deeply shocked. Nishikawa Shacho had religiously maintained that his relationship with the geisha was one of true friendship. Yoshi felt deceived. He could only imagine what the wife was feeling. "I am most sorry."

"He says she's his soul mate and that he can no longer deny his destiny," the wife said, her voice breaking with sobs. "Have you met this woman who has taken my husband from me?"

"Only over dinner," he responded, playing down the numerous times he had met the geisha. "*Si tsu re i si ma su,*" he excused himself before putting the phone down. He was momentarily distracted from the virus and the ransom demand. The wife's humiliation and devastation were heart-wrenching. Her breakdown on the phone, to a virtual stranger, would undoubtedly cause her even more distress. Yoshi hoped her children were there to comfort her. She had two boys, grown up now; the youngest would have finished college this year. It suddenly occurred to Yoshi that Nishikawa Shacho must have planned to leave his wife when the children finished their education. The vice-president was not one to act on impulse.

Yoshi had one more number for his boss. It was a

mobile phone number. Again, it wasn't a number he had dared to call before. He took another deep breath, not sure what reception he would get on the other end. The vice-president answered, his voice raw with sleep.

"Nishikawa Shacho, I am sorry to disturb you. I need your advice. We have a crisis in Australia."

"Just a minute." There was a rustle of bedclothes and then the echo of feet as they padded across hollow floor-boards.

"OK. Tell me what is wrong," he said after a few moments.

Yoshi read out the fax.

"How did this happen?" Nishikawa Shacho demanded when he finished. "This will ruin the company . . ."

Yoshi didn't answer straight away. He chose his words carefully. "It appears to be a collaboration between our legal counsel, Lucinda Armstrong, and the software engineer, Denis Greene – you know, the one who was suing us – that's all we know at this point."

"Is the virus real? Could it be a hoax?"

"We think it is real."

Nishikawa Shacho didn't take any further time to ask questions.

"Pay them the money," he instructed.

Yoshi had been expecting a more in-depth discussion, an interrogation, even a chiding for being the messenger of the bad news. "Is that your final answer?

"What do you expect me to say?" Nishikawa Shacho retorted. "I have no magic formula to make this good. If we pay the ransom money, our profit and share price will plummet and our competitors will almost certainly make a take-over bid. On the other hand, if we let the virus take hold, HDD will be sued to the point of bankruptcy. That's where we are at, Yoshi. Not a good place to be but we'll have plenty of time later to analyse why we were exposed like this – that's only if you and I still have a job left by the end of this. Now, I must go. I'm in Kyoto and I must get into the city as soon as possible. I was to meet with the analysts today to tell them about the ANZ contract renewal. Now I will have to find some reason to cancel."

Bruce went to the kitchen to make himself a strong coffee. An illicit cigarette balanced from the corner of his mouth. He didn't have time to go outside and he couldn't think straight without the nicotine. Armed with the black coffee, he crossed the executive area, stopping off at Niamh's office.

"Do you know where she is?" he asked Sharon, whose desk stood guard outside the empty office.

"She went to get a coffee – that was over an hour ago now," she replied. Helen had also been around looking for her boss. Sharon didn't know what to say other than the truth. Niamh seemed to be having an extra long coffee break and wasn't answering her mobile phone.

Bruce was thoughtful as he took a sip of the black coffee. "I told her some – bad news – this morning," he said quietly. "She wouldn't do anything stupid, would she?"

"I don't think so. God, I hope not. But she hasn't been herself the last few weeks."

Sharon was really worried now. What had Bruce told Niamh? She had assumed that Niamh was having problems at home but maybe, from what Bruce was saying, the problem was with work.

Bruce's cigarette was lying idly between his fingers now and some ash fell onto her desk. "Have they changed the rules about smoking in the office?" she asked, her face a sheet of disapproval amid the wild hair.

"No. Don't tell on me, will you?" he grinned unrepentantly.

"I don't have anyone to tell," Sharon's face was deadpan, "Niamh would give you a right rap on the knuckles but she seems to have disappeared into thin air."

Bruce gave in and stubbed the cigarette out against the side of her rubbish bin. "See? You've got to my conscience. Look, we're probably worrying unnecessarily about Niamh – I'm sure she has just gone off to do an errand or something like that. When she comes back, can you tell her we need her in Malcolm's office?"

Bruce hurried away and Sharon tried Niamh's mobile again. It was still going to voicemail. She decided to go downstairs and check the coffee shop. She didn't expect that Niamh would still be there but it was as good a place to start looking as any.

There was a fine sheen of sweat on Willem Boelhoers' forehead. The computer room at ANZ Bank was very well air-conditioned but pressure always caused the Dutchman to sweat. And this was pressure the like of which he had never experienced before. Bruce had despatched his most experienced software engineers to each of the customer sites listed in the fax. It had taken the engineers ten minutes to run all the standard virus scans but, as expected, there were no corrupt files found. Marcus Diddams had used his considerable skill to create a brand new virus and there was no existing anti-virus software to detect it.

The only other thing Willem could do was to run some ad hoc searches across the enormous web of servers, directories and folders of the bank. If he had more time on his hands, he could have narrowed the portfolio of potentially corrupt files by a process of elimination aided by the LAN administrators at the bank. With only thirty minutes remaining on the clock, time was a luxury he didn't have.

He searched for files with *Lucinda* or *Marcus* in the name. Then he typed *Denis* and *Greene* separately into the search box. There was no success with any of these obvious guesses at the name of the file containing the virus. With a flash of inspiration he remembered that Denis's wife was called Lily. There were a few moments of anticipation before "no files found of that name" flashed on the screen to mock his optimism. He desperately tried to remember the snatches of conversation he had heard through the air-conditioning vent. He typed a few more guesses into the search box before he remembered one of the last things that Lucinda had said.

"It's time to cut the kite loose."

Willem ran a search on *Kite*. One file was found deep down in the layers of directories and folders. It was highlighted on the screen. One click of the mouse would open it. But the bank's systems would come crashing down if it was the virus. He ran a search on the mainframe for a file of the same name. It was there too. He phoned Bruce.

"Tell the others to run a search for a file called *Kite.exe*. Tell them to check the mainframes as well as all the servers. Remind them not to open or delete it at this point. I just want to see if the sites have the file in common."

Willem continued to run random searches while he waited for Bruce to call him back. He was still sweating; his watch told him they had only fifteen minutes left.

Yoshi was the first one back to Malcolm's office.

"I talked to Nishikawa Shacho. I've got the approval to pay the money if we need to," he told the CEO.

Malcolm shrugged, choosing not to respond. For the last thirty minutes, left on his own while the others scurried around, he had done some thinking. He had decided he was finished with all this. It was too much pressure at his age. All for two selfish kids who would do nothing worthwhile with their private education anyway.

"Did you call the police?" Yoshi asked, noticing that Malcolm seemed to be in a world of his own.

"My secretary is on to them."

"You didn't call them yourself?" Yoshi was critical.

"No, I didn't." Malcolm stood from his seat, his large tummy protruding through his striped shirt. "Look, you're running the show here – I don't think I'm needed any longer."

His large frame was remarkably agile in its path to the door.

"You're walking out?" Yoshi's mouth dropped open. "You're walking out, *now*, in the middle of all this?"

"No, I'm resigning," Malcolm corrected the Japanese spy. "It's all yours, Yoshi. It's what you wanted. I'm sure you'll find it harder than you thought – it's not as easy as looking over someone else's shoulder. But have fun, won't you?"

Malcolm passed Bruce on his way out. The services director had his ear glued to his mobile phone and barely looked at the CEO. He saw Helen leave her office, also talking on her phone. Niamh's office was empty as was Lucinda's. He wouldn't miss any of them, he thought to himself as he called the lift. He was retired, finished, done with all the bullshit. The spoiled brats, his children, would have to fund their own education.

Helen and Bruce arrived at Malcolm's office in tandem, both of them speaking on their mobiles.

"It's Keith," Helen put her hand over the mouth piece to update Yoshi. "He's just pulled up outside the international terminal."

Bruce took his cue from Helen and also paused in his conversation to give a quick update. "Hold on a minute," he told the engineer at the end of the line. "Yoshi, we think Willem has found it. Two of the sites have the same file . . . it's looking good. I'll try one more site, the Department of Defence. They have a different profile to the banks. If they've got *Kite.exe*, then we've found it!"

Helen and Yoshi were frozen in a flimsy moment of hope as they waited. Would they be that lucky? Had Willem really achieved the impossible and located the virus?

Bruce finished the call and dialled the engineer out at the Department of Defence. Helen realised that she had a dial tone on her own phone. Keith had got fed up waiting for her to come back on the line.

The Department of Defence confirmed positive to a file named *Kite.exe* on its mainframe. Malcolm's phone directory was open on his abandoned laptop. When Helen saw the way the conversation was going, she took the initiative to call Willem Boelhoers direct.

"Here . . ." she said, handing her phone to Bruce when he finished, saving him precious seconds from having to dial the number himself.

"OK, Willem." Bruce swapped phones. "I'm 99 per cent sure we have it. No more time to sit on the fence . . . yeah, delete it . . ." He waited, his heart hammering. "Anything happen? No? Give it a minute . . . still OK? . . . right, I'll get onto the others to delete it as well . . ."

"Give me the names of some of the engineers," Helen said from Malcolm's desk, the phone directory on his laptop proving very useful. "Yoshi and I can help pass on the message . . . it's to delete any files called *Kite.exe*, is that right?"

Lucinda was waiting for her flight to be called. Her hair pulled back in a ponytail, she wore a navy tracksuit and looked like all the other travellers who were waiting in the departure lounge for the British Airways flight. They were all dressed for comfort, aware of the twenty hours of flying that lay ahead.

She had been unable to get on the same flight as Marcus and Jack. The three of them had left the house together with no sadness on her part. It was an ugly house on an ordinary street. Jack had spent most of his childhood there but he would soon forget it.

She had driven her son and husband to the airport before parking in a local shopping mall. Then she had called Malcolm from the car to say she was taking a week off. He was mildly surprised but didn't ask any awkward questions. She didn't return to the ugly house again, feeling it was safer to sleep both nights in the car.

She was in the ladies' toilet when she heard her flight being announced. Her reflection in the mirror showed her smile as relief flooded through her. She was on her way to Paris at last: to make a new start with Marcus and Jack. Everything would be different over there. They would be free from the likes of Kel Sheridan.

She washed her hands and balanced her cabin bag on her shoulder. She was making her way to the gate when she heard someone call her name.

"Lucinda . . . Lucinda!"

She didn't turn around, couldn't risk it. She kept walking, counselling herself to stay calm.

"Lucinda, wait up." Fingers grasped her arm with a vice-like grip.

She looked around to see Steve Jones, the barrister. He

had a stupid smile on his face. "Imagine bumping into you here. Where are you off to?"

"I'm late for my flight," she hissed, pulling her arm free.

His face fell. His expression was similar to that of a child the age of Jack rather than a fifty-something barrister. "We're going to Fiji," he said, pointing to his overweight wife who was watching from a distance. "Adam was there recently. Do you remember Adam? Do you know he's twenty-one now? And he's engaged to be married. You'd know the girl – Donna Howard. She works in HDD too."

Lucinda shook her head in denial. "No, I haven't come across her. I must go –"

"You're looking great." He had a desperate edge to his voice. "I meant to say that to you when I saw you – but I was caught off guard – you see, I didn't know you were with HDD – you were the last person I expected to see that morning – not that I wasn't very happy to see you . . ."

"Goodbye, Steve."

"Would you like to catch up sometime? Maybe we could have dinner?"

"I don't think so – now, I have to go – my flight . . ."

"Maybe I could help you . . ." he pleaded, his desperation completely unveiled. "I could take you away from your problems . . ."

"I have no idea what you are talking about," she said, pointedly looking in the direction of the wife he seemed to have forgotten about.

"There she is!" a man yelled from close to where the wife was standing.

Lucinda saw a grey-haired, ginger-bearded man run towards her. Her first reaction was panic but then hope shot through her that the strange-looking man was running after someone else. She turned away from the lovesick barrister. She had walked only a few steps when she felt her arm being grabbed again, this time with more force. Her heart stopped. It wasn't Steve's fingers that were curled around her arm. She looked into the face of the ginger-bearded man and saw it was over. If it hadn't been for Steve Jones, she would be on her way to Paris.

Niamh's nose was broken. It was X-rayed, reset and bandaged. When they were happy she didn't have any concussion from the blow, they released her with a warning not to be alone for the next twenty-four hours. Apparently, concussion could occur at any time in that period.

Armed with a prescription for painkillers, she went outside. Morning had turned into afternoon. It was still a beautiful day, the sun was just higher up in the sky now. She sat on a bench overlooking the front gardens of the hospital. It was calming to look at the bursts of colour in the flowerbeds but their scent was lost to her because of the enormous bandage holding her nose in place. She considered if she should call Malcolm or Yoshi. She decided on Yoshi. The Japanese man was infinitely more placid than Malcolm and she needed everything to stay calm for now. She was going to tell him she wanted to

381

take a few weeks off work. It wasn't because of her nose; it was her emotions that needed the break. So much had happened they needed some space to run riot before any kind of normal life could be resumed.

"Yoshi, it's Niamh."

"Niamh! Where have you been?" He sounded frantic.

She was as casual as possible with her reply. "I've just come out of the hospital. I have a broken nose and I'm a little shocked – but I'm basically OK."

"What are you talking about?" he asked, obviously confused. "Have you been in an accident?"

"Didn't Willem come and tell you?" Niamh's heart sank. Had Willem's schizophrenia reared its ugly head again? Was he alone somewhere having a breakdown? Why else would he not have told Yoshi what had happened in the alley?

"You mean Willem Boelhoers? He's been in the ANZ Bank all morning. He's the one who found Lucinda's virus. What was he meant to tell me?" Yoshi's voice was becoming very stilted as he tried to deal with the baffling conversation that wasn't in his native tongue.

"Yoshi, sorry for being stupid but what on earth is Lucinda's virus and how would Willem find it?" Niamh was starting to wonder if she had suffered concussion after all. This conversation was certainly making no sense.

Yoshi could feel Helen watching him and he decided to let the two women speak. There would be tension after their confrontation that morning but at least their command of the English language should help them translate this disjointed string of events into a chronological summary. "I'm going to hand you over to Helen. She can explain what's happened better than I can."

He pretended not to hear when Niamh said, "No. Please don't."

There was some background noise as the phone changed hands.

"Niamh, it's Helen. Did I hear correctly that you have a broken nose?"

Niamh smiled ironically – she should have called Malcolm after all. At least he wouldn't have had Helen hanging off him when he was on the phone. "Yes. I was attacked in the alley this morning."

"You were mugged?"

"No, mugged is when they want your money," Niamh corrected her. "I think he was trying to kill me."

"Are you saying it wasn't a random attack?"

"I think it was a very deliberate attack. Both Willem and I think Lucinda was behind it."

"Lucinda?" Helen's tone changed. "Lucinda got someone to assault you? Good heavens, she's had one busy morning."

Niamh's earlier smile tightened on her face – apparently there was another twist to this very strange day. "What do you mean? What was Yoshi saying earlier about her 'virus'?"

"I'll give you the two-minute version," Helen said, her voice picking up speed. "Lucinda's husband, Marcus Diddams, created a virus and paid Denis Greene to put it on the operating systems of some of the banks and government departments. Malcolm was sent a blackmailing fax this morning . . . *pay thirty million bucks or we'll bring down the systems of your clients!* Lucky for us, Willem Boelhoers found the virus in time."

"Oh my God!" Niamh's animosity towards Helen was lost in her astonishment. "Really? My *God* ... that's incredible . . . but it explains everything – why Lucinda wanted Denis back in his role and her lies about the visa – Denis breaking into the ANZ. It all makes perfect sense. Where's Lucinda now?"

"She was about to get on a British Airways flight to Paris but Keith Longmore caught her just in time. She's being questioned by the federal police as we speak."

Niamh's mind was working fast; there were a lot of questions she wanted to ask but she rationed them down. "You said Keith caught Lucinda at the airport . . . how did that come about?"

"He's been investigating her for the last few weeks," Helen replied. "I hired him . . . it was only a hunch at the start but there was more behind Lucinda than I'd ever thought there'd be."

"Did he know Lucinda was going to have me assaulted? It would have been good if he could have prevented my nose from being broken." Niamh's tone was wry.

Helen risked a laugh. "Sorry, I don't think he knew that . . ."

Niamh was overcome with a wave of gratitude that Willem cared enough to follow her that morning. "I was lucky to get off with a broken nose. The guy was going to kill me but Willem saved me."

"It sounds like Willem saved the day on a number of

accounts . . ." Helen said, then paused. "Look, I know you don't want to hear this now, but I am really sorry about the party and what happened with Chris . . ."

"I know you are. But I just couldn't believe it was you, Helen. I knew he was with someone, but *you*?"

"Please believe how sorry I am . . . and please believe that I didn't know he was your husband."

"We're getting divorced. Did I tell you that earlier?"

"I'm sorry," Helen said again.

"Don't be." Niamh was blunt. "I'm not sorry. I'm relieved."

"OK." Helen seemed to be struggling for words. "Look, I'll hand you back to Yoshi now."

Niamh waited for the phone to change hands again. She jumped in before Yoshi could speak. "I'm going to take some time off . . . maybe a few weeks."

"That's an understandable reaction. Take as long as you need." His kindness was matter-of-fact.

"Can you tell Malcolm what's happened?"

Yoshi paused before saying, "That won't be necessary. Malcolm has left the company. He resigned earlier today."

"Are you the new CEO?"

"Yes."

"Congratulations," Niamh said sincerely. "I'm glad you're staying on in Sydney."

"Thanks . . . mate. Call me tomorrow and let me know how you're feeling."

Niamh's smile came back when she heard the Australian salute. Yoshi was trying to fit in. Helen could only be his motivation. After hanging up, she took a few moments to let the beauty of the gardens seep into her consciousness and then she found she could honestly say she was happy for Helen and Yoshi.

The sun beamed down on the back of her neck and her bare arms. She enjoyed it for a few moments before deciding it was too nice to go home and sit in the empty house.

She phoned Scott. "Hello."

"Hello, yourself." His voice was flirtatious and she felt a surge of happiness.

"What are you doing today?" she asked. An idea had formed as she looked on the brightness of the gardens.

"I've just come out of that interview and I'm on my way to pick up Jenny from Deb's."

"How did it go?"

"Really good," he said. "They sounded me out on salary so I think they're close to making an offer."

"That's great."

"You sound funny – blocked up. Have you got a cold?"

"No – my nose is –" She faltered, it was too long a story to tell over the phone.

"Don't tell me! It's grown too long from telling fibs about not being on the rebound and now you can't breathe through it any more."

"No, it's not that, I swear," she laughed. "Look, I was ringing to see if you want to call round to my mother with me this afternoon . . . ."

"Why aren't you working?" he asked immediately.

"I'm playing truant . . . Yes or no?"

"I'd have to bring Jenny," he said after a small hesitation.

"That's fine. Mum has a lovely garden. I used to play in it when I was a kid. Jenny will love it there . . ."

"Are you sure?" He was still hesitant. "Don't you want time alone with your mother? Don't you have things you should talk about?"

"We can talk while you two enjoy the garden. Mum will be delighted to see Jenny. She loves babies."

"But will she be as happy to see me?" Scott asked. "You've only just broken up with Chris – I don't want her to see me as the other man."

"After what Mum went through to be with Tom, I think that's the last way she'd look at you."

"OK, I hope you're right. Where will we meet?"

They agreed to meet at the playground on the Corso.

"I can't wait to see you," he said.

She smiled into the phone, his words making her brim over with a happiness that transcended everything else. "And me you."

She hung up and started to walk to St Leonard's station. She got a few curious looks on the way. She had one other call to make and had planned to do it later in the day. But now that she had made up her mind, she found she couldn't wait. She dialled the number as she walked; the call was to Ireland.

"Hi, Aisling. It's me."

"Niamh? Is that you? Is it really you?" The voice on the other end started off groggy but was quickly coming alive.

"Yes, it's really me. What time is it there?"

"It's . . ." Aisling paused to check the clock, "it's 4am . . . you wait all this time to call me and then when you do, it's the middle of the bloody night."

"I'm sorry, I rang without thinking . . . I hope I didn't wake the baby."

"I would have killed you if you had . . ."

They both laughed, then Aisling asked, "Why are you calling? Is Mum OK?"

"She's fine."

"Tom?"

"He's never been better. I'm ringing to tell you I'm coming over there for a holiday."

"Really?" Aisling squealed. "That's great news – when?"

"In the next few days . . . as soon as I can organise a flight."

Aisling's tone was more sombre when she said, "Now that you're ready to face your demons you don't want to dally, is that right?"

"Yeah, I suppose that's the way it is. I want to see the garage, put Dad's soul to rest. Then maybe I can get to know that new niece of mine."

THE END

Published by Poolbeg.com

Executive Affair

BER CARROLL

Unlucky in love, Claire Quinlan wants to get far away
from Dublin. And where better to nurse a broken
heart than Bondi Beach!

A finance manager with software giant
Amtech, Claire transfers to their Sydney office.
She loves the sun, the beaches and the lifestyle.
It looks like her life has changed for the better.

But Claire's new job turns out to be a
greater challenge than she imagined. First there's the
complication of the handsome vice-president,
Robert Pozos, and his estranged, neurotic wife
Julia. Then Claire uncovers a scam to defraud the
company and she gets caught in the crossfire.

Can Claire trust Robert? And who has the most
to lose in this *executive affair?*

ISBN 1-84223-180-4